Praise for
NEVER LOOK BACK

"Expertly crafted . . . A mind-bending mystery, an insightful exploration of parent-child relationships, and a cautionary tale about bitterness and blame."

—*Kirkus Reviews* (★starred review★)

"Alison Gaylin's 11th novel perceptively examines family dynamics, the domino effects of violence, and our personal stories—real or invented—that help us maneuver through life. The strong tension that launches *Never Look Back* only intensifies with each surprising twist. . . . *Never Look Back* is another superior outing from Gaylin."

—Associated Press

"Mystery and true crime aficionados will delight in piecing together the puzzle in Edgar winner Gaylin's (*If I Die Tonight*) deliciously twisty novel."

—*Library Journal* (★starred review★)

"An addictive and complex tale related through the experiences of April, Quentin, and Robin, with multiple startling conclusions."

—*Booklist*

"Nothing is as it seems in Gaylin's addictive, shape-shifting thriller . . . a twisty-turny plot that will sizzle your summer."

"Her latest release, *Never Look Back*, is not only her best novel yet, but also one of the best novels of the year-to-date, period."

"New Alison Gaylin is a good reason to set everything aside and give yourself wholly to what promises to be a psychologically riveting and suspenseful read. . . . It's a fascinating, fresh, and intoxicating thriller about motherhood, truth, and the mysteries that shroud those closest to us."

"*Never Look Back* asks us to be unafraid to look deeper, to believe in the healing power of the truth, and to accept the consequences and be good to ourselves regardless."

By Alison Gaylin

THE COLLECTIVE
NEVER LOOK BACK
IF I DIE TONIGHT
WHAT REMAINS OF ME
TRASHED
HEARTLESS
REALITY ENDS HERE

The Brenna Spector Series
AND SHE WAS
INTO THE DARK
STAY WITH ME

Samantha Leiffer novels
HIDE YOUR EYES
YOU KILL ME

NEVER
LOOK
BACK

A NOVEL

ALISON
GAYLIN

wm WILLIAM MORROW
An Imprint of HarperCollinsPublishers

NEVER LOOK BACK. Copyright © 2019 by Alison Gaylin. All rights reserved. Printed in the United States of America. No part of this book may be used or reproduced in any manner whatsoever without written permission except in the case of brief quotations embodied in critical articles and reviews. For information, address HarperCollins Publishers, 195 Broadway, New York, NY 10007.

First William Morrow premium printing: May 2022
First William Morrow paperback printing: July 2019
First William Morrow hardcover printing: July 2019

Print Edition ISBN: 978-0-06-303266-8
Digital Edition ISBN: 978-0-06-284455-2

Cover design by Amy Halperin
Cover photographs © Maria Heyens/Arcangel Images (woman); ©
Getty Images

William Morrow and HarperCollins are registered trademarks of HarperCollins Publishers in the United States of America and other countries.

22 23 24 25 26 BVGM 10 9 8 7 6 5 4 3 2 1

For Myrna Lebov, in loving memory

NEVER
LOOK
BACK

ONE

June 10, 1976
1:00 A.M.
Written Assignment for Ninth-Grade
Social Studies Class (Mrs. Brixton)
A Letter to My Future Child
By April Cooper

Dear Aurora Grace,

It is 1976, the year of our nation's bicentennial. I turned fifteen three months ago. Like many young people my age, I am concerned about some of the issues affecting our country and the planet. The hole in the ozone layer is something that I worry about. The passage of the Equal Rights Amendment could provide equal pay for both you and me. These issues, just like you, are part of a future I can't see from where I am. I try to imagine the world you may be living in: flying cars; picture phones; pills that can make you beautiful forever. I try to imagine you— what you might look like, the clothes you might wear, the sound of your laugh. I try to imagine who your father might be, and I'm hoping with my whole heart that he's someone I will meet many years from now, when everything is better.

I don't know a lot. I'm only a freshman, and my grades are just okay. I don't play any musical instruments and I'm not on a sports team. I've never traveled to a foreign country except for the one time my mom and I went to Mexico, and I was only five years old then, so all I remember is the hotel swimming pool.

But there are things I've seen now. There are things I know.

I heard the gunshots when I got home from school. I was walking up the driveway and there were three loud blasts. Fireworks for the bicentennial, I thought. I told myself the blasts were coming from the park up the block, from someone else's backyard, from my own imagination. But part of me knew that something horrible had happened.

When I opened the door to my house, the lights were off and the shades were drawn, and so the first thing I noticed was the smell. Like sawdust and smoke and something else—something coppery and dark that made my stomach turn.

I felt hands on my back, someone gripping my neck and spinning me to look at him. "I didn't mean to," Gabriel said. "I was just so angry at your stepfather. I know you only broke up with me because he made you. I love you so much, April."

I could smell his sweat. I felt it slick and cold on his hands and on my skin. When Gabriel turned the light on and I got a good look at him, I noticed the spray of tiny red drops across his face.

Papa Pete was on the floor. Blood spreading beneath him. I don't think I've ever seen anyone or anything as absolutely still as his body.

I tried to ask where Jenny was, but I was crying so hard I couldn't get the words out. Jenny is my baby sister. Your future aunt, Aurora Grace. She's only three years old. I don't know what he's done with her.

When I was still crying, Gabriel put the gun in my hand. He wrapped himself around me, the same way he had done back in January, when he taught me how to hit a golf ball at the driving range near his house. He aimed the barrel on Papa Pete and pressed his fingers against mine and made me pull the trigger. Papa Pete's body shook. Mine too. My throat was raw from screaming, but I couldn't hear my own voice.

Hours later now, and my ears are still ringing. Gabriel is asleep, but in my head, he is still saying it, over and over: Now you've done it too. You've shot him too. Your prints are on the gun. We're in this together. He is so close, his lips brush the back of my neck. "We're in this together," Gabriel whispers. "We'll always be together."

When someone is that close, you don't just hear a whisper. You feel it.

It's 1:00 A.M. A half hour ago, I sneaked out of my room and tried to call the police, but the line had been cut. I felt someone watching me. It was Gabriel, awake and standing right behind me. He pressed the gun between my shoulder blades. I felt it so clearly—the full circle of the barrel on the part of my back that leads directly to my heart. It felt heavy and cold and I was scared beyond breathing. Gabriel spoke very quietly. "Jenny is in a safe place," he said. "She's being cared for. Things will stay that way unless I say the word. And I'll never say the word, as long as you are good to me."

Gabriel has the keys to Papa Pete's Cavalier, the money from Papa Pete's wallet, and of course, he has the gun. He says he's leaving, and if I'm good, he'll take me with him, alive. I don't want to ask him where the gun came from, or how he got to my house in the first place with no car. But I'm guessing that it has to do with the people watching Jenny, and so I'm going to try and be good, even though I feel as though my whole life has been pulled out from under me and I can't close my eyes without seeing Papa Pete—the shell of him on our living room floor, blood pooling all around.

I will be good. I will be good. I will be good. Please help me to be good.

A week ago, I was so excited about this assignment. Mrs. Brixton told our class that she would keep the letters and send them to us at our future homes in the year 2000, when we will be the age that she is now.

Aurora Grace, the one thing in the world that I know I want to be is a mother, your mother. The idea of writing you a letter now that you can read someday gave me what Papa Pete would have called "purpose" and "direction" and all kinds of other things I've never had enough of. It made me so happy, I actually thanked Mrs. Brixton for the assignment. But now, I know I'll never be able to turn it in. School is out in less than a week. And one way or another, I will be gone by sunrise.

With love,

April (Your Future Mom)

TWO

QUENTIN

"IT WAS THE GIRL." The old man leaned forward, bracing against the worn-out armchair as though he were trying to escape its grasp. "April Cooper. She was the real killer."

Quentin Garrison watched his face. He was very good at describing people, a skill he used all the time in his true crime podcasts. Later, recording the narration segments with his coproducer, Summer Hawkins, Quentin would paint the picture for his listeners—the leathery skin, the white eyebrows wispy as cobwebs, the eyes, cerulean in 1976 but now the color of worn denim, and with so much pain bottled up behind them, as though he were constantly hovering on the brink of tears.

The man was named Reg Sharkey, and on June 20, 1976, he'd watched his four-year-old daughter Kimmy die instantly of a gunshot wound to the chest—the youngest victim of April Cooper and Gabriel Allen LeRoy, aka the Inland Empire Killers. Two weeks later, his wife, Clara, had decided her own grief was too much to bear and committed suicide, after which Reg Sharkey had apparently given up on caring about anything or anyone.

Quentin said, "Wasn't it LeRoy who pulled the trigger?"

"Yes."

"But you blame April."

"Yes."

"Why?"

Reg stayed quiet for several seconds. Quentin resisted the urge to fill in the dead air. This was a trick that often worked in interviews, the subject finally relenting and spilling his guts—anything to put an end to that awful, uncomfortable silence.

Quentin listened to the hum of the air conditioner and the whoosh of a passing truck. Just outside the shaded window, a bird shrieked—a blue jay, Quentin thought, or some other similar species put on this earth to destroy radio broadcasts. He was glad Summer had talked him into the cardioid mic—it was so much better at cutting out background noise than the omnidirectional he'd planned on taking. *You'd be surprised at how many distracting sounds there are in a typical living room*, Summer had said. And she'd been right. Of course, if Summer had seen this place, she'd never have called it typical.

Reg's living room was a time capsule, from the faded plaid earth-toned couch, to the Formica coffee table, to the avocado-green ashtray and matching coasters that looked as though they hadn't been unstacked since the premiere of the very first *Star Wars* movie. There was a coffee-table book of photography—*The Best of Life Magazine*—and a few dusty *TV Guide*s, one of which had Fonzie on the cover. It was as though Reg Sharkey had attempted to stop the clock on June 19, 1976, before his family had crumbled into a billion pieces.

Quentin took in the line of photographs on the mantelpiece—almost all of them of Clara and Kimmy, holiday photos and vacation shots, birthday party pictures, mother and daughter, smiling and young, forever hopeful, just we two . . . Quentin's jaw tensed, a tiny, bitter seed taking root at the pit of his stomach.

He took a deep breath, willing the tension out of his body as he'd learned in the holistic yoga class his husband, Dean, had forced him to take. *In with the positive energy, out with the negative* . . . God, Dean could be so Californian sometimes, but it was better than nothing. Worse than downing a globe-size martini, or putting one's fist through drywall. But better than nothing.

"They're all I have," said Reg. "Those pictures you're looking at. They're the only family I have left."

"Well . . ." said Quentin.

"You know what I mean."

"Yes." Quentin struggled to keep his tone neutral. "I know what you mean." But the truth was still right here with them, hanging in the stale air and coursing through Quentin's tensed muscles, showing itself in his narrow face and his slight overbite and the thick black lashes that used to get him teased when he was a kid. No matter what Reg Sharkey thought he meant, the truth was with them. It had nowhere else to go.

Reg and Clara had another daughter, a girl ten years older than Kimmy. At the edge of the mantel stood the evidence, a faded professional photo of the Sharkey family: Kimmy as a baby in Clara's arms, posed between Reg and that older daughter, Kate.

Quentin stared at the ten-year-old standing next to her mother, a skinny kid with a pained, buck-toothed smile, a puffy-sleeved pink party dress that seemed to swallow her whole. Thick lashes behind plastic-framed glasses, dark eyes identical to his own.

He gritted his teeth. One picture. Out of this entire gallery, just one picture of Kate in a bent, cardboard frame. Anger bubbled within him, the kind a healing breath couldn't fix, and Quentin had an urge to point that out—*just one fucking picture of her*—but he kept his mouth shut, remembering Reg's rough voice over the phone. How he'd relented, finally, to thirty minutes and not a second more. Quentin needed those thirty minutes if this podcast was going to work. He needed to keep calm.

Quentin cleared his throat. "Back to my original question," he said. "What did April Cooper do to make you think she was the real killer?"

"She didn't do anything."

"I'm not sure I understand."

Reg sighed heavily. "Gabriel LeRoy was all over the place. He was firing at everybody in that Arco station. He was consumed by rage. Out of control."

"Okay . . ."

"She wasn't."

Quentin nodded slowly. "She could have stopped him, but she didn't."

"Yep."

"I'm sorry, sir," he said, "but I'm really trying to understand this. Can you explain to me why that makes a fifteen-year-old girl guiltier of murder than the legal adult who actually killed everyone?"

He drew a long, weary breath. "Think about a house on fire. It's your house. Burning to the ground, taking with it everything you own. Everything you love. April Cooper—a fifteen-year-old girl as you point out—is standing next to the firehose, but she doesn't make a move toward it. She just watches the flames and smiles." Reg ran a hand through his hair and leaned forward, eyes blazing. "Who are you going to blame for all that destruction—the fire? It's a thing of nature. It can't exist without burning."

Quentin took too big a gulp of the iced tea Reg had brought him—lukewarm and bitter. Hard to swallow. *Everything you love.*

"Kimmy was just eleven years younger than April Cooper," Reg was saying. "She could have been her little sister, but that . . . that girl just stood there. Her boyfriend shot my daughter in cold blood. He took away everything I loved and April Cooper stood there, like she was watching a movie. Do you understand me now?"

Dark thoughts whirled through Quentin's brain. He tried another of Dean's deep, healing breaths. "Yes," he said. "I understand."

"Good."

Quentin pulled his steno pad out of his pocket. With shaking hands, he thumbed through the pages he'd covered in notes from the hours he'd spent online, reading old issues of the *San Bernardino Sun*.

"I haven't seen one of those since I was still working." Reg gestured at the pad. "I did the books for a Ford dealership in La Quinta. Spent twenty-five years in that same office, one secretary the whole time. Sweet old lady named Dee. I bet a kid your age wouldn't even know what shorthand is, but Dee was sure good at it."

Quentin cut him off too quickly. "Tell me about June twentieth, 1976," he said, reading from his notes. "It was a hot day, right? Close to ninety degrees."

"Yes. It was."

"And it was a Sunday. Did you guys go to church?"

"Yep."

"How soon after church did you and Kimmy go to the gas station?"

"We went home, had lunch. Kimmy asked if we could go for ice cream. The gas station was a quick stop first. But Kimmy loved it there."

"She loved the Arco station?"

"Yeah. There was a mural there—I think the owner's kid painted it. Noah's Ark, with all the animals."

"That's sweet."

"It was."

Quentin asked Reg to set the scene—to describe the sights and sounds and smells at the Arco station once he and Kimmy arrived. He wanted him to remember it in full, to the point of crying, so that listeners might feel something for this man. That *he* might feel something for this man . . .

Reg obliged, his voice soft and contemplative and weary. Good radio, though Quentin couldn't get himself to concentrate. ". . . steam coming off the pavement," Reg was saying. "His shouts. They echoed. The boy wasn't in his right mind. He was drunk or stoned. Maybe both. He was swaying on his feet. I told Kimmy to get down, and she did. But . . . she was holding her favorite plastic horse. The shiny black one. She dropped it. It made this clattering sound on the pavement, and then Le-Roy just . . . he just . . ." A tear trickled down Reg's cheek. "I begged her. I looked right into April Cooper's eyes and I said, 'Please make him stop . . .' But she didn't. She . . . she gave me this look. Like she expected this to happen. I think she might have smiled."

Quentin closed his eyes for a moment.

"You okay?" Reg said.

Don't say it. Don't say it . . . But he said it. He had to.

"Everything you love." And it was as though Quentin stepped off the edge of a cliff, years and years of pain and anger spread out below.

"What?"

"The burning house," Quentin said. "You said it takes down everything you love."

"That's right."

"What about your other daughter? What about Kate? She wasn't taken down. LeRoy and Cooper didn't get her. Are you saying that you didn't love Kate?"

Reg wiped the tear from his face with the back of his hand, jaw squared, eyes turning to ice. There would be no more crying, Quentin knew that much. He'd mentioned the elephant in the room about twenty minutes too early.

"That isn't what I—"

"Have you ever wondered about Kate? Tell me, sir. Have you ever felt bad about ruining her life?"

"You are nothing but a sleazy, fake-news journalist."

"Do you know what it's like for a child to grow up, completely ignored by her own father?"

"I will not be ambushed."

"Did you ever think about how that might affect her as a person, as a mother? Did you ever think about how it might make her treat her own son?"

"You said this was going to be about the Cooper and LeRoy murders," Reg said. "That's the only reason why I agreed to talk to you. You want to make this into some . . . some kind of family thing."

"The Cooper and LeRoy murders *are* a family thing."

Reg glared at the open laptop on the coffee table, the cardioid mic plugged into it, capturing every last word. "Turn that off," he said.

"Kate was a victim. She not only lost her sister and her mother. She lost her father too. You. You were never there for your daughter, and it ruined her. Jesus, you blame April Cooper for just standing there while horrible things happened in front of her. What did you do during my mother's *entire life*? *You just fucking stood there.*"

"Turn it *off*." Reg lunged for the laptop, but Quentin was there first, unplugging the mic, closing the lid, slipping it back into its case.

"Get out of my house!"

Quentin gripped the case, his palms slick from sweat. He headed for the door and Reg followed him. "There is no podcast, is there?" Reg said. "Your mother put you up to this."

Quentin turned. Stared him in the face. Reginald Banks Sharkey. His grandfather. He'd never laid eyes on him until today. And until today, he'd never realized how little he was missing. "We were both better off without you."

Quentin headed out the door and into the late afternoon sunlight, the old man shouting at his back.

"YOU'RE HOME EARLY," said Dean.

Quentin checked the time on his phone. "Yeah, I guess I am." It didn't feel early, though. In fact, the ride from San Bernardino to their South Pasadena bungalow had seemed to last a lifetime, with Reg Sharkey's angry voice looping through Quentin's brain, along with his own angrier one, that interview playing out over and over, to the point of where he was flipping around the radio—NPR first, then Howard Stern, alternative rock, '80s punk, the Soulful Sixties Station, anything, everything—just to drown it out.

What had he done?

Quentin wasn't normally a combative person. He took hits from his interview subjects without snapping back, and during rare arguments with Dean, he always made sure to listen carefully before responding. Hell, even Quentin's tweets were thoughtful and even-handed. He'd *worked on that*. He'd spent years learning to tamp down the rage that sometimes pressed against his skin, his throat, the backs of his eyes . . .

Man, he'd fucked this one up, though.

The podcast he was working on was called *Closure*. And what had sold the station's director of content on the idea was the personal aspect of it, how the Inland Empire Killers, both of them dead for forty years, continued to impact the lives of survivors and their descendants, including—and especially—Quentin himself.

The reunion with his grandfather should have been tender and surprising—a chance for Quentin to forgive his neglectful, damaged mother and the man who did such a terrible job of raising her and leave the past behind at last.

If the interview had worked out the way he'd hoped, Quentin and Reg would have taken a road trip to Death Valley, where April Cooper and Gabriel LeRoy had perished in a fire at the site of their last attempted murder—a compound owned by a survivalist family called the Gideons.

He'd envisioned his grandfather and himself, reunited after twenty-seven years, watching the sun set over the craggy rocks. He'd imagined them making peace with the ghosts of the murderers, with Kate, with each other. *Closure*, the podcast living up to its title in the most satisfying of ways. But that hadn't happened. Instead, Quentin had engaged in a two-and-a-half-minute-long yelling match with his mother's father—a dumpster fire of an interview that was more Maury Povich than NPR.

When Quentin had finally arrived home, "Candle in the Wind" was playing on whatever station he'd most recently found. That was his mother's favorite song and proof positive that God had a sick sense of humor. He felt his throat tightening, tears beginning to well in his eyes even now in his comfortable home with his sweet husband watching him, concern spreading across his face. *Seems to me, you lived your life* . . . Mom would sing it when she was high, in her cracked, broken voice. Just that one line, over and over, never finishing the sentence . . .

"What's wrong?" Dean said.

He couldn't lose it, not now. Instinctively, Quentin reached for his sunglasses—vintage Ray-Bans that Dean had given him their first Christmas together—but his shirt pocket was empty. "I lost my sunglasses," he said.

"Quentin."

"The ones you gave me. They're gone. What the hell is wrong with me?"

"You'll find them," he said. "Tell me about the interview."

Quentin took a deep breath, then handed the laptop bag to Dean. "On the bright side," he said, "Terry Gross can rest easy."

"Oh, honey."

"Use the headphones, okay?"

Dean looked at him in that kind way of his, and Quentin could almost see the sentences scrolling through his head, the helpful adages and encouraging words thumbed through and rejected. "There's a six-pack in the fridge," Dean said, finally. The most perfect thing he could have possibly come up with. "I just bought it."

"I love you."

As Dean put on the headphones, Quentin went into the kitchen. He opened the fridge and grabbed himself a bottle and cracked it open—a nice IPA, cold and bitter as Reg Sharkey's heart. He pulled a bottle of Cabernet out of the wine cabinet, uncorked it, and poured Dean a glass, and brought both drinks into the living room, where Dean was just removing the headphones. Finished already.

Quentin said, "See what I mean?"

Dean took a long gulp of wine, draining nearly half the glass, which seemed to Quentin more a stall tactic than anything else. "He called you fake news," he said. "I mean who actually says that when they're not intending to be ironic?"

Quentin sighed. "It's funny. People are so much more complicated than characters in movies. But that complexity is what makes them so much less interesting."

"What do you mean?"

"In the real world, you can be both a grieving father and a complete asshole—as Gramps here proves," he said. "But sadly, that combo makes for shitty radio."

Dean looked at him. "Did you ever tell him about your mom?"

Quentin shook his head.

"You could go back. You could tell him. Not like he deserves to know, but . . . I mean . . . He should be told, don't you think?"

"Dean."

"He'll see how much damage he's caused."

Quentin cringed. "I'm not going back. Ever."

"You said you need closure."

"No, honey. *You* said I need closure."

There was a long pause, Dean with those sad, soft blue eyes, Quentin trying to avoid his gaze.

You're too good for me. That's the problem. Quentin would have said it aloud, if it wasn't so true. "I think I may have to pull the plug on this podcast."

"Come on. There are tons of ways to tell a story. You've said that yourself."

"But this is *my* story."

"It still can be," Dean said. "You just need a different way in. Isn't there a book about the Inland Empire murders?"

"Only one that's worth reading. A cheesy paperback put out by a tabloid that came out right after the Gideon fire. They based the TV movie on it."

"So? Maybe there's something in the book you could investigate."

Quentin shook his head. "It's been out of print for years."

Dean sighed. "Oh . . . Wait." He reached into the side pocket of the laptop bag, removed the *Closure* burner phone and waved it around like a prize.

It was Quentin's turn to sigh. He and Summer had one of these for each of their podcasts—a private line for listeners to call in with tips and info. It had been Summer's idea—a way to keep the information for each story physically separated, should they be working on two podcasts at once. Plus, Summer was a bit paranoid—the only twentysomething Quentin had ever known with virtually no social media presence, not even when they were in college together. Summer claimed burner phones were less hackable or traceable than a simple line at the office. Why she thought anyone would try to hack or trace a tipline, she'd never bothered to explain, but that was Summer—careful to the point of not even knowing why. Dean said, "When was the last time you checked the tipline?"

Quentin brought the bottle of beer to his lips and drank, the cool of it sliding down his throat, calming him. Alcohol did him too much good. Same with the Klonopin he was prescribed, allegedly for plane trips. Allegedly.

He settled into the brown leather couch—one of two identical ones, the color and texture of broken-in bomber jackets, that had been in Dean's old apartment when they first met. Quentin loved them. Loved the faux Tibetan rug Dean had found at a yard sale, the bookshelves he'd installed, the bound Shakespeare collection that had belonged to Dean's grandfather. He loved Dean's kind and supportive parents and his aunt's lasagna recipe, his closet full of soft, shareable sweaters and his positive outlook on life. You bring so much to a marriage, so much more than just yourself—and what Dean had brought to this one was almost entirely good. "Three months," Quentin said.

"Seriously? Didn't you buy that phone three months ago?"

Quentin nodded.

"Well then," Dean said as Quentin drained the rest of his beer. "I'd say you've got a lot of listening to do."

THE BURNER'S VOICE mail was full. Quentin explained to Dean that he'd planned on going through it after he'd finished all his other interviews. But he only said that in order to avoid more raised eyebrows and *seriously*s from him. Dean couldn't be expected to understand. He was an assistant professor of philosophy at a tiny private college in peaceful Claremont, far removed from the world of radio and from the world in general. But the truth was, Quentin had always considered these tiplines a waste of time—full of crazies and fame-seeking murder fans and elderly NPR listeners, confusing the number for the station's weekly comment line. The thought of those same calls coming in regarding a crime that had impacted him so personally was unpleasant, to say the least.

But for Dean's sake, he listened.

He listened after dinner at his desk while Dean lay in bed with a book; listened carefully, earbuds in, pen poised to take notes. But the pen proved as unnecessary as he'd imagined it would be and before long, Quentin found himself deleting messages within seconds after they started. The few numbers he did take down were from people with incidental-at-best knowledge of the Inland Empire murders. A down-the-street neighbor of Cooper and LeRoy's third victim, Ed Hart, who admitted they'd only spoken briefly. A former waitress who had served coffee to Carrie Masters and Brian Griggs—the couple's sixth and seventh victims—two months before their deaths. A true crime buff with a theory that April Cooper and Gabriel LeRoy had been murdered by members of the Gideon family in some sort of ritual sacrifice, and that the fire that had burned their house down had been started by the ceremonial pyre. Yes, the voice mail pickings were so slim that he actually took that number down.

When he was close to halfway done, Dean asked him how things were going. Quentin just shook his head.

"Well," Dean said, "it isn't over till it's over."

"What does that even mean?"

"I have no idea."

Quentin put the phone down and moved toward the bed. "Honestly. Who was the lazy bastard who came up with that expression? *It isn't over till it's over.* He didn't even bother thinking of a synonym for 'over.' He basically just ran out of steam midway through the sentence and decided to repeat the exact same word." He was beside Dean now, gazing at his soft lips, his twinkling eyes. "And yes, I'm aware that I said 'he,' but I wasn't being sexist," he said softly. "I know how patriarchal assumptions bother you academics, but actually, I'm saying that a woman wouldn't be lazy enough to come up with that ridiculous, inane expression."

Dean smiled. "You're stalling."

Quentin smiled back. "You're right," he said. "And I could think of better ways to stall."

Dean's grin grew broader.

Quentin took his husband's hand and stared extra meaning into his eyes and started to sit on the bed, his smile turning to something with a more serious intent. He moved in closer, but Dean put a hand on his chest.

"Nope. Not falling for it," he said. "Get back to me when you're done listening."

"Oh come on."

"Just listen. If there's nothing on there, I'm fine

with hearing, 'I told you so.'" Quentin started to protest, but Dean put a finger over his lips. "Either way, you'll get laid."

He pushed himself to his feet. "Why do you care so much?"

"Because no matter how much you pretend not to, I know how much *you* care about it. And I know what it will do to you if you quit before you've done everything you can."

"Maybe you don't know me as well as you believe you do. Ever think about that?"

Dean looked at him.

Quentin's breath caught. Not the right thing to say. Too close to the truth.

"Quentin?"

"Yeah?"

"You're stalling again."

He felt a spark of relief and sighed heavily, dramatically. "I'm holding you to the getting laid thing."

"You can hold me to whatever you want. But you have to listen to those messages first."

Quentin forced a smile. He plodded back to his desk and picked up the burner. Listened to the next message—a woman who went to high school with the actress who portrayed April Cooper in the TV movie. He wasn't sure he was physically capable of making it to the end of these messages. And then his own phone vibrated in his pocket. He glanced at the screen: Summer. "Shit," he whispered. He'd never told Summer about the Sharkey interview.

"So?" she said after he picked up. "So?" He didn't answer right away, so she said it again. "So?" Summer was set a few speeds faster than everyone else, and often used words as a bayonet, jabbing and jabbing. She was from New York City, and though she'd lived here for eight years now, she still hadn't gotten used to the more relaxed rhythm. "Talk to me."

"Um."

"Is that a good um or a bad um?"

"I'm sorry, Summer."

Dean put his book down. "I'll give you your privacy," he said.

"No. Stay."

"I'm right here," Summer said.

Dean nodded, picked up his book again, though Quentin knew he wasn't so much reading it as putting a barrier between himself and Quentin's business. Dean always made a point of not invading his space. But Quentin never minded. In fact, he appreciated it, growing up the way he had, almost always alone.

"I was talking to Dean," he told Summer. "Not you."

"Oh. So, what was the problem? Your grandfather wasn't at home?"

"No, he was at home."

"He refused to talk?"

"Oh, he talked."

"Then that's great!"

"No it isn't."

"Of course it is. If he was home and he spoke to you and you got it recorded, there's absolutely no way that it isn't great."

Quentin said nothing—just plugged the phone

into his laptop and played her the whole of the interview.

He hopped back on the phone expecting a long, awkward silence, or at least a pause. But his coproducer was as unfazed as ever. "His description of the shooting is pretty good. We can use that."

"Summer."

"My job is to be objective when you can't be."

"*Summer.*"

"Okay. Look. Your grandfather turns out to be kind of a dick. I know that has to hurt. I'm not completely insensitive. But we're producing something here, something important."

"It isn't that important."

"You don't mean that, Q. You said it yourself. This podcast is going to change lives, including your own."

"I don't want to change my life." Quentin looked at Dean, his tapered fingers tightening on the book.

"You know what I mean."

"I don't want anybody else to hear that interview," he said. "I don't want to do this podcast."

At last, the awkward pause.

"I thought I could do something," Quentin said. "Change lives, like you said. Or at least learn from it. But . . . I think what I've learned is that I don't want anybody to know about my mother, or my grandfather, or my connection to these murders."

"*Why?*"

"Because," he said quietly, "the one thing I've learned is that my only real family is Dean. And I don't feel like doing a podcast on that."

Quentin took a breath. He could feel Dean's gaze on him, but he didn't return it.

"Okay," Summer said. "What if I told you that we could do *Closure* with hardly a mention of your family?"

"That's not possible."

"It is," she said. "It's why I called you in the first place. I've found somebody."

"What do you mean?"

"Actually, he found us. His name is George Pollard. I forwarded you his email."

Quentin opened his email. When he clicked on his in-box, Summer's forwarded one was at the top—the only unread email in his queue, George Pollard's name the return address. He gaped at the subject line. "Oh, come on."

"Don't judge until you read it."

The email came with an attachment, and Quentin opened that first—a faded, scanned photo from the '70s of a thin, dark-haired boy in a gas station attendant's uniform, posing between pumps.

"Pollard isn't insane," Summer was saying. "I talked to him. He's actually very respectable— hospital administrator from Duarte, married for thirty years with three kids. President of his local rotary club . . ."

Quentin enlarged the picture. George Pollard was also movie-star hot in his youth, especially for a guy who came of age before going to the gym became trendy.

"He knew her," Summer said. "He claims they were in love."

"Yeah, and?"

"The video? The one he sent us the link to? Hello?" She said it as though he were an easily distracted kindergartner, and she was trying to teach him the alphabet.

"I haven't looked at it yet." Quentin zoomed closer in, to the handsome teen's shoulder. His mouth went dry.

"Come on," Summer said. "Have you even read what he has to say?"

Quentin hadn't. But he didn't need to. Over the shoulder of the young George Pollard loomed the gas station's sign. It was an Arco station. He couldn't make out all the details of the mural on the wall beneath the sign, but he could still tell what it depicted: Noah's Ark and all the animals. George Pollard was standing in the spot where Kimmy Sharkey had been killed. Quentin's gaze went back to the subject line, a chill at the back of his neck.

April Cooper is alive, it read.

THREE

June 10, 1976
4:00 A.M.

Dear Aurora Grace,

Did you know that if you were to drop a penny from the top of the Empire State Building and it was to hit someone, it would go right through that person's skull? But if you hold that penny in your hand, it's shiny and harmless. It can even be good luck.

We're going somewhere, Gabriel and me. We're leaving in ten minutes. I am in the bathroom, writing this very quickly, so if I spell things wrong, that's why.

Before I came in here, Gabriel asked me if I'm on his team. I said yes. He asked if I still love him. I said yes to that too, and he took the gun away from my head. He told me I'm the best thing that ever happened to him, that we will escape from here and move far away where we can always be together.

I wanted to tell Gabriel that I'm not a thing to happen to him. I'm a person, a human being. But then I thought about Jenny and changed my mind. I told Gabriel it was Papa Pete who made me break up with him and that I've always loved him and will love him until the end of the world, just like we promised. I hope Papa Pete forgives me for telling that lie, and that when I meet him in heaven, he will understand.

I made myself touch Gabriel. I put my hand to his cheek and felt a tear. Gabriel's tear. I tried to make myself cry too, just to get him to love and trust me even more, but I couldn't. I don't think I'll ever be able to cry again.

Gabriel called me his angel. I called him my lucky penny. He seemed to like that.

5:20 A.M.

We're in Papa Pete's Cavalier. Gabriel is driving. I'm stretched out in the back seat. He thinks I'm sleeping.

He told me to pack a bag, and so I did. Here is what I'm taking, besides clothes and my toothbrush:

1. *Once Is Not Enough* by Jacqueline Susann. (My favorite book. I found it in Mom's drawer after she died, and I've read it three times. If I decide not to name you Aurora Grace, I may name you January Grace.)

2. Papa Pete's college ring. It's gold and it has a big red stone and it's worn down smooth inside from never leaving his finger. I can fit

two of my own fingers into that one ring of
his, and it still feels warm from him. Papa
Pete, I'm so sorry.

3. A picture of Jenny, holding her favorite
   stuffed animal (a fluffy pink dog she named
   Todd for some reason). I will keep the picture
   in the pocket of my denim jacket, and I will
   look at it every day.

4. Shalimar perfume. Gabriel made me take
   that because "my girl should always smell
   the way I like."

5. The big butcher knife from the kitchen,
   wrapped in one of my sweaters. For when
   Gabriel is asleep, and I find the courage.

   With love,
   April (Your Future Mom)

FOUR

QUENTIN

"THE SMILE," GEORGE Pollard said. "The way she runs her hand through her hair. The ring on her finger. See it? That's aquamarine. April's birthstone."

Quentin and Summer were sitting across from Pollard at his sprawling, polished desk at the Duarte Medical Center, watching the video clip of the woman he insisted was the very-much-alive April Cooper. It was well after his usual work hours—close to 8:00 P.M., Pollard having made up an excuse about a dinner meeting with the hospital board that his trusting wife had accepted without question.

Pollard had sneaked around on his staff and lied to his wife in order to meet Quentin and Summer, which said a lot. But he wanted no part of the *Closure* podcast—no visible part of it, anyway. "I feel awful about what happened to your family and I want to help," he'd said to Quentin over the phone that morning. "But if you mention me by name, position, or anything that directly identifies me, I'm afraid I will have to take legal action."

Quentin hadn't pressed. To be honest, he understood where George Pollard was coming from, both in his desire to distance himself from April Cooper and in his need to do something to make up for the damage she'd done. But he also believed he could get Pollard to reconsider. Meeting the man in person, looking him directly in the eyes and witnessing the change in them as he gazed at the woman on his computer screen, Quentin saw a lot of the same emotions that had plagued him since childhood. Longing. Loathing. Guilt . . . The key was to convince Pollard—as he'd somehow convinced himself—that *Closure* was the cure for all of it.

The video they were watching was the same link that Pollard had sent to the *Closure* email address. He'd sent it in response to a call for information Summer had posted on an Inland Empire Killers message board and it was a three-month-old clip of Robin Diamond, the film columnist for the popular website DailyCulture.com, discussing feel-good movies with her mom, Renee, in honor of this past Mother's Day.

It was Renee they were all focused on—softspoken, ash blond, sixtyish Renee. Renee, who had cried over *Bambi* when she was pregnant, who loved *Easter Parade* "above all other movies" and had watched it with her grown daughter "at least a dozen times," and who Pollard swore up and down was a very-much-alive April Cooper. "She couldn't wait to be a mother," he was saying now. "She wanted kids, a house, and a husband. In that order." His eyes clouded for a moment and he smiled. A dreamy, lost, young boy's smile. "Actually, the husband part she said she could take or leave."

Great quote, thought Quentin, who was recording the conversation on his phone. He always did this, even with deep-background and off-the-record and completely unwilling sources. With some of the particularly distrustful ones, he even kept a mini voice recorder running as backup. (He'd bought it from a spy store, and it looked exactly like a pen.) Summer found it unethical, but he didn't. He'd never air the interview without permission. And if he never got permission, he'd destroy the recording. Eventually. What was the harm in that?

"It's strange," George Pollard said as the video ended. "I never go to the Daily Culture website. I so rarely go to any of those sites. But I saw the link to the video on my home page—'Mother's Day Means Movies,' I think it was called. And for some reason I had to click through. It was like someone was guiding me there."

Summer said, "How soon into the video did you start thinking Renee was April?"

"Immediately," he said. "And it was more than thinking. It was knowing."

"Really?"

"It was her voice. It sounds exactly the same."

Quentin studied Pollard's face—a tanned and gently worn version of the teenager's in the photograph, the dark hair gone silver and expensively cut, fine lines around the eyes and lips that looked as though they'd come from years of smiling. Hard to believe that George Pollard was two years older than Quentin's mother would have been. He'd aged well—the way people of health, privilege, and happiness tend to do. Kate had none of those things in her life, and it had shown all over her.

"You're positive it was April's same voice," Summer said.

Pollard nodded, his dark eyes misty. *She was my first love,* he had written in his email. *But I'd rather not say any more than that here . . .*

Quentin said, "You never forget the voice of your first love."

Pollard's gaze traveled to the desk—the one framed photograph he'd placed at an angle, next to his computer. "That's right," he said quietly.

It was always interesting, the personal pictures people chose to frame and display. In his office at Claremont College, Dean had dozens of them—candid and staged photos of his parents, his younger sister and her husband and baby, a cheesy shot of Quentin feeding him cake at their wedding, even a black-and-white of his childhood dog. Reg Sharkey, of course, had a mantelpiece littered with framed pictures from a lifetime ago, while Summer's desk at work held just two: a photo of Joan Didion and herself, taken at a book signing, and a college-era pic of Quentin, his face contorted in laughter. It embarrassed him every time he caught a glimpse of it.

Quentin, for his part, had none. To him, framing a picture was an attempt to make time stand still—something that was neither possible nor desirable. He preferred to keep his personal photos on his phone, ready at any given moment to be deleted forever.

The sole framed picture on George Pollard's desk, the one he stared at now as though he were asking it for guidance, was of his family—his entire family. There were at least twenty people in the shot, ranging in age from elderly to infant, all wearing pale blue T-shirts, the words POLLARD REUNION 2014 emblazoned in white on the front. "Do they know about April?" Quentin said.

"No."

"None of them?" Summer said. "You haven't shown your wife the video?"

"No. And I never will."

"Why?"

Pollard turned his attention to Summer, then Quentin. "You're journalists," he said. "Can't you just investigate this?"

Quentin exhaled hard. "Mr. Pollard," he said. "My mother's younger sister was killed at the gas station where you worked."

"I know. And I'm so sorry."

"Were you there that day?"

"No."

"Did April Cooper and Gabriel LeRoy expect you to be there?"

"No."

"How can you be sure?" Summer said. Quentin glanced at her—those enormous cat eyes, that glow-in-the-dark pale skin, that red hair blazing furiously. Summer's looks were as arresting as her rat-a-tat speech pattern, and she had a powerful effect on the people she interviewed, like a human interrogation lamp. Quentin had seen subjects break under her unblinking stare, revealing more than they ever intended. "Quentin and I always thought it was random," she was saying to Pollard. "The police report says the Arco station massacre was a botched robbery. LeRoy had stopped there for gas and made a spur-of-the-moment decision to hold the place up."

"That may have been."

Quentin said, "You don't think it had anything to do with you?"

"I know it didn't."

"How can you know?"

"I just do."

"Mr. Pollard," Quentin said. "Even if LeRoy went to your station out of revenge or jealousy. Or if April Cooper secretly wanted to see you again—"

"She didn't."

"I'm saying it isn't your fault." He kept his tone low, measured. "None of it is your fault. Just like it wasn't my grandfather's fault for taking Kimmy to the Arco station. You can be honest with us. It will go no further than here."

Pollard's jaw flexed. "Are you recording this conversation?"

Quentin felt Summer's gaze on him. "I'd never record you without your permission," he said.

"I'm going to need you to take your phones out and turn them off."

Summer removed her phone from her purse and placed it on his desk. "It's turned off already, sir," she said.

Quentin removed his phone from his jacket pocket. He powered it down and set it next to Summer's, longing for his pen recorder, his eyes fixed on

Pollard's neat desk, lest someone look into them and read his thoughts. "You aren't being recorded, Mr. Pollard," he said. Which technically was not a lie.

Pollard glanced at the door, then turned his attention back to Quentin, his gaze intense enough to give off heat. When he finally spoke, it was in a voice so low it was barely audible. "I met April after the shooting took place."

"What?" Quentin and Summer said it in unison.

Pollard was staring at his hands, clasped against the polished desk as though he were praying for the strength to say more. "I met her," he said, "after the Gideon fire."

DURING THE SUMMER between his junior and senior year in high school, an honors student, varsity quarterback, and part-time gas station attendant fell in love with a presumed-dead, fugitive murderer and harbored her for twenty-four hours, his parents and younger brother never the wiser. She'd shown up at the gas station where he worked, half dead from hunger and exhaustion. And instead of calling the police, he'd made a gut decision and hustled her out of there before anyone took notice. He'd given her food, shown her around town, shared his deepest secrets with her, and made sure she got out safely, after which he'd gone on with his life, telling no one about his "first love" for more than forty years. It sounded like a pitch for some ill-conceived romance novel, but Pollard swore it was true. Every word of it. And, during the brief time Quentin spent in his presence, he was inclined to believe him.

It wasn't Pollard's respectable demeanor. Quentin had met plenty of people, not just in his career but throughout his life, whose kindly exteriors housed evil, untrustworthy hearts. It was something else—the earnestness with which he talked about April Cooper, maybe—that made Quentin think that, whether or not Robin Diamond's mother, Renee, truly was the infamous teenage murderer, George Pollard believed she was. "We hid out in a movie theater—a revival house on the outskirts of town," he was saying now. "We sat through the same movie for three screenings—at first it was so she could stay hidden. But at some point . . ."

"Yes?" Summer said.

"At some point, she stopped being who she was and I stopped being who I was, and we were just two teenagers, watching an old movie. Holding hands in the dark."

Quentin glanced at Summer. He wished his phone were recording. "You never forgot her," he said.

"Not a single day has gone by when I haven't thought about her. I've read everything I could about the murders. I lurk on all the true crime message boards. I watched that terrible TV movie, back in the day . . ."

"But you never contacted the police," Summer said.

Pollard shook his head.

"You never said a word about her to anyone—not even your wife."

"No."

"You kept her secret." Quentin said it without anger, without judgment. Though the "why" was implicit. "You let her live."

Pollard gave Quentin a slight, sad smile. "Our whole lives, we tell ourselves stories, don't we? I was a kid, and I was in love, and so I told myself the most powerful story I could about her. In order for the story to work, though, she had to be innocent."

Quentin said, "Why would a killer return to the scene of her ugliest murders, less than a week after they took place?"

Pollard's face relaxed. "Exactly," he said. "A guilty person would never do something like that, would they? They would want to put as much distance as possible between themselves and the crime scene. Everybody knows that."

Pollard stood up. Quentin took the cue. He picked up his phone. Summer did the same, and they both thanked him for his time, shook his hand.

"I almost forgot." George Pollard removed a sealed, legal-size envelope from his pocket and handed it to Summer. "This is my stub from the movie we saw at the revival house," he said. "I kept it all these years. But I'm thinking you guys might want it."

When they were alone in the elevator, Quentin spoke for the first time since he and Summer had left the office. "What I said about a murderer returning to the scene of the crime. I hadn't meant it as a rhetorical question."

"I know you didn't."

"Do you think it's true, Summer? I mean . . . I've been on the same message boards and websites as him. Every one of them treats it as a definitive fact that Cooper and LeRoy both died in that fire."

She shrugged. "Nothing is a definitive fact that

happened in 1976. There was no DNA testing back then." She opened the envelope Pollard had given them, slipped the ticket stub out.

"I know that. But." Quentin took a breath. "I mean . . . Look. Maybe George Pollard hooked up with some crazy girl forty years ago, and she told him she was April Cooper. I believe that. But do we really want to fly to New York and freak out this poor woman and her entire family, just because Pollard says her voice sounds familiar?"

"Quentin."

"And anyway. I want to tell the story of the survivors of a forty-year-old killing spree. I don't want to go all *CSI Inland Empire* with this."

Summer said, "We might not have any choice."

"What do you mean?"

She handed him the movie ticket stub, soft as silk from so much holding over so many years. The revival house's name was printed at the top along with the date: June 24, 1976. The exact same day that first responders in Death Valley found the charred remains of April Cooper, Gabriel LeRoy, and what looked to be the entire Gideon family. At the center of the ticket stub was that day's feature—the movie George and April had watched from beginning to end three times in a row, falling deeper and deeper in love with each viewing. The letters were faded and so ghostly thin, Quentin had to remove his glasses and squint in order to read them: *Easter Parade*. "Jesus," he whispered. "Way to bury the lede."

"RENEE LOOKS LIKE someone famous," said Dean, who was watching over Quentin's shoulder as he viewed the Daily Culture video clip for the umpteenth time. They were in bed, and it was close to midnight, Quentin having spent most of the evening chatting up the amateur sleuths on an Inland Empire Killers message board, asking for any possible clues—however shaky, however thin—that April Cooper might have survived the Gideon fire.

TBH, one of the sleuths had written, *I think there's more of a chance that Amelia Earhart survived that plane crash, flew back to the States, and joined the Rockettes.*

The Gideons were all men and boys, another had explained. *Mom died in childbirth six years earlier. The remains were of a girl April's age, height, and build. And her body was right next to the one identified as LeRoy's via dental records.*

Quentin had known all this, of course. It was information found in nearly everything that had been written about the Inland Empire murders, Wikipedia entry included. And it had made for some impressive pyrotechnics in the 1986 TV movie. But hearing it again, from people more genuinely obsessed with the case than even he was, force-bloomed the doubts that had seeded themselves in his mind the moment he dropped Summer off at her apartment. All they had to go on was one ticket stub and the off-the-record musings of a middle-aged man who'd been taken in for a few free meals by some vagrant girl forty-three years ago. That wasn't a podcast. Hell, it wasn't even a decent story to tell at a cocktail party.

"I don't think she looks like anyone," Quentin said, pointedly.

"Come on, honey," Dean said. "Who knows what a fifteen-year-old would look like at fifty-eight?"

"You believe George Pollard. You think I should believe him too."

"I believe," Dean said, "that anything is possible."

On-screen, Renee was waxing on, yet again, about *Easter Parade*. "I know it's not a mother/daughter movie per se," she was protesting over Robin's gentle teasing. "But it's a movie I love to watch with my daughter."

"Love is an understatement, Mom. How many times have we watched it together? I know it's in the double digits . . ."

"At least a dozen, maybe two," Renee said, and as her daughter laughed, she gazed at the vase of spring flowers placed in front of them, probably to add extra color to the shot. Robin looked to be around forty, but Renee was clearly a young mother, and on top of that youthful for her age. For a moment, she looked like a blushing bride, lost in the emotion of her big day. "Some movies are keepsakes," she said. Robin Diamond—a columnist, not an interviewer—didn't ask her to explain.

"Keepsakes," Dean said.

"Yeah, well, we'll never know what that was supposed to mean."

The clip ended. "What are you going to do?" Dean said.

"I'm going to get angry at myself for being so gullible."

"You honestly think George Pollard is lying?"

"Not intentionally. But he said it himself. We go through our lives, telling ourselves stories."

"Come on."

"Sweetheart, let's be real. Couldn't that adorable, lost girl have lied to the hunky gas station attendant about who she really was? And couldn't there be two sixtyish women out there with a special affection for *Easter Parade*?"

"So you need to investigate more. Get yourself another source."

Quentin nodded. "Or, you know . . ."

"What?"

"Drop the whole thing."

"Quentin."

He turned. This close, Dean's eyes affected him the same way the sun did. He couldn't look into them without hurting.

"Why does this story scare you so much?"

"It's not the story. It's the lack of it."

"That never stopped you before," he said. "What about that crazy guy in Kentucky who told you that the mayor of his town was a murderer? You flew out there, exposed him as a liar, uncovered a bigger, better story about the underage prostitutes—"

"That was different."

"How?"

"Well, for one thing, he never claimed that his fucking mayor was the person who turned my mother into a worthless drug addict." Quentin closed his eyes, but not soon enough. He saw the spark in Dean's eyes, that wince, as though he were bracing for a blow. "I'm sorry," he said.

"No. I'm sorry. That was insensitive. I need to be more—"

"You don't," Quentin said. "You don't. What I

need to do is grow up, do my job. Stop blaming everything on Mommy."

"It was only six months ago. You need time."

Quentin said, "I need to stop being so damn scared."

"You're scared?"

Quentin swallowed hard. He hadn't meant to say that out loud.

"What are you scared of?"

He shook his head. "That wasn't the right word."

"Quentin," Dean said. "You'd tell me, right? I mean, if anything was going on with you again . . ."

Quentin took Dean's face in his hands. He kissed him, because it was something he knew how to do, because he could close his eyes to do it and because it felt a hell of a lot better than answering that question. "What are you scared of?" Dean whispered.

Getting found out. Quentin didn't say it, but the words raked at his skin, the backs of his eyeballs. They pushed into his lips as he kissed the man he loved more than anything, so much more than himself . . . Those words, always close to the surface when the topic of his mother came up, her death and what it had done to him, what he'd done . . .

His hands slid down the length of Dean's smooth body, more powerful than his own and yet more yielding. He wasn't all coiled up inside like Quentin was. He had nothing to hide.

Quentin pulled away. "I'll investigate," he said. "I'll look into April Cooper's past. If I can find a compelling enough reason to believe she survived that fire, I'll fly out to New York and track down Renee."

"Quentin."

"Yeah?"

"I know what you're scared of."

Quentin's stomach tightened. "What?"

"Hurting people."

Quentin smiled, tears forming in his eyes. He closed his laptop. Clicked the light off, thinking back to months ago, weeks after his mother's death, when he'd awakened from a nightmare and reached out for Dean, pulled him too close and held on too tight, his lips pressed to Dean's shoulder, his face wet against Dean's neck, both fists jammed into his stomach, hanging on for his life. *Don't leave me, please don't leave me, please . . .* Dean waking, holding him. The gentle *sssh*es and *it's okay*s, and *I won't of course I won't. I'll never leave you.*

But you don't know me. You don't know what I've done.

Neither one of them had mentioned it in the morning. Neither one of them had spoken of it again. "You're right," Quentin said, his eyes open in the soft pitch-dark. "I don't want to hurt anyone."

FIVE

QUENTIN

THE HOUSE WHERE April Cooper had lived with her doomed stepfather and baby sister had been leveled decades ago. But Santa Rosa High School, where she'd gone for what was commonly believed to have been the last year of her life, was still around, located in a dusty little town of the same name—a far-flung L.A. suburb situated between Duarte and Monrovia that was nowhere near as lovely and exotic as its name suggested.

Judging from the old pictures Quentin had found online, it hadn't changed much over the last forty-three years, save for the stores in the strip malls that lined the wide, treeless streets. Back then, it had been all about Perry's Pizza and Sunglass Hut and Good Earth Health Foods (*Now serving frozen yogurt!*). These days it was mostly nail salons, punctuated by the occasional Chick-fil-A or Starbucks, plus a surprising number of crafting shops with overly cute names. Stitches n' Such, Buckets O' Yarn, Trimmin' the Tree. All those apostrophes, cropping up like dandelions everywhere you looked.

Santa Rosa High School was less than a five-minute drive away from St. Xavier, the Catholic boys' school attended by Gabriel LeRoy. But Quentin already knew that. It was part of the lore, how Cooper and LeRoy had met cute at the McDonald's between their two schools. The thing that surprised him most about SRHS was how close it was to Duarte, where George Pollard lived and worked. He'd grown up more than fifty miles away and had gone to college at Stanford, which was 350 miles north of here. Yet when it came time to settle down, he'd somehow made it back to his first love's last-known location. Quentin wondered how often Pollard drove by April's old school on a weekly basis—because that really was the question, wasn't it? Not *if*, but *how often*?

He could imagine Pollard cruising slowly past while talking to his wife on the phone, explaining to her and to himself that he was taking the long way home from work, his sparkling brown eyes aimed at the front steps, hoping to see a ghost.

Santa Rosa High was a beige building, squat and charmless, with slits for windows like a jail. It probably hadn't changed a bit since April Cooper was a student, which made Quentin understand, to a small degree, how she might have run off with a deranged murderer. Anything to escape.

After he pulled into the visitors' parking lot and found a space, Quentin took out his phone and recorded that thought. If this were to become a podcast, the story might very well start here, in the hellhole that spawned April Cooper. The skin prickled at the back of his neck, the feeling a familiar one—the thrill of being onto something, that first spark of understanding that would fire his curiosity, pushing him to investigate further. Quentin was beginning to understand April Cooper. Whether he wanted to or not.

"A place like this," he said into the voice recorder, "might even drive someone to kill."

QUENTIN HAD BEEN wrong about Santa Rosa High School being unchanged since the '70s. While it was definitely true of the décor, not to mention the ventilation system (*How can any of these kids stay awake in class?*), the security at SRHS was 2019 all the way. Intercom. Metal detector. Heavy glass doors that, according to Melanie at the front desk, were bulletproof. "We haven't had an actual school shooting," she said, "but we've had some close calls. The PTA petitioned the school board, and with the help of a wealthy donor . . ."

"You're safe now," Quentin said.

"I guess," said Melanie. "You ask me, they could have spent some of the money on new computers. Maybe a few books."

"Central air-conditioning?"

"Exactly. But the donor was specific."

"Interesting."

She shrugged. "People are scared in this town. Too scared if you ask me." Melanie clashed with her industrial surroundings. Raven-haired and pale-skinned, thanks to a shiny dye job and copious amounts of matte powder, she could have been any-where from twenty-five to fifty years old, though

Quentin figured she had to be on the lower end. She wore glittery cat-eye glasses, bright red lipstick, a vintage '50s frock that looked like something Lucy Ricardo would have worn out shopping with Ethel. A hell of a lot of work, just to sit at the front desk of a stifling-hot high school over summer vacation, talking to absolutely no one for 90 percent of the day. An older person, he thought, probably wouldn't have bothered. "At any rate," Quentin said, "thanks for buzzing me in."

"Are you kidding me?" she said. "You're Quentin Garrison."

Quentin blinked at her.

"I mean it. I'm a fan. *Kentucky Crimes* is my favorite. I've listened to it three times." She picked up the smartphone on the desk in front of her, headphones dangling out. "I think I'd go insane in this place if it weren't for my podcasts."

"You're interested in true crime." He said it not to Melanie, but to the smartphone, its case designed after the cover of *In Cold Blood*.

She smiled. "How did you guess?"

Quentin smiled back. It was always so much easier when they turned out to be listeners. You hardly had to explain anything.

"Are you doing a podcast on April Cooper?" Melanie said, proving the point.

"How did *you* guess?"

She adjusted her glittering glasses. "You're not going to do a hatchet job on her, are you? Treat her like she was whatsherface in *Natural Born Killers*?"

Quentin looked at her. "Any reason why I shouldn't?"

Melanie gave him a long, appraising look. "Come with me."

Quentin followed her down a hallway full of empty lockers, her heels clicking on the floorboards and echoing. A janitor nodded and grinned at her as she passed, clearly an object of interest to him in all her youth and red lipstick and costumey attire. "Hey, Bob," she said, unfazed. Used to the attention.

Near the end of the hallway was the library, which Melanie opened by key. "Librarians get summer vacation." She sighed, switching on the lights. "Unlike Bob and me."

Quentin inhaled the smell of books and plastic and carpet cleaner, memories snaking through him.

When he was a kid, his mother would drop him off at the public library after school and pick him up at closing. It was cheaper than day care, and Quentin never complained. At that age, before he grew tall and came out and learned how to fight, he'd spend full days getting tortured by bullies, then full nights at home with his mother, neither one of them saying a word. But at the library, he could escape. He could sit on the floor between the stacks and read for hours without feeling hassled or ignored.

He used to daydream about staying there past closing, reading all night, the night turning into morning and that morning to weeks, months. He dreamed of living at the library, amongst the Harry Potters and the graphic novels and the grown-up books he was just starting to discover. Shirley Jackson. Edgar Allan Poe. Joyce Carol Oates.

Once, he'd hid out in the back of the adult section and nearly achieved his dream, managing to stay past closing time to 10:00 P.M., when he was found by a security guard, thrown into a cop car, and reunited with his mother. Kate had been underwhelmed—at least that was the way Quentin recalled it—his mother's expression changing as soon as the cops left their home. *"What the hell is wrong with you?"* A roll of the eyes when he tried to hug her. Then off to the bedroom, the latest boyfriend, without a glance back.

Was that true? Like most people, Quentin so often lied to himself—out of protection or self-justification—to make himself the hero of his own story or at least someone deserving of sympathy . . . There were plenty of reasons for it. But regardless, it was difficult for him to put his trust in anything he hadn't bothered to get on tape.

"This was what I wanted to show you," Melanie said. She was standing at a long table to the left of the librarian's station, in front of a section marked *Our School*, which held bound editions of the SRHS newspaper, as well as shelves of yearbooks in chronological order. Melanie was holding one of the yearbooks, thumbing through the pages.

"I knew about April Cooper when I first started working here," she said. "I mean . . . she was probably the most famous person ever to have gone to Santa Rosa, which says a lot about this crappy school . . ."

Quentin moved closer. The yearbook was dated 1975–76. "She's obviously not in here very much," Melanie said. "She was only a freshman, and not exactly an activity queen."

"How many pictures are in there of her?"

"Just one." She laid the yearbook out on the table before him. It was opened to a spread titled "Freshman Homerooms." Quentin's gaze moved between the six black-and-white photos, but he couldn't differentiate April Cooper from the other '70s-era teens until Melanie tapped on her image with a bright red fingernail: a girl with delicate features and lank, dirty blond hair. She was short, but she slouched anyway, a baggy shirt and jeans swallowing up her frame. In the TV movie, April had been played by a twenty-one-year-old actress, and since photographs of the real girl were so scarce, that was the image that had stuck in most people's minds: that of an overdeveloped young seductress, worldly beyond her years.

The real April Cooper had turned fifteen less than three months before the murders. She did not look worldly in any way, but Quentin had already known that. He'd seen the posed picture of the two of them at the St. Xavier High School winter formal—Gabriel LeRoy looming over her at six one, the corsage a shackle on her bird-thin wrist. What surprised him about the yearbook photo wasn't how young April Cooper looked. It was how happy. April's attention was focused on the woman standing next to her—Mrs. Brixton, according to the caption, her homeroom teacher. And she was beaming. "Wow," Quentin said.

"Right?"

Quentin turned to her. "Do you know Mrs. Brixton?"

"She retired before I started working here," Melanie said. "But I've seen her."

"Yeah?"

"At last year's homecoming. I talked to her for a little while. Asked her about April. What she was like."

"You did?"

"I figured it might be my only chance. She's eighty-two years old, you know."

"Ah."

"And when I said the name April Cooper . . . I can't explain it, but her face kind of lit up, like she'd been waiting all her life to be asked about her."

Quentin held up a hand. "Is it okay if I record you?"

"Seriously?"

"It's not for broadcast. Just for my own notes."

Melanie broke out in a grin. "I'd be honored."

Once he'd turned on his voice recorder and placed it between them, Melanie repeated that last sentence—not just a podcast listener, but someone who had a true understanding of the way they worked. Quentin had a passing thought about hiring her at the station, whisking her away from all the drudgery and stale heat and craft stores. "What did Mrs. Brixton say?"

"It wasn't what I expected."

"In what way?"

"Well . . . I always thought of April Cooper as an angry person, you know? Angry at her stepfather for being so strict with her. Angry at her mother for dying. You know what I'm saying? A girl who was pissed off enough to kill. But Mrs. Brixton told me that the April she knew was actually very hopeful. She'd meet with her after class sometimes, and they'd talk about the future."

"Like the distant future?"

"Yes."

"That's interesting."

"Mrs. Brixton said she came up with an assignment. 'Letter to My Future Child.' She wanted the kids to describe their current lives and predict what the world might be like in the year 2000. She said she kept the letters, and sent them back to whatever students she was able to track down twenty-four years later. Anyway . . . she only did it that one year. And April was the one who'd inspired her."

"What about her was so inspirational?"

"Well . . . It's kind of an odd thing for a high school freshman to say. I know when I was that age I couldn't imagine anything worse," she said. "But April told Mrs. Brixton she couldn't wait to be a mother."

Quentin's eyes widened. He turned off the voice recorder. "You, um . . . you said Mrs. Brixton was at last year's homecoming."

"That's right."

"I bet her address is on file here, right? I mean, how else would they have sent the invitation?"

Melanie looked at him for a few moments, ruby lips twitching into a smile. "I can find it for you," she said. "Just don't tell my boss."

"You're the best human being I've met in years, Melanie."

Quentin followed her down the sad, empty hallway and back to the front desk, where she clicked into the school's "Friends of SRHS" database and found Edith Brixton's address and phone number. She wrote them both on a slip of paper and slid it to him facedown, as though they were a couple of wheeler-dealers in a cheesy old movie, negotiating a deal. "No worries," she said, after he thanked her. "Just make something great for me to listen to."

Once he was back in his car, Edith Brixton's address plugged into his GPS, Quentin found George Pollard on his voice recorder. He replayed that wistful voice describing his first true love, using the same words that had been looping through his own mind, the exact words Melanie had quoted Mrs. Brixton as saying about the smiling girl in the yearbook photo, again and again and again: *She couldn't wait to be a mother.*

"AND WHO MIGHT you be?" Edith Brixton's neighbor said as Quentin approached the door to her home—a tidy ranch house amidst a swarm of nearly identical one- and two-story stucco buildings at Serenity Springs, a seniors-only condominium complex in West Covina. He'd spoken to Edith on the phone on his way over and was pleasantly surprised to find her both lucid (you never knew past a certain age) and happy to hear from him. "Come right over," she had said. "Melanie told me all about you." *Melanie, the gift that keeps on giving.* So, when he parked his car on the quiet street outside her home and strode up to her front door, he may have done it with a little too much exuberance and bravado. The neighbor, after all, seemed suspicious. Quentin turned to her—a woman probably in her mid-seventies with a dyed-black updo and a perfectly round face. She sweated into a tracksuit of tight pink velour, her face flushed, glasses dangling from her neck on a rhinestone rope. She clutched a skittish little terrier in her arms that yapped and yapped, as though it had been born into the wrong life and was desperately trying to alert the world about it.

"I'm a friend of the family." Quentin gave the neighbor his most winning smile, but she wasn't having any of it.

"Is Edith expecting you?"

"Yes."

Her face relaxed a little. "Is she . . . uh . . . leaving with you?"

"Excuse me?"

"Are you taking her away?"

The door opened and Edith leaned out of it—a small, wiry woman with thick glasses that made her eyes look enormous. Though much frailer and leaning on a metal cane, she was still recognizable as the teacher in the yearbook picture—those same high cheekbones and wide, upturned mouth, the now-silver hair clipped into the same no-nonsense, chin-length style. She wore an oversize oxford cloth shirt that might have belonged to her husband, an A-line denim skirt, and Nikes, her pale, skinny legs roped with veins, like ivy crawling up fence posts. "Fuck off, Gladys," Edith told the neighbor. "I'm not going anywhere."

Gladys turned on her heel and stomped back into her house, the little dog protesting the entire way.

Edith shook her head. "I'm in one of the few one-story houses in this place," she said. "They all can't wait for me to either move out or kick the bucket, but that bitch is the most obvious about it, pardon my French."

"No offense taken."

She smiled. "So . . . April Cooper," she said.

"Yes."

"I don't think a day has gone by when I haven't thought about her, at least once."

Quentin looked at her. "Really? After all these years?"

She pursed her lips, her eyes going misty behind the thick glasses. "She was a special one."

"What do you mean by special?"

"Come on in," she said. "Excuse the mess."

IN QUENTIN'S EXPERIENCE, when interview subjects said, "excuse the mess," it usually wasn't over anything noticeable. Maybe they hadn't dusted yet, or they were busy sorting laundry on the dining room table and didn't want it mentioned on the air. It was more a sign of performance anxiety than anything else—a last-minute bout of maybe-I-shouldn't-be-letting-a-journalist-into-my-home. He always put them at ease with a friendly laugh. "What mess?" he'd say. Or "Come on. You should see my place!" But the moment he stepped into the small foyer of Edith Brixton's coveted ranch house, he knew that wouldn't fly here. Edith, as it turned out, was a serious hoarder—though her hoarding choices seemed limited to reading material. Newspapers, magazines, paperback books, filing boxes overflowing with ripped-out pages of old spiral notebooks and legal pads, covered with scribbles and yellowing. The whole place stunk of newsprint.

"Wow," said Quentin. He couldn't help it.

"My husband, Carl, was a neat freak. I think

maybe I've been trying to get back at him for dying on me."

He cleared his throat, pulled his thoughts together. "No, no. I get it," he said. "You like to read."

"Well, yes. I do."

"You don't want to forget what you've read, so you keep it around. For reference."

"I suppose that's part of it."

Quentin kept his expression neutral. "Listen, when I'm preparing my podcasts, I take notes on old steno pads. I've done that for pretty much every story I've ever written since I was in college. I've kept all of them. My husband makes me store them in boxes in the attic. He hates the clutter, just like yours did."

Edith smiled.

"But the thing is, I can't get rid of them. It feels like I'm throwing out entire parts of my life."

She leaned on her cane, a sigh escaping her lips. "Do you know something, Quentin Garrison? You are wise beyond your years."

"Nah. I'm just saying I know how you feel," he said, "because I'm the same way." Of course, Quentin was lying. He took notes on steno pads, yes. But only when he didn't have his voice recorder handy. And after he'd completed his stories, he couldn't throw them out soon enough. It disgusted him, really, his sloppy, spidery handwriting on the lined page. Something about him that could be analyzed, dissected . . . "Listen, do you mind if I record you?" he said. "I may have forgotten my steno pad, and anyway, I'd rather focus on what you have to say than on my lousy shorthand."

She answered fast. "As long as your tape recorder works properly."

It always surprised Quentin, how easy it was to get certain people to talk on record. He'd interviewed a guy on death row once, a psycho who'd killed his girlfriend and their baby, yet when Quentin turned on his digital recorder, he started acting as though he were a politician, or a Nobel Laureate, or anyone else who might be famous for doing something that wasn't horrible. *You're getting every word of this, kid? That equipment you got works, right?* Thinking about it now, with this for-all-accounts decent person having the same reaction, he realized it wasn't delusions of grandeur that made them so eager to have their words preserved forever. More likely, it was the knowledge of being on limited time.

"I think the living room has the best acoustics," Edith said. She led Quentin through a long hallway, weaving slowly around the stacks of cardboard boxes, nudging some aside with her cane. They wound up in a room with large windows and the shades drawn—a dark room, the couch stacked high with volumes of *Who's Who in America* and *Encyclopaedia Britannica* on one end, a cardboard Bankers Box on the other. There was a glass-topped coffee table in front of the couch, littered with magazines. It made him think of Reg Sharkey and his old *TV Guide*s, and he imagined introducing Edith Brixton to his grandfather—Reg with his tidy time capsule of a living room, Edith with her barely controlled chaos. Together, they might raise an army of dust bunnies and take over the world. Quentin sneezed.

"Bless you." Edith gestured at the one clear space on the couch, and Quentin settled into it, resting an arm on the encyclopedias.

Across from the couch was a rocking chair with no room to rock. Edith dropped her cane and hoisted herself into it, her thin legs not quite reaching the floor. Quentin turned on his phone's voice recorder and set it on the coffee table, atop a *New Yorker*. "Ready?"

Edith nodded.

"I'm speaking to Edith Brixton on June 28."

Edith said, "You're sitting next to April."

Quentin swallowed. "Pardon?"

"The box."

He looked at it. Then looked at her.

"I wasn't just a homeroom teacher," Edith said. "I taught English, social studies, one dismal year of geography . . . Anyway, I kept boxes of all my favorite students' work. My husband, like yours, made me keep them in the attic . . ." She pushed a lock of hair out of her eyes, a slight tremor in her hand. "That box next to you—that's April. I looked for it after you called. It was easy to find."

"She was in your social studies class."

"That's right."

"She was a favorite student." He tried to keep the disdain out of his voice. "A special one."

She ran a hand across her brow, the index finger quivering. "Take a look."

Quentin removed the lid from the Bankers Box. There was a small pile of papers inside, rounded girlish handwriting on lined pages. He read the first page, her name on it, the carefully formed letters.

Women and the Right to Vote
By April Cooper

As Quentin slipped the pages out of the box, a feeling swept through him—a chill that pressed all the way to the bones, followed by a tightness in the muscles—a faint, simmering rage. *Her handwriting on the page. This girl, who had watched her boyfriend kill a child, who had most likely killed many times herself. This murderer, who dotted her i's with little circles. Her handwriting. She wrote this* . . . He was aware of the silence in the room, his voice recorder capturing it, but he couldn't get himself to speak.

"Can you read it?" Edith said. "I know it's quite faint . . ."

He looked up at her—the big eyes behind the glasses, watching him, expectant. He cleared his throat. *Read.* "Before the 19th Amendment came to be in 1920, women didn't have the right to vote. But because of the suffragettes like Susan B. Anthony and—"

"No, no. Read what she wrote at the bottom of that page."

Quentin coughed. The dust was getting to him, but something else was getting to him too. *A special one* . . . He wondered if Mrs. Brixton kept boxes for Brian Griggs and Carrie Masters—Cooper and LeRoy's fifth and sixth victims, found in their prom clothes, handcuffed together, shot in the head. Seniors at Santa Rosa High, not St. Xavier. Most likely victims of Cooper, not LeRoy. A murderer. The girl who ruined his mother's life. Her handwriting on the page.

"Go on," Edith said.

He took a breath. *Keep it together.* "The efforts of these brave women allowed for us all to be free," he read. "But I don't feel free, Mrs. Brixton, do you? When I am of legal voting age, like you, will I feel free, and equal and strong?" He read the next sentence, looked up at Edith Brixton and recited it out loud. "Is that a reason for me to look forward to growing up?"

Edith removed her glasses and rubbed her eyes. "She was one of those kids," she said. "Always looking out the window, daydreaming. Her body would be in the room, but her mind would be a million miles away."

"Did she talk to you directly in all her school essays?"

"Yes."

"Why?"

"I'm not sure exactly," Edith said. "But she'd lost her mother just a year earlier, and most of the other teachers at that time were younger women. Or men."

"You think she was looking for a replacement."

She put her glasses back on. "Something like that. I asked her to stay after class once, and we discussed the questions she'd written to me. It became a sort of tradition. April staying after class, talking with me about the future."

Quentin thumbed through the slim stack of pages, reading sections from them into the voice recorder. An essay about the Great Depression, and its influence on the American family (*Which would you rather have, Mrs. Brixton—enough money to eat, or parents who truly love you?*) Another, titled the "Arab/ Israeli Conflict." (*This happens so often, I think, but maybe you can explain why: people living side by side, but not bothering to understand each other.*) Another one was called "The Death Penalty in America." And when he read the last sentence, his breath caught in his throat. "Mrs. Brixton," Quentin said, "have you ever met anyone who deserved to be killed?"

She stared at him. "What do you mean?"

"I'm quoting April."

"Oh," she said. "Right. 'The Death Penalty.'"

"Did you ever meet with her about these papers? Did you ever . . . I don't know . . . suggest therapy?"

She gave him a weary smile. "You didn't send children to therapy back then," she said. "Not unless they had real problems."

He leveled his eyes at her.

"I know, I know." She sighed heavily, the breath draining out of her until she seemed even smaller. "I didn't think of her as a child with problems," she said. "The April I knew was sweet and caring. And so very alone."

"Even after she started seeing Gabriel LeRoy?"

"More so."

"Really?"

"He wasn't good for her. She knew it. He was needy and demanding. He wanted to marry her and she . . . she asked my advice about breaking up with him. She asked me how she should do it."

"When?"

"Just before he took her away." Her voice quavered. "I . . . I suggested she simply blame it on her stepfather. Tell Gabriel that he said she was too young to go steady."

Quentin's eyes widened. "You think he kidnapped her?"

"I know he did."

"But the police reports . . . The one from the prom night murders. It says—"

"I don't give a flying fuck about what the police reports say." She took another long, wheezing breath. Her whole body was trembling now. Quentin worried she might collapse. "Pardon my French."

"Can I get you anything? A glass of water? I didn't mean to upset you."

She shook her head, her body calming, slowing. "That poor girl," she said. "All she wanted to do was grow up and have a baby."

Quentin nodded, slowly. There was nothing he could say to that. Except maybe . . . "I hope she realized at some point, how much you cared about her."

"I hope so too, Quentin."

Quentin started to slip the papers back into the Bankers Box when he noticed something at the bottom of it—a postcard, addressed to Mrs. Brixton, not at her home but at the school. He took it out.

Edith said, "Oh, that shouldn't be in there."

The postcard was unsigned and read simply, *Wish you were here!* He stared at the rounded script, the circles over the *i*'s. He turned it over. A photograph of a maple tree with bright orange leaves. "What is this?"

"Wishful thinking," Edith said. "She always used to say that she wanted to go somewhere where they had seasons . . . I got that postcard, and I thought maybe . . . Maybe . . . I know it's crazy."

"You got this after April's death."

"Like I said, wishful thinking."

Quentin looked at the postmark: August 1977. A year and two months after the Gideon fire. And the same month and year, according to Wikipedia, that film columnist Robin Diamond had been born. Quentin's pulse pounded. "She just wanted to grow up," he whispered, "and have a baby."

"Are you all right?"

"Can I photograph this postcard with my phone?"

"I suppose," said Edith Brixton. "But why?"

Quentin forced a smile. "Wishful thinking?" he said.

The postmark read New York.

SIX

Dear Aurora Grace,

They call it falling in love because you really do fall. The ground slips out from under you, and you're in this place you've never been—mysterious and dark as a different planet. It's hard to breathe there. There's nothing to grab on to. You can't pull yourself out. Not until the day you fall out of love. And when that happens, when you fall out of love, it's just as unexpected and hopeless and impossible to get out of as it was when you fell into it in the first place.

For me, that happened a week ago, but it could have happened any time. It wasn't anything Gabriel did or said. It was his face, close up, as we were kissing. Out of focus like that, Gabriel didn't look like a boy or a man at all, but like some sort of animal—wolf mixed with bear. And it was consuming me, that animal. It was holding me in its claws like a piece of meat.

Aurora Grace, never open your eyes when you

kiss a boy. I swear to God you will not like what you see.

The next morning, I broke up with Gabriel. I did it over the phone so I wouldn't have to look at him, ever again. I told him Papa Pete didn't want us seeing each other anymore, because I thought that might make it easier for him, easier for both of us. Mrs. Brixton had suggested it, and she always had the best ideas. A little white lie. That's what she said.

Gabriel cried. Wet sobs I could feel through the plastic. Boys aren't supposed to cry like that. It turned my stomach. When I hung up, I thought, thank God that's over. But it wasn't, was it? My white lie, the thing that was supposed to make it easier on both of us. That lie killed my stepdad. I killed Papa Pete.

Now we're sitting in Papa Pete's car. Gabriel's behind the wheel and Kool & the Gang is on the radio and I'm not going to cry. I can't cry in front of him. I can't even look unhappy, or I'll get shot too, and Jenny will have no one. So I push Papa Pete out of my mind. Kind Papa Pete who tried his best to cook Mom's recipes after she died and who told me he loved me the same as Jenny—that I was his real daughter, just as much as her. I tell myself not to think of him, ever again.

I make myself smile. At first, my lips won't stop twitching but after a while it gets easier. I mouth the words to "Hollywood Swinging" and bop my head to the hey, hey, heys.

Gabriel grins at me. He tells me my smile is

sexy. He sings along with the song and then he says maybe we'll wind up in Hollywood ourselves—a supercouple, like Farrah Fawcett and Lee Majors.

He puts his hand on my knee. The smile stays plastered to my face. "Oh baby," I tell him, "that would be a dream come true."

Once you tell one lie, you wind up lying forever.

SEVEN

ROBIN

WHEN IT STARTS, it's barely perceptible. An unmet gaze. The flushing of his skin at an odd moment. A late-night work call, taken in another room.

The next phase, though, is harder to ignore. You can feel the rift, the cold whistling through it, that awful unbreachable gap. Or so it seemed to Robin Diamond as she scanned her husband's Twitter feed while waiting for her boss, Eileen, to read her column, clicking on his "tweets and replies" with her jaw clenched. Eric Diamond, executive producer on a cable TV "news" show called *Shawn Labatoir's Anger Management*, always said he had little time for social media. He used it solely to plug his stories, he said. No personal pictures or information.

But clearly, he made an exception for GinnyMarie, a "lover of the beach," according to her Twitter bio. *Proud Mama to My Furbabies, Yoga Is Life, God Bless the USA.* The banter between those two . . . Well, it sparkled, didn't it? It scintillated. Apparently, Ginny was looking for a funny movie to see and

Eric was suggesting the works of Ernst Lubitsch, extolling the virtues of *Trouble in Paradise* in five separate tweets, less than a minute apart, all this taking place during lunchtime today, when he'd claimed to be in the throes of a breaking story and too busy to meet up. Granted, a Twitter conversation took moments, while lunch with one's wife was more of a commitment. But was Robin wrong to ask for commitment from a man who seemed so distant lately? Who had worked more late nights in the past two months than in the previous three years? A man who failed to mention in half a dozen tweets about *Trouble in Paradise* that he had seen that very movie with his wife at the Film Forum in NoHo fifteen years ago, that it was one of his wife's favorites, and that when they were both grad students at Columbia, she'd taken him, well, *dragged him to it*, actually, as part of an ongoing campaign to educate this otherwise knowledgeable man on films made before 1990? *What's on your mind?* Robin had asked Eric last night when she'd rolled over to find him sitting up in bed, eyes open, staring. *Nothing*, he had replied, which for all she knew was the truth. Eric the enigma. Unreadable, even as his wife transformed into the type of person who stalked his Twitter feed, who was jealous of a lover of the beach in a red, white, and blue bikini top who called her ferrets furbabies and hashtagged the word *blessed*.

Robin's work extension buzzed. Assuming it was Eileen, she closed Twitter and corralled her thoughts back to her column—about a proposed all-female remake of *The Magnificent Seven*, which she was in favor of, despite (or more likely because of) all the online hate it was receiving from men.

Robin cleared her throat. "That was fast," she said.

"Ms. Diamond?" The voice was male and young. Reedy. Touch of vocal fry.

Robin glanced at the caller ID screen and saw an unfamiliar outside line. A 213 area code. Los Angeles. *Movie publicist*, she thought, readying for the pitch. *What I wouldn't give for a glass of wine . . .* "Yes?"

"Hi. My name is Quentin Garrison. I work for KAMC, an NPR affiliate in the Los Angeles area, but I'm out in New York right now."

"Yes?"

"I'm working on a podcast."

Robin frowned. "Yes?"

"I hear noise in the background. Is it hard for you to talk privately where you are?"

Robin glanced around the room, as though she were seeing where she was for the first time. The Daily Culture offices were set up as an open newsroom—art, copy, and editorial all in the same large space. At the next desk over, Jill the music editor was ordering Thai food in her too-loud voice. David from photo was a few desks away, going over red-carpet art on an enormous screen with Michael the creative director, the two of them complaining about all the rearview poses, the over-the-shoulder. "If I have to look at one more set of ass implants," Michael was saying.

"Believe me," Robin said. "No one is paying attention to this conversation."

"Great." He cleared his throat. "Great, we can talk then . . ."

Robin googled his name on her Mac: *Quentin Garrison*, adding *NPR* and *podcasts* for good measure. A picture popped up at the top of her screen—a bespectacled, sweet-faced young man—along with a bio from KAMC's website. She glanced at it. "I think you may have the wrong person," she said. "Alice Cerulli is our true crime editor."

"Not a chance."

"Excuse me?"

"I'm working on a podcast called *Closure* about the Inland Empire Killers. I have a relative who was one of their victims, hence the title."

"Okay . . ."

"I'm trying to get in contact with your mother."

Robin blinked. "My mother."

"I tried social media, but she doesn't seem to be on it. I found her last name, Bloom, from your wedding announcement, but your parents' number is unlisted."

"You want to talk to my mother? For a murder podcast?"

"Actually, I'd love to talk to both of you. Your dad too of course. He's retired, right?"

"No, he has a private practice now."

"Anyway, the whole conversation can be deep background. I won't record it if you don't want me to. If you want to get your truth out but not your identities, I won't name names or locations. And I have the ability to disguise voices. If you don't want to participate at all, I respect that. But I'd at least love the opportunity to share with you what I've learned."

"Mr. Garrison."

"Call me Quentin."

"Quentin," Robin said quietly. "What the hell are you talking about?"

There was a long pause, to the point of Robin thinking maybe the connection had died. "Hello?" she said.

"You're being straight with me, right?"

Robin's other extension buzzed. Eileen. "Hold on a sec." She clicked on the second line, told the editorial director she'd be in as soon as she ended her call, then got back on with Garrison. "Listen, I've got to go to a meeting."

"Ms. Diamond, how much do you know about your mother's teenage years?"

"She had me at nineteen."

"How about before that?"

Robin's extension buzzed again. "I really have to go."

"Okay," he said quickly. "Okay, look. You have my number on your caller ID. Can you call me back when you're free to talk?"

"I don't know. I'm really busy."

"You can call late if you want. I'm still on West Coast time."

"I'll think about it."

"Can you at least do me one favor?"

"I have to go, Quentin."

"Ask your mother about April Cooper. Ask her if she's ever heard of her."

"*I have to go.*" Robin slammed down the phone, her cheeks burning. The words had come out louder than expected. She could feel eyes on her,

Jill gesturing at her dramatically, the phone still in her hand from the Thai order, mouthing, *Are you okay?*

"Publicist," Robin said, affecting an eye roll. As she stood up and started for Eileen's office, she could still feel the phone in her hand, his voice in her ear, her pulse in the tips of her fingers. And that tingling, as though there were something horrible taking place just out of her eyeshot and if she turned ever so slightly, just enough to catch a glimpse . . .

"Shitty publicist," Michael said.

Robin forced out a laugh. "Right?" She had to shake this off. She was worked up. Emotional. It had to be hormones. Or a chemical imbalance. She'd been on meds for a short time as a teen—low-dose Valium to calm her. Ritalin to help her focus. A rarity in her neighborhood back in those days, but not when your dad was a psychiatrist. Maybe she needed a similar combo now, in early middle age. Maybe she should ask her father for the name of a good shrink . . .

No. What she needed was a decent night's sleep. Robin had terrible insomnia lately, and it was taking its toll. Obviously.

Quentin Garrison was mistaken. Robin's mother was a housewife from Tarry Ridge who baked pies and volunteered at the hospital and had once nursed a baby bird back to life. She'd been married and a mother for nearly as long as she'd been alive. What would she know about the Inland Empire Killers, whoever they were?

Robin gripped the back of her chair, hoping no one was watching her. She took a steadying breath and headed for Eileen's office feeling better, but still . . . Still.

There was one thing she couldn't shake off. That name. April Cooper. She'd heard it before.

"WHAT I'M TRYING to say is, I'm worried for your safety," Eileen said.

Robin was in her office, holding a cup of French press coffee, Eileen's "secret stash" as she called it—they both hated the crappy breakroom coffee. "Like the old song says . . ."

"Stop."

"Come on, Eileen."

"I mean it, Robin," said Eileen, who had just finished reading Robin's column about the *Magnificent Seven* reboot. "This is a legitimate concern."

For someone who walked through the newsroom repeating, "clickbait, clickbait," like a mating call, Eileen was surprisingly squeamish when it came to actual controversy. Robin was probably the only person here who knew that about her. She'd been working for her since the launch of the site ten years earlier, and before that, they'd gone to Columbia Journalism School together, the two of them roughly the same age, the oldest Daily Culture staffers by far, though that too was something only Robin knew. Eileen Rand was assiduously, emphatically ageless.

Robin tried, "How about we run the column as is, and I stay off social media for twenty-four hours or ten minutes or however long it takes everybody to be outraged at something else?"

"It's feminist propaganda."

"It's a *movie column*."

"Not in my opinion, of course. I'm just trying to imagine what the trolls might say."

"We're pandering to trolls now?"

"No," she said. "No, of course not. Let me think here . . ."

Robin brought the mug to her lips. She swallowed the coffee too quickly, searing her tongue.

"Maybe we could just soften the lede a little," Eileen said. "Talk about what a classic the original *Magnificent Seven* was before launching right in."

"Fine."

"Then there's that late reveal, where you announce that you've opted to be . . . you know . . ."

"What?"

"Child-free." She actually said it in a whisper.

Robin rolled her eyes. "Take it out," she said. "Whatever." She might have cared enough to put up a fight an hour ago, or at least to call out Eileen for treating the phrase "child-free" as though it were some type of slur. But now she just wanted to get out of this meeting.

"Okay, you win," Eileen was saying now. "I'm being too nervous Nellie about this. It is a movie column. Not the *SCUM Manifesto*."

Robin looked at her. "So, no edits? We're not going to make it into a listicle or a meme?"

Eileen sighed. "I've gotta stop worrying so much," she said. "And you know what else?"

"What?"

"I really hate the song 'Come on, Eileen.'"

Robin sang the words softly. "At this moment, you mean everything . . ."

"Do that again and you're fired."

"You fire me, you'll be the only one here old enough to remember that song." Robin took a tentative sip. The coffee was cooler now, but she could hardly taste it. Her tongue was still numb from the burn. She remembered being a kid, her favorite meal of grilled cheese and tomato soup, Mom dropping an ice cube into the soup, *So you won't get hurt.* Robin took another sip, that reporter's voice in her head again. Quentin Garrison. *Ask your mother about April Cooper.* What was he talking about? Why had he called her?

Eileen tapped at her keyboard. "Your column is officially live."

"Great."

"Enthusiasm is not your strong suit today."

"Eileen?"

"Yeah?"

"Have you ever heard of the Inland Empire Killers?"

"Wow. Non sequitur."

"Have you?"

"Umm . . . Wait . . . Oh, yeah. From the '70s, right?"

"I don't know," Robin said. "I'm asking you."

"I think there was a Lifetime movie about those murders." She went back to the keyboard.

"You looking it up?"

Eileen nodded. "Here we go." She turned the monitor around and Robin stared at the screen—two picture-perfect young actors in tight jeans and clean T-shirts, pasted-on scowls. A dark-haired boy in a blood-spattered shirt and a blond girl with bee-stung lips and hot pants. Both teens held shotguns, and Robin knew them. She knew those faces . . . "Movie of the Week actually," Eileen said. "We didn't have Lifetime in my house. I remember thinking the girl who played April Cooper had pretty hair."

Robin stared at the picture, remembering. "April Cooper."

"Yeah," she said. "That was the girl killer's name. The boy was named Gabriel and the actor who played him was not all that cute. I remember thinking she could do way better. Maybe that was the point, I don't know. Of course, the women in those old TV movies were always hotter than the guys . . ."

"I . . . I saw that . . . that show." Though the truth was, she had only seen part of it. The beginning. She'd been seven years old. Maybe eight. Curled up on her living room rug, eating a bowl of chocolate ice cream, the announcer's voice, low and rumbling and important. "Coming up next, *The Inland Empire Killers: 'Til Death Do Us Part.*" Her mother was in the kitchen, her father on the couch behind her. The announcer said, "What drove Gabriel LeRoy and April Cooper to murder a dozen people in cold blood?" The way he'd said the names. The way he'd said the word. *Murder.* It was thrilling. On the screen, the boy and girl, standing next to each other, guns aimed straight in front of them spitting bullets and fire and Robin watching, transfixed. *Murder.*

Is this too scary for you?

No, Daddy. I want to watch.

And then Robin's mother had swept into the

room, yanking the remote out of her hand, shutting off the TV like someone else's mean mother, a different person, a stranger. *Mitchell, what the hell are you doing?* Mom, who had never sworn before, at least not in front of Robin. Mom, who *tsk-tsked* at her father if he let a *damn* slip out.

Mommy, please can I watch?

Go to your room right now.

But . . . Daddy said I could.

Go to your room and stay there. No TV for the rest of the night.

All these years later, it had stuck in her mind— the announcer's voice, the teens on the TV screen, the blaze of their shotguns, that very same blaze as in her mother's eyes. The shock she'd felt. The fear. Robin had never seen Mom that angry, not before then or since. Even her father had seemed confused. The way he'd looked at her, something shifting in his eyes. *Calm down, Renee. You're frightening your daughter.*

Robin looked at Eileen. "Your parents let you watch that?"

She shrugged. "It was just a TV movie."

Robin nodded slowly. "You're right," she said. "It was."

She put her mug of coffee down and stood.

"Robin," said Eileen. "Are you okay?"

"I'm fine," Robin said, though she couldn't look at her. "Everything's fine."

ALONE AT HER house in the Westchester County suburb of Tarry Ridge, Robin poured herself a glass of sauvignon blanc, made a Gruyère and spinach omelet for one. Her husband had texted her while she was still on the train:

> Dinner with important source. Will come home as soon as I can. Love you.

Ok, she'd texted back. Just those two letters. She didn't trust herself to type more.

The show her husband worked for, *Shawn Labatoir's Anger Management*, was a barely controlled vent-fest. A rotating group of so-called pundits screaming at each other without listening as Labatoir stood at his podium, smirking out the easiest seven-figure salary ever. The idea that Eric would be dining with an important, unnamed source for the show was, to put it mildly, hard to believe.

But that wasn't what had bothered her most about Eric's text. It had been the *Love you* part, the way it had been tacked on at the end as an afterthought, a covering of tracks . . .

"Stop." She said it out loud. "Just stop."

Robin gulped the wine and took a bite of her omelet and gazed out of her kitchen window. It was 8:00 P.M. but still light out, the clouds blushing with the first hint of sunset. *It's not really that late anyway*, she thought, summer working its magic, making everything seem just a little less serious. She remembered Quentin Garrison asking her about the Inland Empire Killers, and that seemed less serious too. Just an overzealous young reporter, following every tenuous lead he could find. Back at work, she'd looked up everything she could about April Cooper. And in this case, knowledge had wiped away most of her fears. As it turned out, the murderous teen had been three years younger than her mother was. And according to every story about her, she'd died in a fire. *Mom may have known a murderer. Maybe they went to the same school or swam at the same public pool or went to summer camp together or something. Big deal.* But it probably was to Robin's mother, the type of person who would have blamed herself for allowing the murders to happen. No wonder she'd gone ballistic over her seven-year-old kid watching that ridiculous TV movie . . .

Anyway, if Garrison's phone call had taught Robin anything, it was that she needed to talk to her mother more about her past. Here, her parents lived three blocks away, in the house she'd grown up in. She considered her mother her best friend, someone she could talk to about anything. Yet, aside from vague references to foster care and growing up poor, she knew virtually nothing about the life she'd led before meeting her father.

That was strange, wasn't it?

She took another bite of her omelet. The cheese wasn't entirely melted, yet the eggs were too dry. Robin was a terrible cook. She threw out the rest and slapped together a peanut butter and jelly sandwich. She ate half of it, polished off the rest of her glass of wine, and tapped her parents' number into her cell phone. Robin's father answered after three rings. "Oh, hi, Robbie." A strange, sad note in his voice. "I was just watching the Yankees lose the fifth game in a row."

"Oh, I'm sorry, Dad."

"Los Angeles Angels. They're killing us."

"Listen, is Mom around? I just wanted to ask her something."

"She's at the grocery store. We ran out of coffee. Anything I can help you with?"

"Maybe . . ."

"I'm all ears."

"How much do you know about Mom's childhood?"

Robin heard the TV in the background, Michael Kay saying something about a forced out. "Well, that's an unusual question," her father said.

"It shouldn't be, though, should it?" Robin said. "I mean, most people can't get their parents to shut up about the good old days."

"The old days weren't very good for your mother."

"Yeah? What do you know about them? Any more than I do?"

"Robin?"

"You guys met in Arizona, when you were in med school."

"Yes."

"Was Mom from Arizona, or had she moved there from somewhere else?"

"She grew up in a foster home in Arizona. I don't know exactly where."

"How could you not know exactly where?"

"She doesn't like to talk about it."

"But . . . she's your wife."

"So that means I have a right to make her unhappy?" There was an edge to his voice, a tightness in it.

Robin moved to the refrigerator, poured herself another glass of wine. "I'm sorry," she said. "I'm just . . . I'm a little . . ." Robin took a long sip. The silence in her house. The emptiness. She could practically feel it. Who was she to lecture her father about what spouses should and shouldn't know about each other? "You're a good husband, Dad," she said. "You're a good person."

There was a long pause on the other end of the line, the Yankees game blaring. Kay made his way through a player's stats and called strike one before her father spoke. "Robbie?"

"Yeah?"

"Is everything okay?"

"What? Yeah. I'm fine."

"You and Eric?"

"He's fine. We're fine. He's busy."

"Mom seemed to think you two might be having some issues."

"She did?"

"Look, honey, I know she always gives the best advice. But since she's out, you know . . . I'm happy to pinch-hit."

"Oh, jeez, Dad. Pinch-hit. Seriously?"

"I've got a pretty good batting average, you know. In the, uh, game of advice."

Robin closed her eyes. Now in his late sixties and semiretired, Dad maintained a private practice in town, but for most of his career he'd treated the criminally insane on Wards Island, where she was pretty sure metaphors like that one would have gotten him murdered. "I wasn't calling to talk to Mom about Eric."

"I don't mean to pry."

"I swear."

"All right. Sorry. I'll let her know you called."

She started to say good-bye, but he stopped her. "Can I ask you a question?"

"Sure."

"Have we been good parents to you?"

Robin blinked at the phone. "What? Of course you have. What are you talking about?"

"Nothing."

"Dad?"

"I'm just thinking out loud, honey. Looking back . . ."

Robin took another swallow of wine, waiting for more. But there was nothing. Only her father's slow exhale, the muffled sounds of the game. "Everything's fine," he said, finally. "You know how melancholy I get when the Yankees lose."

This was true. He did. Even more so now that he was a little older and not talking to psychopaths all day and therefore no longer feeling the need to keep every emotion in check. After particularly disappointing games, Dad would go on about missed chances, stolen opportunities, how quickly the nine innings went by . . . all in such a way, it seemed as though he was talking about something a lot deeper than baseball. Mom would tease him about it sometimes. *Maybe you and Steinbrenner should start a support group. Or a church.* "They can still turn it around, Dad," Robin said. "The game isn't over yet."

"You're right," he said quietly. "It isn't."

Robin and her father said their good-byes, the sky darkening outside her window and the voice of Michael Kay in the background, groaning over a pathetic, botched play.

AFTER SHE HUNG up, Robin pulled a slip of paper out of her wallet—Quentin Garrison's number, copied off her caller ID at work. She typed it into her phone and called him, but it went straight to his voice mail. She hung up without leaving a message.

She opened up her laptop, went onto Google Images, and looked up Inland Empire Killers. Far as she could find, there was only one photo of April Cooper and Gabriel LeRoy, and it had been taken at his school dance. He wore a brown tuxedo. She wore a high-collared prairie dress with ruffles at the chin. He stood behind her and gripped her shoulders tightly, as though he were afraid she might float away. It was an old, faded picture, the blues gone grayish, the reds rust brown. Robin could barely make out the faces, but they both looked pale for Californians. He had a kind of creepy, closed-mouth smile. She just looked sad.

The girl had blond hair and a prim, rosebud mouth. *Like Mom's*, Robin thought. Robin's mind, playing tricks on her. April Cooper was three years younger than Mom. April Cooper had died in a fire. But why had she never seen a picture of Mom as a child, as a young girl? Why were there no photographs of her taken before her wedding day?

I'll ask her about that, when she calls. Robin took both the cordless and her cell into the den and watched the rest of the Yankees game, both phones on the coffee table. The cell vibrated frequently, but only because of her column. Hate tweets. She read a few, then ignored the rest and continued to wait.

She waited until the game was over and it was

pitch-black outside and headed upstairs, into her bedroom, slipped under the covers of her empty bed, and set both phones on the night table, yawning. "Long meeting with your important source, Eric," she said.

Something about the sound of one's own voice, late at night, all alone in a room . . .

Robin drifted off to sleep, still waiting for her mother's call.

AT 11:45 P.M., Robin's phone vibrated sharply on the bedstand, waking her from a light, fitful sleep. She blinked at it. She'd uninstalled Twitter about an hour earlier. So many notifications, and they'd all turned out to be hate tweets—hundreds of them. People she'd never met before with flags and frogs and porn models as avatars, calling her a bitch, a dumb skank, feminazi, childless slut. The red-pill crowd telling her to get a boob job, get a facelift, to get laid, to eat poison and die . . . Normally, she wouldn't have cared all that much. Insults and threats meant her column was getting clicks, which would ultimately up ad revenues before all the trolls moved on to another target. You just breathe deep and ignore it. She'd been through this before, more than once.

But tonight, the ugly words made her feel vulnerable, even scared. She'd locked all the doors in her house, turned on the alarm, yet still, she felt watched. Hunted. How had he found her anyway, this Quentin Garrison?

Robin lifted her phone, remembering her dream—

flames enveloping her home, everything burning to the ground.

The text was from Eric:

On my way. Meeting went late. Sorry!

Outside, Robin heard sirens—someone else besides her in this quiet suburban neighborhood, awake and having a crappy night. She stared at Eric's text. "Fuck you," she whispered. She thought of Ginny in her patriotic bikini top and typed: Trouble in Paradise. Sent it without hesitation, without thought.

Eric replied: ???

Robin saw it through a blur of tears. I'm not an idiot, she typed.

How had the two of them gotten to this bad place in such a short time? A few years ago, they would have been up and awake together right now, researching the Cooper/LeRoy murders and Quentin Garrison over a bottle of wine—figuring it all out, gazes locked, phones in a drawer. They'd reported stories together in J-school. Sat together at the back of city council meetings, nudging each other in the ribs to stay awake. "We're a team, you and I," Eric used to say. "Like Woodward and Bernstein, but with sex." But now, their texts weren't even on the same wavelength.

Is there anything worse than being alone in one's confusion?

It was nearly midnight. Robin's parents were undoubtedly asleep. She didn't want to wake them or worry them, but it was a tug-of-war, their feelings versus hers. And the state she was in right now. The ugly questions running through her brain, and she was alone with them. All alone.

She tapped in her parents' phone number. No answer. They had an old-fashioned answering machine rather than voice mail, so when it picked up, Robin started talking into it, loud enough to wake them but calm, so they wouldn't panic. "Hi, Mom and Dad. I know it's late, but can you please pick up? Mom? I really need to talk to you. Please?"

No answer.

"Hello?"

Still nothing. "Mom?"

Robin thought about calling her mother's cell phone, but Mom hardly ever had it with her during the night. "I like to give my full attention to Dad, not Candy Crush," she would explain.

Robin was starting to get worried. She tried again, louder. "*Mom, please! It's Robin! Pick up the phone!*"

At last, someone picked up. "Are you within driving distance, ma'am?" A woman's voice. Young. Clinical.

Robin's heartbeat sped up. "I'm a few blocks away," she said.

"Would you mind coming by their house?"

"Who is this? Where are my parents?"

"This is Officer Lebow with the Tarry Ridge Police Department," the young woman said slowly. "I'm afraid there's been an incident."

EIGHT

ROBIN

INCIDENT. **THE WORD** throbbed in Robin's head as she headed out to her car, clicked open the door, and drove the three short blocks to her parents' home. *Incident.* The police officer's clean, clinical voice. *There's been an incident.*

Robin clutched the wheel, her palms sweating, heart pounding so hard she felt it in her face, her throat. It was hard to breathe.

"It's okay." She said it aloud, a harsh whisper, just to drown out that word and the thoughts that came with it, growing too loud as she approached her parents' house, three police cars, two ambulances in the circular driveway, lights flashing in such a way it was almost festive, made her think of Christmas, that one Christmas when they had a tree. Dad had brought it home—a surprise. *How come we can't have a tree, just because we're Jewish?* Robin had said that so many times, begged and pleaded with her parents, but she hadn't thought they'd ever do it, and then Daddy had come through the door smiling. "Come look outside," he'd said, Mom stifling her laughter, eyes sparkling. "Come see what Santa strapped to my car!"

As Robin pulled into the driveway and got out of her car, she heard a voice saying her name. *Dad.* But when she whirled around, it was her parents' longtime neighbor, Mr. Dougherty. "Robin," he said again. "My God, Robin." He wore plaid flannel pajama bottoms, a T-shirt that read DUKE UNIVERSITY. His daughter's alma mater.

Mr. Dougherty's wife had died a year ago of bone cancer. Robin knew this too and it made her feel bad for him, even now, the way he was looking at her, head shaking, cheeks drawn, all the sympathy in the world in his eyes. She didn't want to think about why. "I thought it was a backfire," he said. "Then I heard the others."

"Where are my parents?"

"I don't know." Mr. Dougherty's gaze moved to a point behind her. She saw the lights flashing in his eyes, across his face. "Oh," he said. "Oh my God," and it was as though she were stuck in a dream. An awful dream. Ambulance lights. She whirled around, saw the first ambulance pulling away and then paramedics wheeling a gurney out, a flash of her father's barrel chest—such a big man, though she'd never thought of him that way. A linebacker on his college football team. Big enough to earn the respect of his former patients, the criminally insane. But now . . . the white sheet across his chest . . . the blood . . .

And his face.

"Dad!" It barely escaped her lips, the faintest whisper. Her feet headed toward the ambulance of their own accord and she said it again, louder. "Dad! *Dad!*"

"Ms. Bloom?"

Robin didn't even turn at first, unused as she was to her maiden name. But then she heard it said again, felt a hand on her back. She recognized the same cold clinical voice as she'd heard over the phone, only so much more fragile in the warm night air, the shifting swirling lights.

Officer Lebow caught up with her as the second ambulance sped away, siren echoing, both of them staring after it. Robin gave her a quick glance—a sturdy young girl with a sweet face, the uniform the only thing about her that was truly off-putting. "What happened?"

"We're trying to find that out, ma'am," she said. "There seems to have been a break-in."

Dad flashed through her mind again—on the phone, then on the gurney. The blood-drenched sheet, the speed with which the paramedics attended to him. His face . . . Robin heard herself talking, but it was as though her voice were coming from a different body than her own. A weaker one. "They're still alive, right? They're going to be okay? Did you see my mother? What did she look like?"

"Ma'am, when was the last time you spoke to your parents?"

"My mother . . . They were shot?"

"Yes. They're both on their way to the hospital. Don't worry."

How can you tell someone not to worry? What kind of a bullshit directive is that? Robin gritted her teeth.

Tried to catch her breath, though she had none to catch. Her arms and legs felt as though someone had pulled the bones out. *She means well. Help her. Answer her questions and she'll answer yours.* "About eight P.M., I guess," she told Officer Lebow. "I spoke to my father. He said my mom was at the grocery store. Did you talk to them? Are they conscious?"

"What was your conversation about?"

"The Yankees."

"Did he talk about enemies? An unwanted visitor?"

"Enemies? No."

"How about your mother? Has she mentioned enemies?"

A breeze pushed Robin's hair from her face. Her gaze drifted up to the cloudless sky, the dirty sliver of moon. "No one that I know of."

"How often do you talk to her?"

"Every day," she said.

"So you're close. She would confide in you."

"Officer Lebow?"

"Yes."

"Are you trying to say that this wasn't a . . . a . . . simple robbery?"

"We're still trying to figure that out."

Mr. Dougherty said, "My family. We've lived here twenty years, we've never had anything like this." Mr. Dougherty, still talking about his family when he lived alone in his big Tudor house. Still saying *we*, even though his daughter lived in DC now and his wife was gone forever.

"Did your father or mother know anyone who drives a silver compact car? Maybe a Chevrolet

Cruze?" It was another cop asking now—a heavyset man, easily twenty years older than Officer Lebow.

"It *was* a Chevrolet Cruze," Mr. Dougherty said, "not maybe." But all Robin had heard was that one word. *Did.* The past tense.

"I need to go to the hospital."

"Ma'am."

"St. Catherine's," Mr. Dougherty said. "That's where they are."

"Thank you."

She headed back to her car, jogging then running. No one tried to stop her. St. Catherine's was one town over. But it was physically closer than Tarry Ridge Hospital. She knew where it was, more or less, but she punched it into her phone anyway. She couldn't bear the thought of taking a wrong turn.

Mr. Dougherty was shouting after her. "Is Eric at home? Do you want me to call him?"

Robin pretended she didn't hear. As she started up her car, her gaze fell on the front door: uniformed officers and a few men in suits moving through it, a tall man in khakis and a long-sleeved shirt wearing gloves . . .

A crime scene.

She backed out of the driveway, her mind filling with images she'd never forget: the flashing lights, strangers filing into her parents' home. Those thin latex gloves that came with the man's job. And blood, pooling under the white sheet, spreading across her father's chest, the glimpse she'd gotten of his face, eyes wide as she'd never seen them before.

Did your parents know anyone who drives a Chevrolet Cruze? The questions cops asked. As though it would have been normal for Robin to keep a mental tally of the makes and models of all the cars driven by everyone her parents might know. Chevrolet Cruze, though. A Chevy Cruze. She didn't think she'd ever seen one of those outside of a rental car agency . . .

The thought lingered in her mind, but only for a few seconds before it was replaced by other thoughts, dark and endless.

BOTH OF ROBIN'S parents were in emergency surgery. Questioning the nurse at the front desk about it, she learned it was for "bullet wounds." Nothing more. She couldn't get a straight answer out of any of the nurses about the location of the wounds, about either of their conditions. "We will let you know, ma'am," said the nurse at the front desk, using that curt dismissive tone Robin used to hear from certain publicists when she was smack out of journalism school, working as a reporter for a trashy celebrity weekly.

"These are my parents." She hated the sound of her own voice, the frailty of it. There was quite a crowd in the emergency room tonight—the family of a teenager who'd been in a car accident, a mom holding a toddler, flushed and shrieking from fever, friends of a college student who'd cut her finger on a blender's blades while making margaritas. She'd heard all their stories while waiting at the front desk, and here she was, the only one who'd come here alone. She moved closer to the nurse. "These are my parents," she said again, her voice trembling. "They're all I have."

The nurse's face softened. "I know," she said.

"The doctor will come and speak to you as soon as he can. They're working hard on both of them, I know that much Ms. . . ."

"Diamond," she said. "Robin Diamond."

The nurse's eyes lit up. "From Daily Culture?" she said. "The film writer?"

"Yes."

"I love your column."

Robin made herself smile. "Thanks."

"I read it every week. I knew you were from around here, but boy . . . never thought I'd meet you in person," she said.

"So nice to meet a reader," Robin said carefully. "Please let me know . . . as soon as you hear anything. Okay?"

"You bet." The nurse gave her a smile that was bright enough to restore faith. "And I'm all in for the Femme Seven. Don't listen to the haters."

Robin managed a nod. Today's column. Well, yesterday's at this point. She moved away from the desk, took a seat against the wall, a few chairs down from the wailing toddler. She felt her phone buzz in her back pocket—a text. *Eric.* Something stirred within her, the tiniest spark of hope. She pulled the phone out of her back pocket, looked at the text. It was from an unfamiliar number:

Choke on your piece-of-shit column and die.

Robin closed her eyes. *Speaking of haters.*

And then she put her head down and started to cry, tears spilling down her face, shoulders heaving.

She cried as though she were alone in the room, alone in the world, her sobs rivaling those of the toddler. She was beyond caring or thinking about anything, not the teenagers whispering in the row of chairs across the room, not that bright-faced young nurse standing over her, asking, "Are you all right, Ms. Diamond?" She cried until she felt arms around her, warm and familiar—an answer to a prayer she'd never been aware of.

The arms of her husband. His voice in her ear. "Oh my God, Robin. Oh my God."

You're here, she wanted to say. But she couldn't speak.

Eric held her until her sobs subsided, all the tears drained out of her, her head on his shoulder.

"How did you find out?" she said, finally.

"Mr. Dougherty told me."

"Oh."

"They'll be fine. Your parents are strong and healthy. Your mom's barely into her sixties. And your dad. Come on, he's a bull. He can still beat me at arm wrestling."

"I hope so."

"I swear, honey, they'll be okay. And the police will get whoever did this to them."

Robin said nothing. She wanted to believe Eric. Just like she wanted to believe that all her suspicions about him were unfounded, that he really was just working late over the past couple of months, that he might have been taking his job too seriously but not as seriously as her, as their love, their future, the things they cared about.

"You should have called me, Robin," he said. "I'd have been here sooner."

"I know. I'm sorry."

"I got home and you weren't there and I thought . . ." His voice trailed off.

"What?"

"I thought you'd left me." She turned and looked at him, the beard scruff, dark circles under the bright blue eyes, the concern in them . . . She inhaled his cologne, but she didn't ask herself why he'd put on cologne to meet a source. She asked nothing, felt nothing, other than a yearning to know him again. "I would never leave you," she said. And in that moment, she meant it.

"ROBIN."

Eric's voice. Robin had been having a dream, a bad one. She blinked the sleep out of her eyes and took in the waiting room, most every seat empty now, save for one of the college student's friends—a big bearded redhead, stretched out and snoring on a row of seats across the room.

Eric said, "You were whimpering. Were you having a bad dream?"

"I don't remember." Shards of it stuck in her mind: A rental car backfiring. Her mother screaming. That cop's voice: *How about your mother. Has she mentioned enemies?*

Her own: *We're not going to make it into a listicle or a meme?*

Robin said, "It might be my fault."

"What are you talking about?"

"The break-in. My parents . . ."

"Don't be ridiculous."

"Listen to me. I wrote a column yesterday. Did you read it?"

"I didn't have a chance."

"It doesn't matter," Robin said. "It got a ton of hate. More than usual. I had to turn all my notifications off, and even then, I . . . I got a text." She dug her phone out of her pocket, handed it to him. "Look at the latest text, Eric."

He stared at the screen. "That's terrible."

"How did they find out my cell-phone number?"

"Robin, it's a huge leap to think some troll would be able to track down your *parents*."

"The nurse at the front desk," she said. "She reads me. She said she knew I was from around here."

"Robin . . ."

"I'm serious. If an ER nurse I've never seen before knows where I live, then who's to say some psychopath doesn't know it too? Who's to say that psychopath didn't track down my parents and break into their house?"

"Over a film column?"

"Yes, Eric. Over a fucking film column."

"Robin," he said slowly. "You've got to get a grip."

Her jaw clenched up. "The cops asked if my parents had any enemies," she said. "They told me to think about it hard, Eric. They didn't tell me to get a grip."

He stared at her. "They asked you that?"

"Yes . . ." She stared back. His face was pale, eyes wide. "Are you okay?" she asked him.

"It's nothing."

"Stop it," she said. "You aren't allowed to tell me,

'Nothing.' Not tonight. You have to let me know what's on your mind."

"You aren't the only one who's pissed people off."

"What do you mean?"

Eric started to answer. At least she thought he started to answer, but she'd never be sure of that, riveted as she was by the doctor pushing through the ER doors, asking, "Are you Robin Diamond?"

"Yes." She thought about whether she should stand up to greet him, as though there were some ceremony to this, the Receiving of News. In a type of compromise, Robin half stood up, then fell back to sitting again. "That's me."

"We worked very hard, ma'am," he said. "There's no easy way to put this."

"*No,*" she whispered. Or thought. She wasn't sure. *No, please, no.*

She didn't want the doctor to speak. But the words kept coming. "Ms. Diamond," he said, and then, "your father." And then, "I'm so sorry." And then, "entrance wound" and "blood loss" and "vascular structure," each word as pointless as a scribble on a piece of paper, as pointless as Eric's hollow gasp and his arm across Robin's shoulder, as all the prayers she'd said, all the pleading to a God she was never sure she believed in. Each word he said as pointless as life.

NINE

Dear Aurora Grace,

For the past two nights, we've stayed at a Motel 6 in West Covina. I haven't left the room, and neither has Gabriel. A couple of times he's sent out for Shakey's pizza and paid out of Papa Pete's wallet. When the delivery guy shows up, he makes me hide in the bathroom, just like he made me hide in the car when he checked in to the motel. Gabriel doesn't like anyone looking at me besides him. He says it's a safety thing— witnesses would remember a young couple more than a single guy on his own. But I don't think that's the real reason.

There's nothing to do here and I'm bored. I've asked if we can go out and buy magazines, but Gabriel doesn't think that's safe either. He thinks the cops are after us, and actually, as far as that goes, he may be right. Papa Pete's murder was on the news last night. And even though nobody said anything about Gabriel and me, someone did see a car with two people in it pulling out of the driveway. And the news reporter said the witness gave a description to the cops. The newscaster had also said that both of Peter Cooper's stepdaughters were missing. "It's only a matter of time," Gabriel kept saying. "We have to get out of here. It's only a matter of time." He hasn't turned on the TV since.

It's driving me nuts, the quiet. I've tried reading *Once Is Not Enough* again, but I guess I don't like the book so much anymore. January's life is 99 percent miserable, and as much as her dad may love her, he can't protect her from any of it.

The only other book in this room is the Bible in the nightstand drawer, so I've been reading that, just to look at something that isn't Gabriel's face.

The good news is, he got us a room with twin beds. He said he doesn't want to make me do anything I'm not ready to do. "You're lucky. I'm not like other guys. I care about your feelings." This is what he tells me, this boy who wouldn't let me break up with him, who killed the only father I ever knew and made me shoot him too. Who sleeps with a gun to make sure I don't get away. Who won't even let me buy a fucking magazine!!! Sorry for swearing, but come on, Aurora Grace. My feelings. Sure.

Last night, when G was sleeping, I got the knife out of my bag and I stood over his bed for so long I got light-headed. I kept telling myself it's like opening a door. Just push it and you can be free. The police will understand.

But I couldn't do it.

It wasn't that I was scared. It was something he had said to me, as he was falling asleep. "If you're good, I'll let you talk to Jenny tomorrow." It's 7:00 A.M. He's still asleep. When he wakes up, I will remind him.

Love,
Your Future Mom

June 13, 1976
11:30 A.M.

Dear Aurora Grace,

I spoke to your aunt Jenny! Gabriel took me to a pay phone and called the people who are keeping her. He put me on the phone with her, and she didn't say anything but I could hear her breathing. I know the sound. Back home, I shared a room with her and sometimes, to get to sleep, I'd listen to the way she'd take the air in through her lips and push it out so fast, like she'd changed her mind and wanted it out of her as soon as possible. Shallow, baby breathing. I always wondered how any of it had time to reach her little lungs.

Sweet Jenny. I miss her so much. Talking to her on the phone, I told her I loved her, and I told her not to be afraid. "See you soon, kid," I said, like it was no big deal and she was silly to be scared. She didn't say anything, but I could tell she understood me.

When I hung up with Jenny, I felt a little better about everything. Even Gabriel. He's been telling me how sorry he is for "all the stuff." That's what he calls it. He tells me how he let his passion for me get the best of him, and that he'll make it up to me by becoming a better person after we've escaped. How he'll be the best man he can possibly be, so that he can be deserving of my love.

It's hard to trust him, but when I opened the motel room Bible this morning, this was the first sentence I read: "For I will forgive their wickedness and remember their sins no more." Could it be a sign? I want to believe in signs, Aurora Grace. I want to believe in things.

Right now, Gabriel and I are driving to the house of a man he knows. The man doesn't live far from the Motel 6, which is kind of weird. I never knew Gabriel had any friends outside of Santa Rosa. Anyway, this man we're going to see is a property master for TV shows. His job is to buy and keep track of all the props you see on-screen, whether it's guns on the cop shows or stuffed animals, like Boo Boo Kitty on *Laverne and Shirley*. It sounds like a good job to me. I can't think of a single TV show that doesn't have props in it. And Gabriel says that this man has worked on a whole bunch of them, including *Starsky and Hutch*. I wonder if he's met David Soul, who plays Hutch. In case the show isn't on anymore by the time you're born, I should tell you this: Hutch is my Dream Man. He isn't beautiful, like David Cassidy. But he's good-looking in a subtler, more grown-up way. The thing I love the most about him, though, is the way he acts. Hutch seems so calm and serene all the time, as though nothing could ever upset him—what Papa Pete used to call a "cool customer."

Someday, I'd like to meet a man like that, a man who doesn't let his emotions get in the way of being a good person. Gabriel is more like Starsky.

Anyway, Gabriel swears that this property master guy is superrich and can set us up with another car, more money, maybe even new identities. Gabriel's convinced that, when all this blows over, this property master can help us break into the movie business. I have no idea how Gabriel knows this superrich man with a job in Hollywood, but I'm going to guess he's sold him weed. We're about fifteen minutes away from the property master's house. His name is Ed Hart. I hope he's not as weird as Gabriel (ha ha).

Love,

Future Mom (FM!!!)

TEN

QUENTIN

QUENTIN HAD NEVER met his father, though he did know his name: Hamish Garrison. As a kid, Quentin had believed his mother when she told him that Hamish had been an award-winning investigative journalist for the *London Times* who had been killed in the line of duty while embedded with troops in Iraq. But in truth, he had been a reporter for one of the supermarket tabloids and had met Kate at a bar in Las Vegas while covering the wedding of Richard Gere and Cindy Crawford. She'd admitted that to him nine months ago, when he'd come to visit her in rehab and started asking her questions, taking advantage of her newfound lucidity.

Kate had told him the whole story—insomuch as Quentin's mother could tell anyone the whole story of anything. Hamish had been thirty-eight years older than Kate, who at the time had been living just off the Strip with no real game plan, just a vague idea about setting up residence in a different state. The Garrisons had married the night they

met and stayed together just long enough to con-
ceive Quentin, after which Hamish moved back to
his native Britain and reunited with his estranged
wife. "Your father gave you one thing," Kate had
said, tears in her eyes. "His curiosity. You're a born
reporter." She hadn't meant it as a compliment.

Quentin was in the Rose Main Reading Room
of the New York Public Library, having just found
Hamish's obituary on microfilm, in the August 2,
1996, issue of the *Mirror*. He liked the cool of the
room, the dead, cavelike silence and the location of
the library, at the center of a bustling city where he
knew no one and no one knew him.

He might stay here forever, he thought. Or at
least until no one knew him anywhere anymore.

Quentin finished reading the obituary, his gaze
hanging on the last line: *Mr. Garrison is survived by
Hannah, his wife of 40 years, as well as his two grown
sons Mark and Martyn*. No mention of Kate, or of
Quentin, who at the time of the obituary had been
just four years old. Not even a line about a brief sab-
batical in Las Vegas.

Quentin heard his mother's voice in his head,
weary and mocking, the way he'd so often heard it
in the months following her death.

Seems to me, you've lived your life . . .

Quentin's phone went off in his pocket, drawing
a disgusted look from a nearby security guard—the
only other person in this cavernous room on such
a warm summer day. The sternness in the guard's
eyes, his uniform . . . It spooked Quentin a little.

He took the phone out and glanced at the
screen—Summer, wanting to FaceTime him. He

wished he could turn the phone off, but he couldn't. She'd been trying to get hold of him since last night, and if he ignored her again, she'd probably call the cops.

He hurried out of the room, through the lobby and out of the building, to the safety of the steps and the stone lions and the crowded sidewalks below. Summer was trying Quentin for the third time in a row by the time he finally responded.

"Where the hell have you been?" On the small screen, Summer resembled a horror movie heroine with that paperwhite skin, those huge, wide eyes that seemed to be in a permanent state of shock. She had a way of looking at you too, as though she could see all the way through to your every thought.

Quentin tried not to make eye contact with the face on his screen. "Hello to you too." He reached for his pocket. "I lost my sunglasses."

"Aw, the ones Dean gave you?" She sounded genuinely upset.

"I'll find them. I'm sure they're around."

Summer said, "I hope so."

"I know you do."

"So what happened yesterday? Did you ever talk to Robin?"

"Yes."

"And?"

"She had no idea who the Inland Empire Killers were."

"Are you sure?"

Quentin thought back to his phone conversation with Robin Diamond, which had taken place a million years ago on the previous day. It had been just a few hours past his arrival on a red-eye flight. He'd managed to get thirty minutes of fitful, Klonopin-aided sleep at his Newark airport hotel, and if anything, it had made him feel more exhausted than he'd been in the first place. He probably should have waited until he'd had some real rest before contacting Robin. But back then—when he was taking his first skipping steps onto that yellow brick road of questions-yet-to-be-answered—Quentin had been excited and hopeful and therefore short on patience. Like her parents, Robin Diamond had an unlisted phone number and home address, and Quentin did not want to think about *Closure* or Robin Diamond or her parents, especially her parents. Her father . . .

"I'm positive."

"Okay, no worries," Summer said. "I'm going to go back to Duarte and try and get George to reconsider going on record."

"Do you think there's any hope in that?"

She smiled. It tracked weirdly on his screen, a slow-motion grimace, an image out of a dream. "There's hope in everything, Q."

He cleared his throat. "Listen," he said. "I don't think there's a real story here."

"Are you serious?"

"Yes."

"But the postcard from New York . . ."

"Lots of students loved Mrs. Brixton. That postcard could have been from anyone."

"Come on. You don't believe that."

"I don't know what I believe."

"Quentin, the ticket stub—"

"Do you know what I was just doing, Summer? I was reading Hamish Garrison's obituary."

"What? Why?"

"I found it here at the library. All these years, researching murderers and their victims, I never bothered tracking down my own origin story. I rely on my mother—the most unreliable source on the planet. If I was interviewing her for a podcast, I'd fact-check every word out of her mouth. But here she tells me this random British guy was my dad, and I believe her without question. Isn't that strange?"

"This conversation is what's strange."

"I mean it, Summer. What if Hamish Garrison being my father is just a lie I've been living with all these years? The same way Pollard's been living with the idea that April Cooper is still alive."

"Hey, Q . . ." That tinge of worry in her voice. He closed his eyes.

"Or, hell . . . I don't know. Maybe Robin Diamond is the one who's been living with a lie. Maybe her mother really was a murderer, and she'll never know it. What difference does it make? We all believe whatever bullshit we want to, don't we? We suck up whatever pretty stories we can, just to help us get through the day without throwing ourselves in front of a train."

He opened his eyes to Summer's face in his hand—a mask of concern, eyes bigger than ever. For an awful moment, he wanted to break the screen.

"You need to get some sleep," she said.

"*You have no idea what I fucking need.*" Quentin

said it louder than he should have. He was aware of a group of young kids and their parents on the library steps, stopping their conversation, gaping at him.

"I'm sorry, Summer," he said. "I just . . . Hell, you know how I can get sometimes."

"I care about you."

"I know."

"I mean . . . Your mom. It's only been six months, and we've barely talked since—"

"I don't need to talk," he said. Then, "I swear, I'd tell you if I did."

Summer touched her fingertips to the screen. Quentin did the same. Tried to smile. "I probably shouldn't have looked up the Hame-ster's obit," he said. "I don't even know why I did. What was I expecting?"

"It would be nice," she said, "if it mentioned a son in L.A."

For a moment, Quentin flashed on Mitchell Bloom—the air-conditioned comfort of his office, the professional concern in his eyes. *Do you really think April Cooper and Gabriel LeRoy were to blame for all your mother's troubles?* he'd said. *For all your troubles too?* Like a father. Like a shrink. He'd learned not to trust either. "I've just had a bad couple of days," he told Summer. "I'll snap out of it. Promise."

"Quentin?"

"Yeah?"

"I really hope you find your sunglasses."

He smiled, his throat clenching. "Thank you."

After he ended the conversation, Quentin went to his recent calls and scrolled through them. Most all of them over the past twenty-four hours were from Dean and Summer, but there was one that was unfamiliar, with a Westchester County area code. *Could be Robin Diamond.*

He thought about calling back, and it made him feel tired and hopeless, as though he'd been treading water for too long.

He slipped his digital voice recorder out of his pocket and turned it on. He'd been doing this ever since Dean had dropped him off at LAX— recording thoughts and observations that might make it into the podcast, a type of personal diary as he journeyed to the heart of the murders that so deeply affected his own life. It had been Summer's idea initially, but he'd taken to it quickly. Probably too quickly. Recording his own thoughts was, after all, basically the same thing as talking to himself.

He cleared his throat and spoke into the recorder, the mic catching his voice along with the roar of traffic on Fifth Avenue, the bleat of horns. "All parents lie. That's just a fact. For some of us, the lies are designed to preserve our innocence: Santa is real, for instance. Trying for a baby means praying really hard. Other times, the lies are deeper, more material. Parents tell us those lies not to protect us, but to protect themselves. They don't want us to know who they really are."

Quentin's phone chimed. He looked at the screen. Another unfamiliar number. Another Westchester County area code. And when he answered the call, he heard a man's voice he was certain he'd never heard before. "Hello," the man said, "can you tell me who I'm speaking to, please?"

"Only if you tell me first."

"This is Detective Nick Morasco, from the Tarry Ridge Police Department," he said. "Now it's your turn."

He swallowed. "Quentin. Quentin Garrison . . . Um . . . Is anything wrong?"

"Mr. Garrison, do you know a man named Mitchell Bloom?"

Quentin had the strangest sensation—as though he were outside the conversation, as though he were his future self, listening in. "Why? What happened?"

"Answer the question please, sir."

Quentin thought about lying, but only for a second. He needed to tell the truth. He knew that. But first, he needed to be able to breathe. "Yes," he said. "Yes, I know him."

Mitchell Bloom. When he'd spoken to Robin the previous day, Quentin had managed to pry one piece of information out of her—her father wasn't retired. And as it turned out, he'd found a listing for a psychiatrist named Mitchell Bloom with a private practice in Tarry Ridge and paid him a visit there, during working hours.

"You went to his workplace?" Detective Morasco said. "To talk to him for your podcast? You didn't call first?"

"It hadn't worked out so well when I'd called Robin," Quentin said. "I thought if I went in and saw him, and explained everything, it wouldn't be as easy to turn me away."

"And you wanted to talk to him for a true crime podcast."

"That's right," he said. "About the Inland Empire murders. My aunt was a victim."

"And Dr. Bloom is an expert in criminal psychiatry," he said. "That's why you wanted to talk to him."

The detective said it like a statement, not a question. Quentin decided it was best to agree.

"You didn't speak to Dr. Bloom after that one conversation in his office?"

"Detective Morasco," Quentin said. "Has . . . has something happened?"

He didn't answer right away. Quentin leaned into the silence, his heart pounding. "Detective?"

"He's dead, Mr. Garrison."

Quentin felt numb. "Oh . . . Oh my God."

"Do you think you may be able to come by the station? Or we can meet you in the city, if it's easier."

"What about Mrs. Bloom? Is she all right?"

"I'd prefer to talk more about this in person."

"I can come by the station," Quentin heard himself say. "I have a rental car."

"That would be great. It won't take long."

Quentin said good-bye and hung up, both hands trembling. The phone started pulsing like a beating heart and he looked at the screen. An app he'd downloaded on the plane: news alerts for Westchester County. He clicked on one of them. Read the article all the way through. Noted psychiatrist Dr. Mitchell Bloom and his wife, Renee, had been shot in what was thought to have been a home invasion. Renee Bloom was in critical condition. Mitchell Bloom was dead.

MITCHELL BLOOM, MD. Gold letters on clouded

glass. Dr. Bloom had no receptionist, just a small waiting room and he'd stepped out into it—a big man, a few inches taller than Quentin and with a kind, owlish face. A double take, once he saw the stranger in his waiting room. *I thought you were my four o'clock*, Dr. Bloom had said. And then Quentin had told him why he was there.

They'd talked for around half an hour, with no tape recorder running, Dr. Bloom playing psychiatrist. Quentin trying to play interviewer.

Closure. That's an interesting name.

It was my coproducer's idea.

Do you think closure is possible for you, Mr. Garrison?

Huh?

For all intents and purposes, you're the survivor of a murder that happened nearly twenty years before you were born. Don't you believe it might be wishful thinking for you to think that type of pain can be fixed?

As I said. My coproducer thought of the name.

Your coproducer?

Actually, my coproducer and my husband. They thought of the name together.

Do you think it might be wishful thinking on their part, then? Your coproducer and your husband? Do you think they might care for you so much, they're hoping for the impossible?

Quentin, trying to play interviewer and getting angrier and angrier . . .

As he made his way down the library steps, Quentin's skin flushed even hotter than the stale humid air around him, images flashing through his mind from that same night . . . of the Blooms' Tudor home, the lush green lawn and the big bay window, the TV flickering from the upstairs window, the hum of cicadas outside, the heavy scent of lilies planted along the edge of the yard. That lovely home, that loving family.

How long had Quentin stood outside Dr. Mitchell Bloom's house, remembering that half hour in his office, simmering over the way Dr. Bloom had pried his way into Quentin's darkest thoughts without answering a single one of his questions? Mitchell Bloom, MD, with his lovely, gold-lettered life and no need for closure.

Watching the house from the window of his rental car, Quentin had slipped his recorder out of his pocket. *Mitchell Bloom can sleep at night*, he had said into it, his voice tight with anger. *Whether his wife is a murderer or not.*

Stop thinking like that. Stop thinking. As he reached the parking garage where he'd left his rental car, Quentin told himself that as soon as he could, he needed to find all the recordings he'd made last night. All those observations he'd spoken into his mic, his thoughts burning and popping. Everything he had said. Everything he had done. It needed to be erased.

ELEVEN

ROBIN

IN THE DAYS following her father's death, Robin moved through life as though she were navigating her way through a dark cave, the air around her dank and hard to breathe, the potential for danger beneath every footfall, every brush of the hand, no light to guide her.

She wasn't sure exactly how much time had passed since the shootings. In this endless cave, one hour was the same as the next and the next. She took pills to sleep but it didn't feel like sleeping. Waking up was just an opening of eyes.

There were things to do, though, in Robin's waking hours and so she did them. She signed autopsy reports and answered the cops' initial questions and put off the follow-ups. She spoke to poker-faced doctors about her mother's chances at survival. She met with funeral directors and chose a coffin for her father and signed many, many checks and put flowers into vases. She answered emails she barely read. Typed "thank you for your kind words" over and over and over.

Eric was around. He stayed home from work and talked to people on the phone, telling them, "She's sleeping now. Can I have her call you back?" And, "I know she will appreciate that. Thank you." He cooked Robin meals that she couldn't bring herself to eat and sat by her side in intensive care as she held her mother's cool, dry, mannequin hand. He put his arm around Robin's shoulders and stroked her hair, and he asked her questions like, "What can I do?" and "How can I help?"

It made Robin feel guilty, all the attention her husband was paying her. She'd been longing for just a fraction of it over the past several months, wishing for it, really. And a part of her worried that she'd wished too hard, that she'd brought this on herself, on her family.

Had she?

She probably shouldn't have been entertaining thoughts like these, sitting now in the bright of her kitchen, talking to the two detectives in charge of her parents' case. Their names were Nick Morasco and Ehrlich Baus ("Pronounced Boss," he had told her, as though she gave a damn) and while she really didn't have anything against either one of these men—well, Morasco anyway; Baus was pretty annoying—her main goal was to get them out of her house as quickly as possible. Her father's funeral was this afternoon.

Robin would have preferred not to be talking to them at all, not the way she was right now, with her head all jumbled from grief and worry and the remnants of last night's sleeping pills and the Xanax she'd taken this morning. But at this point, she had no other choice. She'd been putting them off for so long, and, as Baus ("Boss") had explained it to her, if they had to wait any longer to question her in full, it could hinder the investigation. *You do want to find out who did this, don't you?* he had asked, and Robin could have sworn she detected a hint of suspicion in that smirk of his, those beady green eyes, like shards of glass. When she'd asked if Eric could stay in the room while she was questioned, he'd shaken his head as Morasco had said yes. Yeah, *pretty annoying* was putting it mildly.

Baus was smiling at her now. *Smiling.* Gulping the glass of lemonade that Eric had brought him and smiling pleasantly, like it was a church social in here and the square dancing was about to start. "Your husband makes an awesome glass of lemonade," he said. Robin had no idea how to respond to that. She glanced at Eric.

"It's . . . uh . . . a mix," he said.

She turned to Morasco. "Did you look into the Femme Seven column?"

"Yes, ma'am." Morasco, far as she could tell, was his partner's opposite. Where Baus was short, meaty, and florid, Morasco was tall and sinewy, with a pale cast to his olive skin. Where Morasco was polite and laconic, Baus seemed to be in love with the sound of his own voice. Morasco wore a wedding ring and spoke frequently of his private investigator wife, while Baus seemed like a guy who hadn't gotten laid in at least half a decade and hated all women as a result. Morasco seemed intelligent. Baus . . . did not. Maybe it was all just an act. A good cop/bad cop kind of thing. Robin hoped so, for Morasco's sake.

Morasco said, "We've looked into the accounts you received the tweets, texts, and emails from. No red flags yet."

"Really?"

He nodded. "You'd actually be surprised at how many of them are bots from foreign countries and twelve-year-old boys."

"Oh."

"It's funny, you know, the things that get us worked up into a lather and keep us up at night. It's words on a screen. And when you pull away the curtain, and you look at who or what is actually typing those words . . . Go onto one of those private threads with all those frustrated teenagers on it. Tell 'em you're a cop. It's like turning on a light and watching the cockroaches scatter."

"She shouldn't impersonate a police officer," Baus said.

"I wasn't literally telling her to do that."

"The lady might not have known you were kidding."

"Oh my God," Robin whispered. She wondered if Baus was some kind of punishment from the police chief. Maybe Morasco had shown up late for work one too many times.

"Anyway," Morasco said. "We'll let you know if any of these trolls turns out to be a potential suspect."

Baus said, "Tell us about your parents' marriage."

Robin blinked. "Excuse me?"

Morasco gave him a sharp look and took out a notepad. "Your dad was a forensic psychiatrist, right?"

"Yes."

"About how long ago did he go into private practice?"

"Ten years, I think. Maybe more."

"After you left home, though."

"Yes."

"Do you know why he quit his job at Wards Island?"

Robin closed her eyes. Tried to remember. Her mom's voice over the phone. *We have some good news to announce.* Dinner with Eric and her parents at their favorite restaurant—a French place in White Plains they'd just discovered. Cake brought to the table and wineglasses raised. Just the four of them. It had always been just the four of them for dinner. Just the three of them before Eric. When Robin was a kid, her mother had an active social life during the day, with her volunteer work and her PTA friends and her walks in the park. That baby bird. She'd tried bringing home a dog once—a sickly old thing from the shelter. But Dad was allergic, so she'd found it another home. And then there was another time—a babysitter of Robin's, a girl named CoCo who'd come from a bad home. *We have room,* Mom had said, her voice cracking. *She deserves a chance. It wouldn't be forever.* God, Robin hadn't thought of that girl in years . . .

Always taking in strays. Dad always making her take them back. Mom's days were busy, but the nights were reserved for her family. That was the way Robin had looked at it. Her vision blurred. A tear slipped down her cheek. Maybe Dad was jealous of the strays. Maybe he wanted Mom all to himself.

"Ms. Diamond?" Morasco asked.

"I'm sorry. What was the question?"

Baus said, "Why did your father decide to leave Wards Island?"

"I think he just . . . I think he wanted to spend more time at home."

"Did he ever mention feeling threatened?" Morasco said.

She stared at him. "Threatened?"

"Or your mom? Was she concerned about your dad's safety?"

"I don't . . . I don't think so."

"So your dad's patients were never a concern."

"No . . ."

"In his private practice, can you recall your dad ever having any kind of falling-out with anyone?"

"No."

"How about your mother?"

She looked at him. "Everybody loved my mother."

"Okay," Morasco said. "Would you describe your parents as close?"

"Yes."

"Happily married."

"Very."

"They weren't arguing about anything recently that you know of?"

"Not that I know of."

"So your dad sounded pretty happy," Morasco said, "during that last conversation."

Robin remembered her father's voice on the phone, the catch in it. *Have we been good parents to you?* "Actually, he said he was feeling melancholy."

Morasco raised his eyebrows.

"The Yankees were losing," she said. "I know that sounds weird but it isn't. He . . ." Tears sprung into her eyes. This had been happening lately. Grief, pouncing on her when she least expected it. Attacking. A tear trickled down her cheek. She wiped it away. "He always took it personally when the Yankees lost."

Morasco gave her a smile. "I get that."

Baus said, "I'm a Mets guy."

Morasco ignored him. "So just to be clear," he said, "there isn't anything unusual that you can think of that happened in the past forty-eight hours—"

"Well, there was the column."

"Yes, right," he said. "I'm thinking more about anything that might have happened with your parents."

"No."

"You're sure," Baus said. "Absolutely positive."

Morasco scribbled something in his notebook.

The thought crept up on her. The phone call . . . "Wait."

Morasco looked up from his pad.

"This is probably nothing," she said.

"Let us be the judge," said Baus.

"I got a phone call at work from a podcast producer. A guy from California named Quentin."

"Quentin Garrison," Morasco said.

"Yes. How did you—"

"Was he trying to get hold of your father as an expert?"

Robin started to answer, then stopped. "Yeah," she said, her brain creating the lie and her mouth forming the words before she even knew she was saying them. "For some true crime podcast. About some murders in the '70s."

Morasco nodded.

"We knew about that," Baus said. "We talked to that guy. He already told us that."

"He did?" There was a humming in Robin's ears, in her brain. She wanted to ask them if Quentin Garrison had said anything about April Cooper or the Inland Empire Killers, but she couldn't make herself say the name. *Ask your mother about April Cooper*, the voices in her head told her. Quentin Garrison's voice and then her own. *Ask Mom about her. Don't say anything to the cops until you talk to Mom.*

If you can ever talk to Mom . . .

"Okay," Baus said. "I think we've covered the podcast guy."

Robin exhaled. "So, is that it?"

"Nope," Baus said. "Just one more question."

Robin sighed. Always one more question.

"When and why did your mother purchase the firearm?"

Robin stared at Morasco, then at Baus, those beady glass eyes watching her expectantly. "My mother," she said slowly. "My mother doesn't own a gun."

"Yes, she does. Smith & Wesson M&P 45 compact."

"Ehrlich," Morasco said.

Baus grinned. "He won't call me Boss. Everybody else does, but not this guy. Nobody's your boss, huh, Nick?"

"My mother hates guns. My husband knows that."

Her gaze darted around the kitchen. Where was Eric? Why would he sneak out when they told him he could stay? A heat rose from the pit of Robin's stomach and bloomed in her cheeks. She was red-faced, the back of her neck breaking out in a sweat. "She . . . she'd never buy a gun. She wouldn't even know how to shoot one."

Baus said, "Ms. Diamond, try not to get hysterical." And she wanted to leap across the kitchen table, grab him by the throat.

She turned to Morasco. "There's a mistake. There has to be."

He shook his head.

"Where's this gun that my mother supposedly owns?" she said. "I want to see it for myself."

"I'm afraid that's not possible."

"Why? *Why can't I see it?*"

"It's being held as evidence."

"*What?*"

"The gun Detective Baus is talking about," Morasco said. "The one registered to your mother. It's the same gun that was used to shoot them both."

AFTER THE TWO detectives left her house, Robin went looking for Eric. She shouted his name a few times downstairs, then headed up to the second floor and did the same, louder, her throat aching from it. For a few, unbalanced moments, she actually thought he might have left her—jumped into his car and sped away as she was being questioned by police.

But then she saw Eric from the bedroom window. He stood in their backyard with his back to the house, facing their small garden, his shoulders slumped and sad in his somber blue dress shirt and black pants, dressed for the funeral minus his suit jacket. *What are you doing out there? What are you thinking about?* She hurried downstairs and outside into the heat, her heels sinking into the dirt. It wasn't until she got closer that she realized that he wasn't slumped in thought. He was on his phone, texting.

He spun around when she said his name. Dropped the phone in his shirt pocket too quickly. "Hi," he said. "Did the questioning go okay?"

Robin's gaze fell on the phone, glowing beneath the cloth of his shirt, as though it were trying to interrupt. "Why did you leave?"

"I . . . I didn't really think I was needed, and—"

"My mother owned a gun."

"What?"

"The gun that killed my dad was registered to her."

"That's crazy. There's got to be some mistake."

"That's what I told them."

He shook his head. "Your mom would never—"

"I know." Robin felt numb and battered, her mind assaulting her with thoughts she didn't want to have. The call from that podcaster. *Ask your mother about April Cooper.* That Inland Empire Killers movie, the teenage actress on her TV screen, her gun spewing bullets. Her father on the phone, his last night alive. The sadness in his voice. Her father, whom Quentin Garrison had told police he'd wanted to reach. As an expert . . .

Had Quentin Garrison tracked down Dad? Had he told him to ask Mom about April Cooper? Had

Dad asked her? And if he had, was her answer the reason why he'd sounded so sad over the phone? Was her answer the reason why she'd left the house?

Was her answer the reason why they'd both gotten shot?

Robin shut her eyes. She wasn't sure where she was going with this, but she needed to come back.

Eric said, "After the funeral, let's talk about this more. We know your mother better than those cops do. And if they're on a lead like that, I think we might be better off hiring a private eye."

"Maybe."

He stroked her face, kissed her forehead. In her entire life, Robin had never felt so entirely alone. "I'd better finish getting ready," she said.

Robin turned and walked inside, thinking back to the half second when she'd come up behind her husband, how it had appeared to her as though every molecule in his body had been directed into that phone.

Texting as though his whole world depended on it. She didn't know to whom.

Robin didn't know anyone in her life. Not a single living soul.

TWELVE

June 13, 1976
2:00 P.M.

Dear Aurora Grace,

There is something bad inside Gabriel. It's like lava in a volcano. If you don't see it or feel it, it can't hurt you, so it doesn't seem real.

But it is real. This bad thing is always there, bubbling closer and closer to the surface, until finally, it explodes out of him, destroying everything it touches. You know you can't stop it, not any more than you would be able to stop real lava in its tracks. So all you can do is stay as quiet as possible and pray with everything you have that it doesn't touch you too.

I never saw Gabriel kill Papa Pete. I only heard the shots from outside. By the time I walked in through the front door, he was already dead. "I didn't mean to," Gabriel said, and I believed him. I believed him because I hadn't seen him fire the gun. I hadn't seen his eyes as he pulled the trigger. I hadn't seen the veins popped out on his forehead or that smile on his face that isn't really a smile at all, just skin stretching. I hadn't seen the lava.

Through all these months of meeting Gabriel the way I did and liking him and loving him and not loving him and disliking him and even hating him a little, I had no reason to truly fear him, even when he was holding a gun to my head. And that was because I had never seen the lava. Not until today.

We showed up at Ed Hart's house at about 1:00 P.M. It's a small house. No bigger than mine. I asked Gabriel if he was sure it was the right house because it didn't look like a place where a rich Hollywood guy would live, especially not someone who was friends with people like David Soul.

Gabriel said, "He is rich. He's just not showy."

Gabriel said he knew Ed Hart well when he was little. As it turns out, Gabriel's real dad is a hotshot entertainment lawyer who used to take him to movie and TV sets a lot. He stopped doing that a long time ago, when he left Gabriel's mom for a dancer on the *Sonny and Cher Comedy Hour* and never saw the family again. Gabriel hates him, of course, and that's why he never spoke about him to me before. But back when he was in elementary school, Gabriel used to worship his dad, and he and Ed were pals. He met him on the set of some cop show, and while his dad yapped away with his TV producer client, Ed showed Gabriel prop guns, fake handcuffs, even a phony bomb. They got together a few times after that, and Ed told him that when he was old enough, Gabriel could apprentice for him. Become a property master himself.

"He'll be glad to see me," Gabriel said. "He was like a second father." But when he answered the door, Ed didn't seem to have any idea who we were.

Ed Hart was balding and kind of short. He was wearing baggy, Wrangler-type jeans and a green Lacoste sports shirt that stretched tight across his belly. His eyes were wide and bright and his cheeks were very red, as though he'd once gotten so embarrassed that his face froze like that. He had a sweet, confused smile that reminded me a little of Jenny. Even though Ed was old enough to be a dad or maybe even a grandfather, there was something almost baby-ish about him—something that made it hard to look him in the eye for very long. "Can I help you kids with anything?" he said.

I will never understand why he opened the door all the way.

June 15, 1976
4:00 A.M.

From the *Inland Empire Eagle*

WEST COVINA, June 14—Police are investigating the apparent murder of property master Edward Roy-land Hart, 61, after his body was found this morning in his home at 655 Mercer Lane, bound at the wrists and feet and riddled with more than a dozen bullet wounds.

The body was discovered by Mr. Hart's housekeeper, Margaret Ingram, who immediately called police. "This is tragic," Mrs. Ingram said. "Mr. Hart was such a nice man. He had no enemies. I never even heard him raise his voice to anyone."

Though Mr. Hart's wallet and watch had been taken, along with assorted movie and TV memorabilia, police sources say that the crime appeared to be unusually violent for a simple robbery. "There seemed to be an element of overkill," said Lieutenant Barrett Grange of the L.A.P.D. County Sheriff's Department, whose detectives are assisting West Covina police. "Even if the assailant was a complete stranger, the violence visited on Mr. Hart was unusually excessive for a simple robbery." Mr. Hart was shot in both legs, the groin, abdomen, and face, all apparently while bound and gagged.

Mr. Hart was divorced, with no children. Said Lieutenant Grange, "Anyone with any knowledge as to what person or persons may have committed this crime is encouraged to contact the law enforcement team at the tipline, listed below."

Dear Aurora Grace,

Newspapers are strange. They tell you about things after they happen, but when you read them, you feel as though they're happening right in front of you. This article is a good example. Ed

Hart will never be alive again, and yet when you read that article you want to help. You want to save him. Don't you? I want to save him.

I wanted to save him when it was happening but I was too scared. I couldn't move and couldn't speak and I hated myself for that. As we drove away from his house, I wished with all my heart that I'd been brave enough to stop Gabriel. To change things. But now I'm not sure. Now, I'm thinking that maybe it was meant to be. That Gabriel and I were steered by the Hand of Fate down that quiet street and up Ed Hart's driveway and into his house to give him exactly what he deserved. Does that sound crazy? Does it sound like I've been reading the Bible too much?

I was supposed to throw this newspaper out, but I ripped out that clipping when Gabriel wasn't looking. I stole a tube of glue from Ed Hart's house and that's what I used to stick it to the page. When you are old enough, I want you to read the article, but I want you first to read what I am about to write here, so you know and understand the whole story.

After it was done, Gabriel wanted me to help him take Ed Hart into the backyard. He'd found a shovel in his garage, and his idea was to bury him there. When I said I couldn't do that, Gabriel had the idea of pouring gasoline on him and burning him. But then he worried about the fire spreading and hurting innocent people, and so he came up with putting Ed into his own car. We would wrap Ed in one of his own sheets and put him in the trunk of his car. And then we would drive it to a wrecking yard and make sure the car got crushed, with Ed Hart in it. Gabriel had seen that in a movie once, he said. It would be easy.

Gabriel said, "Don't you see? He'll be gone. No one will find him. We won't have to think of him ever again."

I thought it was a terrible idea. I doubted we would be able to carry Ed together. And even if we could, we didn't know the area. How were we supposed to find a wrecking yard? Look it up in the Yellow Pages? Ask the neighbors? I wanted to say all that, but I was crying so hard I couldn't talk.

I couldn't even stand. I was on the floor of Ed Hart's house, curled up into a ball with the stiff shag rug pressing into the side of my face, that copper and smoke smell all around me again, seeping into my skin just the way it had with Papa Pete. Gabriel was standing over me, pleading with me to stand up, all the while talking about throwing Ed into the back of a car like he'd seen in some stupid Charles Bronson movie and I wanted to shut the door on all of it, on him, on this nightmare I seemed to have found my way into.

Finally, I was able to get one word out. I pointed to Ed on the floor, tied up with pairs of his own socks, and I said it. "Why?"

Gabriel's face changed into something I'd never seen before. It was as though he was a jar and sadness was water, and someone kept filling and filling him until it spilled over the edges. "I can't tell you," he said. "I can't say the words."

It turns out Ed Hart wasn't a second father to Gabriel. He wasn't a mentor or a teacher or even a human being to him. Ed did things to Gabriel when he was little that he still can't talk about for the shame of those things, not even to me. "Especially to you, April," was exactly what he said.

Gabriel figured Ed would remember those things he'd done to him and feel guilty enough to give us a bunch of money and some names of people in Hollywood. But when Gabriel saw Ed's face—the blankness and confusion—that small, weird hope of his turned to something else. Something he couldn't control.

Gabriel didn't tell me any of that until we were sitting at a diner off the 10, forty miles away. He bought me a slice of lemon meringue pie and a strawberry milkshake with money from Ed's wallet, and he explained it all to me in a voice so quiet, I had to strain to hear him.

Listening, I understood why he'd wanted to burn Ed's body, to bury it in the ground, to mash it to a pulp. It wasn't enough to kill him. He wanted to make Ed Hart into something that had never happened.

It scares me, how well I understand Gabriel. How perfectly I can read his thoughts. It makes me think he may be right when he says that we were meant to be together, and that we always have been, from the dawn of the world and through many lifetimes up until now.

There's no controlling that, is there? Is there a way to stop something that's meant to be, even if it's something you don't want?

There's something else I need to tell you, Aurora Grace. I am the one who tied up Ed Hart. I got the socks out of the drawer in his bedroom. They were thin, stretchy knee socks, long enough that I was able to do the knots Papa Pete taught me from his days in the navy during the Korean War. I made the knots tight and perfect, leaving him no chance of escape. Yes, Gabriel told me to do it. Yes, he had a gun aimed at Ed and me both, and yes, I do believe that Jenny's life still depends on my obeying Gabriel at all costs. But I could have tied looser knots.

When we were in the diner, after Gabriel finished telling me why he killed Ed Hart, he pulled something out of the duffel bag he'd filled with all the things he'd taken from the house before we left. It was a coffee mug, with a picture of Starsky and Hutch on it. "For you," he said.

A better girl might have thrown the mug in his face. A better girl might have said that she could never accept a gift that had belonged to a murdered man, even if that man had done horrible things to a child. Even if that man deserved to die. But I took the mug, Aurora Grace. I took it, and I thanked him and told him I will keep it with me, always.

THIRTEEN

ROBIN

"LET US PRAY," the rabbi said. He began reciting the Twenty-third Psalm, and Robin mouthed the words, her father's body in a coffin just a few feet away, the coffin she'd chosen based on some musing of Dad's that she vaguely recalled. Something about being buried in a "plain pine box." Though it could have been her mother who had said that. She wasn't sure of anything anymore.

Getting ready for the funeral, Robin had downed a glass of wine to steady her nerves, and now her head felt light and woozy, her peripheral vision pierced by tiny, bright sparks. She hadn't eaten today, and that, combined with the wine and the Xanax she'd taken earlier and forgotten about, was affecting her, that plus her own cartwheeling emotions—confusion and grief and anger and fear, so much fear for her mother. *Please, please, Mom, please wake up . . .*

Wake up and explain to me who you are.

"Are you all right?" Eric put an arm around her

and she leaned into his shoulder and closed her eyes for a few moments, waiting for the feeling to pass, trying not to think of Eric texting furiously on a day off from work or the way he'd dropped his phone into his pocket when he realized she was behind him.

"I'm fine," she said. "I'm fine." So many things Robin couldn't let herself look at, not if she was going to get through the rest of this day.

Robin opened her eyes. She turned her attention to the group surrounding her father's grave, work colleagues of Dad's whose faces looked vaguely familiar, a contingent from her office headed by Eileen, a few shell-shocked men and women she figured for Dad's patients. Morasco was there too, standing in the back of the group with a tall, curly-haired woman Robin assumed was Brenna, his wife. There were a few people from Eric's job whom Robin barely knew, a voluptuous young woman she recognized as Shawn Labatoir's latest personal assistant. Some of her mother's fellow hospital volunteers, her parents' neighbor, Mr. Dougherty. And Nikki. Nikki was a sturdy-looking woman in a black T-shirt dress with sensibly cut silver hair; a weathered, makeup-free face; and blue eyes so bright they were difficult to look directly at. Before the ceremony started, she'd gone straight for Robin, hugged her tight enough to knock the wind out of her. "My God, Robbie," she had said. "Little Robbie."

"Umm . . . I'm not sure I—"

"Of course you don't. It was so long ago. I've been keeping up with you, though. Your school and your career. Your mom . . . She is so proud of you."

Her face was wet against Robin's shoulder, her arms warm and strong. At last, Nikki had pulled away, those otherworldly eyes sparkling with tears, and Robin had hung on to her hands, not wanting to let go of the only person here who seemed as hurt and as lost as she was.

"She *is* proud of you," she had said, leaning on the present tense. "She *is*."

"I wish I remembered you, Nikki," Robin had said.

"We'll catch up. When your mother gets better, we'll catch up, and we'll reminisce."

Nikki was standing by herself now. She was holding a Bible and mouthing the prayer and Robin watched her, the memory of her like the pinpoints of light at the corners of her eyes, so close. Yet she couldn't hang on to it long enough to see it clearly . . .

The rabbi finished the psalm. Workers lowered the coffin into the grave. "*Al mekomo yavo vesha-lom*," the rabbi said. "May Mitchell go to his place in peace."

The rabbi was a young man, rosy-cheeked and earnest. Robin's parents never went to temple that much to begin with, but when Rabbi Isaac left last year and this one took over, they stopped going altogether. *Nothing against him*, Dad would say. *He's just too young to lead a flock*. The new rabbi's last name was Klein, which means "Little" in German—something Robin's father had found hilarious. Mom and Dad had referred to him as the Bar Mitzvah Boy. And yet here he was, the Little Bar Mitzvah Boy, laying her father to rest. Life had a sick sense of humor.

Rabbi Klein beckoned Robin to the grave as the workers lowered the coffin. Eric put one hand on her waist and took her hand with the other, as though she were too frail to walk. He started to lead her to the grave but she shook her head. "I can do it," she said, a little too sharply. "I can stand on my own."

At the edge of the grave, the rabbi handed Robin the shovel. "As is tradition," he said, "Mitchell will be buried by the hands of those who love him."

Just as he was shot by the gun of his wife, who loved him.

Robin shoved the thought away. She pushed the shovel into the dirt, feeling as though she were moving through water, the lack of her father all around her, the gasp of her mother's ventilator running through her head. The shovel was heavy as she lifted it, and the clump of dirt hit the coffin with a soft, crumbling sound. She wanted to cry, but she couldn't, not with all these eyes on her. Not standing next to the Bar Mitzvah Boy. It was easier to keep her head down, her breath even, to focus not on feelings but on what she had to do: hand the shovel to the rabbi, turn around and walk back to her husband, one foot in front of the other, eyes aimed at the ground, at her open-toed shoes. Her chipped pedicure. *Don't think. Just do.*

As she walked, though, Robin found herself remembering again the last phone conversation she'd ever had with Dad—the strange, sad sound of his voice. Yes, he frequently got sad over the Yankees losing. But this had been different and Robin had known it, deep down. *Have we been good parents to you?* Over forty-one years of her life and hundreds of poorly played games, he'd never asked her that question before.

Something had been wrong. Robin had known it at the time. Some part of her had. Yet it had been easier to just believe the lie, the way she always believed the lies her father told her, about everything being okay when it wasn't, about how he and Mom had only been *engaged in a discussion*, during those few times they'd woken her up late at night with their harsh, hissed words. About how mama's baby bird had *flown off to join her flock* or how seventh-grade parent-teacher conferences had gone *just fine*, when Robin later wound up flunking math that year, how her eighth-grade perm made her look *like a movie star* or how the bottomless sorrow she felt sophomore year of high school was nothing serious at all—just *teen angst. Everybody has that.* It had been Robin's mother, with her lack of a medical degree, who had finally taken her to a therapist.

For a person whose job it had been to plumb the depths of criminals' brains in search of the ugly truth, Robin's father had been awfully comfortable telling little white lies. And Robin had made herself fall for them, every time. It was easier, wasn't it, to pretend that things weren't as bad as they seemed?

Some of the guests were lining up now, waiting for their turns to shovel dirt onto Dr. Mitchell Bloom's grave. The others in the group were starting to disperse. She saw Nick and Brenna Morasco heading away from the group and hurried to catch up with them, brushing past some outstretched hands as she did. "Detective Morasco?"

He stopped, turned around. "Hi, Ms. Diamond," he said. "It was a lovely ceremony."

The tall woman stuck out her hand. "Brenna Spector," she said. "I'm so sorry for your loss." She had a strong grip and a steady gaze.

"Thank you." In one of their early conversations, Morasco had mentioned to Robin that Brenna had that Marilu Henner thing—hyperthymesia, or superior autobiographical memory. Whatever you wanted to call it, it basically meant that she couldn't forget a damn minute of her life if she tried. Robin couldn't imagine anything worse. *I bet that puts the pressure on* you, she had said to Morasco, half joking. *You blow it once, she remembers forever.*

But actually she thought that Morasco's wife's condition might have had a lot to do with his demeanor—the way he seemed to think all his sentences through before he said them out loud. As though he ascribed a certain permanence to his comments and actions that other people didn't. "Listen," Morasco said. "I'm sorry about Ehrlich Baus. I'd tell you he means well, but I don't know if it'd be the truth."

Robin smiled. "Yeah, well . . . You have a lot of patience."

"He does," said Brenna. "Believe me."

"Listen," Robin said. "I um . . . I just wanted to get something straight. About the case."

Brenna and Morasco exchanged a look. "I'll see you back at the car," she said, then turned to Robin. "Again, my condolences."

Brenna headed up the small hill toward the parking lot. Robin watched her go, Dad's funeral, his death, and everything her husband had told her about it trapped forever in the amber of her perfect memory.

Morasco said, "What can I help you with?"

"Okay, I didn't really think about this before because I was so surprised by the information," she said. "But the killer . . ."

"Yes?"

"He or she shot both of my parents with my mother's gun."

"Yes. That appears to be what happened."

"So . . . that tells me my mom must have taken it out from wherever she'd been keeping it. You know . . . to defend herself."

He said nothing.

"But you guys were asking me about people my parents know. People they might have had fallings-out with . . ."

"Yes."

Robin was aware of others leaving the cemetery, their eyes on her as they passed. She saw Mr. Dougherty, the bright sun beating down on the back of his bent head. She gave him a weak wave that he returned as he trudged alone up the hill.

Robin turned her attention on Morasco. "Someone broke in," she said. "My mother took out the gun she apparently owned. She tried to defend herself. Wouldn't it make sense that the intruder was *not* someone she or my dad knew?"

"There's a lot of inference in what you just said."

"Inference?"

"No one would be able to confirm that your mother took out the gun or that she tried to defend herself against an intruder," he said. "No one except for your mother. And she's . . . unconscious at the moment."

"Yeah, but it seems pretty obvious. People buy guns to protect themselves."

"Have you been reading the news stories?"

"Not really." She tried to keep the sarcasm out of her voice. "I haven't been surfing the web very much in the past couple of days."

"I asked because the media are treating it as a home invasion."

"Isn't that what it was?"

He exhaled. "I can't really discuss the case with you, Ms. Diamond."

"Detective Morasco—"

"We don't discuss ongoing investigations with—"

"*Please.*" Her voice shook. Her hands clenched into fists. The wine was wearing off and the Xanax was long gone and her feelings were showing themselves again—pain and powerlessness and an exhaustion that was agonizing, as though she'd been swimming against a strong current for hours, days. She took a breath. "I need to hear what's going on, Detective. I won't tell anyone. Not even my husband if you don't want me to. But I need to hear the truth. From someone. Please."

He looked at her. "You can't tell anyone. You have to promise to keep this between us."

"I promise."

He leaned in closer, barely moving his lips when he spoke. "There was no evidence of a break-in," he said. "No broken windows or locks. The alarm hadn't been engaged. No one in the neighborhood heard a noise until the gunshots. So even though we're still looking into every possibility, it seems very likely that the shooter had been invited in."

"Oh," Robin said.

She felt footsteps behind her. Without turning around, she knew it was Eric, before his gentle hand on her shoulder, his shiny black shoes on the grass, the smell of his cologne, her favorite. The same cologne he'd worn the night of her father's death, that late dinner he'd had with a source . . .

"Hi, Detective Morasco," Eric said. "I'm not sure if you heard, but we're having some food and drinks at our house."

"That's really nice of you, but I should be heading out." His gaze moved from Eric's face to Robin's. "We'll be in touch," he said.

Robin nodded. She took Eric's hand and walked up to the parking lot slowly, stopping to accept hugs and condolences, her head resting on his shoulder, inhaling cologne. When they were nearing their limo, she turned to him. She gazed up into his clear blue eyes, and wanted to trust him, wanted to trust someone . . . "Who were you texting earlier?"

"What?"

She didn't repeat herself. She'd said it perfectly clearly, and he'd heard her. That was obvious. She could see him stalling for time, his brain working behind those clear eyes, clicking through responses. At last, Eric opened his mouth, but she put a finger to his lips. "It doesn't matter," she said. "I shouldn't have asked."

"But I was just—"

"I mean it, Eric. I shouldn't have asked. I don't want to know. Not today."

He nodded, slowly. They got into the limo together, neither one of them saying a word. As they headed out of the parking lot, Robin told herself, the way her father would have told her, that everything was fine. That Eric was probably just texting a work colleague about an important matter and even if he wasn't, that was something to save discussing for another time, when there wasn't so much going on.

Robin found herself remembering instead what Mr. Dougherty had told her the night of the shooting, about seeing a strange car near her parents' home. She scanned the parking lot for silver sedans, because that was something concrete and simple to do with her brain. There were many silver sedans in the lot. Next to one of them, she spotted silver-haired, bright-eyed Nikki talking to a tall, young bespectacled man in a dark T-shirt and jeans, who looked . . . Could it be? Her gaze went to the Chevy insignia on the back of the car, the name of the make. *Chevrolet Cruze.*

It could have been important. Or not. During the hours she'd spent in the waiting room at St. Catherine's the night of the shooting, Robin had looked up Chevy Cruze on her phone. Turned out it was the most popular car at East Coast rental agencies by more than 30 percent. If you rented a car to come to the funeral, odds were you'd get a Cruze.

More interesting than the model and make of the car was the young man Nikki had been speaking to and how, in the midst of their rather animated

conversation, he'd raised his head and watched the
limo as it left the parking lot, his gaze intent, as
though he were trying to see inside. Robin pulled
her phone out of her bag. Looked up images of
Quentin Garrison. Sure enough, his headshot from
the NPR station came up first, and Robin saw him
staring back at her—the young man from the parking lot. Her mother's old friend Nikki was talking
to Quentin Garrison. About what, she had no idea.
But Robin wanted to know.

FOURTEEN

QUENTIN

WHEN QUENTIN WAS a kid, his mother would sometimes take him to Westwood Village Memorial Park—a patch of green between towering L.A. office buildings and the eternal resting place of some of Hollywood's biggest stars, including Kate's idol, Marilyn Monroe. He had hazy memories of those visits: Kate's cool hand wrapped around his own, that rare touch of her skin and the whispering breeze, the bright flowers on the graves of the stars and Marilyn Monroe's crypt, the most beloved one of all, the stone gone pink from years of lipstick kisses. He'd been to other cemeteries since, of course. But as he stood under the hot sun that afternoon at Tarry Ridge Cemetery, watching the funeral of Mitchell Bloom from a respectful distance, Quentin found himself feeling much the way he had back then.

It could have been the summer heat or the dewy grass beneath his sneakers, but more likely it was the emotion coursing through him—the same one he'd felt holding his mother's hand as she sobbed and sobbed over Marilyn, a dead celebrity she'd never met. It was a disquiet he couldn't put a name to; an awful, powerless feeling, like pounding on soundproof glass.

Quentin watched Robin Diamond walk to the head of her father's grave. He watched her take the shovel, her matchstick arms braced as she forced it into the earth. It was hard to reconcile this frail, tired-looking woman with the one in the Mother's Day video, same as it was hard to think of the woman in intensive care as Renee Bloom. Both of them tungsten-strong in that video, both impossibly, infuriatingly happy. Now, Robin looked dead on her feet, Renee was fighting for her life. And Mitchell Bloom . . .

I should warn you, the man in the coffin had said to Quentin three days ago, when he'd spoken to him at 4:00 P.M. at his office in Tarry Ridge. *Since I've been in private practice, I'm no longer as up on all the current theories as I once was.*

You think I want your expertise as a forensic psychiatrist?

You don't?

I'm sorry, sir, but no.

Well . . . What do you want then?

Dr. Bloom, how well do you know your wife?

Had that been so wrong of him to ask? It had been a simple question, really. One that could have resulted in Quentin closing up shop, heading back to L.A. and finding himself a new angle for *Closure*. If only Dr. Bloom had been able to answer it. If only he hadn't chosen instead to psychoanalyze Quentin, to dig down into the reserves of his pain and bring it to the surface, where it could breathe and flourish.

Quentin felt a tap on his shoulder. "Here to pay your respects?"

It was Detective Morasco from the Tarry Ridge Police Department, and Quentin jumped a little when he saw him. A day ago, he'd found Detective Morasco good-looking in a Mark-Ruffalo-with-a-hangover kind of way, and reasonably easy to talk to. But maybe that was just compared to his partner, who was—and Quentin normally didn't generalize like this—the worst type of straight man: that guy who'd lived his whole life thinking he was the cleverest and most charming son of a bitch in the room, either because no one had bothered to let him know otherwise, or because in the rooms he frequented (shudder), he was.

Anyway, the partner wasn't here, but Morasco was, and Quentin didn't find his presence as reassuring as he had at the police station. "To be honest," Quentin told him, "I'm not sure why I'm here."

Behind Morasco, Robin was handing the shovel to the rabbi, her head bowed low, as though her neck couldn't take the weight of it. "Me neither, actually," the detective said. "I never knew the Blooms when they were alive."

Quentin's eyes widened. "Is Mrs. Bloom—"

"No, no. I misspoke. I'm just saying . . ."

"Yeah, I get it."

Morasco's gaze moved to the phone in Quentin's hand. "You still working on the podcast?"

"No. I mean . . . I am. I will. But I'm not here in a professional capacity."

"Well, I appreciate you keeping your distance, anyway," he said. "I'm sure the family does too."

Robin had joined her husband. The rabbi was speaking again, urging others to take up the shovel. "I should probably go," Quentin said.

Morasco nodded—probably the reason why he'd come back here in the first place, to politely kick Quentin out of the cemetery before the Diamonds caught sight of him.

Quentin started to leave.

"Listen, Mr. Garrison . . ."

"Yeah?"

"If you wind up including the shooting as part of your podcast . . ."

"I'm not going to do that. I swear. I would never record and report on something as private as this funeral."

"Okay, fine," he said. "But if you change your mind and decide to branch off into this case. And if, in your reporting, you find out anything that might help us . . . Anything at all that stands out to you . . ."

Quentin exhaled. That wasn't what he'd expected to hear. "Oh," he said. "Oh, yes. Of course."

"You still have my card?"

"Yes."

"Great. Thanks."

Quentin looked at him. "You don't have any leads as to who could have done this?"

He smiled a little. "Every lead helps," he said. Which wasn't an answer at all.

They said a quick good-bye, and Quentin headed up the hill and into the parking lot, past rows of cars, the waiting limousine, the empty hearse . . .

"Okay . . ."

"I've been out here working on a podcast. It concerns the Blooms, and I thought maybe I could get some insight from you."

"I don't think I can give you very much insight, Quentin."

"Were you close to Renee?"

"Present tense."

"What?"

"Renee is still alive. I *am* close to Renee. Present tense."

Quentin smiled. "That's the insight I'm looking for. I'd love to talk to you, ma'am."

"I don't think so."

"Why not?"

"Because you didn't know Mitchell or Renee. You're only here to cover the home invasion. I'm not going to fault you for doing your job, but honestly, Quentin, I think you'll get a far better response from the police, the coroner . . . People like you."

"Like me?"

"People who are only interested in the Blooms because they've been shot." She said it patiently, warmly. "I don't mean to cause offense."

The limousine passed them, Robin Diamond and her husband inside. Quentin stared at it. He couldn't help himself. He hoped she wasn't staring back. "No offense taken," he said.

"I know you're just doing your job."

"I've been here since before the home invasion, ma'am," he said. "I spoke to Mitchell Bloom when he was alive. I believe I was one of the last people to do that."

The woman's lips parted, but she said nothing. Her bright eyes drilled into him.

"We only spoke once but he seemed like a very good man."

"Why did you speak to Mitchell? Why are you out here?"

Quentin exhaled. "Can I get your name, please? Can I buy you lunch? I promise I'll tell you everything, if I can just get a few moments of your time."

The woman bit her lip. She gave Quentin a long appraising look, as though she were trying to read his mind. The silence went on for an uncomfortable while. And when she finally spoke, it felt like a victory. "Don't worry about buying me lunch," she said. "I'll pay for my own."

HER NAME WAS Nicola Crane, and Quentin followed her in his identical rental car to Ruby's Diner—a place with Formica tables and orange vinyl booths and waterproof menus thick as doctoral theses. In snooty Tarry Ridge, this place stuck out like a dollar bill in a stack of hundreds, and it made Quentin like Nicola Crane for choosing it. They sat across from each other at a booth next to a window and exchanged business cards—Nicola's consisted of her name, a phone number, and a P.O. box in Philadelphia—and quickly dove into the menus. "I think I may eat every meal here from now on," Quentin said.

Nicola smiled. "You could do worse." She pushed her menu aside. "I've been spending a lot of time here, since . . . well, for the past two days."

The waitress sauntered up to the table—a bored blond teenage girl who wore a Breitling watch with her polyester uniform. "What can I get you two?" she said, flatly, "you two" clearly a feeble attempt to sound homey and welcoming.

Quentin guessed she was a rich Tarry Ridge high schooler, and the summer job was some sort of bug up her parents' collective ass having to do with learning the value of a dollar. "What would you recommend?" Quentin said.

She yawned. "Everything's okay."

Quentin ordered a stack of blueberry pancakes, a side of turkey bacon, and coffee. Nicola asked for coffee and cinnamon raisin toast, with cream cheese and strawberry jam.

The waitress smiled at her. "That's what you ordered last time," she said.

"Comfort food."

When the waitress left, Nicola said, "So . . . is your podcast about Mitchell's work in psychotherapy?"

"Not exactly." Quentin took a sip of his water. "This is going to be a little hard to explain."

The waitress returned with their cups of coffee, a creamer, and a stack of sugar packets. Nicola poured around five fingers of cream into her cup, stirred it in.

Quentin waited until the waitress had left before he spoke. "I'm doing a podcast on the Cooper/LeRoy murders."

She took a delicate sip of coffee. If the names were in any way familiar beyond their historical significance, it didn't show on her face. "You spoke to Mitchell as an expert, then? I know he did quite a bit of research on mass murderers when he was working on Wards Island."

"No, ma'am," Quentin said. "I was asking him about Renee."

Nicola's eyes widened. "Pardon?"

"I'm not telling many people about this. Not yet. But you seem like you might be able to solve this for me."

"Solve?"

Quentin weighed it all out in his mind—the promise he'd made to George Pollard, the potential knowledge Nicola Crane had. "A man contacted our station," he said, exhaling slowly. "He'd seen Mrs. Bloom in a video. It was on the website Robin works for. They talked about Mother's Day movies . . ."

"Yes," she said. "I saw it."

The waitress was back with their food. She set the plates down with a condescending smile, the diamonds on her Breitling glinting. "Anything else I can get you two?"

"No thanks," Nicola said.

Once the waitress was gone again, Quentin leaned forward, watching Nicola's placid face. "The man who contacted us," he said. "He claimed to know for a fact that Renee is April Cooper."

Nicola stared at him frozen, butter knife poised in her hand.

Quentin started to explain more but she stopped him. "I know who April Cooper was."

"Oh. Well then . . ."

"Who is this man who contacted you?"

Quentin took a sip of his coffee. "I'm sorry. That's

the one thing I can't tell you," he said. "But I will tell you this. He claims he met her after her death."

"After."

"Yes."

She took a bite of toast, her face relaxing. "He's insane."

"You'd think so." He poured syrup over his pancakes and started to cut them up in pieces. Nicola didn't say anything, but he could feel her watching him, waiting. She wanted more information from him. But he wasn't here to answer her questions. That wasn't how this worked. You have to give information to get it. He cut off a perfect bite of pancake—just the right size, the right amount of syrup, topped off with a sliver of turkey bacon. He put it in his mouth, taking his time to savor it fully before he put the fork down and met her gaze. "How long have you known Renee?"

She took another sip of her coffee. "Since we were children."

Quentin's eyes widened.

She smiled. "You look like you've seen a ghost."

"It's just . . . You're the first person I've met who can even prove to me she had a childhood."

She shrugged. "Well, it wasn't the happiest childhood."

Quentin's phone was in his lap. He picked it up and tapped at it a few times, trying to make it look as though he was receiving a text. "One sec," he said, as she watched him with her ice-blue eyes. Discreetly, he turned on the voice recorder, then placed the phone facedown on the table. "Please," he said. "Please tell me about it."

Nicola took another bite of her toast, the cream cheese thick, the jam drizzled on. She chewed politely and swallowed, dabbed the corners of her mouth with her napkin. Nicola Crane had the look of a frontierswoman but the manners of a debutante. "This was Renee's favorite dish, you know, when we were kids."

"Really?"

"We used to eat it all the time together—cinnamon raisin toast, cream cheese, strawberry jam. She used to make it for me, which is probably why I'm finding it so comforting now."

"So you're not blood relatives," he said. "You and Renee."

"We were in the same foster home back in the mid-'70s. Little town in Arizona called Brittlebush."

Quentin drank his coffee. "How old were you both?"

"She was older than me—maybe seventeen? There were a lot of kids in that house, but she was . . ." Quentin watched her face, the way her eyes clouded, then stopped, shifting back to the present. She took her napkin and again dabbed her mouth.

Nicola said, "You know what oscars are?"

"Academy Awards?"

She laughed a little. "No, no. Fish. Big ugly, mean-looking things."

"Oh. Yeah, I think so."

"Our foster dad kept two of them, in a tank in the kitchen. Funny. I can't remember what he looked like—the foster dad. But those awful fish . . . I still have nightmares about them."

Quentin took another bite of pancake. "Oscars."

"They eat living things," Nicola said. "I guess all fish do, but these . . . the foster dad fed them live goldfish. Renee and I were in the kitchen—I think we were the only ones who saw. I was young and very sensitive. I'd lost both of my parents and I was still . . . hurting."

"I'm sorry."

She shook her head. "Anyway," she said. "I saw one of the oscars eat the first little goldfish and I started to cry. The foster dad told me to toughen up. 'It's the food chain,' he said. 'It's life.' But Renee wasn't having any of it. These poor goldfish were darting around that tank and the two giant oscars were scooping them up into their jaws and she told the foster dad—his name was Bill, that's it . . . Bill Grumley. God, I haven't thought of that name in forever . . ." She took another bite of her toast, chewed, and swallowed.

Quentin said, "What did Renee tell him?"

"'You're heartless.'"

"Huh?"

"That's what she said. She told Bill Grumley, 'You're heartless.' And he laughed at her . . . 'Nature is heartless, girl. You'd best get used to it.'" A shadow passed over Nicola's face, clouds massing outside the diner. Her gaze traveled beyond Quentin, to some distant point over his shoulder, in the past, a million miles away. "Renee woke me up in the middle of the night. She was holding a paper cup. She shined a flashlight on it and showed me. There was one goldfish inside, swimming around in about four inches of water. 'Those bastards got full,' she said. 'He was the only one left. I saved him.'"

"What did you do with the fish?"

"We sneaked downstairs, out the back door. I knew we'd get in so much trouble if the foster dad or his wife caught us. That was one of the rules. Probably the most important one. No leaving the house on our own."

"But you left anyway."

"She left," she said. "I followed."

"You were younger."

"She was braver," she said. "We were barefoot, in our nightgowns. There was a park down the street. It had a pond. She dumped the cup into the pond and the goldfish swam away."

"That must have felt good."

"To me, it felt wonderful."

"But to Renee?"

"Renee," she said. "Renee . . . When we were walking back to the house she was very quiet. I asked her what was wrong, and she wouldn't answer, wouldn't speak. I assumed she was frightened, you know?"

"Frightened?"

"It was a gossipy neighborhood. Even though I was just a kid, I knew we probably wouldn't get away with it. Someone would notice two girls in their nightgowns, walking to the park at three in the morning."

"Of course."

"That wasn't it, though," Nicola said. "Renee was upset about all the fish that had been eaten. She was upset because she hadn't been able to save the others."

"That's very touching."

Nicola smiled, her face again going familiar. "Quentin?"

"Yeah?"

"Why are you doing this podcast?"

"Well . . . I did tell you about the call from that man."

"I mean . . . why not something scarier—Ted Bundy or Charles Manson? Or something unsolved like the Zodiac? Why not something more recent? Why do an entire podcast on these obscure murders just because you got a call from some lunatic?"

Quentin swallowed his coffee. It wasn't part of his plan, answering questions like this one. But there was something about Nicola Crane—the sunshiny voice, maybe, or the deep, caring lines in her face, the warmth in those strangely bright eyes or the unshakable feeling that he knew her from somewhere, someplace . . . Whatever the reason, he felt eager to do the talking for a change. *Do I want to confess? Is that it?*

Quentin forgot about the voice recorder and talked. He tried to explain what it was like to grow up with a mother who never hugged him and only held his hand at the cemetery and seemed indifferent to his presence in her life. He told her about his many attempts to get Kate's attention—first by getting good grades, then by getting bad ones. He talked about how strung out his mother had been, so wasted she often forgot to feed him or clean the house or make sure he got off to school okay. How even in rare periods of sobriety, she'd been completely disinterested in her own son, and how different that all might have been, were it not for April

Cooper and Gabriel LeRoy and what they had done to Kate's family.

Through it all, Nicola ate her toast and sipped her coffee, nodding occasionally but saying nothing. When he was done, Nicola watched his face, her thin lips pulled tight, her bright eyes appraising. "Do you think this podcast is going to help you?" she said. "Is that why you're doing it?"

"I don't know."

Nicola put the last piece of toast into her mouth and took her wallet out of her purse. "Maybe it's just because I'm older," she said. "But I feel like you young kids would be a lot healthier—a lot happier—if you spent less time wallowing in sorrow over things that are inevitable."

"What does that mean?"

"Parents are human beings. Human beings screw things up. It's inevitable. Your situation isn't special or dire or even all that unusual."

He swallowed hard. "Maybe I didn't explain it properly."

"You explained it fine," she said. "But I'm guessing you're no perfect prince either, and as far as you and your mother are concerned, it's a wash at best."

Quentin opened his mouth, then closed it again. He had no idea what to say to that.

"You want my advice?"

"I suppose?"

"Get over it. Your mother did the best she could. Be grateful to her that you made it into adulthood alive, instead of blaming her for all the troubles you've brought on yourself."

"That's . . . that's kind of harsh, don't you think?"

She tapped at Quentin's facedown phone. "When you get a chance, play back that recording you thought you were being so sneaky about. Take a listen to how harsh *you* sounded talking about your dead mother. Then we can talk."

Quentin stared at her. She dropped a twenty on the table and started to stand up. "This ought to cover me," she said, and he found himself thinking about how much her voice reminded him of Renee's—Renee on the Mother's Day tape, honeyed and calm, telling her daughter how much she meant to her.

"I didn't mean to make you angry," he said.

"I'm not angry, Quentin." She gave him a warm smile. "But you certainly are."

He looked at her. *I am.* He was angry almost all the time, though it was only recently that he was having trouble keeping it buried.

Nicola eased back in her seat. "Quentin?"

"Yes?"

"Did you tell the police everything?"

His eyes widened. His face flushed. For a few seconds, he felt as though he were in the midst of a nightmare. "What are you talking about?"

"Did you tell them everything about where you were the night the Blooms were shot?" She leaned against the table, her eyes beaming into his own. "Did you tell them what you saw? What you heard? What you did?"

He could feel the color draining from his face. Was this why she looked familiar? Had she crossed paths with him at the Blooms'? "How do you know where I was?" he said. "Have you been following me?"

She gave him a tight smile and stood up, her purse clasped in her arms. "I was actually just kidding," she said.

Quentin looked up at her face, the fear creeping into her eyes. *You wanted to confess. And you nearly did.* Quentin grabbed his phone off the table. He checked the screen and slipped it into his pocket, trying to think of something, anything to say that was moderately reassuring. "It isn't like that, Ms. Crane," he said quietly. "It isn't what you think." But no one heard him say it. She was already out the door.

FIFTEEN

QUENTIN

ONCE QUENTIN WAS back in his car, he took a few deep breaths. *There's a story here*, he told himself. *Focus on the story.*

He listened to the earlier part of his and Nicola's conversation, scribbling down every name and phrase that might help in following up on Renee's time in the foster home. Then he called Summer and read all his scribblings aloud to her: *Brittlebush, Arizona. 1978. Bill (or William) Grumley. Nicola Crane. C-R-A-N-E. But that could be a married name. Renee White.*

"You got some rest," Summer said.

"A little."

"You want to do *Closure* again."

"I . . . I think it's worth a shot."

"Yes!" she said, then cleared her throat, back to business. "So how old were Nicola and Renee when they were in the foster home?"

"I think they were teens. Nicola said she is younger than Renee, but she didn't say by how much."

"Teens," she said. "So you still haven't found anyone who knew Renee as a child."

"No."

"This is getting strange."

"Not strange enough to mean anything yet."

"I beg to differ."

"Renee Bloom is a private citizen."

Summer didn't respond. Quentin heard the clacking of a keyboard.

"If we're going to even mention the idea that April Cooper might be Renee, we need harder proof or else it looks like malicious intent."

"Duh, Quentin. Please stop mansplaining First Amendment law to me."

Out of his window, he saw a family leaving the diner, a young woman in jeans, a pink T-shirt, and matching sneakers, holding the hand of a gangly boy in glasses who looked about eight years old. *Mother and son.*

The clacking stopped. "Brittlebush," Summer said. "Sounds like a John Waters movie, am I right?"

Quentin forced a laugh.

"Actually, it's a type of wildflower. The town is near the Arizona border, so it really wouldn't be that long a drive. And it's tiny. I don't think it should be too hard to find out if this woman's story checks out."

"Good."

"Nicola, right? Like the cough drop?"

"That's Ricola."

"Whatever. I'll check it out. I'm assuming there's no change in Renee Bloom's condition."

"Far as I know." Quentin realized that he hadn't

checked since this morning. Since the shooting, he'd called the same intensive care nurse three times, and the last time, which had been this morning, she'd simply said, "Same," and hung up on him. Quentin wasn't making a lot of friends in Tarry Ridge.

"Listen," Summer said. "I've got some news you're going to like."

"Yeah?"

"George Pollard has tentatively agreed to an interview."

"Seriously?"

"Yep."

"Wow."

"His family still doesn't know, so he's asking if we can disguise his voice, not reveal his name . . . I'm fully expecting him to cancel, but I managed to pin him down."

"When is the interview?"

"Tomorrow at five."

"This is great," Quentin said. "You're great."

"Aw shucks." He could hear the smile in her voice.

"How did you do it?" His eyes stayed on the mother and her son. They'd reached their car now, and they were involved in conversation, the woman crouched down so she could look him in the eye. He figured she was giving him a good talking-to . . . until he saw that it was the boy doing the talking. Quentin wasn't sure he'd ever experienced that as a child—a grown-up crouching down to listen to him.

Summer was saying, ". . . so now I'm stuck go-

ing to knitting group with George's executive secretary."

"You don't know how to knit."

"I've been watching how-to videos on YouTube.
I think I can fake it. Oh . . . and I also overnighted
you some reading material. The hotel should have
it when you get back."

"Summer?"

"Yeah?"

"Do I seem angry to you?"

"Well . . . are you?"

"No, I mean, do I seem like an angry person?
Like . . . all the time?"

"Of course not."

"Okay. Thanks."

"Why would you ask me that?"

He drew a shaky breath. "No reason."

She started to say something more, but he didn't
let her. "I'll talk to you later," he said. "Let me know
how everything goes."

Once he hung up, he turned on the voice recorder and played back the rest of his conversation
with Nicola. Listened to his entire, three-minute-
long I-hate-Mommy harangue. Then he erased it.
Nicola was right. It had been very, very harsh.

He was staying at an airport hotel in Newark,
a big block of a building as generic as his rental
car. He tapped its address into the GPS app on his
phone and started up the car without turning on
the radio. He watched the mother and son leave the
lot in their SUV, listening to the rasp of his rental
car's engine and Siri's barking directions and re-
calling, without wanting to, the one thing he hadn't

mentioned in his harangue: his mother's death; his part in it.

As he pulled out of the parking lot and turned left on the busy road, following the directions leading up to the highway, he allowed himself to remember that afternoon six months ago: the acrid smell of Kate's room in the so-called sober living house and the way he'd brushed her hair from her forehead, a tender gesture she'd never feel. He recalled how cold her skin had been and the glassiness of her eyes, like a light had gone off behind them. He recalled how he'd cried out and the helper had rushed in (*What did she like to be called? The resident associate?*), how she'd checked Kate's pulse at her wrist and neck and said, without seeming to bear any responsibility, that it had been their third overdose that year. He remembered how he'd cried for his mother—not because he'd known and loved her and now she was gone, but because he hadn't known her, and now he never would.

It had been Dean who had suggested Quentin do a podcast on the murders. He'd told Summer about the idea first, the two of them conspiring behind Quentin's back as though they were planning a surprise party, then cornering him one night at the bungalow, when Summer had been over for dinner. "It will help you get closure." One of them had said it, Dean or Summer. At this point, he wasn't sure which.

It had made some sense at the time, Quentin supposed. He never would have agreed to it if it hadn't. But now that dinner at the bungalow felt to him like the opening scene in an endless nightmare—the murders, the fallout from them now occupying his every thought, every dream. Closure. What a joke. Mitchell Bloom's line of shrink-interrogation couldn't have been more on the nose.

Battling traffic on the Cross County Parkway, Quentin thought about April Cooper and Gabriel LeRoy—how they'd ruined not only his grandfather and his mother, but ruined him too, turning him into the kind of person who doesn't let an old man know that his only daughter is dead. *Your mother put you up to this*, Reg Sharkey had yelled at him. And Quentin hadn't corrected him. He'd been so full of hate, he hadn't said a word.

By the time Quentin reached his hotel, he was back to his mother's overdose—the part that he never allowed himself to think about, the one part of it that he hadn't told anyone, not even Dean. She'd still been alive when he showed up at the sober house. He had seen her sitting up in bed, her eyelids fluttering—and immediately, he'd known what was going on. It had happened before, twice. He had been angry at the people at the sober house for allowing her access to sleeping pills to the point where she'd been able to hoard them again, angrier still at Kate for planning it this way, right before his weekly visit, as though she were forcing him to save her. Forcing a man to save her, because no man had ever done it voluntarily.

He'd pulled out his phone to call 911, just as he had the other two times, and she'd whispered to him, just as she had then. *You're better off without me. Let me go.*

And this time, he had. He never pressed send on the 911 call, didn't attempt CPR the way he had two other times before. He just stood over Kate, watching the life spill out of her, the way April Cooper had watched Kimmy Sharkey fall to the ground.

Relieved. That's how Quentin had felt. He may have even smiled.

He had felt that way until she was gone, until he brushed the hair from her forehead and gazed into her glassy, wide-open eyes and thought, *What have I done? What kind of person am I?*

Quentin got out of the car and walked through the hotel parking lot, his vision thick with tears, not for himself but for Dean, for Summer, for anyone else who was deluded enough to believe in him.

"Mr. Garrison," the front desk clerk called after Quentin, as he made his way through the antiseptic-smelling lobby to the elevator. Quentin's cheeks were wet. He was a mess. Whatever the guy had to say to him could wait for later. "Mr. Garrison! Mr. Garrison! *Mr. Garrison!*"

"*What?*" Quentin shouted it so loud, his voice went hoarse.

There were a few people in the lobby—a family of three, an elderly couple. They all froze in place staring.

Quentin walked over to the front desk, his head down, his fists clenched. The mother drew her child closer as he passed.

"Jesus," the elderly man whispered. "What a nut."

"Sorry," Quentin said to the clerk, though it hardly seemed enough. *It's not me*, he wanted to say. Because this wasn't him. He wasn't like this. Something was happening to him here on the East Coast. Something dark inside him, surfacing.

Without a word, the clerk held up a FedEx package, his name and the address of the hotel scrawled on the front in Summer's impatient handwriting. "Thank you," Quentin said, remembering it now—Summer telling him over the phone about overnighting him reading material. "I was just . . . I went to a funeral today . . ." he said. "I'm a little out of sorts."

The clerk didn't respond, and Quentin didn't blame him. He wouldn't have. He headed for the elevator, his face wet and burning, guests whispering behind his back.

Once he got back into his room, Quentin put the package aside, opened the desk drawer, removed a piece of stationery, and wrote a long letter to Reg Sharkey. He put it into an envelope and found Reg's address in the contacts on his phone. He took it downstairs and left it with the desk clerk, giving him enough money to send it first class, plus an extra twenty for "putting up with me being such an asshole," which finally earned him some eye contact and a smile. "No worries," the guy said.

Only then, when he was back in his room, did he think about opening the package Summer had sent.

Inside was an old paperback book, accompanied by a note from Summer that simply read: FOUND IT! Quentin looked at the book. The cover had bursts all over it: *A special from the editors of The Asteroid! The true story of the Killer Lovers! Soon to be a Movie of the Week!* And in the midst of them all, the title: *The Inland Empire Killers: 'Til Death Do Us Part.*

"God, you're so good, Summer," Quentin whispered.

He opened the book and read, losing himself in the lurid prose, the carefully chosen details. Gabriel LeRoy's lisp, how it had made him subject to bullying as a kid; the long walks a fourteen-year-old April Cooper liked to take, pushing her baby sister, Jenny, in a stroller, in a bid to escape her stern, somber home. The bloodlust that had consumed April and Gabriel both, making them forget their weaknesses as individuals and turning them into a single, murderous entity, "a two-headed monster, fueled by rage."

He read until the sun began to set and his room grew dark, feeling as though he were on the run with Gabriel and April—Gabriel gripping the wheel of one of many stolen cars, the jumbled thoughts running through his brain as April egged him on, encouraging his madness, driven mad as she was by the untimely death of her mother and the feeling that her stepfather loved Jenny—his biological child—so much more than her . . . He devoured it all, facts and fiction, direct quotes and clear instances of poetic license and paragraphs, pages, where you couldn't tell the difference, truth and lies bleeding into each other, all to tell the best possible story. Much like a podcast. Much like life.

Quentin was in the final third of the book and feeling bleary-eyed and hungry when a paragraph jumped out at him:

The blood from the gas station murders barely washed from their hands, the killer couple found solace in a roadside diner, where Gabriel relished a plate of steak and eggs and a side of apple pie, washed down with a cheap beer. April's last meal on the road was more delicate: cinnamon raisin toast and cream cheese, with strawberry jam. "She said her mother used to make it for her," recalls Gretchen Philips, the waitress who served them. "She said it was her favorite dish."

"Comfort food," Quentin whispered.

He removed Nicola Crane's business card from his pocket and stared at it: A name. A phone number. A P.O. box. The utter lack of information. And he'd never asked her about that—something he normally would have done. He'd gone on and on about himself, his family, without learning about hers. Had she engineered that?

He thought of Nicola's voice, the honeyed sound of it, so similar to Renee's. He recalled her tanned, lined face and her sturdy body, but with something so familiar beneath those years of workmanlike muscle, the skin like broken-in leather. Something Quentin knew.

He turned to the middle section of the book and stared at the winter formal picture—April Cooper in her ruffled dress, pale and bony and unformed.

"Is that you?" he whispered to April Cooper's serious young face. "Is that you, Nicola?"

SIXTEEN

June 16, 1976
2:00 A.M.

Dear Aurora Grace,

There's this ride at Disneyland. It's called Mr. Toad's Wild Ride, and it's supposedly for little kids. Here's how it goes: You get in this car with a cute little frog, and everything seems like it's going to be loads of fun. But the problem is—and this is a huge problem—frogs can't drive. They can't even reach the pedals. So, you and the frog end up on this horrible trip where you're nearly crashing into trees and making fire hydrants explode and getting chased by cops . . . until finally you get into a deadly car accident and you both wind up in hell.

Does that sound like a little kids' ride to you? (I'm not kidding about the hell part either. The very last part of Mr. Toad is orange and red flames and little red demons dancing around and everything.)

Anyway, one of my earliest memories is going on that ride with my mom. My real dad had left years earlier, when I was just a baby. Papa Pete wasn't in the picture yet, so it was just her and me back then. I was maybe three or four and when the car started swinging around, I got so scared I started to cry. By the time we got to hell, I was sobbing. But Mom put her arms around me and hugged me tight and said, "It's only a ride. It's not real. Nothing like this could ever happen."

"Do you promise?"

"I promise."

I stopped crying because if there was one thing I knew about Mom, it was that she always kept her promises to me. So many people had let her down in her life, and she didn't want me to grow up sad like her. She wanted me to feel as though the world was a good place where people kept their word and anything was possible. I believed her. I trusted her with every little cell in my body. I loved her with all that I had.

But then she got into a car accident and died.

Sometimes I still have nightmares about Mr. Toad, only it's just Mom in the car, and it's not some little kids' ride at Disneyland—it's really happening. And then I wake up, and I realize that it really _did_ happen.

I hate to say this, but I am sure that Mom is in hell right now. She was sent there for lying to me. For making me believe that the world is something it isn't.

Gabriel says he doesn't believe in hell. He doesn't believe in heaven either. But I believe in both, and I also believe what Papa Pete used to say: the road to hell is paved with good intentions.

I am going to hell, Aurora Grace. After what I've done, it seems pretty obvious. But I don't feel bad about it. Actually, I'm looking forward. I'll see my mother again, and even though we will be burning for all eternity in a blazing furnace, surrounded, like the Bible says, by the weeping and the gnashing of teeth, she will hold me tight. She will kiss my forehead. And she will tell me that it's only a ride.

Love,
April

SEVENTEEN

ROBIN

"IT'S ALL OVER TWITTER," Eric said.

It was dark out—past 9:00 P.M. Robin had left the postfuneral gathering early in order to sit with her mother in intensive care, and she'd just returned to find the house completely dark except for the kitchen, where Eric stood by the refrigerator, a beer in one hand, staring at his ever-present phone.

"That makes two of you," said Robin.

He looked up at her. "What?"

"Nothing." She had to stop it with the pettiness. It wasn't doing anybody any good. "I'm just . . . I'm tired."

"I know, honey." He started to move closer. She took a step back.

"Any change with your mom?"

She shook her head.

"I'm sorry."

"What's all over Twitter?"

He handed her his phone—which was, Robin had to admit, a sign that he might have nothing to hide. She looked at the screen. A series of tweets, all with the hashtag #TarryRidgeShooting. "Wow."

"I was debating whether or not to show you," he said. "But I figured it's always best to know what kind of crazy you're up against."

She clicked on one tweet, linking to Robin's Femme Seven column and speculating that "some incel POS" had shot Robin's parents in response to it. #TarryRidgeShooting was accompanied by a dizzying array of hashtags, including #RedPillLosers #MicroPenis and #StoptheHate. Another tweet speculated that if it weren't for Robin's "feminist agenda," her parents would "still be alive." Yet another included a #GoodGuyWithAGun hashtag and pointed out that Robin's parents would have been a lot better off had they been armed. She handed the phone to Eric, wondering what that tweeter might say if he knew that the gun that had shot them had actually belonged to her mother. "Hashtag no words," she said.

"Labatoir wants to do a show about it."

She looked at him. "Are you kidding me?"

"I wish I was."

"Well . . . what did you say?"

"I told him to shove it up his ass."

"Seriously?"

"I may have said butt. You know how Shawn hates profanity."

Robin broke into a smile. She hadn't genuinely smiled since the shooting and she almost felt guilty about it.

Eric smiled back at her. For a few careless moments, she felt like falling into his arms, just for the sake of being close to him, of feeling the warmth and strength and promise of his body. "I'm on your side, you know," he said. "I'll always be on your side."

"Eric," she said. "I don't know if I'll be able to live without her."

"You don't have to worry about that. She's going to make it. I know it." He looked straight into her eyes as he said it.

"You really believe that, don't you?"

"I do."

She knew he was telling the truth. Eric had always been like this, the very definition of blind optimism. In the past, she'd found it appealing—contagious too, the belief that anything was possible if you just willed it that way. But then Eric started working for sleazy Shawn Labatoir and changed in ways she wouldn't have willed if she'd had that power. He started showing less of his new self to her and more of it at the office, on social media, wherever else he went to disappear. He worked longer hours and got raises and promotions, which bought them things he, not she, wanted: new furniture for the house, a renovated kitchen, dinners at New York's finest restaurants. Robin didn't care about any of that, and now she was the owner of an expensive home she spent a lot of time alone in; its only real value its proximity to her parents, one of whom was dead, the other so very close to it, for reasons she might never know and that, like everything else, she had no control over.

Robin took a breath. *Enough.* Eric put his beer down on the counter and took her hand in his. She didn't pull away.

"Anybody show up at the house after I left?" she said.

"A few people."

"Yeah?"

He nodded. "Michael from your office. Some lady who said she used to babysit you when you were a kid. A guy who said he was one of your dad's colleagues, but seemed a lot more like a patient if you ask me—"

"A babysitter?"

"Yeah," he said. "She didn't stay long, but she left her card and said she'd love to catch up. It's on the table."

Robin spotted it and picked it up—a plain white card with black lettering. A name: *Nicola Crane*. A phone number. A P.O. box in Philadelphia.

Eric said, "You remember her? Nicola?"

"What does she look like?"

"Gray hair. Your mom's age, maybe? About your height."

"Very bright blue eyes?"

"Yeah."

"Nikki. That's how she introduced herself. And I got the impression she was a friend of my mom's."

"She is," he said. "I think she was a friend of your mom's who babysat you from time to time. Not a babysitter per se."

"Interesting."

"Is it?"

"I saw her at the funeral. I don't remember anyone from my childhood who looked like her."

He smiled. "She probably didn't, back then," he said. "Anyway, she seemed anxious to get together.

She said she's going to be in town until your mom gets out of the hospital. Said you can call her anytime."

"See, now that's interesting too. Who is this old friend of my mom's who I haven't seen since I was a kid—and who cares so much about what happens to my mom, she puts her life in Philadelphia on hold?"

Eric didn't answer, and, when Robin looked up at him, she saw he was absorbed in his phone. Her heart dropped a little. "I'm going up to bed now."

"Wait, what? Sorry I was just—"

"Don't worry about it," she said. "Good night."

Eric said something. Robin didn't hear him and didn't ask him to repeat it. She went up the stairs with Nicola Crane's card in her hand. She tried to remember her, a younger version of this sinewy, silver-haired, tough-looking woman. *Nicola, Nikki. Knickknack, paddywhack* . . . Maybe she'd gone by something else. *Mrs. Crane?*

Robin changed into a big T-shirt, brushed her teeth. She got into bed without taking off her makeup, because the thought of running those moist towelettes all over her face wore her out and anyway, most of her makeup was gone. She was exhausted, physically and emotionally, head to toe, her muscles like wrung-out rags. *Maybe I can get to sleep tonight without any help.*

She lay flat on her back and closed her eyes, the cool of the pillow against her neck, her palms resting on the soft sheets. She listened to the hum of the air conditioner, trying not to let her own thoughts get the best of her, the nursery rhyme playing in her head, over and over, *Knickknack paddywhack, give the dog a bone* . . .

The stray dog her mother had brought home, a pit puppy named Brutus with silver fur and big sad eyes. Brutus, that had been his name, and he'd licked Robin's nose, making her laugh. But her father . . .

I can't, Renee. You know that. My allergies.

But, Mitchell, he has nowhere to go . . .

The baby bird has no mother. Let me help her, she has nowhere to go . . .

She has nowhere to go. She won't be any trouble. She can clean up around the house and help me take care of Robbie. Come on, Mitchell, please . . .

Mom always taking in strays. Dad always making her take them back . . . "Mom," Robin whispered, her voice small and alone in the darkened room. "Mom. Don't go. I need you more than Dad does now. Don't listen to him. Don't do what he says for once. Don't leave me. Please don't leave me."

And then she was sobbing. How fast that had happened, that shift from the brink of sleep to this— Robin bent in two, clasping her knees, her throat aching, all the breath knocked out of her. *This is the way grief is. This is the way it's always going to be. It lies in wait and then it pounces and there's nothing you can do. There will never be anything you can do to make it better . . .*

She reached for the bottle of sleeping pills on her nightstand, dropped two of them into her mouth, choked them down without water. She ran a hand across her wet face and waited for sleep to take her out, thinking again of that young babysitter—a teenage girl. Her mother's last stray. *She can take care of Robbie, Mitchell. She loves Robbie so much.* Her mother's arms around the girl's shoulders. And how old had Robin been? Around eight or nine. The girl had called herself CoCo and she'd played Barbies with Robin and let her watch MTV and she'd let her comb her hair. Such long, pretty blond hair and blue eyes. Bright blue eyes. *CoCo. Nicola. Oh, how you've changed* . . . "Mom," Robin whispered into her arm as she drifted off to sleep. "Your stray has come back."

ONE SUMMER NIGHT, when she was ten years old, Robin woke up thinking that someone was breaking into her house. She'd heard the floorboards creaking when she was still half asleep, and she tried telling herself—as her parents had always told her when she was little and frightened by noises in the middle of the night—that it was just the old house settling. But then there had been a crash downstairs, and Robin had sat up in bed, too frightened to scream. After a few moments, she'd heard the squeak of the back door opening.

Robin had sneaked out of bed and peered out her window. She saw it right away: the shadow of a man, turned away from the house, facing the hedges on the far side of the garden. A shadow that, even from the upstairs window and in such a terrified state, she had recognized as her father.

Robin had put her sneakers on. She'd hurried downstairs and into the backyard, just as he was putting out a cigarette. The shiny red ashtray cupped in his hand, his cheeks flushed, even in the dim garden lights. Dad. Smoking.

Don't tell Mom, he had said, finger to his lips. Standing now in her parents' backyard at two in the morning, thirty years later and with her father in his grave, Robin could practically see him here again, surprised as he'd been on that night, Dad caught in the act in his pajamas and robe, stale smoke hovering between them as he turned to her, shame all over his face.

You never truly know anyone. Every human being who has lived long enough to make mistakes has secrets stashed away in the back of a locked closet or stored in a cloud or crouching in the darkest depths of the brain, moments of weakness that they've worked their whole lives to hide, even from those they love most. Especially from those they love most.

Robin's father smoked. Her mother owned a gun.

Robin shut her eyes tight for several seconds and inhaled the smell of her parents' garden—the pasty scent of tiger lilies hanging in the sticky night air, the same way it had the night of her father's forbidden cigarette break. It had been the same time of year. Summer vacation, Robin biding her time until camp, each day an endless day in an endless summer in which nothing bad would happen. *Promise me you won't smoke anymore, Dad*, she had said. He'd given her a smile. *I'll try not to, honey.* Such a good person. Unable to make a promise to his daughter that he might not be able to keep. When Robin opened her eyes again, they were filled with tears.

The full moon bathed her parents' garden and made it glow like an image in a dream. When she'd left her house, Eric had been asleep in the bed beside her, so thoroughly unconscious that she hadn't even needed to worry about keeping quiet as she escaped. She assumed he'd gotten into her sleeping pills, which was understandable. He had work in the morning.

At 1:30 A.M., Robin had woken up from a fitful half-sleep, the pills not working quite as well as she'd hoped. She'd watched Eric for a few moments—his pained, twitching face—wondering what he could possibly be dreaming. And then she'd left. Threw some yoga pants on, some sneakers, along with the big T-shirt she'd been sleeping in—one of Eric's, from a marathon he'd run back in 2004. She'd driven to her parents' house without thinking, as though drawn here by a magnet with no real idea why. She'd parked about a block and a half up, in front of the small public garden she sometimes played in as a kid, jogged from there to the house on the opposite side of the street, so as not to alert Mr. Dougherty of her presence.

She hadn't come here to investigate. The police had swept the house days ago, after all, bagging anything noteworthy and taking it with them. No. Robin had devised an entire plan to get here unnoticed, just so she could breathe in this air and see if her parents' home still held the same magic . . . the only place, all these years, where she ever truly felt calm.

It wasn't the same. Of course it wasn't. Tire tracks on the front lawn, remnants of yellow crime scene tape hanging from the front and back doors in tatters. The whole house dark, empty. Lifeless.

Who shot you, Dad? What were your last thoughts?

In her mind, she saw this place the way it had looked the night of the shootings. The whirling lights of the police cars, the rush to the front door. All those cops she didn't know, pushing into her parents' home. And Dad on the stretcher. The wide-open eyes. Whose eyes had he seen last? *Who killed you, Dad?*

Robin moved across the garden, to the line of hedges where she'd caught her father smoking. She could still smell cigarettes—clearly some miswired synapse, fried from grief.

She noticed something glinting between two of the hedges—a hard, shiny thing, reflecting the moonlight—and bent down for a closer look.

"Dad," she whispered.

It was the ashtray. The same one.

Robin picked it up. An ashtray of red ceramic with black, white, and gold dice painted on it, the words *Las Vegas* swirling across one side in '60s-glam cursive. So unlike her scholarly, quiet father. But then, it hadn't been like him to smoke either.

It was a good-size ashtray, and there was easily a pack of butts in it. She wondered when he'd smoked the last of these, which were all the same brand. Dad had been a Marlboro man, apparently.

Robin thought about taking the ashtray home with her as a souvenir. But instead she decided to replace it, crouching down and setting it gently back in its spot behind the hedges, hidden from Mom, from the world.

As she did, Robin noticed something on the ground that had either been underneath the ashtray or beside it—a piece of lined paper, folded into eighths.

Robin picked it up and unfolded it—a clean, dry, pristine sheet that clearly hadn't been outside long enough to survive a rain. And it had come from one of Robin's father's notebooks.

When it came to his patients, Mitchell Bloom was an old-school Freudian notetaker, scribbling on a pad while they poured out their souls on his couch, not a laptop or a voice recorder in sight. He'd been using the same type of classy stenographer's pad for years—leather-bound, the pages a pale aqua. He bought them in bulk from an office supply chain, and in his home office, he kept the used-up ones in a locked cabinet, each notebook labeled with a patient's name. More than once at her parents' home, Robin had seen Mitchell opening the cabinet when on the phone with a patient, thumbing through one of these books as he listened.

Robin had expected to find a page filled with her father's illegible doctor's scrawl. But when she opened it, she saw a phone number with a 213 area code. She recognized it from the caller ID at her office, three days earlier. Knew it without having to double-check. Quentin Garrison's number.

Below it, her father had written three names in careful capital letters, with arrows drawn from one to the next, from the bottom up. And though she wasn't quite sure what it all meant, it gave her the most overwhelming feeling, as though each name were a wave sweeping over her, knocking her down.

QUENTIN GARRISON
KATE SHARKEY ↑
APRIL ↑

ROBIN SAT BOLT upright in bed, the remnants of a nightmare running through her head—a spray of bullets, a wash of blood. She couldn't remember any more of it than that. Light streamed into the room. She was alone in bed, Eric long gone. The house silent. She checked her phone. 9:00 A.M.

She rubbed her eyes, confused, but only for a few seconds—only until she saw the folded-up piece of lined, pale aqua paper on her nightstand, and then it all came crashing back.

Last night, she'd jogged back to her car and sped all the way home, heart racing, eyes bolted open.

Once she got back to her house, she'd taken out her laptop and looked up everything she could regarding the Cooper/LeRoy murders. Wikipedia entries about each of the twelve victims—among them a teenage couple on prom night, a property master for TV shows who volunteered for children's charities in his spare time. A young police officer. An elderly man and his paid caregiver. A four-year-old girl . . .

Each killing more senseless than the previous, the couple's motives a complete mystery. Robin had looked online for *The Inland Empire Killers: 'Til Death Do Us Part*, but had only been able to find one three-minute clip: Gabriel LeRoy—the TV actor version of him—shooting a bound and gagged middle-aged man who lay prone at his feet. A slick of bright red blood on the floor. The TV actress version of April Cooper squealing with delight. *"Get him, baby."*

She'd watched the clip again and again, to the point of where it worked its way into her dreams. You'd think it was pure Hollywood hackery—*Natural Born*

Killers strapped onto an after-school special. But to Robin, it seemed like it may have been an accurate portrayal. She had read eyewitness accounts describing the gleam in April Cooper's eyes, the serene smile as she watched the bodies fall. Some speculated Stockholm syndrome, but every article, every police report she could get her hands on, every credible account of the killings described the girl—a fifteen-year-old high school freshman—as not only a willing accomplice but an enthusiastic one. April's former classmates and teachers spoke of someone who was almost disturbingly standoffish, a middling-to-poor student frequently caught daydreaming in class, a girl who rarely spoke, even when spoken to. A dead-eyed girl whose feelings remained a mystery.

Had she always been that way, or was the antisocial behavior the result of the untimely death of her mother, Grace, killed in a car accident just one year earlier? Hard to say, but according to one article, when April met Gabriel LeRoy—in the parking lot of a McDonald's that was walking distance from both their high schools in Santa Rosa, California—the evil within her blossomed.

The more her stepfather, Peter Cooper, objected to their budding relationship, the more April and Gabriel drew closer to each other. The same article described them like this: *two dry sticks rubbing together, insistently enough to create a lethal flame.*

Throughout her search, Robin had only been able to find one photo of the couple—that same faded prom picture she'd seen days ago, April's and Gabriel's pale features ravaged by years of exposure, barely distinguishable on the screen. For the longest time, Robin had stared into the unsmiling face of that young girl as Eric lay sleeping beside her, enlarging it until it looked like a mess of pixels. She didn't like the thoughts that kept running through her head. She refused to put a name to them.

Robin plucked the piece of paper from her night-stand, unfolded it, stared at the number. Her father's handwriting. *April*. No last name. Quentin Garrison's name and phone number, another name: Kate Sharkey. And then April. Simply April. All written on a fresh piece of paper, untouched by the elements, most likely the same day Garrison had called Robin. The day of Dad's death.

And Garrison was still here. She'd seen him in the cemetery parking lot, just after the funeral. Standing next to his silver Chevy Cruz. Talking to CoCo.

Robin didn't know a lot about this investigation. When it came to discussing details with her, the cops all seemed squeamish about it, even Morasco. *The investigation is still active*, they would say, which may indeed have been part of the reason. But Robin still sensed that there was something else going on. A great big elephant in the room that threatened to crush her memories to a pulp, to subvert and destroy everything she thought she'd understood about her family. And even a bunch of cops didn't seem to want to be part of that just yet. They had time, after all. Mom wasn't going anywhere.

Mom.

One of the doctors in the ICU had told her. She wasn't sure which one. Everything was such a blur these days, lack of sleep and grief and wine and pills

muddying the line between dreaming and waking, between nightmares and reality to the point of
where she felt like she had to grab hold of events
and stare at them, just to make sure they were real.
But this doctor, whichever one, had told her that
Dad had been shot through the lung, shoulder, leg,
and abdomen, while Mom had been shot just once,
in the abdomen. Just once. Robin hadn't thought
much about it then. She'd figured the shooter, the
murderer, had gotten scared and run. But that was
before she learned that the gun had been registered
to her mother. And it was before she'd learned that
no one had broken into the house. It was also before she'd found Quentin Garrison's phone number, written in her father's handwriting, along with
those other two names . . .

She grabbed her laptop from her nightstand.
Googled *Kate Sharkey*. Then *Kathryn Sharkey*. Then
Kathleen. She found a lot of them. She added Quentin Garrison's name and *California* and that's when
she found the obituary: Kathleen Sharkey Garrison, dead at the age of fifty-seven at the Mountain
View Sober Living Facility in San Bernardino, California. Her gaze settled on her survivors: Kate's father, Reginald, and her son, Quentin.

She recalled the one conversation she'd had with
Quentin Garrison. The podcast title, *Closure*. How
he'd explained it: *I have a relative who was one of their
victims, hence the title*. She googled *Inland Empire
Killers + Names of Victims + Sharkey*. And then she
stared at the screen. "My God," she whispered.
"The four-year-old girl."

Had Quentin Garrison and Dad discussed Mom's

connection with the Cooper/LeRoy murders? Had he told him what had happened to his mother's little sister? Had he confronted Mom with that information and had she . . . *No. She wouldn't.*

Still, she couldn't tell the police about this. Not until she knew more.

Robin grabbed her phone from the charger and tapped in the number. The 213 area code.

"Hello?" The voice on the other end of the line was quiet.

"Quentin."

"Yes?"

"What did you say to my father?"

"Oh. Ms. Diamond. I didn't . . . I didn't recognize . . . Listen, I'm so sorry for your loss."

"You talked to my father on the day he died. He wrote down your number and your mother's name."

"I'm sorry."

"What is my mother's connection to April Cooper? What did you tell my father about it?"

"This isn't a good time."

"Are you fucking kidding me?"

"Can we meet? Maybe in an hour?" His voice cracked. "Please. I'll meet you anywhere you'd like."

Robin thought for a few moments, listening to Quentin Garrison's trembling breath, louder than it should be. She heard noises in the background. Children shouting. *A park?*

"Okay," she said. "I can meet." Robin directed him to the same place she'd eaten nearly all her meals in the past few days: the cafeteria at St. Catherine's, two floors down from the ICU, where her mother still lay fighting for her life.

EIGHTEEN

June 16, 1976
9:00 P.M.

Dear Aurora Grace,

We've moved motels. We're now in Pico Rivera, in a place called the Drop Inn that makes the Motel 6 in West Covina seem like the Beverly Hills Hotel. Papa Pete would have called the Drop Inn a fleabag, though "roachbag" would be more accurate. Every time you go in the bathroom and turn the lights on, hundreds of them scurry under the cabinets, into cracks in the walls, behind the toilet, down the drain. It's the most disgusting thing I've ever seen.

"Live with it." Gabriel keeps saying that to me. And I suppose I have to. We both have to. Someone saw us walking up to Ed Hart's door and told the police—so now there's a composite sketch of us that's all over the nightly news and probably in the papers. I don't know if anybody has connected Papa Pete's murder with Ed Hart's, but I do know that even more people are searching for me and Jenny. There are search parties. Gabriel and I heard that in the car. (That name. Search parties. Like they're making a big celebration out of looking for my sister and me.) As soon as the report finished, Gabriel turned off the radio and punched the steering wheel so hard it made my insides jump.

We're both fugitives now, Gabriel says, so we have to live like fugitives. We're at the roach motel because the guy at the front desk didn't ask for ID. We're eating food from drive-throughs so no one behind any counter will see us in full. We wear baseball caps and sunglasses when we go out, and we're driving a pickup truck that Gabriel stole out of the parking lot of a strip mall because it has a different license plate than the one on Papa Pete's car. And Gabriel keeps his gun loaded all the time, because if the cops do come for us, we're not going to go willingly.

I feel so strange—as though I got dragged into someone else's bad dream, and since I wasn't able to fight my way out of it, it's my dream now too.

I don't hate Gabriel anymore. I'm not even that scared of him—not unless I see the lava, and I haven't seen that in days. I can't get myself to leave him, though. And that's the thing that DOES scare me. Gabriel LeRoy is all I have in the world. Well, him and Jenny, but I'm not allowed to talk to her. Gabriel says for all we know, the police could have tapped the phones of the people watching Jenny, so we have to lie low until we can sneak back and steal her away.

Aurora Grace, my school's senior prom is tomorrow night. Back when I was getting ready to break up with Gabriel, I was secretly hoping that this one senior boy would ask me to go with him. He's tall and quiet. Blond curls like Peter Frampton. Blue eyes like David Soul. He isn't like the other boys at my school, tripping me when I walk past, wolf-whistling and snickering or whispering stuff like "slut" or "white trash," just loud enough for me to hear. When this boy passes me in the hallway, he says, "Hey, April, how's it going?" Sometimes, he even carries my books.

He has a girlfriend. She's rich and beautiful and mean. I think if she ever saw him carrying my books, she would pitch a fit. But then again, so would Gabriel. "Love makes you crazy," Gabriel says. "I think of someone else touching you, my heart crumbles into dust."

What's strange about that is, Gabriel never touches me. He never even kisses me anymore. He says that if we were to kiss, he might not be able to stop himself from going further. But we used to kiss a lot, so I don't think that's the reason. I think it's because of Ed Hart. I think that when Gabriel looked him in the eyes again after all this time, it was like stirring up a hornet's nest. Those ugly memories that he'd put to sleep got woken up—and they've been buzzing around in his head ever since, stinging him and stinging him, making him confused and weak. I know he's done some bad things, but I'm not sure that even Gabriel deserves to be in this much pain.

Anyway . . . Like I was saying, prom is coming up soon. That boy will buy his mean, rich girl-friend a corsage. Wrist, so she won't poke holes in her fancy dress. Orchids or red roses, because they are the two most romantic flowers in the world. He will wear a tie to match her dress, and she'll stash little airplane bottles of booze in her beaded purse. The two of them will sneak out of the gym and drink those bottles so quickly they won't even taste them. And then he will take her face in his hands, and he will gaze into her eyes. He will tell her she's the most beautiful girl he's ever seen. And she won't even say thank you.

I believe that if you think about someone hard enough, they can feel it. My mom used to say that when she was at work and I was missing her, she always knew. And these days, I feel Jenny thinking about me all the time—it's how I know she's still alive. So here is what I'm going to do: After Gabriel falls asleep tonight, I will lie on my back in bed. I will stare up at the ceiling of our motel room as though it were a sky full of stars. And I will think about that boy. I will think about him so hard that he will appear to me in three dimensions and in my mind, I will call out his name: Brian Griggs.

He will feel my thoughts, and that will make him think of me. And no one else will ever know.

Love, Future Mom April

June 17, 1976
8:00 A.M.

Dear Aurora Grace,

This morning, Gabriel woke me up with a glazed donut from Winchell's and a Styrofoam cup full of coffee with cream and lots of sugar, the way I like it. Then he got down on one knee and asked me to be his prom date.

At first, I was scared that he'd read my letters to you. But when I looked into his eyes, I didn't see the lava—not the slightest sign of it.

It turns out Gabriel's prom is tonight too, which makes sense. His school is a Catholic boys' school called St. Xavier and it's practically walking distance from mine. Our teams play each other all the time and girls from our school can audition for their plays and we can even take certain classes there if we want.

Gabriel had been thinking about his prom just like I'd been thinking about mine. But unlike me, he was imagining us going to it together—and the images in his brain were so beautiful, he said, it made him know that it was meant to be.

If Gabriel ever joked about anything, I would have assumed that was what he was doing. His school is just a few miles away from my house, where Papa Pete's body was discovered. And obviously, he knows all about the police investigation, the unnamed witness, the search parties. He's said it himself: we're fugitives.

But Gabriel doesn't joke. "I know we can't go to the actual prom because we don't have tickets," he said. "But we can go to the park afterward." He was talking about Pullman Park, which is a big field on the outskirts of town with a baseball diamond on one end, tennis courts on the other. After prom every year, the seniors from both our schools crowd into that park and stay there till dawn, drinking six-packs and blasting their car radios and fooling around. "We can stay on the outskirts where no one will see us," he said. "We can watch everybody and it'll be like we're there."

I was worried about Gabriel, and also a little frightened. His baseball cap was pulled low over his forehead and as he spoke, his eyes shone out from under the bill in a strange way I'd never seen before. Had he lost his mind? It sure seemed like it. And the panic I felt right then . . . It made me realize again how much I need him and what a sorry, sad state my life is in that Gabriel is the only person in the world who can keep me safe. I said his name quietly and calmly, as though he had a bomb planted under his skin and if I spoke too loudly, he'd explode and kill us both. "Don't you think someone might spot us?"

He started laughing. And then he pulled off his baseball cap. His hair, close to shoulder-length before, was cut very short and bleached so blond it was nearly white. I still can't get over it. He looks like a different boy entirely. "You're next," he said. He showed me the scissors. The box of drugstore hair dye in Darkest Copper. Gabriel's in the bathroom right now, mixing up that dye. He says I'll make a gorgeous redhead.

Love,

April Your Future Mom

5:00 P.M.

Dear Aurora Grace,

I am in a dressing room at Mervyn's right now. I am trying on a pale green dress with spaghetti straps. I'm not crazy about it. It makes me look sickly white and it clashes with my hair (although you can't really blame the dress for that. Everything clashes with my hair). But the good thing about it is, it fits under my clothes.

Gabriel is standing right outside the dressing room, and I am looking at myself in the mirror. My haircut is horrible—like I've got a copper bowl on my head. My skin is broken out from all the fast food I've been eating, and I'm so pale, like someone who's been living in a cave her whole life. I don't recognize my reflection, and I'm about to shoplift my own prom dress. Gabriel just asked how it's going in here and I have no idea what to say.

I just took the picture of Jenny out of my jacket pocket. I am looking at her smile and her pink stuffed dog, Todd, in the hopes that it will make me feel stronger like it has in the past. But the only thing I can think of is that if Jenny were to see me now, she wouldn't know who I was.

I don't know how to steal. I'm going to get arrested for shoplifting, and the cops will find out who I really am, and Gabriel and I will be tried as murderers.

"We're both in this together." That's another thing Gabriel says a lot, and he's right about that. If someone pulls you into a room with them and locks the door and sets the room on fire, it's still true that you're both in it together.

Love,

Your Future Mom

6:00 P.M.

Dear Aurora Grace,

I didn't get caught! I wore the dress out of the store under my biggest T-shirt and jeans and no one stopped me.

This is going to sound weird, and I know I shouldn't say this to my future daughter. But I found it kind of thrilling. There's something about walking past a department store security guard, a stolen dress under your clothes, that makes you feel both powerful and invisible at the same time. And it's been so long since I've felt either of those things.

Gabriel says that we're transforming into true outlaws, the two of us. He believes that we'll be folk heroes, like Bonnie and Clyde.

I don't know about that. But it is true that I'm becoming someone else—a different person, unlike anyone I've ever known.

Love,

April

NINETEEN

ROBIN

"HOW LONG CAN she be like this?" Robin asked the nurse.

The nurse, whose name was Verity, didn't say anything right away. They were in the ICU at St. Catherine's, the two of them, watching Robin's mother, pillows propped up behind her head, her chest rising and falling, the ventilator working away. Over the past few days, Robin had asked this question repeatedly of doctors, but every response had been both hasty and tentative. "It varies." "There are many factors." "I can't predict the future."

One doctor had offered up "Time will tell," which had possibly been the most infuriating answer of all. Couldn't even be bothered to come up with a noncliché.

Verity, though, took the question seriously. "I've seen people taken off the ventilator after more than a week and they're just fine," she said.

Robin looked at her. "That's good."

"But . . ."

"But."

"Look, I'm not going to lie to you. Every hour she's on that thing, the weaker she gets."

Robin swallowed hard. "Have they talked about trying to wean her off it?"

"She's on light sedatives, but from what I've heard, she hasn't given them anything." Verity looked at her. "She doesn't react. Doesn't move."

"Maybe she would if they took her off the breathing tube," Robin said.

Verity shook her head. "If they thought she'd survive it, they'd do it."

Tears began to well in Robin's eyes. She'd almost have preferred a cliché, but then again what had she expected? The woman's name literally meant truth.

"Ms. Diamond."

"Yeah?"

"You love your mom, don't you?"

"Very much."

"Before she got in here, you spent a lot of time with her?"

"She was . . . she *is* my best friend."

"That's good," she said. "You're lucky."

Robin nodded.

"Have you told her everything you need to tell her? Because . . . you know . . . if you haven't, I'm a firm believer that they hear you. A part of them hears you, even when they're like this."

Robin's gaze stayed on her mother's placid face. "I have told her everything," she said quietly. "I'm not sure she's done the same."

Verity put a hand on her arm and gave it a quick squeeze—a gesture Robin might have found patronizing in the past. "Be with her," the nurse said. "Hold her hand. Let her know you'll be okay no matter what."

"I don't know that I will be okay . . ." Robin said. But Verity had already left the room.

Robin glanced at her watch. 10:00 A.M. On any other Monday at this time, she'd have been at a morning meeting at the Daily Culture office, listening to the reporters pitching ideas, taking notes as she thought about this week's film column. Such a different world she used to live in four days ago.

She couldn't remember whether or not she'd called in sick to work, couldn't imagine herself ever returning. The thought of putting on something other than a T-shirt and yoga pants, of making up her face and getting on a train, of traveling that far from the hospital and talking and thinking about movies for God's sake, about anything other than what was happening to her mother and why it was happening and who had done it to her . . .

Robin had forty-five minutes before she was supposed to meet Quentin Garrison in the cafeteria, but she wasn't sure she wanted to speak to him anymore. She didn't necessarily feel like hearing what he'd told her father. She didn't know if she was strong enough for what he had to say.

She pulled a chair up next to the hospital bed. The room was curtained off, and on the other side of it, she could see the shadows of broad, dark-clad shoulders. Police guards. In case the killer came back to finish the job. Or, at least, that's what she had assumed. Thinking about it now, with all these strange new fears in her mind, Robin wondered if they were out there to make sure her mother didn't escape . . .

She took her mother's hand in her own and gripped it tightly, hoping, as she always did, for the slightest squeeze back. Nothing.

Robin watched her face, so utterly still, the breathing tube taped to her lips—something Mom never would have stood for had she been aware, the way it infantilized her, like a bottle shoved into a baby's mouth.

She listened to the sound of the ventilator, trying in her mind to liken the hollow whoosh of it to something other than what it was. Closing her eyes made it easier. Without the visual, the ventilator could be the sound of someone deep breathing while meditating, or the sound a seashell makes when you hold it up to your ear.

Of course, it isn't the seashell that makes that sound—it's your own blood, moving through your body. But there had been a time in Robin's life when she hadn't known things like that.

She squeezed her eyes shut and she was a kid again, at her family's summer rental in Sarasota, Florida, Mom tanned and strong and smiling, handing her a conch shell she'd found on the beach. *Put the shell up to your ear, Robbie. It wants to tell you about its home.*

Robin opened her eyes. She kept Renee's cool, limp hand in her own like a gift she didn't want to part with. "Tell me about your home, Mom," she whispered, in a voice too low for the police guards to hear. "Tell me who you are."

THIS MORNING, AFTER hanging up with Quentin Garrison, Robin had washed her face, changed into a cleaner T-shirt, another pair of yoga pants. She'd brushed her teeth and pulled her hair back, put on her sneakers, and she'd driven again to her parents' house—a repeat performance of the previous night. This time, though, she'd gone inside. Robin hadn't thought about it first, not enough to prepare herself for what she might see. She was simply drawn in through the back door, into the kitchen as though by a magnet, then through the living room, where the shooting had taken place. The cops had removed everything they needed to, but they'd done a terrible job of cleaning up afterward, and so Robin had to make herself turn away from the chalk marks and the tape, the pushed-around furniture. The throw rug—a bright, handwoven thing her parents had picked up on a trip to India—was no longer there. She didn't want to think about why.

She'd hurried upstairs and into her parents' bedroom, which she'd found nearly as hard to look at as the wreck downstairs. It was untouched, the bed still neatly made. Her parents had never gone to sleep that night, which of course she had known. But to see the bed like that. To see the drawers closed, the closets shut, the reading material on the two nightstands—a Lincoln biography for him, a stack of *New Yorker*s for her—as though the room still hadn't heard what had happened, as though it were patiently waiting for the two of them to come to bed . . .

It had been so much harder than she'd imagined

it would be. But she'd gone there with a purpose, and so she'd headed straight for it—the top right-hand drawer in her mother's dresser.

This drawer of her mother's held socks, tights, and stockings, and in the very back, a small wooden box filled with old keepsakes. Her father had no reason to know about it and most likely he never had. Robin, though, had known about the box since she was twelve years old. She'd caught her mother looking through it once and stayed in the back of the room like Harriet the Spy, watching. Her mother had been trying on a pair of earrings—big gaudy clip-ons made of painted seashells. Not Mom's taste at all, which had piqued Robin's curiosity enough for her to sneak back into the room and take out the box weeks later, when she was alone in the house . . .

Robin had found it fascinating, the idea that her mother would have a tiny collection of things no one knew about, not even Dad. And for a few weeks during that hot, sleepy July between sixth and seventh grade, the box had been a summer romance—something Robin would sneak in to look at whenever she could and think about whenever she couldn't. She'd never said a word about the secret box to anyone, just like she'd never said a word about her father's pack of cigarettes. Grown-ups kept secrets, apparently. It wasn't her right to reveal them.

By the time September rolled around and school started again, she'd stopped sneaking in to look at it. The box became something she kept in the back of her mind in the same way Mom kept it in the back of

the drawer: not thrown away and certainly not forgotten, but never dwelled on, never spoken of.

This morning, Robin had opened the drawer and
found that box in the exact same spot, as though no
time had passed. She'd pulled it out, removing the
seashell earrings and the add-a-pearl necklace, the
souvenir penny pressed into an oval and embossed
with a star and the word *Corsica*. She'd removed the
tiny magnifying glass, the rainbow rubber ball, and
a few more pieces of costume jewelry—gently, as
though these were living things, deserving of kind-
ness.

With the box mostly empty, Robin had found
what she'd been looking for. She'd put everything
back except for that one item—a Polaroid picture,
so faded at this point, you could barely make out
the image. She'd placed the box back in its spot and
shoved the picture into her bag—where it still was
right now.

ROBIN LET GO of her mother's hand. She unzipped her
bag, removed the picture, and gazed at it—a girl
with short blond hair, smiling for the camera. The
girl was young and coltishly skinny, as though she
still hadn't found her true form. The photo was
blurred, the blonde's features almost completely
faded, but Robin could make out the smile—her
mother's dreamy, warm, slightly crooked smile.

Renee White couldn't have been more than fifteen in the picture, but she looked as though she
was trying to be older than that. She wore a halter
top and tight jeans that were too mature for her and
there was something about her stance too, the way

she cocked her hip, that said less about her than the person taking the Polaroid.

With her left hand, young Renee made the sign for "I love you." With her right, she held a gun.

As a kid, Robin had been unfazed by the gun, a small silver thing she'd fully believed to be a toy. But now, she didn't know what to believe.

Robin took hold of her mother's hand again. She placed the Polaroid in it. "Who took this picture?" she whispered, thinking of the faded photo of April Cooper she'd seen online—a young, unsmiling girl with blond hair like Renee's. "Was it Gabriel Le-Roy, Mom? Did Gabriel take your picture?"

Robin started to tremble. She knelt down and placed her cheek against her mother's cool wrist, the hand at her neck like the hand of a mannequin. "Was it Gabriel?" Robin's voice cracked, and soon she was crying silently, each sob sinking deep into her abdomen, a bottomless, never-ending despair. The Polaroid dropped to the floor. She watched it through the blur of her tears and imagined it burning.

Robin cried until she was simply too tired to cry anymore, and only then did she hear it. A low, soft moan. Robin froze. Looked at her mother's face. Took her hand again. Squeezed it again, expecting nothing.

Mom squeezed back.

The squeeze was weak, but it was real. "Verity!" Robin yelled. "Doctor!" And within moments she was in the hallway with the guards, one of them bringing the radio to his lips, contacting the station. "She's waking up," she was telling them, telling anyone she could. "My mother. I think she's waking up."

ERIC SURPRISED ROBIN. When she called him at work to tell him that the doctors had said her mother seemed to be stabilizing and that they were in the process of weaning her off the ventilator, she'd expected, at the most, some encouraging words and a promise to come home early tonight. But instead, he'd taken the train back immediately, making it to the hospital cafeteria around the time Quentin Garrison was supposed to show up.

Robin stood up, surprised and relieved that it was Eric, not Quentin, calling out her name. There was only so much tension and uncertainty she could handle, and she'd had her fill for now. Eric, though . . . He'd come home.

He took her in his arms and she held him tightly and lost herself in the rare feeling of not being alone. "How is Renee?" he said. "When can we see her?"

"I'm hoping soon. The nurse promised she'd come get me."

"I told you," he said. "I told you she'd be okay."

"Eric."

"Yeah?"

"You're not in trouble, are you?"

He pulled away, his features tensing, as though he were bracing for a blow. "What do you mean?"

Robin stared at him. She could tell they weren't on the same page. "You left work in the middle of the day. I don't want you to be in trouble with Shawn."

Eric's face relaxed. "Oh, I can handle Shawn," he said. "He's the last thing you need to worry about."

"What's the first thing?"

"Huh?"

"Nothing." She sat back down. He sat across from her, taking both her hands in his. "Renee's life is more important than Shawn," Eric said. "You're more important than Shawn."

Robin gripped Eric's hands and shut her eyes and thought of her mother, the rise and fall of her chest. "I hope she makes it."

"She will," said Eric. "I told you. She has to."

Robin opened her eyes and gazed across the table at her husband—those sparkling blue eyes that had roped her in from the first time she'd seen him, sitting across the table from her in RW1, which stood for Reporting/Writing 1—the most time-consuming class in journalism school. He'd winked at her—*winked*—and she'd told herself that he was too pretty, a player, not to be trusted. He'd spent the better part of that year convincing her otherwise. He'd been single-minded back then. Believing fully that if he willed it, it would happen. And it had happened. Of course it had. They'd had sex for the first time after talking all night, sharing their corniest dreams, their most embarrassing experiences, their goals, their fears, their deepest wishes . . . Unrealistic as only young, in-love people can be. *This is going to make me sound like a jackass*, Eric had said, *but I want to write stories that save lives.*

She smiled at him, remembering the earnestness in his voice, wishing she could bring back that night, when there were no filters between them and no secrets, when there were no unexplained late nights or suspicious Twitter exchanges. When nothing went unsaid and all they both wanted was to know each other thoroughly.

Eric said, "I think it's going to be hard for her to go home."

"Huh?"

"Your mom . . . I mean. Because of everything that happened there. Your dad . . ."

"Yes. You're probably right."

"If she wants to stay with us for a while. For as long as she wants, really, it's fine with me."

"Eric."

"I know, I'm putting the cart before the horse. She's not out of the woods after all, and . . . man, could I use any more pastoral-themed clichés?"

Robin smiled. She stroked Eric's stubbled cheek. "Thank you," she said.

She heard her name called again—by Verity this time. She knew it without looking up. "Ms. Diamond," Verity said, and the sound of it made her heart pound.

Verity had piercing dark eyes, a downturned mouth. She was a naturally somber-looking person, but when Robin looked up at her, she was smiling. "Mom's off the tube and alert," she said. "She wants to see you."

Robin jumped up from her seat, Eric along with her. His arm stayed around her shoulders as they followed Verity to the elevators, and Robin breathed deeply, thinking of new beginnings.

Once they reached their floor and the elevator doors opened, Quentin Garrison crossed her mind—the fact that he'd never shown up for their meeting. But it was one fleeting thought of many. And when Verity briefly stopped her, showing her the old Polaroid she'd found under her mother's bed and asking if it was hers, Robin was so intent on slipping it into her purse before Eric noticed that Quentin disappeared from her thoughts entirely.

TWENTY

ROBIN

"HI, SWEETIE." Mom's voice sounded deep and croaky, as though she were just getting over a terrible case of laryngitis. She looked frail still. But awake, animated. Without that tube taped to her lips, Renee White Bloom looked like herself again. It was thrilling, really, to see her breathing on her own.

Eric squeezed Robin's hand, and her eyes started to blur. "You're back, Mom," she said. "You're back with me."

Robin moved toward the bed and took her mother's hand in hers. She wanted to hug her, but she was aware of how frail she was.

"You look so thin," Mom said. "Have you not been eating?"

Robin glanced at Eric. He smiled, and she smiled back. Classic Renee Bloom. Lying in a hospital bed having just come off life support, yet still fretting over her only daughter.

"Where's Mitchell?" Renee said.

Eric's smile dropped away.

One of the doctors stepped forward—a tall, distinguished surgeon with silver-framed glasses that matched the streaks in his black hair. He'd introduced himself to Robin in the hallway as "Dr. Wu, like the Steely Dan song"—an icebreaker he'd no doubt used hundreds of times in his career, but one that Robin still appreciated. She was positive she'd seen and spoken to Dr. Wu at some point early in her mother's hospitalization, and he hadn't bothered introducing himself at all. But now that Mom was officially no longer a goner, it was as though a human decency switch had been flicked and Robin merited not only introductions but classic rock mnemonic devices. "Mrs. Bloom," Dr. Wu said. "Do you know why you're here?"

Mom's gaze darted around the room, resting finally on Robin. "I . . . I had a heart attack?" She looked up at her with pleading eyes, like a grade-school kid trying to come up with the right answer.

Robin was still holding her mother's hand. Eric slid her a chair, and she eased into it without letting go, without breaking eye contact for fear of upsetting her more than she was about to. "There was a break-in at your house, Mom," she said slowly. "You and Dad were both shot."

"Oh . . . Oh my God."

Dr. Wu said, "Why don't you try and tell us what you remember."

She closed her eyes. Robin watched her mother's gaunt face, the skin shiny and paper thin. This close, she could see it—Renee was nearly herself, almost herself but not quite, and Robin could actually feel how hard she was working to get there. "I remember . . . burning."

"Mom?"

"Red and orange flames. Smoke so thick I couldn't breathe . . . and demons. Little red demons dancing around . . . Oh . . . Goodness. I guess it was a dream."

Verity turned to Robin. "She did have a fever at one point," she said. "Sometimes, the mind fills in the blanks."

Her mother's hand was still in hers. "How are you feeling now, Mom?"

"Tired. Very tired. Where's Dad, honey?"

Dr. Wu started to say something, but Eric stopped him. "Can we talk outside for a little bit?" he said. "I have a few questions."

"Of course," he said. And the room cleared quickly, maybe too quickly for Robin's liking, unsure as she was how to say what needed to be said. Verity told Renee she'd be back to check her vitals in a few. And selfishly, pathetically, Robin wished that the nurse could be the one to let Mom know that her husband was dead.

Once Verity left, Robin's mother gave her a weak smile. "I'm awfully thirsty."

"I can imagine."

"All that time in hell will do it to you."

"What a terrible dream."

"I don't know," Mom said. "Those little demons were kind of cute."

"Let me see if I can get you some water." She started to stand but her mother grasped her hand with a surprising strength. "No," she said. "Stay."

"Of course, Mom. I'll do whatever you—"

"Robbie."

"Yes?"

"Daddy died. Didn't he?"

Robin exhaled. Gently, she brushed a lock of hair from her mother's forehead. And then she nodded. She didn't say anything else. Didn't need to. Her mother was making things easy on her, just like she'd always done, ever since she was a little girl. Watching her now, struggling to hold back tears for her daughter's sake, *for my sake*, Robin remembered the death of her father's mother, her most beloved Nana. It had been sudden and unexpected and after Dad had gotten off the phone with whoever had called to tell him, he'd locked himself in his study for such a long time that Robin, then only six or seven years old, feared he might never come out. She understood now that he'd gone in there to cry. Mitchell Bloom never cried in front of anyone back then. Which left it up to Mom to explain what had happened—Mom, an only child and an orphan, whose only family besides Robin and Dad had been Nana too. But she'd held back her tears then, same as she was doing now. *Nana's gone to heaven. She's very happy up there, because instead of visiting a few times a year, she can see you and watch over you always.*

"I'm so sorry, Mom," Robin said.

Two tears spilled down her mother's cheeks—escapees. She didn't seem to notice. "Was he buried?"

"Yes."

"There was a funeral. You held a funeral."

"Yes."

"With that child rabbi . . ."

Robin smiled a little. "The Bar Mitzvah Boy."

"You poor thing. Having to handle those arrangements, all alone."

"It went all right. Eric was a big help."

"I'm glad to hear that, honey." Another tear, yet her face was calm, placid. There was a box of Kleenex on the nightstand. Robin pulled out several sheets and dabbed gently at her mother's cheeks.

"Were there a lot of people at the funeral?" She said it so mildly, as though she were asking about a dinner party she'd missed. It must have been residual sedatives, Renee's true self still struggling to the surface, the slow trickle of her memory returning.

Robin's chest tightened. *Mom. Poor Mom.* "There was a big crowd," she said. "He was very much loved."

"That's nice."

"I'm so glad you're with me now, Mom. I don't know what I'd do without you."

"You'll never be without me. I'll do everything I can to make sure of that." She closed her eyes, struggling between sleep and waking until finally, Robin thought of something she could talk to her about.

"Do you know who was at the funeral, Mom? CoCo."

"Huh?"

"That girl who used to babysit me when I was eight? She's . . . well she's aged since then obviously.

She said you two are friends. That you've kept in touch."

"CoCo?"

"She calls herself Nikki now. Lives in Philly?"

She opened her eyes. "Nicola. I forgot she ever called herself CoCo . . ."

"Who is she?"

"We've been close since . . . since we were girls . . ."

"You have?"

"Yes." Her eyelids fluttered, a dreamy smile crossing her face. "Lovely Nicola. Little doll."

"I didn't know you had anyone from childhood. Friends or family or—"

"Honey, I'm sorry, but can you get me that glass of water now? I'm just so thirsty."

"Of course." Robin hurried out into the hallway, past the guards. Dr. Wu wasn't around, but Eric was.

"Hey, how did she take it?" he said.

"Not terribly," Robin said. "But I think she's still pretty drugged."

She hurried to the nurses' station, where Verity handed her a cup of ice chips, explaining, "Her throat is still weak from being intubated. She can probably have water in an hour or two."

Robin thanked her, took the ice chips, and headed back toward her mother's room, her pulse quickening as though she were on the verge of something life-changing, something big. *Lovely Nicola.* Her babysitter had been her mother's childhood friend. She'd seemed young for that, but then again Renee had been quite young herself. And thinking back on CoCo, so thin and wan, she could have easily looked more youthful than she was. Robin headed into the room—dead quiet now, without the whoosh of the ventilator. "Mom, I was wondering," she started.

But Renee had fallen asleep.

She felt movement behind her—Eric joining her at her side, as Verity made for her mother's hospital bed, clipboard in hand.

"You okay?" Eric said.

"Yeah." She watched her mother sleeping, the rise and fall of her chest. She hoped she wasn't dreaming of hell again.

"SHE LOOKED AS though she was coming out of it," Eric said. "When the nurses were shooing us out and she was saying see you tomorrow, it seemed like . . . I don't know. Like her battery finally got recharged. You know?"

"I was thinking the same thing," said Robin. They were at home now, just the two of them, eating an early dinner that Eric had prepared—grilled tarragon chicken, mashed sweet potato, fresh asparagus. Eric was an excellent cook. Much better than Robin, though of course that wasn't saying much.

"This is really delicious," Robin said.

Eric put his wineglass down, reached across the kitchen table, and squeezed her hand—something he used to do all the time when they were dating. *I just want to make sure you're real*, he used to say. Cheesiest line ever and he knew it. They both knew it. Robin would respond, *You're just trying to get me in bed*. And he'd prove her right every time.

Robin smiled at Eric. *This could work again*, she thought. *We could work again*. But then she remembered the past year, how lonely it had been.

She used to tell herself that it was normal, natural, this separation between the two of them. And it was, at first. After the honeymoon period, all couples reach the same fork in the road and they make a choice: they either grow apart and develop their own interests, or, like April Cooper and Gabriel LeRoy, they become codependent, feeding off and fueling each other's weaknesses until neither one of them can stand on their own.

But Robin and Eric had gone overboard. They'd started growing apart, ever so slightly, before he'd taken the job at *Anger Management*, a show they'd both made fun of, but one that paid very well. He'd assured her at first that he was only doing it for the money—a short-term fix that could take care of both their student debts. And though the old, scrupulous Eric never would have considered a move like that, it was one that Robin, fresh off a stint at a trashy celebrity mag, completely understood.

What neither of them had figured on was how Eric's job would accelerate the growing apart until it became unnatural, unhealthy. How as the months, then years went by, the job would absorb him the way a lover would. How Eric would grow defensive of *Anger Management*, of creepy, cleavage-ogling, whiskey-stinking Shawn Labatoir, whom Robin couldn't bear to be in the same room with. But that's what had happened. Responding to her complaints about his long hours, his dubious "scoops," his devotion to a man they had both considered a fraud, Eric had turned argumentative, then secretive, then absent most of the time. And eventually, Robin had stopped complaining. It was easier to nod and simmer, to rely on the support of her parents instead of her husband, to glare at his Twitter feed and ply her mind with suspicions and pull even further apart. Only now did she really feel how much damage had been done—now that her father was gone and she wasn't sure who her mother truly was—and beyond anything else she needed someone to talk to, to trust.

Robin felt Eric watching her.

"Penny for your thoughts," he said.

She looked at him, millions of dollars of thoughts running through her mind but only the strongest one escaping. "I miss you," she said. "I miss us."

Eric moved closer to her. He took her in his arms as though she were made of glass and kissed her very gently.

"Stop."

He let go. "I'm sorry."

"That's not what I mean." Robin grabbed hold of his shirt. She pulled him to her, with a force that surprised them both. "Stop treating me like I'm going to break."

THEY NEVER MADE it out of the kitchen. They were rough and urgent, zippers yanked open, mouths searching, buttons popped and skittering, as though Robin and Eric had been simultaneously possessed and, in a way, they were. It had been such a long time, the space widening between them with each day, week. Month. God, had it really been that long?

Robin felt the tile counter against her bare back, then the granite island, and then she was riding him on the hardwood floor, a need roiling within her that she hadn't felt in years, maybe not since the first time she'd been with Eric—a longing so intense and unfillable that it bordered on pain.

After they finished, they lay beside each other, Robin drained, fileted, the stress sapped out of her, replaced by a sense of well-being that, considering the reality of her situation, proved what simple, physically driven creatures human beings truly are.

"Wow," Eric said. "That was . . ."

"Yeah."

More silence. But that was normal. Neither of them had ever been big sex-talkers. Not during, not after, both preferring the sound of each other's breathing. It was good to know that in this area at least, Robin and Eric hadn't changed since they met.

"Eric?"

"Yeah?"

"Can I trust you?"

"What? Of course you can."

"Eric . . ."

"I don't know what you think was going on with me, but—"

"I'm not talking about a month ago or a week ago. I don't care what was going on back then. Well, actually, that's not true, I do care." She took a breath. "But I'm willing to just . . . shut the door on everything that happened before the shooting. Okay? I won't think about it. I won't ask you about it. As long as I can trust you from here on in."

"Robin," Eric said. "I never cheated on you."

She rolled over on her side and gazed at his pro-
file, strong arms folded behind his head, eyes aimed
at the ceiling. Outside the kitchen window, the sun
was starting to set, casting a pink glow across the
room. Eric's blue eyes shined in it. She wanted to
believe him. But.

Eight months ago, at the height of their estrange-
ment, three friends on three different nights had
spotted Eric at Chez Chas—a Midtown restaurant
with a celebrity chef and seriously dark lighting. Two
had seen him entering the place, one had seen him
leaving. That friend, the one who had seen him leaving, was the one who had seen him with a woman.

Eric's reasons for being there could have been innocent, even though he'd claimed to be working late
on all three nights. The woman could have been a
fellow producer. She could have been a source. But.

When Robin had oh-so-casually mentioned
Chez Chas a month after the last sighting, told him
she'd heard good things about the food, Eric had
gulped so hard she could see his throat moving.
He'd told her he wasn't sure if the place lived up
to its rep, or even where it was located, because, he
claimed, he'd never been there before.

It's the past. Shut the door and move forward.

"Yes." Eric rolled over onto his side, his gaze
resting on her face. "Yes. You can trust me."

The door was shut. Locked. Robin put her shirt
back on, slipped her purse off the back of her chair,
keeping her gaze connected to his. The old, faded
Polaroid was in the side pocket—the skinny young
girl in the too-old-for-her halter top, flashing the "I
love you" sign. Holding the gun.

Robin pulled it out and handed it to Eric.

He stared at the photo. Straightened up to sitting. "Who is this?" he asked.

"My mother."

"Are you sure?" he said. "It's so blurry."

"I'm positive."

He held it away at arm's length so it caught the light. "That's a toy gun, right? She's trying to act like . . . I don't know. Charlie's Angels or whatever."

"I have no idea what she's trying to do."

"Why are you showing me this?"

"Because I need to tell you about a call I got four days ago. I need to tell you about a podcast producer." She told him everything, all the way through to that morning, the notes from her father, the research she'd done.

When she was through, Eric said, "You didn't show Quentin Garrison that photo, did you?"

"I only spoke to him over the phone, so no."

"Good."

She heard herself say it out loud for the first time: "Do you think my mother is April Cooper?"

"No." He said it in that voice of his, that power-of-positive-thinking, will-it-and-it-will-happen voice that had been driving her crazy for the last couple of years. But at this moment, she found it comforting. "Absolutely not."

"You're not just saying that?"

"It's a toy gun. April Cooper was a crazy teenager who died in a fire more than forty years ago. I remember that stupid TV movie. She was nothing like your mother."

Robin looked at him. "Your mother let you watch that movie?"

"It was a TV movie. Why wouldn't she let me watch it?"

Robin winced. She looked at Eric. "I think Quentin Garrison got to my dad."

"What?"

"That day. It must have been that same day. My dad had his phone number written down, along with some other names . . . I found it at their house. I think Quentin Garrison asked him if my mom was April Cooper. And I'm wondering . . . what if Dad confronted her about it?"

His eyes widened. "Did you say that to the police?"

"No."

"Good."

"Why?"

"Because I don't want them expending a bunch of their time and energy trying to prove it was your mother who was responsible for the shooting," he said. "Because I want them to catch the real killer."

She wasn't sure she'd ever loved him more.

"Have you talked to Garrison? I mean . . . since the shootings?"

Robin stared at him, all of it dawning on her . . . "I was supposed to." She made for the counter. Unplugged her phone from the charger and clicked on her recent calls. Quentin Garrison's number was near the top. She clicked on it. Called him again. "I was supposed to meet him at the hospital this morning," she said. "He never showed up."

The call went to Quentin's voice mail. *Mail-box full*, the voice said. Strange. When she turned around, Eric had grabbed her laptop off the counter and was tapping away. "What are you doing?"

"You remember Dave Nixon?"

"Who?"

"We booked him to be a special guest on *Anger Management* about a year ago—he was part of true crime week. Shawn was trying to hop on the whole *Making a Murderer* thing, remember?"

"Not really."

He sighed. "I might not have mentioned it to you."

"You might not."

Eric pressed on. "Dave Nixon's wife was killed in a hit-and-run, back in the 1990s. Unsolved. We did a one-on-one interview, but we never wound up airing it."

"Why?"

"Dave was unhinged. He wanted to track down his wife's killer so that he could get revenge. He said, 'Pain like this is a cancer. It doesn't die until you kill what's causing it.'"

"Scary."

"Incredibly." He cleared his throat. "I talked to Shawn and we wound up deciding not to air the interview. We realized we were feeding into this guy's obsession, that it was dangerous. And if we encouraged him in any way, we'd be potentially responsible for a murder." Eric's eyes drilled into hers.

"Why are you telling me this?"

"Because I think Quentin Garrison might be something more dangerous than a dirty journalist," he said. "I think he might be utterly sincere in his beliefs."

"Like Dave Nixon," she said.

"Yes." He brought the laptop to her. On the screen was a page from KAMC's website, the words *CALLS FOR SOURCES* at the top. There were several short posts beneath, reporters asking "listeners and others in the know" to call various tiplines for podcasts-in-progress. "Look at the fourth one down," Eric said.

The post had been dated six months earlier. Robin read it aloud, the back of her neck tingling. "Every day of my life, I suffer the pain that these two killers inflicted . . ."

Robin looked up at Eric. "Quentin Garrison sounded normal over the phone."

"So did Dave Nixon. And not only that, he had a good job. Just like Quentin Garrison." He took the seat beside her. "The thing is, Robin," he said. "Normal people go off the deep end all the time. Half the tragedies in this world are because of regular guys who lose it."

"Yeah . . ."

"It's something to think about."

She stared at him. "Mr. Dougherty said he saw a Chevy Cruze outside my parents' house the night of the shooting."

"Yeah?"

"I saw Garrison in the cemetery parking lot after the funeral. I'm pretty sure he was driving a Chevy Cruze."

Eric stared at her. "He came to the funeral?"

"Yes . . ."

"That's strange, Robin. Don't you think that's strange?"

"I thought maybe he was reporting on it."

"Still."

"I saw him talking to Nicola Crane."

"Your babysitter."

"Yes."

"Okay, listen. When she came to our house for your dad's gathering, she told me she'd just had a very disturbing conversation with someone. A reporter. That he'd taken her out to interview her about the shootings and she couldn't leave soon enough. She said he scared her, Robin."

Robin exited the radio station's website, the back of her neck tingling. "You think it was Garrison?"

"She didn't say, but, I mean who else could it have been?"

"Do you think he went to my parents' house?"

"I don't know."

"Do you think he got into some kind of argument with them and lost control?"

"I'm just saying, he's not exactly looking like an objective reporter."

Robin's phone buzzed—a text message. "Probably Eileen," said Robin. "We need to figure out when I'm going back to work."

She picked up the phone. Looked at the text.

I'm sorry for any pain I've caused you and your family. I am not a good person.

Robin felt weak, her head spinning, an uncomfortable feeling spreading through her.

Eric said, "Who texted you?" A question she would have found surprisingly invasive a week ago, four days ago. But not now.

"Quentin Garrison," Robin said. Then she showed it to him.

"I think we should talk to the police," he said.

TWENTY-ONE

June 17, 1976
6:45 P.M.

Dear Aurora Grace,

The police are onto us. I don't know whether someone saw me shoplifting at Mervyn's and put two and two together or if we got recognized from a composite sketch or what, but when we got back to the Drop Inn, there were three police cars in the parking lot. I don't know if I've ever been as scared by the sight of anything, and you need to think about that, Aurora Grace. Think about what I've seen.

I'm changing. Faster than I ever imagined I could. Three days ago, I would have felt nothing but relief at the sight of the flashing lights. I would have opened the car door and run for those police cars with everything I had. But now I'm telling Gabriel to drive away faster, faster. My voice is hoarse from screaming. "Fast as you can," I tell him. "Don't look back."

We are close to the freeway now. My heart is pounding so hard I feel like I may pass out from it, but I know Gabriel is more nervous than me.

I can't see his eyes behind the mirrored aviator sunglasses and baseball cap, but his skin is a deep red and there are sweat rings on the collar of his T-shirt and under the arms and he keeps saying "Oh shit," over and over again.

I just told him we'll be okay. I said it in a calm, steady voice. He asked me what I was writing in this notebook. I told him it's lyrics to a song about the two of us and that I'll show him later. He believes me. He asks me what the song is called. I tell him "Outlaws." "I like that," he says. It seems to calm him, and I need him to be calm. I wish I could drive.

Now we are on the freeway, the 134. I think we are safe, but Gabriel is still driving superfast just to make sure.

"We'll have to buy new clothes and shit," Gabriel says. It makes me think of everything we left behind. All the clues and evidence. Gabriel's marked-up map. Papa Pete's wallet, his driver's license in the little plastic window, clear as day. That damn Starsky and Hutch mug. And buried deep at the bottom of my suitcase, between the pages of Once Is Not Enough, the knife I'd planned to kill Gabriel with.

A scene runs through my mind: Gabriel has been arrested. He's in one of those brightly lit interrogation rooms, like on the cop shows Papa Pete and I used to watch. There is nothing in this room but a table and some chairs, two mean and angry detectives on one side, Gabriel on the other. One of the detectives takes out a plastic evidence bag. He shows it to Gabriel. "Do you know anything about this?" He smirks when he says it. Inside the bag is my knife. "Your girl-friend had it hidden away in her things. What do you suppose she intended to do with it?"

Oh, Aurora Grace, if we are caught, I will lose Gabriel. They'll show him the knife. They may even show him my letters to you. He will no longer stick up for me. He will never let me know where Jenny is. I'll have no one and I will die alone.

We can't get caught. We won't get caught. We'll keep moving forward and we won't look back and I'll never again think about what we've left behind.

Here's what we have with us: The stolen prom dress. Ed Hart's wallet, which still has some cash in it. In the trunk, a duffel bag full of Ed Hart's things: clothes that don't fit either one of us, some props from the shows he'd worked on, a decent-looking transistor radio, two stereo speakers, and a watch Gabriel says is expensive. Also in the trunk: a six-pack of Coke; two bags of Lay's potato

Oh my God there's a cop car following us. We just exited the freeway and he followed us off the off-ramp, a right turn, a left turn, and now he's flashing his lights. Drive faster, Ga-briel. Don't look back. But he won't listen to me. DRIVE FASTER GABRIEL PLEASE PLEASE PLEASE DRIVE AWAY!!!!!

We're on a quiet street now and Gabriel is pulling over. The cop car pulls over too. It's so dark outside, I can barely see my writing on this page. I ask Gabriel what he thinks he's doing. He shushes me. He tells me to keep writing my song, which makes me feel sad for him. I am quiet and now the whole car is quiet. There's nothing in the world but the two of us and the flashing lights and the slam of the police car's door.

Gabriel just told me to get ready—I don't know what for. I think of home, of Hollywood. Of anywhere but here.

TWENTY-TWO

ROBIN

MORASCO WAS AT Robin's house less than twenty minutes after she called. As soon as he came through the door, she and Eric showed him the text. "I know who Quentin Garrison is, but I don't understand," he said.

They told him everything, starting with that first phone call she'd received at work, leaving nothing out—well, nothing as far as Quentin Garrison was concerned. The old Polaroid of Robin's mother stayed hidden, as did any dim suspicion either one of them had that Garrison may have been onto something. Through it all, Morasco watched them, his jaw flexing—an attempt, Robin thought, to maintain a poker face.

When they were more or less through, Morasco said, "Any idea why he believed that your mother had a connection to April Cooper?"

Eric jumped in before Robin could say anything. "There was a video of her on Robin's site back in

May. It got a lot of views. Maybe it was something she said, the way she looked."

"So . . . You think he could be obsessed?"

"Well, I'm not a psychiatrist." Eric winced, looking at Robin as though maybe he shouldn't have said it. "But you know . . . if I'd had Kathleen Sharkey for a mother and I believed there was someone out there who was to blame . . ."

"Yeah. I get it." Morasco looked at Robin. "Can you do me a favor? Screenshot that text and email it to me?"

Robin did, Morasco staying long enough to make sure the email had gone through.

Once he left, Robin sat back down at the kitchen table. Eric came up behind her and put his hands on her shoulders, his thumbs resting at the base of her neck. "Do you think we did the right thing?" she said.

"No question." His voice was firm. This was another thing about Eric, and it went hand in hand with the blind optimism. He never questioned a decision he made, whether it was the color swatches for their new kitchen or opting not to have kids or working for Shawn Labatoir or turning the cops on Quentin Garrison. Robin was more the type to agonize and second-guess, probably because she was an analyst's daughter. "What if Garrison's innocent?"

"Then the truth will out."

She looked up at him with flat eyes. "Sure," she said. "That always happens in law enforcement."

Eric kissed the top of her head. "You've got to trust someone, Robin," he said. "And given the choice between Nick Morasco and his partner . . ."

"Good point." Robin closed her eyes, a sense of calm sweeping through her. It helped, right now, to see the world the way Eric did—without self-doubt, questioning nothing. She thought back to what he'd said to her at the emergency room, just before she got word that her father had died and her entire life came apart at the seams. *You aren't the only one who's pissed people off.* He had said it without elaborating. Hadn't brought it up again and, as far as Robin could tell, hadn't given it another thought. Who had he pissed off? Had it been professional? Personal? "Eric . . ."

"What?"

But she realized that she didn't want answers from him, not now. She just wanted to be able to trust him, to lean on him a little. Let him have his secrets. It seemed like a fair trade. "I'm going to have a glass of wine. Do you want one?"

"Sure."

Robin removed two glasses from the cupboard and got the sauvignon blanc out of the fridge. It had been a long time since she'd poured two glasses of wine. It felt good, as did the fact that he hadn't checked his phone once—not one single time since they'd started dinner, and that was hours ago.

She handed him a glass, and he raised it to her. "To your mom's full recovery."

She smiled. Raised hers. "To new beginnings," she said.

THE NEXT MORNING, Robin headed to the hospital after dropping Eric off at the train station. He was no doubt getting an earful from Shawn today for "leaving his post" (for someone who'd lied his way out of Vietnam, Shawn Labatoir was awfully fond of military phrasing) but, he told her, he didn't care.

"Come home soon," she had said. "I can't wait to see you."

She was thinking those same words as a cheery nurse led her from the waiting area to the private room in the new wing where her mother had been moved. *I can't wait to see you.* "Mom is really looking great," the nurse said. "She should be able to go home soon."

Robin felt that spark of hope within her growing as she approached her mother's room, guards stationed outside the opened door, the curtain drawn behind it. She could hear her mother speaking to someone—a man, a doctor probably, her voice stronger and clearer than it had been the previous day. "I think so," Mom was saying. "But I don't want to commit to anything if I'm not certain."

Soon, she'd be coming home with Robin and Eric. She'd stay with them for as long as she needed, and they could figure out their lives, postshooting, post-Dad. They could settle into their grief together, help each other through. It wasn't a situation she would have imagined inspiring hope within her in the past, but that's what life does. It throws things at you. You adjust and scar over because that's how you survive.

You bend, or you break. There are no other choices.

She started to push the curtain when one of the guards stopped her. "Just a minute, ma'am." She looked at him. He was young, with good posture and rosy cheeks. He was in full uniform, though his hat was off, revealing a light blond military haircut that sparkled under the flat hospital lights, as though someone had sprinkled glitter over the top of his head. "Mrs. Bloom is being questioned."

"She's what?"

"And this was around what time that you returned?" said the man in her mother's room—not a doctor. She recognized the Jersey accent. Nick Morasco.

"Probably eightish?" her mother said. "I was out for around half an hour. Not long."

"And you can't be positive," said a different voice, louder and higher pitched, "whether or not this handsome guy was at your house, talking to your husband?" *Baus*.

"Oh hell no," Robin said.

"Robbie, is that you out there?"

"Yes, Mom."

Robin moved the curtain and stepped into the room.

"Ma'am," the guards said in unison, but Morasco stopped them. "She can come in," he said.

Robin's mother was sitting up in bed in her hospital gown, the color back in her cheeks. "Hi, honey."

Robin moved past the two detectives to hug her mother, Renee's grip even stronger than it had been the day before. On the tray in front of her was Quentin Garrison's headshot, pulled from the NPR website and blown up. Robin stared at it as she pulled away. She knew she probably shouldn't say anything, but she couldn't help herself. "Do you know him, Mom? Have you seen him before?"

"He looks familiar, I . . . think?" Renee said it, not to Robin, but to Morasco and Baus. "I wish I could remember more of that night."

Baus said, "You're pretty sure he came by the house, though?"

"No," she said. "I'm not sure of anything."

"I understand," Morasco said. "If you remember anything at all, call. Please. Any time of the day or night."

Renee tried to hand the photograph back, but Morasco shook his head. "Keep it. Maybe it will jog your memory."

They said their good-byes and left the room, and for a few moments, there was just quiet. Robin's mother stared at the photograph.

"You don't remember?" Robin said.

She shook her head. "Your father and I," she said quietly. "We had a disagreement. I left to get some fresh air. I remember driving home. After that . . . nothing."

Robin looked at her, thinking of her father's sad voice on the phone, the ashtray full of cigarettes, the handwritten names on analyst's notebook paper. Quentin Garrison. Kate Sharkey. April. *Have we been good parents to you?* "What was the disagreement about?"

Her mother looked at her, her eyes pinkish, the color fading from her cheeks, as though that simple question had weakened her. "I don't remember."

Robin moved closer. She took Renee's hand in her own and squeezed it. "It's all right, Mom," she said. "You just rest."

Renee's hand was icy cold, but of course they'd

always been like that. Bad circulation, but Dad viewed it more romantically. *Cold hands, warm heart*, he used to say . . .

Renee said, "You want to know something funny?"

"Yeah?"

"When the detectives got here, I was waking up from a nap. One of them was talking to the guards, and I heard his voice . . . I assumed it was your father." Renee's eyes glistened. A tear escaped. Robin grabbed a piece of Kleenex from the box at her bedside and dabbed at it, as though she were a child. She didn't know what else to do.

"We had a fight," Renee said in a small, choked voice. "We never fought, but we did that night, and it will always be the last thing we did together."

"It's okay, Mom."

"It's not."

"You can say good-bye to him. Make your peace."

"How?"

"Once you're out of the hospital, I'll take you to the cemetery."

"We can't."

"Why not?"

"We're supposed to wait a year. Then we have the unveiling."

"Who cares what we're supposed to do? An unveiling is a Jewish tradition, and you're not even Jewish."

"Dad is."

"I guarantee you, it doesn't matter to him now."

Mom laughed a little. Then she started to cry. She cried silently, shoulders shaking, tears spilling down her face, her lip trembling like a child's. Robin knelt next to her and put her arms around her, stroked her hair. She kissed her wet, salty cheek and wished she could think of the right thing to say, but there was no right thing.

"I keep telling myself he's just away on a business trip—at a conference," Renee said. "I dream that's where he is. Over and over, I have this same dream, where he walks through that door and tells me his flight has been delayed. And then I wake up and there's no one there, or maybe there's a nurse, and my first thought is always the same. He'll never walk through that door. I'll never hear his voice. I'll never see him again."

"I know, Mom. I know." Robin grabbed more Kleenex—a big wad of it—and handed it to her mother. She let her dry her own tears.

Robin said, "I spoke to Dad that night."

"You did? Did he sound angry?"

"Not at all," she said. "He didn't even mention that you'd had a fight. He just said you went out to buy some coffee."

Renee blew her nose. "That was your father," she said. "He never wanted you to hear anything bad."

"I should have come over and watched the Yankees with him. We could have waited for you to come home."

"I'm so glad you didn't."

"No, Mom, no," she said. "I mean . . . maybe if I'd have been around when it happened, I could have helped."

"Don't even say that."

Robin looked at her mother. She was calmer now, her face dry, her breathing steady. "Mom."

"Yes?"

"Why did you buy a gun?"

Renee's eyes clouded for a moment, then cleared again. "What do you mean?" she said softly, gently. "I hate guns."

"How are we feeling?" A freckle-faced nurse who looked about twelve stood just behind Robin, her timing horrible. "We just need to run a few tests and check our vitals." The nurse peered at the screen by her mother's bed and took her pulse and temperature, taking notes after each step. She was fast and efficient, but to Robin, it felt endless.

At long last, she left. "Mom," Robin said.

"What?"

"The gun you both were shot with. It was registered to you."

Renee exhaled heavily, twisted a piece of Kleenex between her fingers. Robin watched her, twisting it tighter and tighter. It was like watching a jack-in-the-box, waiting for it to pop open. "It was your father's idea," her mom finally said. "He bought it for me. He was going to a lot of conferences at the time, and he was worried about me being at home alone."

Robin opened her mouth, but she couldn't find the words. Mitchell Bloom had always despised guns, to the point of where he'd complained to Robin's high school about the use of prop guns in a production of *Hedda Gabler*. He'd always said it was the thing that had bothered him most about Wards Island— not the murderers, but the armed guards, the ever-present firearms. The idea of her father buying a gun made even less sense than her mother buying one. But what could Robin say? Renee knew it as well as she did.

"I know it sounds strange," Renee said. "That's one reason why we never mentioned it to you."

"It was Dad's gun."

"Yes."

"He registered it to you."

Renee met her gaze, her blue eyes steely. "Yes."

"Okay," Robin said. "Thank you for being honest."

Renee's eyes narrowed. *"What is that supposed to mean?"* She practically hissed it, her face hard and angry and unfamiliar, Robin feeling the way she'd felt as a kid when her mother had railed at her for watching a movie on TV. As though she'd suddenly dropped character, turning into someone Robin didn't know, someone she couldn't trust. Someone who scared her.

"Nothing," Robin said. "I swear."

Renee's face relaxed. She ran a hand across her eyes and gave her daughter a kind smile and settled back into herself again, as though a mask had slipped off and she'd snapped it back in place. "I'm sorry, honey," she said. "Sometimes, I don't know who I am anymore."

TWENTY-THREE

June 17, 1976
9:00 P.M.

Dear Aurora Grace,

He's dead. The cop who pulled us over. His name was Officer Nelligan. He was probably just a few years older than Gabriel. I killed him.

He's lying in the middle of some road we never learned the name of. He is a skinny guy with freckles, a gap between his front teeth, a Timex watch. A wedding ring. A name tag that says Officer Nelligan. I learned all those details about him after he was dead, and those details made him alive. When he actually was alive, he didn't even have a name. He was just a shadow that yelled.

"What do you think you were doing back there?" Officer Nelligan yelled into our car. "Do you realize you were going eighty in a forty-mile-per-hour zone? What is wrong with you? Are you on drugs?"

I'd never known cops could be so loud, so terrifying. Before now, the only ones I'd seen up close had been the ones who came to school every year for the first assembly. When we were little, they told us to look both ways before crossing the street and not to talk to strangers, and once we got into junior high they added "don't do drugs" to the mix. There were different cops every year—usually a young one who tried to act "cool" and an older one who was a little more serious. But no matter what kind of thing they were telling us to do, those cops' voices had always been calm and kind. This one, Officer Nelligan, was as loud and mean and scary as the siren that blared from his black-and-white car. It was dark out. The sun had just set. His face was hidden by the brim of his hat. Maybe it's just the way I remember it, but I swear to you that when he was talking to us, all I could see were his eyes, glowing like a rat's eyes in the dark.

He had a flashlight in his hand. He aimed it through Gabriel's opened window. He pushed the beam of it around the inside of our stolen car, over our bodies, into my dyed orange hair so that I could feel its burn. He aimed the beam into my eyes until the pupils squished up. Held it there good and long, so that when he finally moved it away, my eyes didn't work for at least a minute, and all I could see was this hovering cloud of white.

Gabriel apologized to Officer Nelligan. He said he hadn't realized he'd been speeding, and that he was a new driver. "Please forgive me, sir." He said it so calmly, I was proud of him. I thought to myself, *Everything is going to be all right. We will* escape with a warning and we will drive far away and he'll never even know who we are.

But then the cop asked Gabriel for license and registration. I knew we'd never escape this. Remember, Aurora Grace, we are wanted. Fugitives. And as soon as he got one look at Gabriel's driver's license and called in the name or whatever it is that cops do when they take people's licenses to their cars, Officer Nelligan would know that about us. We were doomed.

Gabriel stalled a little, pretending like he couldn't find his license. I sat there, sweat pouring out of my underarms, slipping down my rib cage and into the belt of my too-baggy jeans, the vinyl seat of this cheap stolen car sticking to the backs of my arms and my neck. It felt like the whole car was trying to hold me down, to punish me for stealing it. Without moving my lips, I prayed for something. A miracle to save us. I wasn't sure what that miracle would be, but I wasn't picky. I told God, *You decide.*

And then I saw it happen: Officer Nelligan recognized us. I knew it before he said anything, just in the way he stopped talking, the way his back straightened, and he seemed to change shape, growing bigger and taller and meaner than he'd been just two seconds earlier. I pictured buttons popping on his uniform, his rage turning him into a giant, a monster that could, would kill Gabriel and me.

"Get out," he said. "Get out of the car now. Both of you. Out." I could hear the crackling of the radio at his belt. I saw the handcuffs in his

holster, the gun. He told us to get out of the car
again, and then everything seemed to slow down
like gears grinding, each movement a freeze-
frame, so I could see it super clear. Gabriel opening the door. My hand finding the gun on the seat
between us—the gun that had killed Ed Hart.
The gun I'd been forced to shoot Papa Pete with
after his death, so that it now felt familiar in
my hands and I knew what to do. It was a sign.
At least that's how I felt in that moment. Like
God was showing me what needed to be done.

I told Gabriel to move out of the way. I think
I must have screamed for him to do it. My
throat still feels raw.

The cop reached for something—his radio or
his gun, I wasn't sure which. I had the gun in
both hands. I released the safety the way Gabriel showed me. Time froze into a still photograph. I was standing at one end of a tunnel
and Officer Nelligan was at the other and there
was no one else in the world but the two of us.
I pulled the trigger and we both fell back. It
was like a weird dance, only he kept falling. My
shoulders jammed into their sockets, same as
with Papa Pete. And again, my arms went all
weak and tingly and my head got light and I felt
like I might pass out. It was only then, when I
saw him fall to the ground, the blood spreading
across his chest and pooling beneath him, his
mouth opening and closing and then stopping—
all of him stopping—that time started moving
normally again.

You watch movies where someone kills another person for the first time, and if it's a girl like me, they get hysterical. They scream and cry and say "Oh my God, what have I done?" again and again until some man has to slap her across the face.

Aurora Grace, it wasn't like that for me.

I could hear Gabriel saying, "Oh my God, babe, oh my God." And he sounded like a baby, like someone who needed taking care of. It made me want to slap him across the face. Or better yet shoot him. I might have done it too, if he didn't know where Jenny was.

I didn't say a word, didn't feel a thing, until we got closer to the cop, and I saw his face. His eyes were big and still, the eyelids unblinking. His mouth was open, like he was about to say something but had forgotten what. That's when it all became real for me—what I had done. The Timex watch. The wedding ring.

I hadn't done God's bidding. I hadn't saved us from a monster. I had killed a man. I looked into his still, staring eyes and without saying a word, I told him I was sorry. I told his wife I was sorry. His kids, if he had them. I hope he didn't have them. I put my hand over his eyelids, and I closed them so he could sleep.

Gabriel told me to cut it out. He warned me about fingerprints and went for Officer Nelligan's gun, his handcuffs, and his wallet. I hope that shows you how different we are—that I'm not really like him. I think that spending all this time with Gabriel has made me turn a little, like when you leave a glass of milk out in the sun.

I think about that day in the future when you are born—when Jenny will be in my life and Gabriel won't be, and I will be free and safe. In that future time, I will go to church every day. I will pray for Officer Nelligan and Papa Pete too, who when you think about it, wouldn't have been killed if I hadn't used him as an excuse to break up with Gabriel. I will even pray for Ed Hart. Every day, I will do something good for a person or an animal. I won't go to sleep until I've made someone's life better. And all those good deeds will turn me back.

For now, though, I just have to live through this. I have to be what I have become.

Love,

April

TWENTY-FOUR

ROBIN

"I'M SO SORRY," Renee said again, and it felt as though that momentary outburst had been a passing cloud, a few drops of rain, nothing more.

Robin smiled. She took her hand. "It was probably just the drugs," she said.

"No," she said. "It's your father."

"Mom?"

"Him being gone, I mean. He's been a part of me for all these years. He's known me longer than anybody and I feel like . . ." Tears streamed down her face. "He was my anchor. He kept me in place." Her eyes fluttered and closed. "I don't know what's going to happen to me with him gone. I don't know where I'm going to go . . ."

Robin kissed her cheek, took her hand in hers. "You still have me," she said.

"Yes," her mother said as she drifted off to sleep. "Yes, Robbie. And the truth is, you're all I've ever really wanted."

Robin backed away from her mother's bed and

headed toward the elevators, taking one downstairs to the cafeteria. On her way down, she thought about the weather, about upcoming summer action movies and this week's column and what she planned on wearing tomorrow or the next day, when she finally returned to work. She thought about nothing important, nothing worth remembering because sometimes, not remembering was best.

TWENTY-FIVE

June 17, 1976
11:30 P.M.

Dear Aurora Grace,

We're at prom now. Well, not prom. We're at
Pullman Park, where everybody goes after prom.
Gabriel and I have kept up with our plan to come
here together, but for different reasons now. We
are here to get a new car.

After Officer Nelligan, we found a gas station
and parked our car behind it. We took turns, Gabriel and I, cleaning up in the restrooms, changing into our prom clothes in order to fit in. We are
here now. "Just two prom kids in love, looking for
a place to park." Gabriel says this over and over,
trying to hypnotize us both into believing it, as if
the two of _us_ believing that we're "just two prom
kids in love" is the important thing. Gabriel is
wearing a burgundy sports coat he swiped from
JCPenney over a checked plaid shirt and jeans.
His bleached blond hair makes him think he can
pass for a surfer boy, and maybe he can from a
distance, but up close he looks deranged. I am

wearing the dress I shoplifted, and I've pinned my jagged orange hair behind my ears. I'm wearing mascara and blush and so much Bonne Bell Lip Smacker, the whole car smells of strawberry. But every time I catch a glimpse of myself in the rearview mirror, I don't see a prom girl. I see a murderer.

The area of the parking lot where we are right now is packed, couples drinking and smoking in the cars or leaning back and looking up at the sky from the seats of open convertibles. Other kids are roaming around the area on foot, laughing and shouting, jumping up onto hoods and leaning into windows. In the distance, I can see a group on the baseball diamond, a guy in a pale blue tux rounding the bases. Everyone is wasted and happy. Not a grown-up in sight.

Music blasts out of car radios. All of them are turned to the same station—the AM Top 40 station I used to listen to at home. "Oh, what a night," Frankie Valli sings, and he isn't kidding. The air outside is warm and smells of pot smoke and beer and I wish I could escape into it. I wish I could turn my body to powder and float away forever.

Gabriel is muttering to himself very quietly. I almost feel like I can hear his brain working as we reach a more secluded area, the make-out area, where cars are parked far apart from each other and the windows are steamed white. Gabriel drives slowly behind the parked cars, eyeing each one—a shiny vintage Mustang, a green VW beetle, a long black Cadillac that has to belong to someone's dad. I can't take my eyes off one car, though. It's a powder blue Honda Accord, and I know it belongs to Brian Griggs because I've memorized his license plate. If I squint hard enough, I swear I can see through the fogged-up window—his silhouette in the front seat, his rich, mean, beautiful girlfriend, Carrie Masters, leaning into him. They kiss and he holds her face in both his hands as though it's precious and delicate. Something tightens in my chest, a dull pain in my heart. Carrie Masters called me a dumb whore once. I passed the two of them in the hallway and said hi. I normally don't say hi to Brian when Carrie is around, but I said it that time. He said "Hi," back. And Carrie said, "Why would you say hi to that dumb whore?" She didn't even bother to whisper it. She didn't care if I heard.

Gabriel is watching me now. I expect him to ask me what I'm writing, but instead, he asks me who I'm looking at. How do I answer without upsetting him? "Nothing," I say. "No one." But the pain is still there and I'm sure Gabriel can feel it radiating off me.

If Brian Griggs loves someone as awful as Carrie Masters, he must be kind of awful too.

Gabriel is parking our car now, about twenty feet away from the other cars. He parks in the shadows, cuts the lights. He tells me to take all the stuff out of the back. I ask him where he's going. He won't tell me, but I know. I'm watching him heading toward Brian's Accord. I see the

gun in his hand. Officer Nelligan's gun. In the
other, he is holding the handcuffs. A different girl
would stop him. A better girl would. But I don't.
I just watch, and I sing to myself.

Oh, what a night.

TWENTY-SIX

REG

"ARE YOU FEELING all right, Mr. Sharkey?" It was Mrs. Bowen from next door. Always sticking her nose in everybody's business, especially Reg's. She'd lived in that house for God knows how many years, and for as many of those years as he could remember, Reg couldn't go outside to mow the lawn or turn the sprinklers on or even get his mail out of his damn mailbox—which he was trying to do right now—without Mrs. Bowen popping up out of no-where, her mouth open like a baby bird, ready to feed on his misery.

One time, he'd gotten her good. Just like always, she'd tapped him on the shoulder while he was watering his lawn and asked, "How *are* you, Mr. Shar-key?" leaning hard on the *are*, each word dripping with fake concern. But that particular time, Reg had turned around too fast and accidentally-on-purpose sprayed her with the hose. Made him smile just thinking about it. The sight of her in her sopping wet housedress, her roller-set curls all stuck to her face. "Well, I never!" she'd said. Like she was Scarlett O'Hara. But now that he thought about it . . . Boy, that had to have been a long time ago. Had to have been before he'd put the sprinkler system in, and he'd put the sprinkler system in just about a year after Kimmy was born . . .

Reg stared at Mrs. Bowen, wondering how it could be that she looked exactly the same as she had forty-five years ago. How was that possible?

"Mr. Sharkey?" she said again, and it dawned on him like a thick fog clearing. Mrs. Bowen had died a couple of years back, and this wasn't her talking to him at all, but her daughter, Karen. No, not Karen. Corinne. Corinne Palmer. That was her married name. Reg was fine. His brain was fine. He just wished he didn't have to talk to nasty Corinne Palmer, with her shitty TV shows blaring out the window all day and all night. *Hoarders. My 600-lb Life. 16 and Pregnant.* People flaunting their misery for a few bucks and some attention—there was nothing more depressing than that. But Reg supposed that for a nosy person like Corinne, who lived off the misfortune of others, these TV shows were a regular opiate. Her mother, at least, had never blasted the TV.

"I'm fine, Corinne," Reg said. "Why do you ask?"

"Well, I heard you arguing with that young man a couple of days ago, and I haven't seen you since. You usually mow your lawn on Mondays, but you weren't out there yesterday."

"Lawn didn't need mowing."

She just kept talking, as though he'd never spoken. "I was worried for your welfare. That young man sounded so angry . . ."

"I'm fine."

"If I'd gone another day without seeing you, I was going to call the police."

"The lawn didn't need mowing. What the hell more do you want me to say?"

She took a step back, blinking like someone who'd just dodged a punch. Her nose was red and bulbous like her mother's had been, and something about her expression too, the way she opened and closed her mouth like a dying fish on a dock . . . What had Mrs. Bowen's first name been again? Had Reg ever learned it?

"Who was that young man?" How old was Corinne when he'd doused her mother with the hose? Twenty maybe. Did she have any idea, back then, how cruel her own DNA would turn out to be? "You can tell me, Mr. Sharkey. Who was that young man?"

"Kate's son."

"My God. Really?" She sounded deliriously happy. He said, "This better than *Hoarders*?"

"What?"

"Nothing."

Reg opened his mailbox, which was what had brought him out here and into this unpleasant conversation in the first place. Maybe if he threw all his energy into opening his mail, Corinne would feel ignored and go back inside her house.

Reg thumbed through his letters: phone bill, electric, brochure from Home Depot.

Corinne Palmer said, "I don't think I've seen Kate's son since he was a little boy."

Reg thought, *Why can't she take a hint?* But then a memory flickered in his mind: a little boy. Chubby cheeks. Thick glasses. Black hair flopping like a puppy's ears. *Pleath can I have a doggy oh pleaaatttth?* The funny way he used to talk, that kid. But no. Reg was wrong again. It wasn't Kate's son with the funny voice. It was. Oh, it was . . .

"Mr. Sharkey, are you sure you're okay?"

"I'm fine." Reg swiped at his eyes, at the wetness on his cheeks. Tears. Mortifying. *The way the body betrays you at this age.* Reg thought of that song Kate used to blast when she was a teenager, about only the good dying young. Wasn't that ever the God's honest truth . . . He looked at his neighbor. "Run along, Corinne," he said.

She blinked again. "Remember, Mr. Sharkey, if you ever need me, I'm just right over—"

"I know where you live."

Corinne started to say something, then stopped. "All righty then." She turned on her heel and huffed away. Those pistonlike legs of hers, just like her mother's.

With some effort, Reg was able to back away from the memory. So many things he'd destroyed in his life, that little boy being only one of them.

He looked through the rest of his mail: an ad for a home security device, a book of coupons from Vons, a postcard from his dentist, telling him he was due for a cleaning, his Social Security check, a brochure about the world's most comfortable shoes. At the bottom of the pile was a letter, addressed to

Mr. Reginald Sharkey in neat capital letters. A man's handwriting, Reg decided. A professional man. He looked at the postmark, turned the envelope over. Strange. The return address was South Pasadena, but the postmark said New Jersey.

He waited to open the envelope until he was back in his own house. It had been written on nice stationery, a watermark and everything. Hotel stationery, as it turned out. *Garden Suites* embossed on the bottom. It was two single-sided pages long and it began, "Dear Mr. Sharkey" and ended with, "Your grandson, Quentin," and though Reg wasn't sure he had any interest in reading it (*That boy and his mother. Always up to some scam . . .*) he did anyway:

> First of all, I want to apologize for my behavior at your house the other day. I had no right to speak to you like that. It was very unprofessional.

"Okay," Reg said to the letter. "That's a pretty good start."

> Second, there is something you need to know.

Reg read on. A group of sentences he would never be able to read again. "Oh God," he whispered. "Oh Katie."

He made it through the rest of the letter, the talk about how difficult life was, and how everyone had done the best they could, Reg included. *It's all just a matter of surviving. I know that now. I'm not sure that*

Mom ever wanted to survive. But you are a survivor, and I'm like you that way. He read about how Quentin still saw his mother's face in dreams, and how he'd live the rest of his life wondering if he could have said or done anything to ease her sadness and heal her addiction. *I don't think either one of us was the right man for that job.* He read too about the podcast Quentin was making—how Quentin now felt that it had been a mistake, lifting all those rocks just to look underneath, disrupting so many lives in the process. He said the only reason why he'd decided to make the podcast in the first place was that it seemed like a way to better understand Kate and Reg—the huge parts of them that had been stolen by April Cooper and Gabriel LeRoy. *It's not your fault, Mr. Sharkey,* Quentin had written. *We all make our own choices in life. My mother made hers. Please stop blaming yourself for everything. The only thing you did was go to a gas station.*

Reg's face was wet again, and he was sobbing, convulsing.

Katie, his Katie. All of his children, gone. And Quentin was wrong. It was Reg's fault. All of it. From the very beginning.

Once Reg caught his breath, he picked up the kitchen phone. Called the number Quentin had given him, back when he'd first set up their interview. *I'll tell him,* he thought. *I'll explain everything.* But then Quentin's voice mail was full, and Reg's brain got the best of him, that gnawing, ever-present fear. *I can't do it,* he thought, the secret staring him in the face, baring its sharp, yellowed teeth. *I'm not strong enough. I can't.*

He hung up, pulled his bottle of Dewar's out of the kitchen cupboard, poured himself a glass. Reg drank a toast to Katie. Then another, to everyone he'd ever loved and ruined, from that little boy on. "May they all rest in peace," he said.

TWENTY-SEVEN

ROBIN

IT WAS ROBIN'S fourth day of scrambled eggs and wheat toast in the hospital cafeteria. She'd ordered it her first morning here because it had seemed like a safe choice, and since she'd barely touched it at breakfast, she ordered it again for lunch. It had gotten to the point where the women behind the counter gave her a plate of scrambled eggs without even asking, and she didn't want to be rude by correcting them. Like any safe thing, the plate of scrambled eggs and toast had begun to get oppressive with time, and now Robin could barely stand the sight of them. Luckily, the coffee wasn't bad.

The cafeteria was close to empty—just a few members of the hospital staff grabbing a quick bite between shifts. But Robin had a long table all to herself—the better to be alone with her thoughts. She'd been sitting here for a good half hour, maybe longer, thinking about her mother, how she'd snapped at her in the hospital room, then recovered, thinking about what she'd said as she was drifting off, about her father being an anchor and not knowing where she'd go.

She wondered if this was something she might have to get used to, these sudden bursts of rage and worry. Renee had lost a lot of blood in the shooting and had been on life support long enough that it could have affected her brain chemistry. Anxiety and anger issues weren't uncommon for survivors of traumatic attacks, and the very fact that she couldn't remember a good portion of the night she was shot seemed like proof—at least to Robin—that she'd been changed in ways that the doctors here hadn't taken into account. Therapy, that's what she needed . . .

Interestingly, Renee had never gone in for analysis when Robin was growing up. Despite the fact that she'd obviously had a sad, bleak childhood, Robin's psychiatrist father discouraged her from talking to anyone about it. Robin could distinctly recall the topic coming up—her mother mentioning a friend of hers, a fellow volunteer at Tarry Ridge Hospital, who'd been going to group therapy and loving it. *You don't want to do that, Renee.* Her father had said it as though it was a fact he was reminding her of. Which was strange, now that Robin thought about it. She'd gone for therapy herself as a high school student. And Dad too saw an analyst for a while. But not Mom. Maybe she'd suffered for it. Maybe it was time to change things, to find out who Renee Bloom truly was without that anchor holding her in place.

Last night, Robin had woken up from a dream

that felt more like a memory. Her mother sobbing behind her parents' closed door, and her father urging her on. *That's it, Renee. That's it. Let it out. Don't run from it . . .*

Had that really happened?

"Mind if I join you?"

Robin glanced up from her eggs and into those sharp blue eyes. "Nikki."

"They told me your mom was resting, so I thought I'd grab a little bite."

Robin gestured to the seat across from her and Nicola Crane eased into it, setting her tray down. Like Robin, she had a cup of coffee, along with a donut that looked like a reconfigured version of Robin's wheat toast. She took a delicate bite. "I should have stopped at Dunkin'."

Robin smiled. "Tell me about it." She took a sip of her coffee. "So I remember you now."

"You do?"

"Why didn't you introduce yourself as CoCo?"

"Oh, I practically forgot about that nickname," she said. "Only you called me that, you know."

"Really?"

"I mean, I came up with it, of course, but you were the only one nice enough to call me by it. Everybody else thought it was silly. Your mother included." She smiled, her teeth white against her tanned, lined skin. She wore jeans and a plaid shirt, rolled up to the elbows, revealing muscular arms, a long scar on one of them. To Robin, she had the look of a farmer or a rancher or maybe a lifelong surfer.

"How did you know my mom?" Robin said.

Her bright eyes shimmered. "We were in a foster home together, years ago," she said. "And then we reconnected once she'd settled down. She saved me from a terrible situation. Gave me money for my education. Got me on my feet."

"So you were friends," she said, "when you both were kids."

"Yes," she said.

Robin took another sip of her coffee. She leaned forward, wanting to ask the question, but fearing the answer at the same time. "What was she like?"

"She was the kindest person I'd ever known."

"Oh thank God." Robin exhaled, relief spreading through her.

"Like there was ever a question?"

"It's just . . . Someone asked me about her past recently. They thought she . . . Well obviously they had her confused with someone else."

"I don't understand."

Robin swallowed. "They thought she'd associated with some unsavory types when she was a teenager."

"Well," Nicola said, winking, "they must have been talking about me." She laughed—a startlingly loud, shrieking laugh that seemed to pop out of nowhere, far too hearty for the situation or the surroundings. Whereas Nicola's smile was disarming, her laugh was downright off-putting, and Robin could feel people staring at them. Her face flushed a deep red. *I am having breakfast in a hospital cafeteria with Robert De Niro from* Cape Fear.

After a time, Nicola calmed herself. "I'm sorry," she said. "But that just tickled me. The idea of your mom, hanging out with some criminal . . ."

Robin relaxed. "It is kind of ridiculous."

"I mean, what? Was she pals with a drug dealer? I mean . . . could you even imagine your mom smoking a joint?"

Robin giggled. "Not a drug dealer, just—"

"A prostitute?"

They were both laughing now.

"Numbers runner? Carjacker? Hired killer?"

"Okay," Robin said, laughing harder. "Okay, I see your point." They laughed together for quite a while, Robin growing used to Nicola's shrieks, along with the other cafeteria patrons. It did something, laughing with another person like that. It bonded you.

Once their laughter died down, Robin leaned in close and said it. "I spoke to this guy. He was making a podcast about these killings in the '70s."

"Quentin." Nicola said the name like it was a rotten piece of meat in her mouth.

"You know him?"

"Met him. Don't like him." She leaned in. "Don't trust him. At all."

"Yeah?"

She glanced around the cafeteria and nodded slowly. "He said something, Robbie. It made me very suspicious."

"What did he say?"

"Something about being in your parents' neighborhood the night they were shot."

"What? Are you serious?"

"I mean, he could have just been snooping, like journalists do, but—"

"Did you tell the police?"

She smiled. "I am the police."

Robin stared at her. "You are?"

"Don't look so surprised. Gray-haired ladies can be cops too. And yes. I spoke to an irritating detective from the Tarry Ridge Department."

"Baus."

"Bingo."

"Try Morasco next time."

"Thank you. That Baus is a jackass."

Robin forked some scrambled eggs into her mouth and choked them down. She took in the tanned face. "I can't believe you're the same CoCo," she said.

Nicola took a bite of her donut. "Life rides some of us harder than others."

"No, no. I didn't mean that," Robin said. "I just can't believe you've been in touch with my mom, after all these years."

"I'm good at tracking people down," she said. "And I'd never have let your mom slip away."

Robin thought of her father, the anchor. "I'm sorry you couldn't stay with us."

"Listen, I never had any hard feelings over your dad not letting me, if that's what you're thinking."

"Well . . ."

"If Mitchell hadn't said no, I'd never have gone to the Police Academy, never would have made detective or met my darling ex-husband or seen as much of the world as I have," she said. "Hell, if he'd said yes, he'd probably be long gone, and your mother and I would be in that house, pulling a Grey Gardens and . . ." She shook her head. "I'm an idiot," she said quietly.

"What?"

"I'm so very sorry about your dad."

"It's okay."

"It's not. I speak before I think sometimes."

Robin took a swallow of her coffee. Nicola's hands were folded on the table, and Robin placed one of her hands over them, squeezed. "I'm glad you're here with us now," she said.

THE NAP SEEMED to have done Renee a world of good. Robin and Nicola spent more than an hour with her, reminiscing over old times, the two of them embarrassing Robin with childhood stories, Nicola's maniacal laugh erupting sporadically. From time to time, Renee would get quiet or teary and Nicola and Robin would simply sit with her, holding her hands, waiting for the moment to pass. Nicola cracked terrible jokes with the nurses and showed pictures of her three dogs to Robin and Renee, Renee in particular cooing over them—a yellow lab, an Australian shepherd, and a standard poodle. Renee who'd spent her entire adult life with an allergic husband, longing for a dog. She seemed to love the lab especially.

When Dr. Wu came in to run some tests on Renee, Robin and Nicola kissed her good-bye and promised to come back in a few hours—at which point, she'd hopefully be well enough to be released. Walking down to the parking lot together, Nicola and Robin made small talk, complaining about the heat and the food in the cafeteria, and sharing restaurant recommendations in the area. Once they reached Robin's car, they hugged and Robin's mind returned again to Quentin Garrison, what Nicola had said about him earlier. "Do you think he might have done it?" Robin said, her hand on the door.

"Let's put it this way," she said. "I have no idea who else would have done it."

It wasn't until Robin was driving away that she realized she'd never said Quentin Garrison's name or what she thought he'd done, but she hadn't needed to. Nicola had known.

DRIVING HOME, ROBIN listened to the news on NPR, all those dumb grief clichés running through her head—doors closing and windows opening, silver linings and brand-new days. She'd never get over the loss of her father. It was a pin stuck in her forever, one that hurt only marginally less if she didn't look at it directly. But her mother was going to be okay, and that was her window opening, her silver lining. Renee was going to live, and she had a dear old friend that Robin had never known about to help her pull through.

Robin was starting up her car and thinking about getting a yellow lab for Mom when her phone rang. She answered it, Eric's voice coming through the Bluetooth. "Guess what?" Robin said. "I spent the whole morning with Nikki the babysitter. Did you know she's a cop now? How bizarre is that?"

There was a long pause on the other end of the line. "How's your mom?" Eric said finally. His voice sounded strange. Hollow.

"Um. Fine? They're probably going to release her soon."

"That's great," he said.

"What's going on with you?" she said. "Shawn didn't fire you, did he?"

"No."

"So . . ."

"Listen, Robin. I got a call from Detective Morasco. He'd been trying to call you, but I guess your mailbox is full."

"And?"

"Quentin Garrison confessed."

"*What?*"

"He said he shot both your parents during a dispute at their house. It's all on tape. Morasco says he's going to let you listen to it. And he wants to talk to your mom again."

"Oh my God," she said. "Well . . . is he in custody? Has he been officially charged? Are there going to be a shitload of reporters at my mom's house when I go to get her clothes?"

"Well, see, Robin, this is the thing."

"Yeah?"

"They have his confession on tape because he emailed the audio files to the cops," he said. "But Garrison's not at the station. He isn't at his hotel. Nobody knows where the hell he is."

TWENTY-EIGHT

ROBIN

"WHEN DID YOU talk to him?" Morasco said.

Robin pulled out her phone, checked her recent calls. Found the one with the 213 area code and read out the time. "9:13 A.M.," she said. They were sitting in the waiting area on her mother's floor, Morasco having met her here about twenty minutes after she'd spoken to Eric. He'd agreed to be the one to break the news to Renee about Quentin Garrison and question her again, free of Baus, plus he'd agreed to do it with Robin present. Morasco's priority was finding Quentin Garrison, while Robin's was making sure her mother wasn't traumatized into a relapse—and those two priorities didn't need to be at cross-purposes.

Plus, from what Robin could gather, she had been the last person to have any contact with Garrison.

"Why did you call Quentin Garrison?" Morasco said. It was for the benefit of his voice recorder. She'd told him already.

"I wanted to know why the hell my father had

his phone number and his name, and his mother's name written down," she said.

"And what did he say?"

"He said he couldn't talk. Which really made me angry. He said he'd meet me in an hour, anywhere I wanted."

"Where were you going to meet?"

"The cafeteria at St. Catherine's. Downstairs from my mom's room."

"And he agreed to that location."

"Yes," she said. "But he sounded weird. Nervous. And you know . . . he never showed up."

"Did he say anything to you on the phone that sounded like an apology?"

"No. But he texted me later."

"And when was that?"

Robin checked her phone. "Looks like nine thirty P.M."

"That same night."

"Yes."

"We have a screenshot of the text."

"Right."

Morasco took a breath. "All right, Ms. Diamond. Is there anything else you remember about that call? Anything that struck you as unusual?"

Robin started to say no, then stopped herself. "Actually, yes," she said.

He looked at her.

"I heard noises when he was talking. Children playing. It sounded like he was in a park."

"Okay," he said. "That's helpful." Though she wasn't sure whether he meant it or not. There were hundreds of parks in the tristate area. And he'd spoken to her from one of them more than twenty-four hours ago. God only knows where he'd been when he'd texted her.

Robin said, "Why would you confess to a murder and just disappear?"

"Why is for psychiatrists," Morasco said. "What I'm interested in is how, when, and where."

MORASCO AND ROBIN waited until Dr. Wu had examined Renee, declaring her to be in excellent health and ready to be released the following day barring setbacks. And even then, Robin was nervous.

"I didn't expect to see you back so soon," Renee said. And then she noticed Morasco, lingering near the doorway. "What now?" she said, her face going pale.

Robin watched her. *What's wrong? What are you thinking?*

"Mom," Robin said. "Quentin Garrison confessed to shooting you and Dad."

Slowly, her color came back. "He did?"

"Do you remember anything about that night?"

"No . . ." Renee's eyes went to the detective. "Why don't you ask Quentin Garrison about it? He'd probably have a better memory of it than me."

"He's not available, ma'am."

"Not available?"

Robin said, "They haven't found him yet."

Renee sat up in bed, her eyes blazing. She stared at Morasco. "How could you lose a confessed murderer?"

"Mom, please calm down."

"Don't tell me to calm down. There's a man who tried to kill me, and no one knows where he is."

"We have you under constant surveillance, ma'am. We're doing everything we can to ensure your safety."

"Except catching a damn murderer."

"Mom."

"I need to rest, Robbie. I need you both to leave."

"Do you remember anything from that night, ma'am? Any tiny snippet, any image . . . anything at all . . ."

Renee closed her eyes. She took a deep breath, her thin body expanding and settling with it. Robin thought she might tell them to leave again, but when she spoke, her voice was calm. "We had a fight," she said quietly. "Your father and me. That's all I remember. The last image I have in my mind of him is full of anger. It isn't fair . . ."

"Do you remember, ma'am," Morasco said, "what the fight was about?"

Robin watched her, the rising and falling of her chest, her neck and arms frail beneath the hospital gown.

"Yes," she said quietly.

Robin's eyes widened.

"It was that podcaster, Quentin Garrison," she said. "That's what we were arguing about. He'd spoken to him. He thought we should speak to him. I didn't."

Robin looked at Morasco.

"We," he said.

"Excuse me?"

"I just noticed that you said 'we.' Not he. Your husband was a forensic psychiatrist and this was a true crime podcast—"

"Mr. Garrison was delusional, apparently," she said quietly. "He saw me online. He thought I looked like someone I'm not. He'd had a tragedy in his family and I felt sorry for him. But I was leery about meeting him face-to-face. He sounded . . . unbalanced."

"Mom?" Robin said. "You're just remembering this now?"

She stared up at the ceiling. "Yes."

"But you still don't remember the actual shooting."

"No," she said. "Can you please leave, Detective Morasco? Can you find that poor, delusional young man and bring him to justice so I can take a nap without getting murdered in my sleep?"

"Thank you for your time, ma'am," Morasco said. He nodded at Robin and slipped out the door.

After he was gone, Renee took the pitcher of water from her bedside, poured herself a plastic cupful and drank until it was empty. Then poured herself another and did the same. "I'm sorry for that young man. I'm sorry about what happened to his family," she said. "But that doesn't give him license to try and destroy ours."

"Did you know her, Mom?" Robin said. "Did you know April Cooper?"

"Of course not, Robin."

"I didn't think so."

"Your father felt very sorry for that young man," she said, a tear leaking down her cheek. "I did too, but I didn't think . . . It felt like your father wasn't taking my safety into consideration . . ."

"Mrs. Bloom? Are we okay?" It was that young, freckled nurse, who apparently had no knowledge of second person singular.

She wiped her face. Smiled. "I'm . . . fine. Just tired." Renee turned to Robin. "I'm going to take a little nap, honey. Is that okay with you?"

"Of course, Mom."

As Robin left the room, she heard the squeak of the nurse's shoes on the slick hospital floor. "Oh, we do look like we could use some rest," the nurse was saying. "Let's take our vitals."

As Robin took the elevator down to the first floor where the cafeteria was located, she thought about something her mother had once told her, when she was going through some junior high school drama. *At your age, you don't even know who you are yet. That's what growing up is—getting closer and closer to becoming yourself.*

On her way into the parking lot, Robin nearly bumped into Detective Morasco. He nodded at her.

"I got kicked out too," she said.

"I don't blame your mother," he said. "If I were her, I'd be pissed off too that this guy is on the loose."

"Hopefully, he won't be for long."

"Yep . . . Something you might want to tell your mother, though. The shooting wasn't about her, or who Quentin Garrison might have thought she knew."

She looked at him. "It wasn't?"

"In his confession, he says he went to your parents' house to interview your dad, as an expert. He says they got into an argument, and things got out of hand. For what it's worth, it sounds like he never intended to cause them any harm, but his anger issues got the best of him."

She exhaled. "Doesn't do us much good at this point."

"True," he said. "But it might help your mother feel less guilty over it all. He apologizes to your family directly. You both can come by the station and listen, any time you want."

Robin winced. "I don't know that I'll be ready until he gets captured," she said. "I don't know that I'll ever be ready to listen to him."

"I hear you," said Detective Morasco. "And I'd like to be able to say you'll get over this. But I lost my dad more than twenty years ago, under a lot less violent circumstances."

"We just have to move forward," Robin said. "Right?"

"Hang on tight to your mom, Ms. Diamond. She fought hard to stay with you." He gave her a quick wave and headed for his car, and Robin got into hers, a song running through her head. "Hang on, to what we got . . ." Frankie Valli and the Four Seasons. A song her mother used to sing with CoCo, when all of them were young.

TWENTY-NINE

June 19, 1976
2:00 A.M.

Dear Aurora Grace,

I'm a blonde again. I'm going to tell you about that first, because it's the easiest thing to talk about. Prom night, Gabriel and I drove for miles and miles. We picked up some hair dye from a Sav-on all the way in Ventura. At dawn, on a long road that was all cactus and sagebrush, we got our tank filled at a gas station with old-fashioned-looking pumps, by an attendant who didn't speak any English but knew enough to give Gabriel the bathroom key. We went in there together. and colored our hair. I had chosen Diamond Blond—a color as light and shiny as the hair of a Barbie doll. It doesn't look quite like that on me, though. Since I didn't have a lot of time to leave it in, the bleach kind of blended with my old copper color and came out strawberry blond. It isn't bad, though. Gabriel dyed his hair black. He looks kind of like a tall Eddie Munster now, but I wouldn't tell him that. He probably wouldn't think it was funny and besides,

I'm not talking to him. (You'll know why when I tell you about the next thing.)

Not far from the gas station, we found a new motel. It's called the Bristol Arms. Don't let the fancy name fool you. It's a step down from the Drop Inn. Our room doesn't have a TV, for one thing. There are no cockroaches in the bathroom, but guess what? The bathroom is down the hall. The last time I went, I had to wait twenty minutes for some skank to finish doing whatever it was she was doing in there. (I think she was probably shooting up.) She wore hot pants and cork sole platforms and a bandanna tied across her boobs. When she finally left the bathroom and saw me waiting there, she got right up in my face. "What are you looking at, you little bitch?" which was kind of funny, since she's the same size as me. She stank of cigarettes and cheap perfume. Spit flew out of her mouth when she talked and it reminded me of bullets spraying out of a machine gun.

There are times when I think about the girl I was before this whole thing with Gabriel happened. That girl would have backed away from that skank without saying a word. She may have even apologized for staring or said something really lame like, "Please don't hurt me. I won't do it again." She would have run.

But not me. Not the girl I am now. I grabbed that skank by her skinny neck and told her in a low, calm voice that if she ever takes that long in the bathroom again, I'll cut her, forehead to belly button. She walked away fast.

Anyway, Gabriel is asleep now, so I can tell you about the next thing, which is a lot harder to talk about than the color of my hair.

Back at Pullman Park, Gabriel told me to take all the things out of our car. He walked up to Brian Griggs's powder blue Honda Accord, and tapped on the window. I couldn't hear what he said to Brian and Carrie and I couldn't see if he showed them the gun. But for whatever reason, they let him get in back. And then, they drove away.

They never saw me. I hid in the shadows and listened to the music playing on the car radios. I leaned the duffel bag full of Ed Hart's things up against a tree and put my head on it like a pillow and inhaled the warm air that smelled like beer, pretending I belonged there.

I didn't think Gabriel would be that long. I figured he'd probably make Brian drive some-where secluded and then show him and Carrie the gun, make them get out of the car and walk home. But ten minutes passed, then twenty, then forty. Then an hour. I closed my eyes, just as a way to relax. But I wound up falling asleep instead. I don't know how long I slept. I don't even know why I'm telling you all this, other than maybe I'm stalling.

When I woke up, the parking lot was empty, everything glowing from the rising sun. Gabriel was standing over me, the powder blue Honda Accord parked in one of the spaces. He looked pale. His hair was wet. And when I followed him to the car, I noticed a red drizzle on the back of his jeans, his white sneakers. "Did you send them home?" I asked.

He didn't answer.

"Brian and Carrie. Did you kick them out of the car and send them home?"

Still no answer.

"Where are Brian and Carrie?"

I felt it before I saw it happen. Like a door slamming into my face. The shock of it was worse than the hurt, but I can feel the pain of it now, my swollen, tender jaw, the metal taste in my mouth. At least I didn't lose any of my teeth.

After it happened, Gabriel kept saying he was sorry, over and over and over. He said he was just nervous and upset and he didn't mean to hurt me. "I'd never hurt you, you have to believe me."

I just stared at him. He wasn't even making sense. How could I believe he'd never hurt me when hurting me was exactly what he'd just done? The worst part, though, was this: Gabriel would never have hurt me like that unless he'd completely lost control. And what had made him lose control? My asking him about Brian and Carrie.

I don't want to think about it. Instead, I will tell you what I said to Gabriel. The last thing I said to him, through all this driving and coloring our hair and finding and checking into the Bristol Arms. What I said was this: "I want to see Jenny."

He said it was dangerous, driving back to where he'd left her. That if we did that and the police caught us, they'd separate me from Jenny forever. He promised, though, that he'd let me talk to her again.

And he kept his promise. Once we got checked in to this fleabag, we went to the pay phone outside. Gabriel dropped a bunch of coins in there and dialed a number that I secretly wrote down. I heard him talking to someone, telling them to put Jenny on. Just like before, she didn't speak to me. But I heard her breathing again and I told her I love her and that I'm going to come for her soon and when I did, we'd be together forever. I would never let her out of my sight again.

That was enough. It had to be.

Oh, Aurora Grace, I don't want to get into bed. I don't want to go to sleep again, until life is normal and there's nothing to be afraid of and nobody gets hurt for asking simple questions. Until no one gets hurt at all.

Love,

Future Mom

4:00 A.M.

Dear Aurora Grace,

It turns out the girl from down the hall isn't a skank at all. She's a hippie or something like that, I guess. But she's super nice. Her name is Elizabeth.

Just after I finished that last letter to you,

she knocked on our door and told me she noticed how swollen my jaw was. She'd brought an ice bag and a bottle of lime-flavored vodka, and we sat on the bed, drinking and talking while Gabriel snored on the floor. She asked me if Gabriel was my brother or my boyfriend, and I sat there saying nothing for quite a while. Thinking. Finally, I said, "He's kind of both. And neither."

Luckily, she didn't ask me any more about my life than that, because I didn't want to lie to her and at the same time, I didn't want her to run away. We talked about so many things. Our hopes and dreams. Where we see ourselves in ten years. We talked about witchcraft too, because Elizabeth is into witchcraft. She says she thinks our meeting each other was an act of magick because we look so much alike—same size, same color hair. Same smile, even. It turns out that for years, she's been wishing for a sister.

Elizabeth keeps a deck of tarot cards in her purse, and she read mine. I got Death, which Elizabeth says is not a bad card at all. In the Aquarian tarot deck, she said, the Death card means rebirth. A new beginning.

Elizabeth is going to Hollywood. She doesn't want to be an actress, though. She wants to be one of those people who take still photos on movie sets. After about an hour of talking, we went to her room, and she let me try on some of her clothes and we did a photo shoot. I brought over some of Ed Hart's props with me—a whip, a fake gun, some phony-looking handcuffs. I didn't tell her where I'd gotten them, and she didn't ask. She took some Polaroids of me, and then I took a great one of her—posing with the fake gun like Sergeant Pepper Anderson from *Police Woman*. (She insisted on making the "I love you" with the other hand, though, because like I told you, she's a hippie.)

Elizabeth says she grew up in a commune in the desert. They raised llamas and chickens there. They made all their own clothes, and if anyone there used violence on each other, they got shut in the fruit cellar overnight. Elizabeth left, she says, because it was boring. No one to talk to except her brothers—she was the only girl—and she wasn't allowed to smoke cigarettes or wear makeup and she had to read the Bible from cover to cover. I understand what Elizabeth was saying, but except for all those boys, it sounds like a perfect life to me. The Gideon compound, the commune is called. Just like the name on the cover of that motel Bible I read, back in West Covina, before I'd ever killed a man. It has to be some kind of sign.

THIRTY

ROBIN

Just three days earlier, Santa Rosa High School's golden couple had been crowned king and queen of the prom. Now, the lifeless bodies of Carrie Masters and Brian Griggs lay handcuffed together in a vacant lot, both shot in the back of the head execution style. In one of life's cruelest ironies, the bleak, overgrown plot of land was just eight miles away from the school where Brian and Carrie had fallen in love, most likely oblivious to a quiet, sullen freshman by the name of April Cooper.

Had the hair-trigger temper of April's lover Gabriel Allen LeRoy gotten the best of him yet again? Or had it been April herself who had done the brutal deed? Experts speculate that April Cooper trained the gun on the terrified teens as LeRoy bound them, using the handcuffs they'd stolen from Officer Neil Nelligan. And when she caught LeRoy ogling beautiful Carrie, the lethal wallflower flew into a jealous rage, murdering the angel-faced cheerleader and her adoring boyfriend in quick succession as her lover watched, aroused.

ROBIN SHOOK HER head at the article on her screen—the cheesiest and most offensive one yet, from a 1979 issue of a *True Detective* knockoff called *Crime Stoppers* that some murder nerd had posted on Reddit. It wasn't the best way to use her downtime on her first day back at work, but Robin couldn't control it, the urge to search for information on the couple that had driven Quentin Garrison to kill her father.

He was all over the news now, Quentin—the "true-crime-podcaster-turned-true-crime-subject" angle impossible to resist. Leaving Grand Central Station on her way to work, Robin had seen Quentin's bespectacled young face on the cover of both the *Daily News* and the *Post*. On one of them, the headline had read, "SERIAL" KILLER. The other had included a still from that cheesy old TV movie her mother had refused to let her watch—actress April and actor Gabriel aiming pistols at the camera—accompanied by a caption block titled, *Killer Quentin's Final Podcast*. Lower on the front page had been a picture of "the victim." Dad. No picture of Robin's mother, thankfully. Though she guessed that was only a matter of time. Mom was at her house, where she'd agreed to spend "one night only, for your sake" the previous afternoon after her early release from the hospital. There was a police detail outside their place, a cadre of armed guards watching her nervous mother—a necessary evil.

At this point, there had to be at least a few intrepid reporters thrown into the mix, who had learned Mom was staying at Robin's. She imagined them camped at the foot of her driveway, phones poised, waiting for shooting survivor Renee Bloom to go out for a breath of fresh air. Maybe the cops would scare them off.

Robin's screen beeped—an incoming email to her work address, the sender (somebody from the *National Enquirer*) and subject (Quentin Garrison) flashing briefly. This had happened so many times today already, she was starting to think she was being overly optimistic in her belief that there were just a few reporters outside her house rather than dozens. Poor Mom.

At least Quentin's mother wasn't alive to see this—her son in the lead role of psycho killer. As a journalist, Robin found it troubling how quickly the press had jumped on Quentin Garrison, bending and molding him into something that had to be so much simpler than who he was. She wondered if Quentin had seen the newspapers wherever he was. And as a daughter, she had to admit, she hoped he had. She couldn't find it in her to fret too much over inaccurate press coverage when it came to the man who'd murdered her father. But she did feel sorry for the people in his life who had trusted him. His friends. That handsome husband. Had they known he'd just implode?

Robin's phone extension buzzed. Eileen, again. "You okay, sweetie?" she said for probably the tenth time today—a real achievement considering it was only 11:00 A.M.

Robin quit out of the article as though Eileen could see her screen. "Fine," she said. "Just coming up with column ideas."

Eileen said, "How do you feel about the idea of writing a personal essay?"

Robin's jaw tightened. Last night, she and Eric had sat bolt upright in bed, awakened by a scream. Robin had hurried into the guest room to find Mom still asleep, thrashing and mumbling. She'd tried to wake her. *Mom?* she'd said. *You're having a nightmare.*

But Renee had stayed trapped in the dream. *Put it out,* her mother had said in a rough, unfamiliar voice, her eyelids fluttering open and shut. *Put out the motherfucking fire.* Her whole life up until that moment, Robin had never once heard Renee swear.

Some personal essay that would be.

"I'll think about it," Robin said.

Eileen didn't say anything for several seconds. "You know what, Robbie?"

"Yeah?"

"I don't want a personal essay."

Robin exhaled.

"To tell the truth, I really hope something happens to knock this story out of the headlines, so we can all just go back to normal."

Robin smiled. She'd arrived at work to a big flower arrangement on her desk—lilacs and white roses, her favorites. There had also been a sympathy card from the whole office, but clearly it had been engineered by Eileen, who was the only one in this place who knew what her favorite flowers were. "Maybe Beyoncé will drop an album," Robin said.

"I'm praying to her as we speak."

"You're a good friend, Eileen."

"Stop it."

"I mean it," she said. "Also, I never thanked you for the flowers."

"What? Oh . . ."

"Seriously. You didn't have to do that."

"Actually, hon," Eileen said, "the flowers were from your hubby."

Eric . . . Robin thanked Eileen for her honesty anyway and hung up the phone, thinking again of the previous night. Her mother, so thin and frail, her whole face clenched up, as though she were trapped inside and trying to burst out. How shaken Robin had been—not so much by the swearing or even the talk of fire but by that strange, husky voice. *Who are you, Mom?* She'd returned to the bedroom to find Eric wide awake, sitting up in bed, waiting for her. They'd talked—or rather he had—about Renee, about everything she'd been through and how she'd lost the person she loved and depended on in a violent act and how therapy might be a good idea for her and how her physical body may be healed, but emotional scars last so much longer . . . Something like that. Robin couldn't recall the exact words Eric had said because she hadn't really been listening. The important thing had been the soothing tone of his voice, his arms around her. His being there. That had been what mattered.

Robin stared at her computer screen. She needed to get out of her own head, think of a column idea. She typed out a few sentences about the new *Batman* movie, deleted them, wrote a few more about a proposed *Poseidon Adventure* reboot, then deleted them too. She pulled the flowers closer to her, inhaled their lush scent and typed the only sentence that made sense: *It's hard for me to care that much about movies right now, when my own life seems to have lost its structure.* Great. She was about to write a personal essay.

Her head was starting to throb. Robin grabbed her phone and purse and got up from her desk, moving past Michael and David mapping out a slide show on Jennifer Lopez's marriages, past Jill on the phone with a pop music flack, begging for a phoner with some former Mouseketeer.

Once Robin made it outside the newsroom, she ducked into the small, empty hallway that led to the bathrooms and breathed in the quiet. It smelled of pine floor cleaner in there—a vaguely antiseptic scent that reminded her of the hospital. She called Eric, and he answered after one ring. "How are you holding up?" he said.

"Okay, I guess. Thank you for the flowers."

"I wish I could take you to lunch."

"But you can't because Shawn will ruin your life."

"Actually, I want to stick around so I can keep my eye on him," he said. "I feel like the minute I let him out of my sight, he's going to do a show about your parents."

"You should stay then."

Robin slid down the wall and sat on the floor. She had an urge to spend the rest of the day out here in this hallway, filing stories from her phone.

Eric said, "I talked to your mom today."

"You did?"

"Yep. She called, asking where we keep the tarragon," he said. "She sounded fine."

"She's probably in better shape than we are."

"Well, she did have a better night's sleep."

Robin slipped the Polaroid out of her purse, gazed

into the young girl's eyes. *Put out the motherfucking fire.*

"I think she's going to be okay," he said. "I mean . . . okay as she can be."

Robin thanked him for saying that, which was the only response she could think of. The truth was, she wasn't sure Mom would be okay, or even that she ever *was* okay, with this big chunk of her past tamped down so tight, packed away from the world. And the only person who could help her, gone. *That's it, Renee. That's it. Let it out. Don't run from it . . .*

"Eric?"

"Yeah?"

"Are you sure my mom doesn't have some weird connection to April Cooper?"

"Robin, come on."

"Well, why was Quentin Garrison so convinced that she did?"

"You know Occam's razor," he said. "What do you think the simplest explanation would be in this case?"

"Quentin Garrison is a nutjob."

"Bingo."

"In his confession, he said he'd wanted to do an expert interview with my dad."

"Maybe on some level, he knew he was being crazy."

"Or maybe he just didn't want the cops to find out about this giant bombshell until he had proof."

"Honey?"

"Yeah?"

"What do you want for dinner tonight?"

Robin sighed. "Way to change the subject."

After they ended the call, Robin pulled herself to her feet, the subject still unchanged in her mind.

She headed back to her desk thinking of her mother, of all the things she didn't know about her, and then Quentin's mother.

Last night after they'd gotten Mom to bed, Eric couldn't sleep. He'd used a service they paid for at *Anger Management* to see if Kate Sharkey Garrison had a rap sheet. He'd only found one arrest, but it was a strange one.

Fifteen years ago. Quentin was probably about twelve . . .

Drugs?

Actually no, though I'd guess there were drugs involved.

Huh?

She broke into a wax museum on Sunset Strip. Tried to steal a life-size figure of Marilyn Monroe. Looks like it made the papers. It was in some column called Weekly Weird News . . .

Once she was at her desk, Robin did an advanced search for the column and found it. Kate Sharkey Garrison's drugged-out mug shot was front and center. Robin wondered if this wasn't part of Quentin's illness—the belief that everyone else's mother was like his own, weak and deviant.

The headline read, MARILYN'S BIGGEST FAN. Robin started to read. When she got to the third paragraph, she stopped breathing. "Oh my God," she whispered. Then she hit print.

"Everything okay?" asked Jill as Robin was folding up the article and slipping it into her purse.

"Fine," Robin said. "Be back later. I've got a publicist meeting."

Robin headed past the rows of desks, some chipper new intern on one of the phones, talking loudly and excitedly about an exhibit of mosaics made entirely of cat food. Robin's heart beat in time with her staccato delivery. She could feel the intern watching her as she passed, could feel everyone watching her, those looks on their faces, that wary concern, as though at any given minute, she might just detonate.

Robin kept her eyes aimed straight ahead of her, smiling stiffly as she passed the front desk and heading fast for the elevator. Once she was on the sidewalk, where it was crowded enough to make her feel anonymous and she could finally breathe again, Robin slipped Nicola Crane's business card out of her wallet and tapped the number into her phone.

"Robin?"

"Nikki."

"Hey, it's great to hear from you!"

"Listen, can you get together?" Robin said. "I really need to talk."

"DO YOU THINK she'll like this?" Nicola said. She opened a red velvet box and showed Robin a necklace—an aquamarine heart on a delicate silver chain. The two of them were in a Starbucks on Madison Avenue, a few blocks away from where she'd been shopping when Robin had called her, asking if they could meet. *It just so happens, I'm in your area*, Nicola Crane had said. *I'm just buying a little something for your mom, you know. To cheer her up.*

The necklace glittered against a white satin pillow. Aquamarine was her mother's favorite, her birthstone. She had an aquamarine pinkie ring, worn as long as Robin had known her. And the necklace itself . . . it reminded her of something she'd seen in Mom's secret box—a plastic heart on a string, that same blue-green color. "She will love it."

"Oh good," she said. "Maybe the blue stone will take her mind off all the Blue Meanies."

"Blue Meanies?"

"You know. The cops." She shrieked with laughter. Several customers turned to stare. Robin was tempted to laugh along with her, but she couldn't. Not after what she'd found.

"Hey, what's wrong?"

"I thought we were friends."

Nicola frowned at her. "Of course we are."

"Well, where I come from, friends don't keep important information from each other."

Robin removed the Weekly Weird News column from her purse and handed it to her. And then she waited for her to get to the third paragraph—the one that described a young police officer named Nicola Crane who had posted the bail for Kathleen Sharkey, the mad wax figure thief. *Kate's a good friend*, Officer Crane had said back then. *She's a good person. She's just going through a difficult time.* Nicola looked up from the page, her expression calmer than Robin had expected.

"All right. You got me. I knew Garrison's mother."

"How?"

"She helped me out when I was young. Got me into foster care. We spoke occasionally as grown-ups. I tried to help her . . . Look, I haven't brought it up with anyone because I don't want word getting around. Poor thing can't rest in peace even as it is."

"Did my mom know her?"

"You'll have to ask her," she said. "But I'll tell you one thing. That son of Kate's was a handful and then some. Pretty much scared me off having kids of my own."

"What was so bad about him?"

"He was always sneaking out. Never minding her. Got into fights at school all the time, and not because he got picked on. He was just . . . mean. His mother was endlessly upset by him. Endlessly disappointed."

"Couldn't he have been acting out to get her attention?"

"First of all, Kate was a single mother working two jobs while battling an addiction. She gave him all the attention she possibly could." She took another sip of her drink, cringing this time. "Also, as someone whose parents died when she was very young, I'd have killed for half the attention that little brat got." She cleared her throat. "Screw it if that sounds harsh."

Robin took a swallow of her coffee. "Really?"

"Okay, think about this," Nicola said. "I probably saw Quentin Garrison at least half a dozen times, and I was in contact with Kate right up until he was a young teenager. And I know we all age, but when he approached me after the funeral, I recognized him instantly. He, on the other hand, had no idea who I was. I know I look different than I did fifteen years ago. But I have the same friggin' name, and it didn't even register with him. Now if that isn't the dictionary definition of narcissism . . ." She took another wincing sip. "God, this latte should be a criminal offense."

"You want some of my coffee?"

"Yes, please." Nicola took a sip. "Nothing like getting a bad taste out of your mouth."

Robin gazed at the opened red velvet box, the necklace inside, sparkling serenely. "How long are you in town for, Nikki?"

"Just a few more days. My dog-sitter says they're about to mutiny."

AS ROBIN WALKED back to her office, she thought of what Nicola had said, and of what she hadn't said back: Not remembering someone you've seen several times isn't the dictionary definition of narcissism. Some people simply have bad memories for names.

She hadn't remembered Nicola either, not at first. She pulled Morasco's business card out of her bag and called it on her phone. He picked up after one ring. "I don't know if this information is important at all," she said, "but my mother's old friend Nicola used to be friends with Quentin Garrison's mother."

"Is that right?" Morasco sounded distracted and strange. She heard voices behind him. People shouting to each other.

"Are you outdoors?" she said.

"Ms. Diamond," he said. "You have to clear out your voice mail. I tried to call you a few times, but I couldn't leave a message."

"Oh, sorry."

"Listen," he said. "We found Quentin Garrison."

Robin stopped in the middle of the sidewalk. "You did?"

The shouting got louder. Someone saying, "Stand back."

"Detective Morasco? Has he been arrested?"

"No," he said. "Quentin Garrison is dead. He appears to have shot himself."

THIRTY-ONE

June 20, 1976
Midnight

Dear Aurora Grace,

Jenny is dead. Gabriel told me. He said she's been dead from the beginning of our trip. He said he killed her before Papa Pete came home, that he buried her body in our backyard.

The times he's called her on the phone, the times she's listened to me and I could hear her breathing . . . He said that was just dead air. A random number that he'd called.

I don't know whether he was telling me the truth, or if he just said it to hurt me. He was angry at me for so many things: Not forgiving him for hitting me. Spending the day with Elizabeth. Getting drunk with Elizabeth when I was supposed to be with him. "You can't abandon me like that," he had said. "You're Bonnie. I'm Clyde."

And because I was drunk, I didn't lie and tell him how much it meant to me for him to say that. I didn't make big sad eyes at him like I normally would. I didn't say I was sorry, that I'd never abandon him again.

What I did was this: I pointed out to Gabriel that Clyde Barrow couldn't get it up. Just like him.

That was when he told me about Jenny. Because he knew he couldn't hit me anymore without Elizabeth cutting him in his sleep with her sewing shears, which she's sworn to him she'll do. Because he knew he couldn't shoot me in the Bristol Arms because there would be too many witnesses. But most importantly, because he knew that telling me he'd killed my sister would hurt me more than hitting or shooting ever could.

At first, I didn't believe him. I told him I know what Jenny's breathing sounds like, and I can feel that she's alive. I told him that he's a liar and that lies can't hurt me. But he just laughed. "She's dead," he said. "Whether you want to believe it or not."

"You will chase your enemies and they will fall before you by the sword." That's what the Bible says. Jenny was never his enemy, even for a second. She wasn't anybody's enemy. She wasn't big enough.

Never trust a boy, Aurora Grace. Even if it's the one boy in the world you've been forced to rely on. Don't turn your back on him. Don't confide in him. And whatever you do, do not believe that he is interested in keeping you safe. A boy will use you. He will hurt you. He will lie, and worse.

Love,

April (Your Future Mom, but only when she is living another life, far away from here)

THIRTY-TWO

ROBIN

BY THE TIME Robin got back up to her desk, Quentin Garrison's death was all over social media. The facts of it first: his body discovered in Tarry Ridge Park, dead of a single gunshot wound to the head. Then came the players: Quentin's coworkers at KAMC in Los Angeles. His coproducer, Summer Hawkins, leaving the station in tears. His husband, Dean Conrad, photographed in the parking lot of the university where he taught, his face pale, his jaw slack, as though he'd had the life knocked out of him. The old mug shot of Quentin's mother.

The hot takes on Twitter and then the reporters—dozens more of them direct messaging Robin, emailing her at work, still more calling in, to the point where Eileen suggested she go home early without her even having to ask. Robin headed for Grand Central and took the 2:45 P.M. train home, Quentin Garrison on her mind the entire time—how he'd been found dead in a park near a playground, and when she'd spoken to him two and a half days ago, she'd heard children's voices in the background. Had he still been at the same park when he'd texted her that night? Or had he left, then returned after emailing his confession?

At least the police detail no longer seemed necessary. And once she got past the two reporters who remained at the foot of her driveway and entered the house and saw her mother sitting in the living room watching the news, a blanket thrown over her waist, she felt a bit relieved over that. "I was trying to make salmon tarragon," Mom said. "But I got a bit tired."

"You rest, Mom," she said. "Rest for as long as you like."

Her mother was heading home tonight—there was no stopping that, so Eric and Robin had insisted on joining her. But it was good to see that she wasn't pushing herself to pack just yet. Renee said, "Did you hear about him?"

Robin sat down on the couch beside her. Tried to read her face. "Yes," she said. "I did."

"That poor boy. He never had a chance."

Robin looked at her. On the way home, she'd read as many articles as she could about her parents' shooting—making up for lost time—and she'd learned that an anonymous caller had spotted Quentin driving through her parents' neighborhood the night of the murders and, at another point, stopped in front of the Blooms' home. As though he were staking it out. "Mom," Robin said. "He killed Dad in cold blood. And he tried to kill you."

But she didn't appear to hear her. "Such a violent, ugly way to go. He can't even have an open casket."

"Are you okay?" Robin said.

Renee stood up. "Not really," she said, moving toward the stairs. "There's been too much death lately. That poor boy. It isn't fair to anyone." She shook her head and trudged upstairs, her thoughts as much a mystery as ever.

AS RENEE LAY napping upstairs, Robin heard Eric's footsteps jogging up to the door. She'd been reading a Jodi Picoult book she'd bought a few months ago and it had been nice, getting lost in the pages, avoiding the flood of messages and news alerts, the inescapable, constant buzz. Her mother wasn't on social media—barely ever even checked her email, and Robin felt she lived a better life for it, especially now.

"I've been trying to call you," he said. "Your voice mail is full."

"I don't even know where I put my phone."

"You've heard the news," he said. "Obviously."

"Obviously."

He headed into the kitchen. "Your mom must be relieved," he called out from inside.

"You'd think so, but not really," Robin said.

"It probably just hasn't hit her yet."

He came out with two glasses of wine.

"How did you know what I wanted?"

"It doesn't take a mind reader."

Robin took a long sip, the wine white and crisp and cold. Eric sat next to her on the couch and put an arm around her. They drank in silence for several minutes. "I should probably order a pizza," he said.

"How about Chinese?"

"You got it."

He didn't move, though. "I've got a proposition for you."

Robin smiled. "My mom is literally right upstairs."

"No. I mean . . . Don't you think it's time we got out our side of the story?"

She took a swallow of wine. "What do you mean?"

"There are wingnuts on Twitter still saying that Garrison shot your parents because of your column."

"Who cares?"

"I'm just saying. You've got a great chance to set the record straight."

She put her glass down. "Are you seriously asking me to go on *Anger Management*?"

"It isn't such a bad idea, is it? And it wouldn't be you. It would be your mom. She's the one everyone wants to hear from."

She stood up. "You'd better be joking."

He gave her a tight smile. "Yeah," he said. "Yeah. I'm just kidding around."

"Seriously?"

"I am. Yeah."

"Why would you even joke about something like that?"

"It was just a dumb joke, Robin. Let it go."

ONCE THE THREE of them had finished dinner, Renee and Robin and Eric headed to their rooms to pack up, Eric unusually quiet all the while. Robin waited till she heard the door to the guest room close before she turned to Eric. "Hey," she said. "What's going on with you?"

He sat down on the bed, motioned for her to sit next to him. Beneath his clean soap scent, she smelled sweat. Fear. "I didn't want you or your mother to come on *Anger Management*," he said. "I hope you believe me on that."

She looked at him. "You said you were joking."

"I wasn't."

"What are you talking about?"

He stared at his hands. "Look, if I don't tell you this now, you're going to hear it from somebody else."

"Tell me what?"

"One of Shawn's producers. A new girl. Young. Her name is Ginny."

Robin's eyes widened. *Proud Mama to My Furbabies, Yoga Is Life, God Bless the USA.* "GinnyMarie?" she said.

"Yeah. How did you . . ."

"I don't want to know."

"If I don't tell you, she will."

"Why? Does she think I'll leave you?"

"Probably." He took a deep breath, in and out. "Look, she's a big fan of yours. She reads your column. She loves it when you get the hate tweets. She thinks it's awesome you can so routinely stir up controversy over something as safe and benign as films."

She glared at him. "Are you trying to get me to be friends with your mistress?"

"What? No. She's not my mistress." He sighed. "She's fucking trying to blackmail me."

"What?"

"She wants you on the show. She always has. But now more than ever. Obviously."

"Not gonna happen."

"Right. So . . . if I can't get you, which I can't . . . She's going to tell the whole world about me. Page 6. The Cut. But worst of all . . . you."

"What are you talking about?"

"My job."

"I know about your job."

"No," he said. "Listen." He took another deep breath. "About a year ago, I was contacted by a woman. She worked at a fancy restaurant in Midtown. One of Shawn's favorites, and the type of place he would like."

She nodded. "Yeah?"

"So anyway, I met with her. She'd been a waitress there for years, and she gave me an earful. Unsanitary conditions in the kitchen. Bullying atmosphere. Sexual harassment like you wouldn't believe. She couldn't place an order without getting a dick in her hand."

"Ugh."

"And it wasn't just her. She said she came to me because she drew the short straw. Everybody was terrified of the owner, but they all agreed that it couldn't go on."

"That sounds like a great story. If she was telling the truth."

"I had her take a polygraph test. She passed with flying colors."

"Wow."

"It didn't end there. A second source came forward. A dishwasher. She said the owner had raped her. Didn't want to give her name. But she said she'd appear on camera if we blurred her face, disguised her voice."

Robin frowned. "I don't remember this story airing."

He looked at her. "It never aired."

"Why?"

He exhaled. "Because the owner—Charlie Maxwell—is a buddy of Shawn's."

"Oh . . ." Robin said, the name clicking in her head. Charlie Maxwell. Celebrity chef. Had his own show on the Food Network for about three minutes. Owner of Chez Chas. "This was last year."

"Right."

"I'd . . . Someone told me she'd seen you there. At his restaurant . . ."

"She took me to the place. Introduced me to Maxwell, so I could see for myself what a douchebag he was. She told him I was her brother. He grabbed her ass right in front of me. She did everything but give me a thumbs-up. She thought I was filming him with my phone."

"You weren't?"

He shook his head. "Shawn told me to convince this woman we were going to take the story, wine her and dine her, do anything and everything I could to get her to trust me enough to sign a nondisclosure agreement and a noncompete."

"Eric," she said. "I don't know that I want to hear any more."

"I sweet-talked her. Told her Charlie wouldn't even be able to run a McDonald's when we were through with him. She signed the NDA. Gave us exclusive rights to the story. Then we killed it. Shawn told Charlie. She lost her job."

Robin couldn't speak.

"She told me I was an embarrassment to journalism. A total sleazebag. I couldn't disagree, because I was. I am."

Outside the door, Robin's mother called out, "You guys ready soon?"

"Just a minute," Robin said, returning her gaze to her husband. All these months, she'd thought he had an affair. That might have been preferable. At least he would have still been the person she thought he was.

Eric took her hand in his. It was warm, his palm sweaty. "I don't want us to have any more secrets."

Robin closed her eyes, trying to wrap her thoughts around it, all kinds of memories moving through her head of the old Eric, the man she'd fallen in love with, the crusading young journalist who wanted to help good people, not destroy them. *This is going to make me sound like a jackass, but I want to write stories that save lives.*

She opened her eyes. "We all start out so pure, don't we?"

"I want to find my way back."

"So do I."

He kissed her, softly. "You're already there, Robin," he said. "You've always been there."

"No. I haven't."

"I've never cheated on you."

"All right."

"I've done some shitty things for Shawn, but that Charlie Maxwell thing was by far the worst."

"It's bad, Eric."

"I told you I'd pissed people off," he said. "Do you still love me?"

"We need to pack up," she said. "My mom needs to get to her house." She was well aware that she hadn't answered the question.

RENEE'S HOME NO longer looked like a murder house. She'd had a cleaning service come in during the day, and so when they arrived there at 10:00 P.M., the place was spotless, everything smelling of pine, the missing Indian rug the only clue that anything bad had ever happened there. There were no reporters outside either. And so, after her mother had gone to bed and she and Eric had set themselves up in the comfortable guest room that had once been her bedroom, it was easy for her to imagine her dad alive, one room over, snoring beside her mom, a book open in front of him.

Robin threw a T-shirt on and got into the double bed next to Eric, who was wearing his boxer briefs, nothing else. "Do you still love me?" he whispered in the dark.

"Yes."

"I love you too."

She inhaled the scent of his cologne, her favorite, worn only for her. "Eric?"

"Yeah?"

"What are you going to do when the news comes out?"

"It won't."

"Huh?"

"If that story comes out, it's not just me that goes

down. It's Shawn. It's the show. And Ginny doesn't want to lose her job any more than I do."

Eric snuggled into Robin's side, his arm against her belly. She closed her eyes and tried to find sleep, because she didn't want to be awake with Eric. Not anymore. "What about the waitress?" she said finally. "She lost her job." But Eric didn't answer. He was already asleep.

THIRTY-THREE

SUMMER

SUMMER HAWKINS HAD known about Quentin's death for twenty-four hours, but she didn't allow herself to cry about it until after she'd dropped Dean off at the airport. It felt like an indulgence, weeping over a friend, even a best friend (and Quentin had been Summer's very best friend), with his husband right beside you, unable to cry or even speak.

Summer had been the first person Dean had called, right after he'd heard the news from the Tarry Ridge police. He'd told her before his sister, before his parents. "I am letting you know first," he had said. "I know you're hurting as much as me."

She wasn't, of course. How could anyone be hurting as much as Dean? But what she felt over Quentin now was nearly as painful—a mix of sorrow and anger and worst of all, guilt. This was what Summer would never tell Dean: as awful as she felt about Quentin's suicide, it hadn't surprised her.

Ever since she'd met him, at a friend's party during their sophomore year of college, Summer had

sensed something off in Quentin Garrison, something broken. It may have been what had drawn her
to him in the first place, fixer that she was—that
faraway look he'd get when he thought no one was
watching him, the way he'd deflect personal questions with jokes or how sometimes, when he'd had a
few drinks, he'd get tears in his eyes . . .

Most people didn't see Quentin as troubled, or
even unhappy. They thought he was an overachiever
and a bit of a grade grubber, his hand constantly in
the air during their creative nonfiction class, always
asking overly complicated questions. But Summer
knew people. She could see them for who they truly
were, and there was so much to Quentin. So much
he refused to show.

Senior year, he finally told her. The two of them
had been sitting on the floor of her tiny studio apartment just before dawn, stoned out of their minds
and talking endlessly as they always did, about poli-
tics and philosophy and the hidden meanings behind old Talking Heads songs. And then Quentin
had gone quiet. "I want to tell you something," he
had said. "It's hard for me to say."

Summer had taken an enormous hit off the bong,
her mind racing with crazy imaginings—the sort of
unrealistic expectations that embarrassed her now,
but had seemed entirely possible back then, when
she was a self-absorbed, twenty-one-year-old virgin
with an all-consuming crush on her gay best friend.
Say it, Summer had thought. *Say it, and I will run
away with you*. But what Quentin had said was this:
"My mother hates me."

Quentin hadn't said any more than that, but he

hadn't needed to. Summer finally had a reason for the sadness that lurked just beneath that cheery surface, ready to pounce and devour. And now that she knew where it came from, she could defeat it. She could put him back together.

Summer had a big, noisy family back in New Rochelle, New York, and she took Quentin there for Thanksgiving and Christmas, convincing them to accept him as one of their own. When she got a job at KAMC immediately after graduation, she dragged Quentin in too as a package deal. And five years ago, she'd done something even better than either of those things. She'd gone onto his Grindr, found Dean Conrad, and sent him the message that had started their relationship. ("9.5" it had said. A slight exaggeration, probably, but screw it. It had worked.)

Summer had fixed Quentin. Or so she'd convinced herself. She'd been halfway to Brittlebush yesterday when she'd gotten the call. Dean's voice over the phone, cracking, breaking. "It isn't like him," he kept saying, over and over. "None of this is like him."

She'd turned around, sped back to her apartment to find Dean waiting there for her. She'd taken him inside, the poor guy, so genuinely hurt and confused. She'd made the plane reservation for Dean so he could identify Quentin's body and bring his ashes home and stayed up with him all night drinking scotch and staring at CNN, and then she'd taken him to the airport at 4:30 A.M., her head throbbing. The entire time, the two of them had barely spoken.

Summer had been glad for the silence. What was she supposed to say? There was so much that Dean had never known about his husband. He had no idea that two weeks after his mother's funeral, Quentin had told Summer he wanted to drive his car off an overpass. He hadn't known how many times she'd had to cover for Quentin when he didn't show up at work during that same period, or about the empty bottles of Klonopin she'd found in his desk. When Summer had talked to Dean about convincing Quentin to do *Closure*, he had no clue how desperate she was to get him fixed again or that she saw the podcast as a lifeline, a last chance. How could she tell Dean about all that now? How could she say that it actually *was* like Quentin to kill himself?

Shooting the Blooms, though. That wasn't like him at all.

She thought about that as she got on the on-ramp for the 405, her eyes blurred from crying, her cheeks wet and stinging, her throat feeling as though it had been rubbed with sandpaper. As argumentative as Quentin could be when you backed him into a corner, as self-destructive as he could become if given half a chance, he'd never hurt another person. Not the Quentin she knew. And though he had a tendency to hide things, shooting two people and killing one was simply too big a thing to hide. Wasn't it? Did she not know her best friend as well as she thought she did?

She recalled all the conversations she'd had with him since Mitchell Bloom's death. All the updates and exchanges of information and the thinking aloud they'd done on the shooting. Not one of those conversations had made her feel as though there were something Quentin wasn't telling her.

Except for the last one.

Summer dried her eyes on the bottom of her white T-shirt. She breathed slowly, carefully, as though the end of her crying was something fragile and tentative and the slightest move could start her up again. The thing was, Summer wasn't a crier, not usually. She probably vomited more frequently than she cried, and she found them both equally unpleasant.

If she didn't think of that last conversation with Quentin, Summer figured she could make the rest of the ride home without losing it again. But then she turned on the radio. Rihanna. "We Found Love." Quentin and Dean's wedding song.

"Jesus Christ," she whispered.

As she turned off the radio, a phone rang. Not her iPhone, but an old-fashioned beeping like a cell phone from the '90s. Summer thought it had come from inside her own brain until she realized it was the burner she kept in her purse. The *Closure* tip-line. *Well, that's ironic.*

She hadn't gotten a call on that phone in at least a month. She glanced at the clock on her dashboard. 5:50 A.M. Quentin had called her at that hour when he'd first arrived in New York, apologizing when he remembered the time difference, and for a moment, she allowed herself the fantasy that it was him calling again, that all this was some big misunderstanding on the police's part that he and Dean would laugh about once he arrived in New York.

She slipped the phone out of her purse and put it to her ear. "This is the *Closure* podcast. May I help you?"

"I heard about Quentin." It was an older man's voice, ragged and sad. "I heard it on the news."

Summer switched lanes, her eyes on the rear-view, then on the near-empty freeway in front of her, the sky blushing pink from the recent sunrise. "Who is this, please?"

"Kate's dad. Quentin's grandpa." He coughed a few times. Cleared his throat. "My name is Reg Sharkey. My whole family is dead."

Summer gripped the steering wheel. "I know who you are, Mr. Sharkey."

"Linda's dead too. I called her old number. Incredible, isn't it? Most of the time these days, I can't remember what year it is. But her phone number's still in my head, forty years later. Clear as day."

"Who is Linda?"

No response. Summer wanted to cry again, and she hated Reg Sharkey for that. Hated him for a lot of reasons, actually. "Mr. Sharkey, I'm not sure why you called this number, and I have no idea why I answered. There's no more podcast, so—"

"What?"

"There's no more *Closure* podcast."

"Why?"

"Because it was about Quentin," she said very slowly, "and Quentin is dead."

"Please." His voice cracked. He started to cry. "Please interview me."

Now it was Summer's turn not to respond. She listened to the old man's sniffles, his labored breathing, and thought back to the day Quentin had interviewed him, his voice in her ear. How she'd cringed when he'd played her the interview, the old fuck yelling at him, calling him "fake news" of all things, and how despondent Quentin had sounded when he got back on the line. *I've learned that my only real family is Dean.* Summer clutched the phone tight in her hand, wishing she could squeeze the life out of this entire conversation. She said, "Haven't you been interviewed enough already?"

Sharkey struggled to catch his breath. "I have a secret," he said. "An old one. I need to confess."

Go to church, then. That's what Summer wanted to say. But she couldn't make herself do it. She didn't have it in her today to be that mean.

"I need to confess," he said quietly. "For the sake of all my children."

All your dead children. Against her own will, she found herself pitying Reg Sharkey, if only for his age, and for the loneliness and desperation that drove him to call a tipline at dawn. "All right, fine," she said.

"Oh, thank you. Bless you." As he gave her his address, Summer took into account how far it was from her home in West Hollywood. Two hours at least, but strangely, she was glad for it. Summer was in no hurry to be at her own apartment, all alone with her thoughts.

On the drive to San Bernardino, she thought of the name he'd mentioned. Linda. From her months-long immersion in all things Cooper/LeRoy, Summer knew that Linda had been the name of Gabriel LeRoy's mother. Following her son's death, she'd declined a number of interviews—one with Barbara Walters—before subsequently disappearing off the face of the earth. Two years ago, she'd died a recluse, her body found in a shack in the desert—a place she'd bought years earlier, just a half mile away from the Gideon compound, where her son had burned to death.

It was probably just a coincidence, though, Reg saying the name. There were a lot of people called Linda, after all.

THIRTY-FOUR

June 20, 1976
2:00 A.M.

Dear Aurora Grace,

I dreamed I shot Officer Nelligan again. I watched him fall and bleed and die, just like before, and I felt awful. Sick to my stomach. Only when I got closer to the body and looked at his face, I saw that it hadn't been Officer Nelligan at all. I'd shot Gabriel.

7:30 A.M.

Dear Aurora Grace,

Gabriel is angry. All morning, he has been pacing around our room, back and forth, back and forth, a gun in each hand, Officer Nelligan's and his own—which, as it turns out, he stole from his mother.

I think he expects me to ask him why he is so mad, or at least to talk to him. But I can't do that. I can't speak at all. Oh my God. He just asked me if I'm still writing the song about us. Can you believe that? Doesn't he even remember what he said to me last night?

Aurora Grace, I've been awake ever since that dream, and I've been doing a lot of thinking. I believe it was a prophecy.

I am going to kill Gabriel LeRoy. I don't know when or how. But the moment will present itself to me, and when it does, I will not be afraid. And as he takes his last breath, I will say Jenny's name to him. I will show him her picture. I will make sure that my sister is the last thought he ever has.

Love,
April

11:00 A.M.

Dear Aurora Grace,

It's Father's Day. That's why Gabriel is mad. Because it's Father's Day and he doesn't have a father. He's always said that his dad left his mom for a dancer, but apparently, that's just another lie. He'd said it to "save face," he told me. It was his mother who was the cheater. His dad left because he found out she'd been having an affair with a married man for years and years—and guess what? She still is. A few days before I broke up with him, Gabriel found a box at the bottom of his mother's closet. Inside was a necklace, a sexy nightgown, and a letter from the married man she's having an affair with—Gabriel's real father. In it, he says to Linda, "Take good care of our son. But don't ever let your husband know."

I think that was what drove Gabriel crazy, not me. I think the lava started bubbling up inside him when he found that box, and then when I broke up with him, it was an excuse to explode.

Gabriel's mom and her lover have a code: She calls him twice. The first time, she hangs up after one ring. The second time, she hangs up after two. They meet at an Arco station in San Bernardino and they usually go to a motel from there, but not always. Sometimes, they just sit somewhere and talk. If she calls on a weekday, he goes to the gas station during his lunch break. If she does it on a Sunday, they meet after church. Gabriel learned some of this from the letter, some of it from putting "one and two together." That's what he said. One and two. He doesn't even know the right expression.

It's a Sunday today and it's Father's Day, and this morning, Gabriel called his real father from the pay phone downstairs. One hang-up after one ring. Another hang-up after two. After he made the call, he spent the rest of Ed Hart's money on a shotgun. He bought it from a guy on our floor who I think is a gang member. The shotgun is in the back seat of the powder blue Accord, strapped in like a passenger. We are driving to the Arco station. Neither one of us speaks, and it's an awful, ugly silence.

When Gabriel told me the story about his father, he was crying. He said it was the first time he'd ever said it all out loud. "Baby Blue, you are the only person in the world who I can trust with the truth." He said this. Gabriel did. The boy who killed my entire family.

I don't have a father either, Gabriel. Have you thought about that?

The bruise on my face has mostly faded. Elizabeth helped me cover up the rest with makeup. But if I touch my cheek, it still hurts. Gabriel LeRoy hasn't just killed my family. He's turned me into someone I no longer know. A weak person and a murderer. He's turned me into him.

Elizabeth says that if I can get away from Gabriel, she'll take me to the Gideon compound. It's something to look forward to, I guess. But right now, all I want to do is make it out of this Arco station alive, so I can kill Gabriel. So I can become me again.

　　Love,
　　April

2:30 P.M.

Dear Aurora Grace,

　　Gabriel is a monster.
　　Love,
　　April

THIRTY-FIVE

SUMMER

SUMMER SAT ACROSS from Reg Sharkey at his kitchen table, her digital recorder between them, listening so intently that she often forgot to blink, to breathe. "He was your son." She said it for the second time, just to make sure she'd heard him correctly. "Gabriel LeRoy was your son."

"Yes. His mother, Linda, and me. We went to high school together. We never quite lost touch."

"Did you ever visit him?"

"Once, when he was a little boy. He had this funny way of talking. This lisp. He asked me for a doggy . . ."

"Did he know who you were?"

"No, of course not. I had a little girl at home at the time. My Katie. She was just a baby."

Summer gritted her teeth. She'd just had the strongest urge to call Quentin. Put him on speakerphone and get him in on this. Then she'd remembered. "So, you thought Linda had called," she said. "But when you showed up at your meeting place. The Arco station—"

"She wasn't there, no. The two of them were. Gabriel and that girl. I didn't see them at first. It was crowded at the station. We were at the pump when they . . . when they got out of their car." The morning light streamed through the kitchen window, beams of it, infested with dust motes. There was so much dust in this house. So many old, neglected things. "It's funny, you get into these situations when you're young," Reg said. "You know they're wrong and they're dangerous, but you think, 'Just this once. Just for a little while.' But then a little while becomes a long while and all of a sudden, you're no longer young. It just feels normal, this dangerous thing you've been doing. It feels like it will go on forever."

Summer's mouth was very dry and her eyes ached. It all wore at her, the cobwebby remains of the scotch, the lack of sleep, the crying. She longed for a glass of water, but she didn't want to interrupt Reg's train of thought by asking for it. This was probably the best interview she had ever done. If only Quentin were around . . .

"You thought no one would ever find out about the affair," she said. "Even though Linda's husband left her because of it."

"He wasn't going to tell anybody. He was probably more ashamed about it than we were and besides, I think he was looking for an excuse to leave."

Those dust motes. Like angry little ghosts. "Okay," Summer said. "So when you got that call on Father's Day, you thought it was Linda, wanting to meet."

"What's that expression? No bad deed goes unpunished? And the longer you keep doing it, the worse the punishment is."

"It's 'no good deed,' actually. No good deed goes unpunished. It's sarcastic."

"Oh. Well, add that expression to the list of things I've been getting wrong for much too long."

"You were at the gas station, waiting at the pump. When did you first notice your son?"

"Not until he started shooting. An old man went down. Then the woman with him. A Mexican lady in a white pantsuit. I think she was his nurse. Then somebody else. A young woman. It was like . . . some kind of sick dance. One body falling after the next. The sound of the gunshots. I turned to where the sound was coming from and there he was. I looked at the girl. I begged her to get him to stop shooting. My daughter. My little Kimmy . . . She dropped her plastic horse . . ."

"Did you recognize Gabriel?"

He stared at his hands. "Yes," he said. "I saw his face and I recognized him right away. Even though I hadn't seen him since he was a little boy. He looked . . ."

"Yes, Mr. Sharkey?"

Reg dragged the back of his hand across his closed eyes and stared up at the ceiling and said it very, very softly. "He looked like me."

"Do you want to take a break?"

He nodded. Summer was glad for that. She needed a break too.

Summer pulled two glasses out of the cupboard, plastic ones with the Anaheim Angels logo on them, both of them as dusty as everything else in the house. She rinsed the glasses, dried them with a kitchen towel, and filled them with water from the tap. The kitchen towel was clean and white, with little strawberries across the bottom. It looked as though it had never been used, and it was hard to imagine Reg Sharkey doing anything with it, that delicate piece of cloth in those scarred, meaty hands. Summer imagined the towel was part of a set his wife, Clara, had bought, before their kids were even born.

When she returned with the glasses, Reg took his quickly, but instead of drinking, he held it to his forehead. "Hot in here," he said. Although it wasn't. For all its dust and old appliances and '70s décor, the place had a good, strong central air-conditioning, which had been turned up high enough to ease some of the pain of Summer's hangover. She gulped her water, until her glass was nearly empty while Reg watched her, waiting.

"Ready?" she said, and when he nodded, she turned the recorder on again.

Reg started talking right away. "His face was red—a true red, like a tomato. He wouldn't stop. There were people screaming and crying but he didn't seem to hear. He just kept shooting. And that girl. That awful April. She just stood there . . ."

"Mr. Sharkey."

"Yeah?"

"Why did you bring Kimmy?"

He put the glass down.

"I mean . . . had you ever brought her to meet Linda before?"

"Of course not."

"Well, then why—"

"It was Father's Day. I was only going to talk to Linda. Tell her it wasn't a good day for me."

"I still don't understand."

He exhaled hard. "She made me," he said. "Clara made me. She said, 'Look, if you're just getting some gas, why not take Kimmy? You know she loves that mural.' She didn't say it like a suggestion, though. She may as well have said, 'Take Kimmy, or else.'"

"So you did what she said."

"We were having a lot of trouble at home. I think she might have figured it out about me and Linda, I don't know. But yeah. Yeah, I did what she said. To . . . keep the peace."

Summer took another swallow of water, lukewarm and metallic, and carefully set the glass down, the truth sinking in. This was why Clara Sharkey had killed herself—not because she couldn't live without Kimmy. Because her jealousy and anger had led to Kimmy's death. So much guilt in one family. So many secrets that Quentin had never known. "What about your other daughter?" Summer said. "How did she react to her sister's death?"

He looked at Summer, a hard smile crossing his face. "My other daughter didn't react at all," he said, "because you see, she wasn't around."

"What?"

"Katie had run away from home. She'd been gone for two weeks. We'd been worried sick about her at first, but then we'd gotten one phone call. She said to quit looking for her. Leave her alone, Katie said. She sounded high."

"She ran away?" Summer said. "She didn't tell you why?"

"She had problems. Christ, she never stopped having problems," he said, and Summer heard it again, just a hint of what she'd heard during his interview with Quentin, that frustration and rage. Reg had made so many stupid mistakes in his life, though. He'd lost so many people and still he kept on living. Who wouldn't be angry?

"You know, when we'd gone to church that Sunday, Clara and I both prayed we'd have our family together again. For Father's Day. God has quite a sense of humor."

Summer took another sip of water. "When did Katie come home?"

"A few days after Clara died. I couldn't even look at her. Didn't ask her where she'd been. The whole rest of her life, I always found it so hard to look her in the eye without my stomach knotting up. I know that sounds terrible."

"You were hurting," she said. "Looking for someone to blame."

Reg took a sip of his water and wiped his mouth with the back of his hand. Summer's gaze drifted to the kitchen counter behind him. The dusty, empty pasta cylinders, the avocado-green phone with its twisted, old-fashioned cord. And next to it, a pair of sunglasses. Vintage tortoiseshell Ray-Bans. *That's where you left them, Quentin. At your grandfather's house.* She shut her eyes for a few seconds. *God has quite a sense of humor.*

"It's the one thing I'll never understand," Reg said. "Gabriel had gone to that gas station with the purpose of killing me, and from where he was standing, he easily could have done it. But he didn't. He didn't aim the gun at me. He aimed it at everyone else."

"Why do you think that was?"

"I think he knew that letting me live would be worse punishment."

A tear leaked down his cheek. Summer found herself leaning across the table, taking both his hands in hers. She found herself feeling for him, this scared, stupid, selfish man. What a strange turn this interview had taken—almost as though Quentin had engineered it himself. Closure for someone, anyway, if not for him.

Reg said, "Was he close to his mother?"

"Quentin? He was there when she needed him."

"That's good. They had each other."

Summer was still holding his hands. This was starting to feel like group therapy, and so she let go. Leaned back in her chair. "Quentin never knew, though," Summer said. "He never knew about her running away."

"She never told him?"

"No."

"Wow."

"Any idea where she may have gone for those few weeks?"

He nodded. "We had a second home," he said. "A little cottage out east. We went there a lot when Katie was little, but maybe only once after Kimmy was born. After . . . what happened . . . Oh, I didn't go out there for years. But once Katie left for good, I decided I should probably get it cleaned up so I could sell it. I found a whole bunch of Katie's old clothes in there. Back from when she was fourteen years old."

"So she was staying at your second home?"

He smiled a little. "Here I thought she was out on the streets somewhere. But she was at our place the whole time. She used to love going to that cottage when she was little. You wouldn't think a little girl would be so crazy about the desert, but she was a strange kid."

"The desert," Summer said. "You said out east, I was picturing a cabin in Vermont."

"Nah, it was driving distance," he said. "Or I guess hitchhiking distance in Katie's case. Little town on the Arizona border. Brittlebush it's called."

FOR SUMMER, LIFE so often seemed to move in loops. For instance, now. This drive. When Dean had called her with the news of Quentin's death, she'd been on her way to Brittlebush, where she planned to see if she could track down information on Nicola Crane and Renee White, who had apparently lived there with a foster father by the name of Bill Grumley.

All that had been canceled, of course, along with the podcast. But a day and a half later, here she was, looping back, taking the same drive in search of the same information, the podcast alive again with possibility. She was wearing Quentin's sunglasses, and she found herself talking to him in her mind, planning out questions as she drove, her arm resting against her open window, warm air blowing in, feel-

ing more focused and tougher than she ever imagined she could feel. Looping back to her old self.
Quentin at her side, or the spirit of him, anyway.

She'd asked Reg for the sunglasses, and he'd
gladly given them to her, along with the address
of his onetime second home and, since he apparently saved everything, some of the old clothes he'd
found of Kate's there. He'd given her something
else he'd found at the cottage with the clothes—a
fluffy pink stuffed dog that looked like something
a toddler would own. "I swear this didn't belong to
either of my girls," Reg had said. "I don't know what
it was doing there."

We're gonna figure this out, she told Quentin in her
mind. *We're gonna report the hell out of this, together.*

Summer flipped on the radio. Aimee Mann's
version of an old song called "Baby Blue"—which,
oddly enough, had been Gabriel LeRoy's nickname
for April Cooper. Summer knew that from her research, and she saw it as a sign.

Summer usually wasn't one for magical thinking.
But imagining signs from above and messages from
the great beyond and speculating about divinely
choreographed podcasts was easier than spending
any time on the fact that before killing himself, her
best friend had apparently gunned down a defense-
less couple in their own home. It felt like fiction to
her, less believable even than the existence of ghosts.

At least, that's the way she wanted it to feel.

The very last conversation she'd had with Quentin had been at 11:30 P.M. her time, the day before
his death. He'd been up all night reading, he told
her, and he'd thanked her for finally finding the

book. "You kill someone," he had said, "and you become a different person. There's no lag time. No subtle transformation. In those few seconds it takes to end someone's life, you go from being someone who has never killed, to a murderer."

Summer had assumed he was talking about Cooper and LeRoy, and so she'd said, "Imagine how that feels if you're just a kid."

But he'd ignored the comment. "What I'm wondering, Summer, is this. How do you live your same life after you've become that other person? Because it seems impossible to me. It seems like, if you're evil enough to kill someone, you probably shouldn't live at all. Right?"

She shook the thought away, replacing that sad, tremulous voice with that of another Quentin, the imagined one in her passenger's seat. The Quentin that she knew. *Just focus on the story*, said the imagined Quentin—smiling, strong, and unafraid. Her best friend, who would stay with her, always. *We've got a lot of work ahead of us.*

THIRTY-SIX

ROBIN

ROBIN WOKE UP to the smell of bacon and the sound of muffled laughter. With her eyes still closed, she lay in bed for a few moments, believing she was a kid again and it was Sunday morning, both her parents downstairs, her mother in her apron, freshly cooked bacon lined up on a stretched-out paper towel. In her mind, she saw Mom giving Dad a playful push as he tried to swipe a piece, and it felt real, as though adulthood had been a long, problematic dream she was finally waking up from.

But the feeling dissolved as soon as she opened her eyes. When she threw on her robe and headed downstairs, she saw that it was Nicola who was in the kitchen cooking the bacon, one of her mother's aprons tied around jeans and a denim shirt. Mom stood beside her in her robe and pajamas, cracking an egg into a bowl. She was easing out of a recent bout of laughter, wiping a tear from her cheek. "Oh, Nikki, you're just crazy," she said. It was strange how Nicola affected Renee. She made her happy, clearly. But unnaturally happy, Robin thought, especially given the circumstances. It was starting to annoy her, which made her angry with herself.

Eric sat at her mother's kitchen table in his work clothes, reading the *New York Post*. Her parents subscribed to the *Post*, the *Times*, the *Daily News*, and the *Wall Street Journal*. On Sunday mornings, after breakfast, they'd go back to bed with all the papers and read them to each other. According to Mom, Dad secretly loved the gossip on Page 6 and would always try and guess the blind items . . . Robin swallowed hard. Tried to tune out her mother's laughter, Nicola's shrieks. *Everyone grieves in her own way. You know this. Be kind.*

Eric stood up. Took a last gulp of his coffee and grabbed his phone. "I gotta go to work," he said. "See you tonight, Renee?"

"Only for as long as it takes you to pick up your bag," Mom said. "You guys need to go home. I'm fine."

Robin said, "It's no trouble."

Renee looked at her. "Yes, it is." She said it quietly and firmly, as though she were scolding a child. Then her face relaxed. "Honestly, honey. I'm fine. Nikki is taking me to the doctor this afternoon, and I'm sure I'll pass my checkup with flying colors."

"What about the reporters?" Eric said. "They'll be back, as soon as they find out you're home. At the very least, we can call the cops, run interference, say 'no comment.'"

"I can do all those things," Renee said.

Nicola smiled. "And so can I."

"Okay, I guess." He gave her a quick kiss on the cheek. Waved to Nicola. "Have a nice day."

He kissed Robin next—gently, carefully. Then he took both her hands in his own, touched his forehead to hers. "It'll be okay," he whispered, less a statement than a plea.

"What will?"

"Everything."

After Eric left, Robin moved to the kitchen table, bringing the platter of eggs and bacon that Mom and Nicola had made, along with some paper plates and plastic cutlery for easy cleanup. The *Post* was still open to the article Eric had been reading—a one-pager headlined PODCAST KILLER'S LAST WORDS. There was a large photograph of a letter, typed up and printed out, the words blurred except for Quentin Garrison's signature, and the closing: *Good-bye.* Someone had leaked his suicide note. Morasco could not have been happy about that.

At least the article was a short one—just four inches, and print outlets tended to hang on to stories a little longer than online ones. Last night, #PodcastKiller was no longer trending on Twitter. The shootings were fading from the news cycle, Robin thought. Or at least hoped.

Interesting that Eric hadn't shown the article to her, though. Or even mentioned it . . . Then again, it took Eric a long time to mention things, and even then he sometimes had to be blackmailed into it . . .

She shooed the thought away. She'd come back to it later, she knew. But right now, she had to focus on Garrison. The note that had been found next to his body—a "mini-confession," as the papers put it, with a signature to make it binding. An audio file emailed to the cops, plus the note, which had been pinned to the jacket of his ruined body. Even for the most thorough of journalists, Quentin's confession felt a bit excessive.

Robin sat down and started to read, as Mom and Nicola joined her at the table, Nicola carrying a fresh pot of coffee and a bowl of cut-up melon. Mom said, "What are you reading, sweetie?"

Robin showed her the article, and she winced.

"Did Detective Morasco show you this note, Mom?"

"Yes," she said. "He also played me the recording he made."

"Did it help you remember anything?"

Renee glanced at Nicola. "No more than I already have," she said. "I think the detective was hoping the sound of Quentin Garrison's voice might trigger something. But, honestly, I can't remember anything from that night now. It's worse than when I first came out of the coma."

Robin nodded. It did make sense. The human body was full of defenses.

The article paraphrased what was in the suicide note and began with a direct quote from it: *My apologies to friends and family, who have been so good to me, but I've done something unforgivable. I can no longer live with myself.*

As Robin continued to read, her mom complimented Nikki on the bacon. "How do you get it so crispy without burning it?" she said, as though her husband's killer's suicide note weren't sitting inches away.

Besides apologizing to the Bloom family, and saying he didn't deserve someone as wonderful as his husband, Quentin had also gone into some detail about the events of that night: How he'd parked his car a block over and walked quietly to the Bloom residence, digital recorder in hand. How he'd surprised Mitchell in the kitchen as he prepared a sandwich, how Renee had heard them arguing and burst in with the gun and how Quentin had gotten it away from her and shot them both. All over an interview request. *I wanted to speak to Mitchell Bloom to gain insight into human rage—something that's long been festering within me*, he had written. *Ironically, that rage caught fire and transformed me that night, into something I've worked my whole life not to be. The presence of the gun made for the perfect storm. May God forgive me.*

Mom and Nicola were discussing the best way to make eggs à la française. "Mom," Robin said. "In Quentin Garrison's suicide note, he said you brought the gun in the room. Did you?"

"He's a liar," Nicola said. But Robin didn't even glance at her.

Her mother looked pale, her eyes sad. "No, he isn't," she said. "I did."

Robin said, "You said Dad bought the gun."

"It actually wasn't Dad," she said quietly. "It was Nikki."

Robin looked at her. Nicola put a hand over Mom's and squeezed. "It's okay," she whispered.

"There was an incident. It scared me. I called

Nikki, and she advised me to purchase a firearm. She took me to a range so I could practice. Nikki's a former police officer. She knows these things."

Robin looked at Nicola. "What incident?" she said. "When?"

"Years and years ago. A man attacked her."

"In a parking lot." Mom gave Robin a tender smile. "You were away at college."

"He attacked you?"

"He hit me. Nearly broke my jaw."

"Trying to get her purse," Nicola said.

"He hit me. There's nothing like that feeling, Robin . . . A man's fist. The cruelty of it. It's worse than the pain."

"Why didn't you ever tell me?"

"Because thank God, I got away from him."

"She fought back," Nicola said.

"I didn't want to scare you while you were away at school. And anyway, I hate guns. I was embarrassed to own one. I kept it hidden. I didn't tell your father."

"Why?"

"I didn't tell anybody, honey. It was in the safe in the basement. I forgot I even had it."

Robin had grown up in this house. She had no idea that her parents had a safe in the basement.

Nicola put an arm around Renee, rubbed her shoulder.

"I was frightened," Renee said, tears forming in her eyes. "I mean . . . I had to be, right? I . . . I had to have felt threatened. Terrified. I had to have felt like that gun was my only hope."

Robin moved closer. She put her arms around Renee and drew Nicola in too. "Of course you did,"

Nicola said. And the three of them stayed like that for a long while. Robin felt safe. Like a child.

There was something else about the article that bothered Robin, but it wasn't anything Mom or Nicola could help her with. It was the phrasing on the note.

Mom pulled away, wiped a tear from her cheek. "Oh honey, I forgot. You must see what Nikki gave me." She stood up, and Robin's eyes went right to it—the glittering aquamarine heart at her throat. "Isn't it beautiful?"

"Very," she said, her gaze moving from the necklace to Nicola's smiling face. "Nicola showed it to me right after she bought it. I told her I knew you'd love it."

Mom's eyes widened. "Really?"

"You love aquamarine. Everybody knows that. It's your color too."

Nicola winked. "I swore her to secrecy," she said, and Mom's smile grew bright enough to hurt.

"I'm so happy that you two have been getting to know each other again."

Nicola said, "Robin and I talked about Kate Sharkey. Quentin Garrison's mother." Robin thought about the Polaroid she'd shown Nicola. She'd put that back last night, finally, while Eric and Mom were asleep.

Mom said, "You did?"

"I was quoted in an old article that Robin found about Kate. Remember the wax museum in L.A.?"

"Not really . . ."

"Anyway, she asked if you knew her too, and you know what? I wasn't sure whether you did or not."

Renee said, "I only knew her through you."

"And you never mentioned that either, Mom? You never told the cops?"

"It wasn't relevant," she said. "Kate was Nikki's friend. I never even knew she'd ever been married or had a son."

Robin started to respond, but Nicola spoke first. "Robin's right," she said. "It is strange. Me knowing that family like I did. So many years ago. Isn't it strange, Renee?"

"It's a smaller world than we realize," she said. "You know, Detective Morasco's wife has perfect autobiographical memory. She literally never forgets a face. And he said that she once told him that there are only a handful of people in the entire world she hasn't seen at least twice."

Robin thought of Quentin Garrison's small family and her own small family, orbiting each other for so many years before finally colliding. She thought of April Cooper and Gabriel LeRoy, somehow fueling it all. All these connections . . . Strange seemed a mild word for that, "small world" even milder.

Renee moved to her and stroked her hair. She put a warm hand on her shoulder and kissed her on the cheek, her lips cool and dry on her skin. "Life is full of coincidences, honey," she said. "We try and put them all together and we hope they'll add up to make something meaningful. But the sad truth is, they hardly ever do. They're just coincidences, that's all. Stupid, pointless coincidences."

ROBIN HAD NO intention of going to work right away, but still she drove all the way to the train station before calling Detective Morasco. She wasn't sure why, but she felt compelled to follow her regular routine. Maybe because she had told Renee she was on her way to the office, and making that initial effort felt less to her like she was lying to her mother—something Robin got a lot guiltier over than most forty-one-year-old women. "I'd like to listen to that recording Quentin Garrison made," she said, once Morasco picked up. "Is this an okay time to come by?"

He agreed, and Robin called Eileen and let her know she'd be coming in late. "I've been asked to go to the police station this morning," she explained, which was only a half lie, really. And she needed to hear the audio recording.

When she was just a few blocks away from the Tarry Ridge station, Morasco called her and told her not to go through the front door, that he'd meet her in the parking lot, and when she got there, she understood why. There were two news vans out front, along with a handful of reporters. *Guess the story hasn't faded from the news cycle.*

There was a parking lot behind the station, and Robin checked her Twitter once she'd pulled into a space. #PodcastKiller was trending again. #Dean-Conrad was too, his picture popping up all up and down her feed. A ringer for Jon Voight in *Midnight Cowboy*, with a little Steve McQueen thrown in to make things interesting. *Handsome, heartbroken Dean . . .* Morasco greeted her at the back entrance. "Quentin Garrison's husband is coming in later today, and the press found out about it," he explained, though she'd already figured that out.

He ushered her in, leading her through an enormous squad room with floor-to-ceiling windows, gleaming hardwood floors and executive-size desks, many of them empty. Like every municipal building in town, the Tarry Ridge police station was ridiculously sleek and architectural and far too big for what was needed of it. There had been a scandal involving a developer a few years back, but before his arrest, most all of Tarry Ridge had been supersized and overrenovated, losing all the charm Robin remembered it having when she was growing up.

She found the town borderline monstrous in its perfection these days, a gracious matriarch who'd undergone one too many facelifts. And the Tarry Ridge police headquarters was a perfect example. She remembered visiting the station with her fourth-grade class, and it had been a third this size back then—a simple brick colonial building with a patch of lawn out front. Perfectly reasonable for its purposes. Now, it had a rose garden out front—ten varieties of roses!—and the inside was even sillier in its excess. The interview room where Morasco had taken her could have probably held an entire New York City precinct house. She peered around the room—the freshly painted cream walls, the leather cushions on the chairs, the enormous plexiglass table that looked as though it had been shipped in from MoMA. One chair had been pulled up to the table, on which had been placed a digital recorder and some bagged items—a belt, a watch, a wallet, and wedding ring, and various other items that had been found on Quentin. "Thanks for setting this up for me," Robin said.

"Actually," said Morasco, "this is all for Dean Conrad. I'm sneaking you in early."

"Oh yes. Of course."

"How's your mom doing?"

Robin looked at him. "She says she remembers less now about that night than when it actually happened."

"That's a blessing."

"I guess."

"If you don't mind my asking," he said, "what made you decide to listen to the recording?"

"Well . . . I read about the note in the *New York Post*."

"Yeah, we're thrilled about that."

"I know. The leak sucks," Robin said. "But I was glad I saw it because there was something weird about the note. I want to see if he talks the same way in the audio."

"What do you mean by weird?"

"Okay." She set the headphones down. "So, I did a little research on Quentin Garrison online. This was before the suicide. Back when I was just curious about him."

"Yeah?"

"He doesn't seem like the kind of person who'd apologize to 'friends and family.' I mean, what family?"

He blinked at her.

"I guess when I say it out loud, it doesn't exactly sound like a smoking gun."

Morasco gave her a sad smile. "He was a troubled guy," he said.

"You're sure about that."

"He had a record. We didn't see it right away because it happened when he was a minor. Shoplifting. Selling pot. An assault charge—a street fight, I guess. After a concert."

That son of Kate's was a handful and then some. Pretty much scared me off having kids of my own. "None of those things were murder," Robin said.

"No. But he was only sixteen." Morasco moved toward the door. "Also the clerk at his hotel said that a couple of days after the shootings, right before he disappeared, he came storming into the lobby and shouted at him for no reason. Scared the hell out of the other guests."

"Oh . . ."

"Yeah, and some witnesses said they saw him freaking out outside the New York library, the day after Mitchell died."

"Oh."

"Okay, anyway, I gotta go check on a few things, but go ahead and listen. I'll be back in about ten minutes to walk you out."

After he left, Robin put the headphones on and pushed the play button. She heard a rustling sound at first, and then Quentin's voice. "So. This tape will be my formal confession to the police. But first I would like to make an apology." Robin shifted in the chair, struck by the flatness of his voice, the lack of emotion. "I want to apologize to Robin and Eric Diamond. Robin Diamond in particular. I'm sorry, Ms. Diamond. Robin. They loved you very much." Robin swallowed hard. Gripped the arms of her chic, cushioned chair. "They gave you a stable upbringing, with summer camp and family vacations. I bet you never woke up in the middle of the night at just five years old, realizing you were all alone in your house." He coughed. Took a breath. "It's interesting . . . I read in this book that Gabriel LeRoy had a nickname for April Cooper. He called her Baby Blue, which had been his name for the baby blanket he used to carry around with him everywhere when he was a little boy. He called her Baby Blue because she made him feel the way that blanket did. Comfortable. Safe. You had that with your parents, Robin. I never had a Baby Blue, so in my anger and confusion and hurt, I destroyed yours. That isn't an excuse. If anything, it's the opposite. I'm telling you that I did what I did for the most selfish of reasons."

Robin shut the recorder off. Rewound it. Played the last section again. "You had that with your parents, Robin. I never had a Baby Blue."

Rewound it again. Played it again. "You had that—"

She hit pause. Then played it one more time, just to make sure—not about what Quentin had said, but about the sound in the background. It was kids, shouting. Same as she'd heard during their last phone conversation. Was he in the same park? Had he recorded this confession right after hanging up with her?

Robin listened to the rest of the recording. "This next part is for the police. I am now formally confessing to the murder of Mitchell Bloom, may he rest in peace. And I am confessing to the shooting of Renee Bloom." He didn't mention friends and family, but as she could tell now, it didn't matter. It was his tone, the hopelessness in it. "Mitchell Bloom had his back to me when I entered the kitchen. It was very late. Eleven P.M. It had taken me that long to get up the courage to talk to him, and I was still used to West Coast time. He was making a sandwich. Listening to the BBC World News on the radio. I said, 'I'm sorry to bother you, sir, but if I could have a moment of your time.' He was scared, then angry. Asked me what the hell I was doing in his house . . . I told him I wanted to talk about my mother. And he said, 'Who gives a damn about your dead mother?' I . . . I know I was an intruder. But I lost hold of my senses . . ." The story went on. Renee entering with the gun, the fight ensuing. "I was consumed with rage and jealousy and hurt," he said. All in that same monotone, the voice you use to surrender.

After he was through with the confession, Quentin apologized to Dean for ruining their wonderful life together, to his in-laws and baby niece for bringing them shame, and finally to "Summer Hawkins, for being undeserving of her friendship." And then he started to cry. Deep, racking sobs that tore at Robin as she listened. Had the shouting children heard him? Had anyone heard him? After several seconds, he caught his breath. "I love you all," he said before ending the recording. "Please don't hate me."

Robin thought back to the phone call again, how his voice had cracked. *Can we meet? Maybe in an hour? Please. I'll meet you anywhere you'd like.*

Quentin had never met her at the hospital. He'd never seen her again. Had he recorded his confession in a public park, right after speaking to her?

Had he known at that point that he was going to kill himself?

Robin glanced at the door, then looked at the plastic bags on the table. She slid open the one that held his wallet and wedding ring. She removed the ring first—a thick band of yellow gold, very old-fashioned. She held the band up to the light, read the inscription inside: YOU ARE MY EVERYTHING, DC. "You did have your Baby Blue, Quentin," she whispered. "You idiot."

She dropped the ring back in the bag, opened his wallet, and started going through it. Nothing that said "suicidal," or "troubled," or, for that matter, "fucked-up teen." She slipped out a California driver's license, two credit cards, an ID from the radio station he had worked for, $300 cash. A cloth handkerchief like her father's father used to carry. No pictures. Who carried pictures in their wallets these days? Though she'd figured a guy with a cloth handkerchief might. There were a few business cards, many of them clearly from this trip. Someone from the New York Public Library. A woman named Edith Brixton. Detective Morasco. Nicola Crane. Behind the business cards, she found a movie ticket stub. She set it on the table and read the faded print, her throat tightening. 6/24/76. *Easter Parade.* A ticket stub for her mom's favorite movie. From close to twenty years before Quentin had been born. "Nothing weird about that," she said out loud.

Then she saw the name of the theater.

She heard footsteps outside the door and shoved everything back into the wallet, the wallet into the plastic bag. By the time Morasco came in, every-thing was in its place.

"Everything work out okay?" Morasco said.

"Fine," she said. "Thank you."

Behind him stood several other cops, plain-clothes and uniform, among them a blond, hand-some, devastated-looking man she recognized instantly as Dean Conrad. "I'm sorry for your loss," he said to her.

"I'm sorry for yours."

She aimed her eyes at the ground and started to pass. "I'm going to tell you what I told these de-tectives," he said quickly. "I spoke to Quentin a couple of days after the shooting. It was the last time I talked to him. He said he was feeling guilty because he hadn't told the police everything about that night."

"Yes?"

"He went to your parents' house. He watched them from outside. Your mom left at one point—she kind of stormed out of the house and he fol-lowed her in his car until he lost her. Then he went back to the hotel. That was all he did."

"Why did he confess to killing them?"

"I don't know."

"Why didn't he tell the police that he'd been out-side their house?"

"I think he thought it made him sound like a stalker. Which he was, kind of . . . But he wasn't a killer. I know Quentin better than anyone. And he isn't. He wasn't . . ."

Robin looked into his eyes, red-rimmed, as though he hadn't slept for days. *I thought I knew my husband better than anyone too.* She didn't say it, of course. But she understood him. She knew how he felt. "Thank you," she said. And then she quoted Eric. "The truth will out."

After she left the building, Robin quickly called her mother's cell phone. "Oh hi, honey," she said. "I can't really talk. I'm on my way to the doctor."

"Oh, that's okay," Robin said, thinking of her mother's home, her empty house. "I was just calling to see how the appointment went."

"I'll let you know," Mom said, and before long Robin was pulling into her mother's driveway, barreling up the walkway, through the front door and up the stairs and into her parents' bedroom where she rooted once again through her mother's sock drawer. She was slipping the box out of the back of the drawer, her mother's secret box. And she was pulling out the seashells and plastic mementos and tiny pieces of costume jewelry until she found what she wanted: the souvenir penny pressed into an oval and embossed with a star, the word *Corsica.* That had been the name of the movie theater on Quentin's ticket stub. The Corsica. *Easter Parade.* 6/24/76. On the movie stub, there had been an identical star logo.

"My God," she whispered.

"Robin?"

She whirled around and saw her standing in the doorway. "Hi Nikki," Robin said, calm as she could, the penny burning in her hand.

THIRTY-SEVEN

June 20, 1976
11:00 P.M.

Dear Aurora Grace,

We're going to Death Valley. Elizabeth and me.
Gabriel is in the back seat sleeping. But we're not
going to keep him around for long.

We are in Elizabeth's car, driving to the Gideon
compound, where there is no phone and no TV and
no helicopter surveillance. No cops. If we make it
all the way there, Elizabeth says, I will be free.
Elizabeth and I look so much alike, we could be sis-
ters. Twins, even. She says I'll fit right in with the
other Gideons because they're all blond like us. She
says they will give me a place to hide without asking questions. And she'll like it better there, with
another girl to hang out with. Elizabeth says the
Gideons hate the government, and therefore they
will love anyone who is on the run from the law.

Once we get to the Gideon compound, I will
kill Gabriel and bury him in the desert.

Aurora Grace, I hope there never comes a time
in your life when circumstances force you to escape
your own body. When you feel so powerless that

your soul acts on its own and pushes out through your skin, just to get away from YOU. That was what happened to me at the Arco station. I told Elizabeth about it, and she understood. She said, "I have felt that exact thing." But I think that in her case, it was for physical reasons.

My beautiful, sweet future daughter, I don't want to tell you what happened at the Arco station. I can't find words to put on this page that won't start me shaking and crying and wanting to die. What I can tell you is this: Gabriel definitely killed Jenny. Before Arco, I had the tiniest spark of hope that I had been right about hearing Jenny's breathing over the phone, that she really was out there somewhere with people taking care of her, that Gabriel had only told me he killed her because he wanted to hurt me. Before Arco, I thought, *He wouldn't do that. Gabriel LeRoy may be a lot of terrible things. But he would never kill a little child.* I was wrong, though. He would. He did. He killed his own half sister. And now, I feel such strangling hate toward him, I will never be able to breathe again until I snuff him out like a match.

June 21, 1976

3:00 A.M.

Dear Aurora Grace,

We are here, at last. Everyone is asleep, and I am using a lantern to see the page. There is no electricity. The water comes from a well, and the compound itself is just a few tents set up on the desert sand. It's much smaller than I thought it would be, but just like Elizabeth said, there are llamas and chickens who live behind fences. They are so cute. I want to play with them all. It was cold when we got here, but Elizabeth and I built a fire in the pit. It warms my skin and smells like home is supposed to smell, and I may finally sleep for the first time in days. But not yet. I can't sleep yet.

Aurora Grace, I need to tell you something, and it starts with Gabriel sleeping. He was sound asleep and snoring in the back seat when Elizabeth first pulled through the metal gate. When she parked the car, he woke and said, "Are we there yet, Baby Blue?" And, to be honest, my heart melted a little. I blame it on all the unhealthy things I've been doing for the past few days—the lack of sleep and the lack of food, the drags off Elizabeth's cigarettes and the swigs from her vodka bottle and constantly worrying about cops and the awful things I've seen, the way those things have changed me. I think all that poison mixed up in my head like ingredients thrown into a blender, and my brain drank it all and turned to mush. So when I looked at that monster, that child-murderer, he just looked like a boy to me.

"We're here," I told him.

Gabriel got out of the car, and he looked around. "Where are we?" he said.

I told him Death Valley, and his eyes started

darting around like he'd suddenly gone insane. I told him we're at the Gideon compound, just like we talked about, and he got even crazier. "No, no, no, no. I never said we could come here."

So I said, "What are you talking about? This is the only safe place there is."

And he said it again. "I never said we could come here. I never gave you my permission to take us here."

And I said, "I don't need your fucking permission."

He hit me. Again. Knocked me down, and it was like the ground came rushing up into the whole side of my body. My legs were all scraped up. My jaw ached from the punch. There was a ringing in my ear too, and when I put my hand up to it, it was wet from blood.

Elizabeth had been looking for firewood, but she came running back when she heard him slug me. You could HEAR it from far away—that's how hard he'd hit. "What the hell do you think you're doing?" she yelled. Gabriel started yelling back. I was surprised no one in the tents were waking up because even with my ear the way it was, I could hear them loud and clear.

Anyway, Gabriel's gun was out of bullets, but Officer Nelligan's was in the back seat of Elizabeth's car, right next to where Gabriel had been lying. I crawled over to the car and threw open the door and grabbed that gun, and when Gabriel called Elizabeth the c-word, I shot him in the stomach. He fell to the ground. I pushed myself up to my feet and stood over him for a while, trying to figure out how I felt. He said something I could barely hear—my ear was still ringing. So I leaned in closer and he said it again: "Jenny is with my sister."

That hurt worse than my ear. It hurt worse than anything. At the Arco station, I'd watched him shoot his own baby sister as his dad stood there, pleading with him to stop. He said it again. "Jenny is with my sister." I shot him in the face.

Aurora Grace, it's been about half an hour since I killed Gabriel. I'm sitting next to Elizabeth in front of the fire she built. I've shown her all these letters, and she says you're a lucky girl to have a mother like me. She says I'm a good person, even though I've killed. She said God knows that. And she's read the Bible cover to cover at least five times.

After we get some more energy, we will burn Gabriel's body. I'm drinking from her bottle of vodka, and my ear's starting to feel better. Elizabeth is looking through Gabriel's wallet, and she just showed me something she found in there: a scrap of paper with a phone number written on it, and the letter K. Elizabeth thought maybe Gabriel had a secret lover, but I told her that wasn't likely. From what I knew of Gabriel, one lover seemed like too many. Then she said something that made me stop breathing: "Maybe he has another sister besides that little girl."

Jenny is with my sister. Was that what he had been trying to tell me—that she was alive and with some other sister, not the one he had killed? Was this number the same one that he'd been calling?

4:00 A.M.

It's another hour later. I am finally feeling like I really could sleep. Elizabeth and I built a much bigger fire and dragged Gabriel's body into it—a very long and exhausting ordeal. The fire's burning higher than we thought it would, and the smoke is thick and choking. I put my head on Elizabeth's shoulder. We talk about our short-term plans. Mine is to find a working phone somewhere and call the number on the scrap of paper. Elizabeth's is to leave this place again forever. "I was away from here so long, I forgot," she said to me. "My father hates me because I'm not a true believer. And some of my brothers are bad. I will need to protect you." I don't feel like I need protection, though. Not anymore. I feel like I can do the protecting.

The sky here is so beautiful—like someone spilled a jar of silver glitter over a black velvet cape. I've never seen stars like this before, Aurora Grace. It's like I'm looking straight up at heaven.

THIRTY-EIGHT

ROBIN

ROBIN FELT AS though she were standing on her tiptoes at the edge of a cliff, and any movement at all—any word in this case—was certain to make her fall.

"Robin?" Nicola said. "What are you doing?" And Robin realized how agonizing it was, standing on one's tiptoes forever.

Robin opened her hand. Held it out to reveal the souvenir penny, older than she was but still shiny and smooth in her palm. The star. Corsica. "Do you know what this is?" she said.

Nicola took a few steps closer and peered into her hand. "A souvenir?"

"It's from a movie theater called the Corsica," she said. "I found it in Mom's things."

Nicola's eyes narrowed. "Why were you going through your mother's things?"

"Because when he died, Quentin Garrison was carrying a 1976 ticket stub from the Corsica in his wallet. And I have a feeling it had something to do with the podcast he was making."

Nicola moved over to Robin's parents' bed and sat on the edge of it. She motioned for Robin to sit down next to her, but Robin didn't move. This was all stall tactics, probably an interrogation technique Nicola had learned as a cop, and Robin wasn't buying it. "I want to know about my mother," she said quietly. "I want to know about her past."

Nicola exhaled. "She met your father at a coffee shop in Tucson. She was nineteen and waiting tables. He was finishing up a residency at the University of Arizona . . ."

"I know how my parents met," she said. "Before that."

"We were in foster care together."

"What was she doing in 1976?"

Nicola smiled. It didn't reach her eyes. "Going to the movies?"

Robin took a step closer. "Look," she said. "I heard Quentin Garrison's confession. He says he shot my parents when an argument between them got out of hand, and fine. It sounds a little over the top, but I can believe that. But I don't believe that argument had anything to do with my dad. I believe it had something to do with my mom, and this movie theater and 1976 and April Cooper."

"You do, huh?"

"And I believe you know the truth." She leveled her eyes at her. "CoCo. You know her better than any living person."

"Aren't you supposed to be at work?"

"I'm going in late today."

"They let you do that?"

"You're avoiding the question."

Nicola exhaled. "She loves you. I know that much. I also know that as many times as she's been over at your house, she's never gone through your personal things."

"Because she's never needed to."

"*Neither have you.*" Nicola's cheeks flushed. She tucked a lock of hair behind her ear, took a breath. "Look, Robin. You know I used to be a cop. These days, I do a little private investigating work. And from time to time, I've helped out your mom."

"You have?"

"Yes," she said. "And last year, she was very concerned about you."

"What? Why?"

"It was your husband. He was working a lot of late nights. Your friend Eileen mentioned to her that she'd seen him at Chez Chas with a woman . . ."

"Eileen said that to my mom?"

"She was worried. She said she'd mentioned it to you, but you didn't seem to believe her."

"Jesus."

"Your mom asked me to look into it, and . . . Well I don't know how else to put it, Robin. Your husband is a real schmuck."

Robin swallowed. Her cheeks felt hot. "I know about it. He told me."

"And you're staying with him?"

She didn't answer.

"Oh, I'm sorry, did he get that woman her job

back? Did he help her sue? Did he actually do the reporting he should have done, and did Charlie Maxwell lose his restaurant and his reputation, like he deserves? I guess I must have just missed it."

Robin walked to her mother's dresser. Carefully, she put the penny back in the box and slid the sock drawer closed.

"I'm not trying to be mean," Nicola said. "I'm just making a point."

"Which is?"

"Are you better off for knowing what a schmuck your husband is?"

She turned around. Stared at her.

Nicola was standing now, hands crossed over her strong chest. "You're not, are you? I mean honestly. It isn't like you're going to leave him over it. And now you're stuck with not only knowing about this shitty thing he did in the not-too-distant past—but that you're the type of woman for whom that type of shittiness is not a deal breaker."

Robin's mouth felt dry. Her face throbbed red. "Thanks a lot." Possibly the most impotent comeback she could have come up with. But there wasn't anything else she could say. Nicola was right.

Nicola took a few steps closer. She brushed a hand against Robin's cheek, as though she were comforting a child. "The point I'm trying to make, Robin, is that we all have pasts," she said. "And very often, the people we love are better off not knowing about them." She drew her lips into a smile. "Your mother loves you. She would do anything for you. Isn't that what's important?"

"I don't know."

"No one should be an open book to their children. That isn't healthy for anyone."

Robin closed her eyes for a moment, her head pounding. She craved an Advil. "I thought you were taking my mother to the doctor's."

Nicola shrugged her shoulders. "She decided to go alone," she said. "I think she's getting tired of me."

"I don't blame her."

"Don't be like that."

"How is it you've stayed friends with my mom all these years, Nikki? Even after her husband kicked you out of her house?"

"I told you, honey," she said. "Foster care. Nothing makes you closer."

Robin and Nicola were in the hallway when Robin's cell phone rang. She glanced at the screen. Detective Morasco. "It's work," she told Nicola. "I'll need to take this in the other room." She slipped down the hall and into her old room, closing the door behind her. "Hello?"

"Robin?" His voice sounded strange. Agitated.

"Is something wrong?"

"That text you sent me, from Quentin Garrison. 'I am not a good person.'"

"Yes?"

"You sure the time on it is correct?"

"Excuse me?"

"I mean, it says 9:13 on it. You're positive that's 9:13 P.M., not A.M."

"Absolutely. It was nighttime. I was at home with Eric. I'd called Quentin, but his mailbox was full. He sent me that text about fifteen minutes later."

"Wow . . . Okay."

"What's the problem?"

"We have an estimated time of death back from the coroner, and it's between eleven A.M. and one P.M." Robin thought back to their phone call, the children's voices in the background—same as on the audiotape.

"The text came in eight hours later."

"You see the problem."

"Yes," Robin said, her skin going cold. "I see the problem."

ROBIN TOOK A SHOWER. Changed her clothes, the whole time thinking about the text she'd received, that first apology. Someone else had sent it, eight hours after Garrison's death.

And if someone else had gotten Garrison's phone, only to replace it so it could be found on his dead body, who had that person been? If someone had gotten his phone, that same person could have easily forced him to confess and shot him. That same person could have shot her parents. She hadn't gone over all that with Morasco, because like most cops, Nicola included, he kept things close to the vest.

Nicola Crane, what a cop she must have been—with that crazy laugh and that cool blue gaze, steady as a gun sight . . . *The point I'm trying to make, Robin, is that we all have pasts. And very often, the people we love are better off not knowing about them.*

Nicola Crane, the opposite of an open book. A sealed, locked journal, with God knows what written inside. These past few days had been so emotional. Yet not once had Robin seen her shed a tear outside of laughter. Not even as her dear foster sister lay in intensive care, on the brink of death.

Had she known more than she let on?

She heard voices outside the entrance to the kitchen and as she got closer, she saw her mother and Nicola, involved in an intense conversation in the foyer, just inside the front door. They stopped talking when they saw her.

"Oh hi, honey," Mom said.

Robin gave her a quick tight hug. "What did the doctor say?"

"Flying colors." She smiled. "Just like I said."

She exhaled. "Thank God."

"And you know what? I think I'm starting to get my memory back."

"Really?"

"When I was driving home, I had a sudden flash. Quentin Garrison in my kitchen. The gun in his hand . . ." She exchanged a glance with Nicola. "I was just telling Nikki."

"That's right."

Robin turned. She leveled her eyes at Nicola. "When did you get here, Nikki?"

"Excuse me?"

"When did you arrive in town from Philly?"

"You saw me at the funeral."

"Yeah. Felt to me like you'd already been here for a while, though. For at least a couple of days."

Nicola stared at her.

Mom said, "What do you mean?"

She thought about letting them know what Morasco had said, but decided not to bother. Mom would find out soon enough that Quentin Garrison probably hadn't shot her and Dad and hadn't shot himself unless he'd been forced. "Just thinking out loud," Robin said, giving them both a smile, Nicola's much smaller than the one she gave her mother. "I've got to head out. I'm needed at work."

Once she got in her car, she called Eric—not because she was dying to talk to him, but because she had no one else to say it to who might even begin to understand. "I'm suspicious of Nicola."

"Your mom's friend? That's crazy."

You wouldn't think it was crazy if you knew that she investigated you.

"Think about it, Eric," she said. "Someone got my mom's gun away from her, but they shot my dad first, not her. My dad's wounds were almost instantly fatal. My mom was shot once in the abdomen. Now she's fine."

"You think she made sure your mom would survive her injuries. That she only shot her . . . why? To keep her from protecting your dad?"

"Why not?"

"Okay," he said slowly. "But why would your mother's old friend walk into her house and kill her husband?"

"I'm thinking my mom might be remembering things wrong. I'm thinking it might have been Nicola who had the argument with Dad."

"Why?"

"It turns out Nicola was the one who got my mother the gun. Who taught her how to shoot. She's an expert shooter. I've looked at old pictures of her, and beneath those muscles and that tan and that gray hair . . . Nicola could be the associate of mom's Quentin Garrison was talking about. Mom's dear friend Nikki could be April Cooper."

There was a long stretch of silence on the other end of the line. And then, "I don't understand."

"You should."

"What? Why?"

"Because, Eric," she said. "You know what it's like to have secrets."

Robin thought about her mother, all the things she never knew about her that she'd only just learned in the past few days: She had fought off an attacker. She owned a gun. She'd hired a PI to investigate Robin's husband. Her closest friend may have been a mass murderer in the '70s. She was a woman with important movie tokens and sexy teenage Polaroids, a past she never spoke about, and many, many secrets.

As she reached her stop, Robin remembered what Nicola had said about Renee. *Your mother loves you. She would do anything for you. Isn't that what's important?*

It was important. Of course, it was. But it wasn't everything. There was also the truth.

THIRTY-NINE

SUMMER

SUMMER STOOD OUT in Brittlebush. She stood out everywhere on the West Coast, with her bright red hair and pale skin, but here, in this tiny desert town where it looked as though sunblock had yet to be invented, people kept gaping at her, as though she were some alien species. It didn't help either that most everyone who lived here looked at least sixty and seemed to have known each other since childhood. Summer couldn't have blended in if she tried.

What Summer normally did when reporting small-town stories was to hang out in one of the local diners, order a piece of pie and a cup of coffee, bum a cigarette off the waitress during her break and get her talking. Summer didn't even smoke, but she could fake it. And she could talk a good game if she did say so herself. By the end of the conversation, she could have that waitress feeling like her best friend, a Deep Throat–style whistle-blower, a freedom fighter who would go down in history,

Quentin's secret crush—whatever Summer needed her to feel like in order to get the info.

She was a little nervous about doing that here, though, in Brittlebush's only diner—a place called Heidi's that looked like Denny's and IHOP had a baby, shoved it in a time machine, and sent it back to 1983. There were a few leathery old guys in here, sitting at the counter. One waitress, who, despite the perfectly good air-conditioning, looked dangerously overheated in her polyester uniform and didn't move her face when she spoke, seemingly out of spite.

The booths were a sickly yellow and made of the type of vinyl you stuck to if you sat on it for too long, and everybody in here kept shooting her looks, as though they were daring her to say something stupid.

Summer slipped her phone out of her purse. No bars. Still. She wasn't sure she'd ever felt this isolated. *Hell of a place for a second home*, she thought. And the fact that Quentin's mother had loved it here . . . Well, Summer didn't necessarily know if that was true. Reg Sharkey had been the one to say that Quentin's mother had loved it here, and he wasn't the most reliable of narrators.

"Are you lost?"

Summer glanced up to see the waitress standing over her, a look in her eye like they'd drawn straws back in the kitchen and she was the loser.

"No." Summer tried smiling. "I'm not lost."

"Your car break down?"

She shook her head. "Nope. Just hoping for a piece of key lime pie."

"Usually, when a stranger comes here, they're either lost or broken down."

"Sounds like the lyrics to a country song."

The waitress frowned at her. "Key lime pie, huh?"

Summer nodded, the conversation officially over. When the waitress returned, though, she decided to try again. "Look, I'm working on a story for the radio," she said. Careful to leave NPR out of it, lest it start some political argument. "I'm looking into a very old story. From the '70s. And I was wondering if you might be able to help me with it." Summer peered at her name tag. "Lena. That's a pretty name."

One of the old guys at the counter said, "The '70s isn't a very old story."

The waitress ignored him. "It's short for Marlene," she said. "I was named for Dietrich."

"I'm Summer. Named for my least favorite season."

This time she got a chuckle out of her. Lena took the seat across from her. "I'll try and help," she said. The '70s aficionado slid off his counter stool and sauntered over, as Summer slipped her notepad out of her purse, trying to make out her own scrawl. "Okay," she said. "If you could just tell me if you know a Nicola Crane, a Renee White, or a Bill or William Grumley."

The waitress smiled. "Well, I know a Grumley, that's for sure."

"You do? You know where I can find him?"

She started to laugh, Mr. '70s joining in. "Honey, if you don't mind my saying, for a reporter, you're not all that observant."

"Huh?"

"Two doors down from here," the old man said. "The general store. It's called Grumley's. Helllooo?" He said it like some teen wiseass on a Nickelodeon show. He knocked on his own head. "Anybody in there?"

"No need to be rude, Freddy," the waitress said. "The store's owned now by Bill Grumley's son, Stephen. Bill passed away about five years ago."

"He was one of my closest friends," Freddy said. "We drove cross-country one summer on our Harleys."

"That's awesome," Summer said. "I'm wondering, though, if you knew Bill when he ran a foster home?"

He frowned at her. "Bill didn't run a foster home."

"Wait, what?"

"Nah. He had five kids of his own. They were enough trouble."

"That's weird. A woman told my colleague that as a kid, she'd lived in a foster home run by Bill Grumley."

"She?" Lena said.

"Bill had boys," Freddy said. "Nothin' but loudmouthed, troublemaking boys in that house. Their poor mom . . ."

"Oh, Freddy, you remember." Lena looked at Summer "You're talking about the '70s, right?"

"Yes. '76 or '77."

"Remember, Freddy? Right around the bicentennial. Bill and Mary took in those two girls."

Summer's eyes went big.

Freddy said, "I thought there were three of them."

"No, that was Kate. The kid with the summer

home. Jesus, Freddy, I remember the '70s better than you do, and I was just a child back then." She smirked.

Summer looked at her. "Kate Sharkey?"

"That's right. Is that who your story is about?"

"A little bit. Yes."

"Oh, well, then in that case," Lena said. "I got stuff to tell you."

SUMMER TOUCHED THE phone in her lap, turned on the voice recorder, and set it on the table.

For the next few minutes, she sat there, rapt, as Lena told her about fourteen-year-old Kate Sharkey hitchhiking to town and staying in her family home for two weeks before anyone realized she was there all by herself. "I worked behind the counter at Grumley's, and she'd buy food there. Say it was for her family," Lena said. "She was coming in almost every day, buying not just food but toys. Coloring books. Candy. Plastic pants. Said it was for her little sister, Kimmy."

"I don't remember that at all," Freddy said.

Lena shot him a look. "You didn't work behind the counter with me, did you?" She turned back to Summer. "Anyway, Kate comes in one day. She's exhausted. In tears. She's got a little girl with her who's about Kimmy's age, maybe a year younger, and she confesses to me that she's been staying in the house alone. That she's been 'hiding from her cheating asshole dad'—that's her words—and waiting for her brother, but she doesn't think he's ever going to come meet her."

"Kate Sharkey didn't have a brother," said Freddy.

Summer's eyes felt salty and dry. She realized it was because she hadn't blinked in several seconds. *Quentin. If you are out there, I hope you are listening to this.* "Kate did have a brother," she said, very quietly. "A half brother. She didn't know about him, though. I mean. I didn't *think* she did . . ."

"She said her brother asked her to take care of this little kid. I guess the two of them had gone to his girlfriend's house. It was the girlfriend's little sister, and he'd asked Kate to take her away and watch over her till he and the girlfriend could come and pick her up. Well, weeks went by and she couldn't handle it anymore, so she gave the little girl to Bill and Mary and they took her in. No one could get a handle on who this kid's sister was, because she wouldn't talk. Wouldn't answer questions. But then a day or two later, the big sister actually shows up. Kate brings her over to Bill and Mary's. Hitchhikes back home. Fourteen freakin' years old." Lena looked at Freddy. "Say whatever you want about her, but Kate Sharkey was a true badass."

Summer said, "Did you ever find out who the girls were?"

She nodded. "They were both from that crazy Gideon compound. The one that those two murderers burned down?"

Summer touched her phone, thinking, *Oh my God. Oh my effin' God.* "The two girls," she said softly, waiting. "Were their names Nicola and Renee?"

Lena shook her head. "I mean, they could have changed them to that," she said. "I'd sure as hell change my name if I were a Gideon."

"What were their names when they lived with the Grumleys?"

Lena smiled, the memory so clearly alive and glittering in her mind. When she spoke, she sounded like a grade-school kid, thrilled with herself for knowing the right answer. "The big one was named Elizabeth," she said. "And the little girl was named Jenny."

ONCE SHE WAS back on the 405 and she had service again, Summer's phone began buzzing wildly with voice mails. She listened to them over her Bluetooth—five messages from Dean, almost all of them repeating the same information: Quentin hadn't killed himself. And most likely, his confession for Mitchell Bloom's death had been coerced.

She stared through his sunglasses and smiled. *I knew it*, she thought. *I knew that wasn't you.*

Summer called Dean from home and updated him on all the information she'd learned. When she was through, he said, "So you're doing this right? You're continuing with *Closure*?"

"Do you think I should?" she asked. Because honestly, that had been her reason for calling. To get his permission to go ahead with this podcast, in spite of everything it had caused.

"I think Quentin would have wanted you to," he said. "Don't you?"

"Yes," Summer said, relief sweeping through her. Then she hung up, climbed into bed, and slept for twelve solid hours.

FORTY

Dear Aurora Grace,

I haven't been able to write for days. I haven't been able to speak or do anything other than walk. Stick my thumb out. Jump in the back of trucks. None of the truck drivers bother me because I look like shit and I smell of smoke. And when the few pervs who stop for me try to talk me into a trade, I start crying like a crazy person and they drive away.

Whenever I close my eyes, I see Elizabeth— my last glimpse of her. I see the tents burning and I hear the screams, and Elizabeth in the middle of all of it, her beautiful hair on fire, waving her arms at me, yelling at me to run. Sometimes, in my imaginings, she turns into Papa Pete or Officer Nelligan or Ed Hart. Sometimes Brian Griggs or Carrie Masters, who I know must have met a terrible fate. Worst of all is when she turns into Jenny.

After we put Gabriel's body in the fire, I fell asleep, and woke up to the sound of Elizabeth's screams. Her father was awake—Elizabeth's knapsack in one hand, a burning torch in the other. He kept yelling "Witch!" over and over. I saw him do it. I saw him burn his own daughter. Elizabeth was dying and I couldn't get near her, because her crazy father had dropped the torch and it was a windy desert night and the flames kept growing and spreading, from one tent to the next to the next. Her brothers shrieking.

"Run!" Elizabeth yelled. And so I ran and I ran, thinking about what had happened. Torch in one hand. Elizabeth's knapsack in the other. That psycho freak of a father had found her tarot cards.

Now, I am trying to get back to the Arco station, because I have decided to let that spot determine my fate. If the pay phone there is working, I will call the number in Gabriel's wallet. If it's not working, or if there are police officers there, I will turn myself in and go to jail. If I die before ever arriving there, well, that's fine too. I haven't slept in days. My best friend burned to death. Another life I've ruined. I can't make decisions. All I can do is keep moving.

June 25, 1976
9:00 A.M.

Dear Aurora Grace,

Aurora Grace, there is a wonderful old movie called *Easter Parade* (I saw it yesterday), and in it, this goofy girl named Hannah Brown falls in love with a famous dancer named Don Hewes. And he loves her too, but she refuses to believe it because why would a famous dancer love a goofy girl like her? So, Hannah says to Don, "Why do you want to dance with me when you can have the very best?" And he says, "I don't want the very best. I want you."

I'm writing that down in this letter to you so I can remember that line and the movie, and what happened after the movie. I want to take that day and wrap it up in a box that I can keep with me always.

You know, it's funny. I thought I had to get back to that Arco station so I could either rescue Jenny or receive the punishment I deserve. I was leaving it up to God. But God had other plans. I think God brought me back to that Arco station, so I could experience one full day of perfect happiness. Everyone should have one full day of happiness, Aurora Grace. Even somebody who deserves to lose everything and probably will. Even somebody like me.

Love,
Mom

June 25, 1976
1:00 P.M.

Dear Aurora Grace,

    I found a pay phone. I called the number.
Jenny is alive!!!!!!!!!
    Love,
    Mom

FORTY-ONE

ROBIN

WHEN ROBIN ARRIVED at her parents' house, she didn't see her mother's car in the driveway or, for that matter, Nicola's. The only car she did see there was her father's sensible blue Volvo, which gave her a fresh stab of grief that made her doubly glad to be alone.

No reporters either—probably too busy trailing after poor Dean Conrad. But on her way up the walkway, she heard Mr. Dougherty calling out her name. She sighed. Waited in the driveway as he jogged up to her. A nice man. She shouldn't be so impatient. "How is your mother holding up?" Mr. Dougherty said.

"Surprisingly well," said Robin, which made his jaw drop. Of course it did. He had lost his wife a year ago, and still mourned her, every day. That was normal. He was normal. Her mother . . .

"I guess it helps having family around."

"Yeah, it comes in handy being a few blocks away," she said. "My dad used to call this neighborhood the Bloom family compound."

"Actually, I meant that lady. The one with the loud laugh."

"Nicola," Robin said. "She's not family. She's my mother's old friend."

"Your mom introduced her as her foster sister."

"Oh."

"Was it the pain pills talking?"

"No," she said, "that's accurate." Robin headed into the house, thinking of her new family: Mom, Eric, Nicola. Of the three of them, she knew Nicola best.

Once she was inside her parents' home, Robin found herself in her father's study, standing in front of his glass-enclosed bookcases, her gaze trained on the shelves. All those leather-bound notebooks. What would happen to them all, now that he was gone?

She imagined a bonfire in her parents' backyard, years and years of his patients' secrets and fixations and recurring nightmares all gone up in smoke, turned to ash like the Gideon compound, before April escaped, changed her name to Nicola, found herself a foster home and befriended an innocent, slightly older girl named Renee White.

It made so much sense. It made too much sense.

She sat down on his soft leather couch, breathing deeply, the way she sometimes used to do when she was feeling panicky as a kid.

As hard as she tried to calm herself, though, she couldn't contain her thoughts—images of Nicola Crane flinging open the back door, opening fire on Dad, shooting at Mom when she runs into the room, trying to stop her. Nicola Crane holding a gun to Quentin's head as he confesses to the crime on tape, the two of them in a park, Nicola so sweet and jovial that nearby children take no notice. *That laugh* . . . Nicola Crane threatening Mom in her hospital room: *Keep quiet or else. Laugh with me, or else. Say you remember nothing, Renee, or I will finish what I started.*

And why had she started it? Why had she shot Dad? Because he'd just been told that his wife had some connection to a teenage mass murderer. And he thought of that stray babysitter who kept coming back and put two and two together.

Robin knew Nicola better than anyone else in her family, and this was what she knew: She was April Cooper. Mom knew it. Just like she knew about the safe in the basement—some hidden place where she could hide a gun from her husband and daughter for more than twenty years.

She left her father's study and headed for the staircase, the basement door behind it. She stumbled down the dark, rickety stairs and into the musty space, knocking into boxes and broken furniture until she finally found the light. She breathed in the moldy air, pushed cobwebs from her hair— this room the neglected sibling of every other room in this otherwise spotless house. It used to scare her as a kid, this basement. She remembered coming down here once with a boy from her seventh-grade class. A football player she'd been helping with math. He'd dared her to come down here, and then he'd dared her to kiss him and she had, just to get back upstairs again. *What was his name? Grant something,* she thought, her gaze coasting from an old changing table to a toybox to an enormous stuffed bear that she never remembered owning, all of it down here for years. Lurking like ghosts. Like memories.

She saw a clothing rack, hung with her parents' old Halloween costumes. His and hers surgical scrubs, his and hers pirates, Groucho and Harpo Marx—her parents always a team, inseparable. Though, as she remembered it, the costumes had always been Dad's idea. She collapsed onto the dusty floor and looked at that costume rack—easily twenty Halloweens' worth of his and hers outfits, worn once and never again . . . except . . . Robin put a hand against the ones at the end—a pinstripe suit. A pencil skirt and sweater. A fedora and a beret and two fake machine guns. *Bonnie and Clyde.* Robin could remember her dad bringing those costumes home, when she was young enough not to have understood the cultural reference. Mom had taken one look at them and locked herself in their bedroom.

How could you, Mitchell? How could you?

Young as Robin had been then, Mom's reaction had stuck in her mind—the drama of it. Robin had always assumed it was because of the guns.

She pulled herself up to standing. And that's when she caught sight of it between her feet. A trapdoor. She lifted the door open, and saw it, glaring at her from within. A small, industrial-looking safe. Robin hoisted the safe out. She placed it on the floor in front of her and crouched down. Looked it in the eye. "Nice to meet you after all these years," she whispered.

The safe had a digital combination lock. She tried her mother's birthday, then her father's. Then their anniversary. Then her own birthday. None of them worked. She glanced at the costumes again and tried Halloween. 1031. The door drifted open.

Robin crouched down and looked inside, unsure of what she was expecting to find. The gun, after all, was in police custody . . .

The safe held a single, leather-bound notebook, identical to the many that lined Dad's office bookshelves. She slipped it out. Looked at the cover. The taped label, just like the others, the patient's name in mechanical print:

APRIL COOPER

The notebook fell from Robin's hand, but she picked it up again. Opened it to the first page. She saw her father's handwriting at the top in ballpoint pen, barely legible: "April Cooper, aka Renee White: Forensic Case Study #1 February 28, 1977, Borderline Personality Disorder. Patient exhibits . . ."

Robin slammed the book shut.

"Do you remember what I said, Robin, about how no one should be an open book to their children?"

Nicola stood behind her.

Robin turned to face her. Nicola Crane, who wasn't April Cooper after all. Just an angry-looking woman with bright blue eyes, speaking with studied menace, holding a gun. "You want to know?" she said. "You really want to know that badly?"

Robin stared at her.

"Mitchell wanted to talk to Quentin Garrison. He wanted to come clean. You're grown, he said. He's semiretired. He said he believed he could help

Quentin Garrison. As though some selfish little podcaster were more important than your mother."

Tears seeped out of the corners of Robin's eyes. "My mom was . . ."

"He didn't think things through. Mitchell never really thought things through, not when they didn't concern him. Your mother is a fugitive. There's no statute of limitations on the shit she did when she was a teen."

"I . . . I don't want to hear any more."

"Oh no, Robin. You wanted to know. You came all the way down here and nosed your way into that safe just like you got into your mother's jewel box."

"Jewel box?"

"Each item in that box is a reminder of someone from her youth that she loved and lost. Well, some of them she just lost. That little aqua heart necklace? That was a gift from Gabriel LeRoy. He said it matched her eyes."

She swallowed. "The penny from the movie theater."

"A gift from George. Her soul mate. She used to carry a Polaroid of him, until your dad made her throw it out. Said it was unseemly. Made it look like they were something other than husband and wife . . . even though that's exactly what they were."

Tears slipped down her cheeks.

"Your father didn't care at all about your poor mother. Doing this podcast will be best for us, he said. It's the right thing to do. He called her from work, told her that and, of course, she called me right away. To vent, she said. But I knew she wanted more than that."

"No . . ."

"When your mom picked me up at the train station, he'd come home, and they'd been fighting. He wasn't backing down. He didn't care if he ruined her. Her own analyst and he was ready to throw her in jail."

"Her analyst."

"Yes. That's what he was. And she was his research topic. Mr. Forensic Psychiatrist. All the papers he'd never have been able to write without her. And now that he was retired, he was ready to be rid of her. That, my dear, is what you call a marriage of convenience."

"You shot them both."

"To save Renee. It's hard to make it look like a home invasion if only one of you gets shot."

Robin exhaled. A deep, shuddering breath. She heard the front door opening above, her mother calling out for Nicola.

She thought of her father's voice over the phone, the sadness in it. *Have we been good parents to you?* "He felt bad for Quentin because of the way he was raised."

"Please. He just wanted someone new to study."

Footsteps tumbled down the basement stairs. "Nikki?" Renee said. "What are you doing?"

"Just asking Robin if she has any more questions," Nicola said.

"About what?" Renee said.

Robin shook her head.

"Oh, I almost forgot. There was no man in a parking lot. That was your dad. Let's just say he got impatient with his patient."

"That . . . that can't be true . . ."

Nicola released the safety. "I've always loved you, Robbie," she said. "It's not personal. But I'm afraid it's necessary."

Robin stared at the barrel of the gun.

"*My God, Jenny, stop!*" Renee screamed. She fell on her, the two of them rolling on the dusty basement floor. The gun went off, and Renee fell back, blood spreading from her chest, pooling under her body.

"Oh my God," Nicola cried out. "Not April. Please, God, please not April . . ."

Robin rushed to her mother. She grabbed one of the costumes off the hangers—the surgical scrubs—and pressed it to the wound. In seconds, it was drenched. She heard Nicola. Or Jenny. Her mother's sister, weeping behind her. "I can't. I can't. I couldn't have. No . . ."

Robin threw her arms around her mother's neck, Mom's lips against her ear. "It wasn't like that," Mom said, in a voice so weak and quiet, it was more pressure than sound. "He never hit me. He cared about me," she whispered. "Jenny . . . was trying to . . . hurt you . . ."

Robin kissed her mother's forehead, the skin burning her lips. "Don't leave me," she said. "Please, Mom. Please stay."

"I killed a cop. Shot him. He had a family. Two little girls. I . . . I didn't . . . deserve a life like . . ."

"Sssh."

"Daddy was a good doctor, Robbie. He was a good man. And he loved you so much."

Her mother's body went still. Robin put a hand

against her neck, her wrist. She put her head to her chest and heard nothing. She screamed, wailed. Her throat scraped raw from it, mingling with Nicola's cries . . . "April, no, no, no . . ."

She heard footsteps above her. Eric's voice calling her name, but she couldn't move. Couldn't breathe. She wanted to die.

Across the floor, she saw the gun—the heavy dark threat of it, smoke lifting from the barrel. She started to reach for it, but Nicola grabbed it first. Grabbed it off the floor, her mouth wrenched open. "April."

Behind her, Robin heard Eric's footsteps on the stairs. She heard her name again. This time from Nicola. "I'm sorry, Robin," Nicola said. "I ruined everything."

And then she put the barrel to her chin and pulled the trigger.

FORTY-TWO

Eight months later

SUMMER

DEATH VALLEY HAD a perfume to it—sand and baked earth and at this time of the year, the strawlike sweetness of desert spring. Back when Quentin had told Summer about his dream podcast—Reg Sharkey and himself, making peace with the spot that had once been the Gideon compound—she'd had one response: *You couldn't pay me enough money to fry in that sweatbox.*

But as she saw now, Quentin had been right. As usual. She wished he were here now. But in a way, she liked to think, he was. She was sitting in the back of a rented convertible Mustang, the sun heavy and warm on the back of her neck. Robin Diamond was beside her. They were recording the eighth and final installment of the *Closure* podcast, Robin having described the series of events that ultimately brought her here, to Southern California, where she planned on living indefinitely, even though her estranged husband tried, on a weekly basis, to reconcile. "He says we're each other's only family," Robin was saying now. "But after everything that's happened, I don't know that that's such a selling point."

Robin wasn't anything like what Summer had expected. She was tanned and easygoing and didn't seem traumatized at all. Grief hit everyone in different ways, Summer supposed. And when the people you're mourning are as complicated as Robin's parents, moving three thousand miles away from the scene of the crime is probably the healthiest thing you can do. Robin was smiling now, a perfect California girl, her big sunglasses glinting. "I have a dog—a yellow lab that used to belong to my aunt. I think that's pretty much all the family I need."

"What about your mom?" Summer said. "How do you feel about her now?"

"I feel like she was someone who did a lot of bad things. But she knew it. And she spent her whole life trying to make up for them. I mean, you compare that to my ex-husband, who . . . okay, he didn't kill anybody but he did a *really shitty thing*. And all he says is, 'I'm going to quit my job soon.' You think that poor woman who lost her entire livelihood because of him gives a shit whether or not he's adding to his 401(k)?" Robin took a breath. "Wow. Let's make that last bit off the record."

"Sure." Summer took a swig from her thermos of water, and Robin did the same, composing herself. "After she married my dad," she said, "my mom spent close to ten years, and with two different private investigators, trying to track down her little sister. Did it without his knowledge, apparently. And when she finally found her—a deeply unhappy kid, on her third or fourth foster home—she flew her out to New York, took her in, and tried to convince my dad to let her live with us."

"But he said no," Summer said.

"Dad was a shrink," she said. "Apparently, he knew crazy when he saw it."

"Yes."

"Still, though. He paid Jenny's rent for more than five years out in Los Angeles. Recommended her to the Police Academy out there." She picked at a nail. "Jenny never told me that."

"They did some good things, your parents."

She nodded.

"People are complicated."

"Families are complicated."

Summer smiled a little. It reminded her of Quentin. After his body was discovered, the police had found a pen stashed in one of his pockets that was actually a tiny voice recorder he'd bought at a spy shop. He'd recorded his own murder—Jenny, aka Nicola Crane holding him at gunpoint, forcing him to confess to the shooting of the Blooms before placing the gun in his own hand and making him shoot himself. Summer had eventually been able to obtain a copy of the recording from a police source and while there were many parts she still couldn't bring herself to listen to, there was one that stuck in her mind. When Nicola had asked him if he had any last words, Quentin had said, "I'm looking forward to seeing my mom again." Families were nothing if not complicated.

"So," Summer said. "You ready for the letters?"

In Renee's will, she'd left Robin a sheath of letters she'd written to her "future daughter" when she was April Cooper. She'd been keeping them in a safe deposit box since Robin's birth, unbeknownst to anyone, including her husband. "Share them with whoever you want," she had instructed her. And so Robin had agreed to read them aloud, the letters interspersed throughout the podcast. "Is it okay if someone else reads them with you?" Summer had said.

Robin had agreed, and now he was driving up in a red minivan: George Pollard. Or, as Robin insisted on calling him, "The *Easter Parade* man."

Pollard stepped out of the van, smiling, his black eyes glinting in the sun. Robin took off her sunglasses and looked up at him with the same black eyes and Summer wished, not for the first time, that radio was a visual medium. A series of taglines ran through her mind—about mirror images and missing pieces and nothing staying hidden forever. About how you can't move forward without ever looking back. And about how family can spring up anywhere, at any time, whether you want it to or not.

FORTY-THREE

August 30, 1976
2:00 A.M.

Dear Aurora Grace,

Things aren't too bad right now. Jenny and I are living in a place called Brittlebush, Arizona, with a couple called Bill and Mary Grumley who are nice (even though I hate their pet fish). Their sons are pretty annoying, but they're all terrified to talk to a girl, so they don't bother me very much at all.

Bill and Mary believe Jenny and I ran off from the Gideon compound because I took Elizabeth's name. And since they think the Gideons were a bunch of weirdo cult members, they're taking care of us, feeding us, sending us to school. They've even helped us to change our names. Mine will be Renee, which means reborn in French. Jenny's will be Nicola, after her favorite doll. There's lots of good food in this house. And Mary lets me have my favorite whenever I want—cinnamon raisin toast, cream cheese, and strawberry jam. My mom used to make it for me. It reminds me of her.

Here's the thing, though, Aurora Grace. I'm not going to be able to stay here for very long. I'm trying to tell Jenny that she'll be fine without me. Better off without me, probably, if anyone ever finds out who I really am.

I've told one boy who I am, but I'm never going to see him again. And I think he'll keep my secret. He is sweet and kind and funny and gentle. And he is, after all, your father.

Aurora Grace, you have decided to show up in my life a lot sooner than I thought you would. So here is my plan: Buy a bus ticket to Tucson. Lie about my age. Get a job at the university and do it fast—before I start showing! Use my new name. Make new friends. Start a new life as a new girl. A new woman. I've been thinking about going to night school at the university. I'd like to study to be a psychiatrist, but that could always change.

I leave later this morning, my growing daughter. Are you ready for our future? I know I am.

Love,

Mom

ACKNOWLEDGMENTS

My gratitude as ever, to my wonderful agent Deborah Schneider, as well as to the brilliant Lyssa Keusch, Mireya Chiriboga, Maureen Cole, and everyone at William Morrow, the amazing Francesca Pathak and everyone at Orion, and also Alice Lutyens at Curtis Brown, who is truly the best.

Thanks also to James "My Main" Conrad, Jackie Kellachan, and my favorite bookstore, The Golden Notebook. I couldn't write these things without the support of friends and family, including (but not limited to) James (again) and Chas Cerulli, Paul Leone (who answered many vital questions), Wendy Corsi Staub, the everlastingly never-ever-all-uncool FLs, Sheldon and Marilyn Gaylin, Ronald LeBov, my terrific mom, Beverly LeBov Sloane, and of course Mike and Marissa, without whom . . . Well let's just say I'm #blessed.

NOTE FROM THE AUTHOR

The Murder Spree That Inspired
Never Look Back

If April Cooper and Gabriel LeRoy seem at all familiar, it could be because of the case that inspired me to create the characters—or because of the numerous other writers, from Terrence Malick to Bruce Springsteen, who derived inspiration from the same case.

In December 1957, nineteen-year-old Charles Starkweather murdered the family of his fourteen-year-old girlfriend, Caril Ann Fugate, escaped with Caril, and embarked on a month-long killing spree that took the lives of eleven people in Nebraska and Wyoming. The pair was eventually captured, with Starkweather receiving the death penalty. Caril became the youngest person ever to be tried for first-degree murder and was sentenced to life in prison as an accomplice—a decision based largely on testimony from Starkweather himself.

What fascinated me most about the case was not so much Starkweather, but Caril—who by many accounts was not an accomplice but a kidnapping victim and, in my own reading of the story, tragically misunderstood.

In Malick's marvelous *Badlands*, Sissy Spacek's Holly is a guileless romantic who willingly runs off with troubled Kit (Martin Sheen) after he offs her cold-hearted, dog-murdering stepfather. In Springsteen's bleak "Nebraska," a brooding Starkweather hopes the "pretty baby" who abetted his murder spree is "sitting right there on [his] lap" when he goes to the electric chair. In movies like *Kalifornia* and *Natural Born Killers*, the Caril Fugate–based character is portrayed as a psychotic Lady MacBeth–in-training, for whom senseless murder is a type of turn-on.

But are any of those depictions close to reality? By all accounts, Caril was a shy, sweet girl and a loving daughter until the day Starkweather killed off her entire family—three-year-old sister included—before she returned home from school, hiding their bodies in outbuildings on her property. Throughout her seventeen years of incarceration, Caril Fugate insisted that Starkweather had lied to her, claiming her parents and sibling were being held captive by mysterious associates and would survive only if she ran off with him, cooperated with his plans, didn't attempt to escape.

In the book *The Twelfth Victim: The Innocence of Caril Fugate in the Starkweather Murder Rampage*, authors Linda M. Battisti and John Stevens Berry paint a horrific scene of the couple's capture by police, describing how Caril was vilified in the press and grilled by prosecuting attorneys without being told she had a right to counsel. The book tells of the young girl's overwhelming, dizzying exhaustion, of screaming hordes outside the courthouse, of flashbulbs popping and hurled epithets, and the slowly dawning revelation that her entire family was gone, that she was being charged rather than rescued, that she was, for all intents and purposes, completely alone in the world . . .

It's a narrative that sadly makes more sense than the darkly romantic one I'd come to know through movies and song—one more in keeping with the fate of the real Caril Fugate, who went on to marry and lead a quiet life after being paroled in 1976, finding work as a janitorial assistant and medical technician before retiring. And it was a narrative that felt too hopeless and pointless and unfair for fiction.

In creating April, I saw a girl around the same age as Caril but in most other ways very different. While April too is robbed of her family and kidnapped by a boyfriend she no longer loves, I saw her as someone who might adapt to her captivity more quickly than the real-life girl, finding hope wherever she could—in the pages of the Bible, in the idea of a future child, in her own simmering rage, and in the chambers of a gun. I saw her as someone who could find within herself the capacity for murder, someone who can—and does—kill. I saw her as a furious survivor—someone who emotionally (and, in a way, physically) goes to hell and back.

In writing the rest of the book, I thought to myself: *How would I feel if I knew this girl?*

And then, I thought: *How would I feel if she were my mother?*

—Alison Gaylin

FIVE TRUE CRIME PODCASTS THAT WILL KEEP YOU UP ALL NIGHT

I've been a true crime addict for years, and a commuter for nearly as long. Put both of those things together, and you'll understand how happy I am that true crime podcasts have become so popular in recent years. As someone with a degree in journalism, I appreciate the way these producers do a deep-dive into the subject matter, combining research, deft interviewing skills, suspenseful structuring—and often a touch of memoir—to provide an immersive experience, much like the Tom Wolfe, Joan Didion, and Hunter S. Thompson New Journalism pieces I fell in love with when I was younger. There are many of these podcasts I could recommend, but here are a few to start out with . . .

Dirty John: This one has all the makings of a great noir movie: a glamorous protagonist whose thirst for love gets her into deep trouble at the hands of a dangerous man. But rest assured, it's a lot more than that. Brilliantly structured, it kicks off with a shocker of a police scene and repeatedly throws you off balance, culminating in a final episode that's a true jaw-dropper. The interviewing is wonderful too: I felt as though I knew all the people involved in this shocking story—and often wanted to shake some sense into them.

You Must Remember This: Charles Manson's Hollywood: I've long been obsessed with old Hollywood, so this podcast—which explores Tinseltown tales like nothing else—is one of my favorites. And this season, which devotes itself to the con-artist-turned-cult-leader, is, in my opinion, the best one of all. Specifically, the thirteen-part season focuses on Manson as a music business wannabe, the surprising connections he made among Hollywood's elite, and how all of it led to some of the most horrific murders the town has ever known. It's completely absorbing, and completely terrifying.

S* Town: This utterly original podcast kicks off in classic true crime fashion: producer Brian Reed gets a call from a man by the name of John McLemore, asking him to investigate a murder in his hometown of Woodstock, Alabama (which he less than affectionately calls Shittown). Though the murder itself is questionable, McLemore himself turns out to be a fascinating and brilliant character, full of secrets and contradictions. His life story—and Reed's exploration of it—proves to be as mysterious, twisted, and heartbreaking as any work of crime fiction.

Happy Face: How would you feel if you found out your father was a serial killer? This twelve-part podcast from *How Stuff Works* answers that question as it follows Washington state writer Melissa Moore—who learned, as a teenager, that her truck-driver father, Keith Jesperson, was the notorious Happy Face Killer. Brutally honest about her difficult upbringing and the traumatic revelation that's taken her years to process, Moore provides listeners with unique insight as to how violent crime affects the families of everyone involved.

Serial (Season One): The mother of them all. I'll be the first to admit that *Serial* doesn't always deliver on its promises. I personally found the structure to be a bit meandering, with a letdown of an ending, and I would have preferred a bit more focus on the victim. But listening to it (and I did, every week, when it was first released by *This American Life*) may be one of the most addictive experiences I've ever had. Producer Sarah Koenig's growing obsession with Adnan Syed—who was convicted for the 1999 murder of his onetime girlfriend Hae Min Lee—is contagious, to say the least. And if you're wondering why true crime podcasts have become so popular, look no further than the first episode.

READING GROUP GUIDE

1. *Never Look Back* begins with a letter written by April to her future daughter, and her story is told exclusively through those letters. Why do you think the author decided to use this device?

2. We are introduced to many principal characters in this novel. What were your initial impressions of them, and did they change by the end of the book?

3. What were your reactions to April's participation in the Inland Empire murders, especially after reading the letters? Do you believe she was as guilty as Gabriel?

4. Gabriel repeatedly assures April that he loves her. Do you think there ever was any love between them?

5. What are your thoughts on Robin's marriage? Did you feel confident about it from the beginning and, if so, how did that change as the story progressed?

6. Early in the book, we find out Quentin's aunt is a victim of the killings, creating a personal interest in the Cooper and LeRoy murders for Quentin. In Chapter 14, more information is revealed about his childhood and relationship with his mother. Do you think Quentin's motive behind the podcast stems from his childhood experiences in a deeper way than he sets it out to be?

7. What was your reaction to Quentin's last text message to Robin? Were you taken aback by it?

8. What do you make of Quentin's ultimate fate—did you find it surprising?

9. In Chapter 23, April and Gabriel run into the cops. How did you feel during this scene?

10. Did the identity of the killer surprise you?

11. A lot is revealed at the end of the book. What were your feelings about the conclusion? Did you find the ending satisfying?

12. The book was, in many ways, centered around the idea of family. What do you think it says about that theme—and did you find the message hopeful in any way?

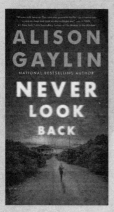